# Rebel Love

# SCARLETT SCOTT

**Rebel Love**
Heart's Temptation Book 2

This book is a work of fiction and any resemblance to persons, living or dead, or places, events, or locales, is purely coincidental. The characters are productions of the author's imagination and used fictitiously.

# Dedication

For Sandy, with infinite gratitude for Chaucer, poems,
endless rounds of dinner, and so much more.

# Contents

# Author Note

Much of *Rebel Love* occurs within the same timeframe as *A Mad Passion* since the two stories are told concurrently to each other. As Thornton and Cleo were rekindling their old passion at Lady Cosgrove's country house party, Bella and Jesse were secretly falling in love.

## Chapter One

*England, 1880*

MAMA N WANTED TO MARRY HER OFF. THERE WAS no kind way of phrasing it, no hope for it. The dowager had tired of Bella's failure to wed. Her maxims were legion, ringing in Bella's mind like an endless bell pull in the servants' hall.

*No lord will wed a bookish miss. Never wear spectacles. Powder is vulgar. Nothing complements an innocent lady's complexion better than white. Don't slouch.*

Alas, her mother's tireless crusade had thus far proven fruitless through several seasons. Bella had no wish to make polite conversation with boring fops in search of fortunes. They were deadly dull, the lot of them. But the plain truth remained in her mind with an attic rat's gnawing persistence. No man, she feared, could ever compete with the incomparable Mr. Jesse Whitney. From the moment she'd first laid eyes upon his golden good looks and heard his butter-smooth Virginia drawl four years before, she'd been hopelessly, impossibly infatuated.

"Bella, do pay attention."

1

The dowager's scolding voice shook her from her reveries, bringing her back to the present with a snap. She turned from the countryside slipping past her carriage window and looked to her mother. "Pray forgive me. My mind is often wont to wander when I'm trapped in carriages."

"A wandering mind is simply unacceptable. A proper young lady's mind should always be empty."

Bella tried hard not to smile at the dowager's pronouncement. "Indeed, *Maman*. I shall endeavor to always have an empty mind from this moment forward."

Her mother pinned her with a glare. "So much cheek. Where did you learn such ill manners? I'm afraid I have failed altogether as a mother."

"Never, *Maman* dearest." She attempted a smile she could not quite feel. "You have been a boon, truly."

"You would call your own mother a baboon? Dear Lord, how am I to find a husband for an uncouth girl such as this?" Her mother addressed the ceiling of the carriage as if she were having a direct audience with the Lord Himself.

Bella would dearly have liked to offer some choice words of her own on the matter, but she wisely refrained. Instead, she counted to five in her head, took a supporting breath, and attempted to correct the dowager. "*Maman*, I said you've been a boon, not a baboon."

"Just so," her mother huffed, "but how like you to say so now I've heard your true feelings. You only seek to abfuscate me."

Bella didn't bother to correct her mother. It wouldn't do a bit of good and she knew it. She simply remained silent and settled back into her seat as the verdant fields continued their endless undulations outside. They were on their way to the great Shakespearean-themed country house party held by Lady Cosgrove, and Bella knew better than anyone that it wouldn't do to upset the dowager now. Indeed, house parties quite set her mother on edge. As did life in general, but that was beside the point.

At times like these, Bella was certain her brother Thornton owed her a great deal. It was just as well he'd finally been forced to do his part and attend this country house party as well as she. Bella didn't wish to be put on display to the grasping remnants of England's aristocrats. Many of them had been cast to penury and she was well aware the only positive quality they'd be likely to find in a bookish young miss was the dowry her brother had provided her.

She wasn't content to be settled upon as if she were no better than a house with a leaky roof. She'd read a great many novels, and she wanted more than resignation. Bella longed for adventure, love and above all, passion. Of course, she could never tell her mother as much, or she'd be cast to Bedlam for being frail-minded.

Most importantly, there was a grander plan in her mind. Her brother had written that he planned to bring his friend and business associate Jesse Whitney for companionship. Because her mother despised him, she'd wisely kept that particular gem of knowledge to herself. Until now.

She slanted a glance at the dowager, who resembled nothing so much as a large bird. She had been wearing gray half-mourning for seven years, and her sole ornamentation was jet and feathers. A *stuffed* bird, Bella decided, was truly what her mother personified.

"*Maman*, did you know Mr. Whitney shall attend?" Bella asked, knowing it was sly indeed of her. Everyone thought her bookish and mild-mannered, but in truth, she had layers. She was a parsnip in reverse, she'd decided some time ago. Thick skin on the inside, sweet and soft on the outside. She preferred it that way, for then, everyone underestimated her.

"The awful American?" The dowager straightened her posture and raised her nose. "You shan't know him, my dear. I can't think why Lady Cosgrove should extend an invitation to such a blackleg, truly I cannot."

"Certainly not," Bella concurred, not meaning a bit of it. "I should never know someone so low."

"Wise girl." The dowager wore a satisfied smile. "I despair of your poor brother, with his dabbling in trade with that American vulture. But not my dear Arabella, thank the Lord. For you, I have expectations."

Bella was not sure she liked this news. "Expectations, mother?"

"You'll have a duchess's coronet and nothing less."

Her stomach cramped at the very thought, and it had little to do with the extra-tightlacing done by her lady's maid that morning or the stiffness of her travel dress. "Yes, *Maman*."

"I have it on good authority that the Duke of Devonshire will be in attendance," the dowager announced in a pleased tone.

Truly, Devonshire had always seemed altogether too proper even if he was handsome. He'd probably never even so much as sneezed at the wrong time of day in his life. But Bella knew it was wiser to smile and concur. It was what the dowager expected. "Wonderful news, *Maman*. I shall ask after his estate."

"Just so, my dear daughter." The dowager marchioness beamed. "Just so."

Because her mother had delayed their arrival over a briefly misplaced trunk, Bella missed the first day's festivities, but she didn't mind. After settling into her chamber, she ventured through the immense Tudor revival wing in search of the library. No matter where she traveled, the library was always her home. Hostesses no doubt thought her strange as it was ordinarily considered a masculine domain, but Bella didn't care. The dowager had settled in for a nap, and while she'd told her mother she would do the same, she had no intention of sleeping when there was a new collection of books to be scoured.

With the help of a kind footman, she located her quarry.

The library was immense, its mahogany walls lined with books. Bella stepped inside and took a deep inhalation of the familiar, comforting scent of leather and paper. She slid her spectacles out of the hidden pocket in her gown and settled them on the bridge of her nose.

"I wonder," she mused aloud as she slowly examined the spines nearest her, "if Lady Cosgrove has any Trollope. Likely not. It wouldn't be my luck. She's probably like Mother and thinks him too fast."

"Interesting," drawled a deep, familiar, honey-slow drawl. "I wonder if you ordinarily hold conversations with yourself."

The book she'd taken off the shelf fell from her fingers to the floor with a loud thump. He was here. She spun about, gaze searching the still seemingly empty room for him. "You have me at a disadvantage, Mr. Whitney. Where in blessed angels' sakes are you?"

"Up here." There was laughter in his tone.

He was in the second level, she realized, following his voice with her eyes. She hadn't known she wasn't alone. Goodness, he must think her an utter featherhead. Of course, of all audiences and much to her embarrassment, it had to be Mr. Whitney. She had not seen him in some time, but even from so far away, she found him as wickedly compelling as ever.

"I'm quite bemused that you've been eavesdropping on my private conversation," she quipped, striving to maintain the pretense she was unaffected. She very much did not want him to think her a fool.

"Perhaps I'm the one who should be bemused." He made his way down the narrow staircase. "I was having a heated debate with myself when you walked in and interrupted it."

She snatched the spectacles from her face as he sauntered toward her, two books in his hands. "Indeed, sir? What debate was that? I confess I didn't hear a single word."

"Poetry or fiction?" He grinned as he reached her and

stopped with a respectable distance between them.

Bella couldn't help but notice the way his grin produced a charming divot in his right cheek. His smile transformed his ordinary handsome charm into melting masculine beauty. After all the time she'd spent with her brother's friend over the past few years, she was still not immune to his magnetism. He possessed some indefinable quality she'd never seen in another man. It was as if beneath his polite exterior there was a wildness he barely kept contained. Maybe she was fanciful, but she'd always found him fascinating and even a trifle frightening.

"Who is the poet?" she asked, trying to keep her mind where it belonged. He had no interest in her and he never would. She would ever be his friend's younger sister and she'd accustomed herself to the unwanted role.

"Matthew Arnold." His grin deepened. "I do like your English bards."

"Arnold is a wise choice," she agreed, having harbored a secret love of poetry for years, against her mother's strict edict. "One of my favorite lines is in *Dover Beach*. It's the last stanza, I believe, where he writes, 'Ah, love, let us be true to one another! For the world, which seems to lie before us like a land of dreams, so various, so beautiful, so new, hath really neither joy, nor love, nor light.'"

She was aware his stare was suddenly intense upon her and she flushed, wondering if perhaps she'd shared too much. "I beg your pardon," she hurried to say, "I didn't mean to wax on."

"No need to beg my pardon." He winked at her, lightening the moment. "I like the sound of poetry on your lips."

For some reason, his words sent a delightful heat simmering through her veins. She had an inkling it was caused by his mentioning of her lips. "Thank you. I know the sentiment is a dark one, but I find it terribly compelling just the same."

"Life is dark." There was an underlying emotion in his

voice she couldn't define.

Her life had not been, but she had a suspicion his past was indeed marred by darkness. Thornton had said his friend had fought for the Confederacy in the War Between the States. She couldn't even imagine the horrors he'd witnessed in combat. He wore the look of a gentleman well, but she wondered if beneath the polish there hid a deeply tarnished soul.

"What is the fiction title?" she asked, attempting to return their conversation to its earlier levity once more. She didn't want to pry, after all, and she feared her curiosity would get the better of her tongue soon.

"*Our Mutual Friend*." He held up the volume for her inspection.

"Dickens." She wrinkled her nose. "I must admit I've never been partial to his writing. *Great Expectations* was a vast lot of endless sentences if you ask me."

He laughed, a rich, velvety sound. Her heart kicked into the mad gallop of a runaway mare. Goodness, he really was far too compelling for her composure's sake. Perhaps she had read one too many romantic novels. It was making her maudlin and foolish. She caught herself staring at his mouth.

"I appreciate a lady who knows her mind," he said, his tone low and intimate.

Oh blessed angels' sakes. What to say to that? *Stop staring at him like a duffer*, she ordered her wayward mind. "You're too kind, Mr. Whitney."

"I wouldn't call myself kind." His tone was wry. "I count myself a number of things, but kind isn't one of them."

Her interest was piqued. She'd always known him to be proper and considerate. A perfect gentleman. "Then perhaps you do yourself an injustice."

"If you knew the thoughts in my head, you wouldn't think so."

That intrigued her in a way she knew could be quite dangerous indeed. "What thoughts?"

His gaze dipped to her mouth. "That you're one of the

loveliest women I've ever seen."

Her lungs nearly failed her. His pronouncement had a stupefying effect upon her. She wanted to say something flippant or clever but couldn't find the proper words. Instead, she opted for candor. "That's rather a kind thing to say, actually. You've bollixed it up."

"Not truly." His gaze met hers and for the first time in the years she had known him, she recognized the awareness she felt for him reflected back in his eyes. Or at least she hoped she did. "It's the thoughts I haven't said that are the problem."

"I'm sure I shouldn't ask what they are." But it didn't mean she didn't want to know. Every part of her clamored with curiosity. Oh, how she wanted to know.

"No, you shouldn't, Lady Bella."

She found she rather liked the sound of her given name in his honeyed Virginia drawl.

"You're not playing fair," she accused quietly. "I do so hate suspense. It's why I always flip to the last page of a novel before I start reading it."

He laughed again and his dimple reappeared. "You ruin each book you read?"

She'd never confessed her peculiar habit to anyone before and she wasn't certain why she'd chosen to bestow her secret upon Jesse Whitney just then. But there was no help for it. She'd already said too much.

Bella tried to keep the telltale blush from her cheeks. It wouldn't do for him to know the effect his mere presence had on her. She wasn't fifteen anymore, fresh from the schoolroom. "I prefer to think of it as preparing myself."

Jesse took a step closer to her, still holding the books he'd been discussing. He was impossibly handsome. "Ah, I believe I understand you."

Bella fought the urge to step back in retreat. He was now too near to her to be observing the proprieties any longer and that made her rather nervous. "Indeed?"

He closed the remaining distance between them,

absconding with her ability to breathe as he did so. "You seek to avoid an unhappy ending."

She faltered, as shaken by his nearness as she was by his perception. "Perhaps you're right."

"If it's a happy ending you desire, I'm afraid you're doomed to be disappointed in life, my dear." He startled her by sinking abruptly to his knees and retrieving the forgotten book she'd dropped. "Here you are."

As she accepted the volume from him, their fingers brushed. "Thank you." She struggled to appear calm, trying with all her might to remain unaffected. "You sound remarkably cynical, Mr. Whitney."

"Merely older." He winked, breaking the intensity between them. "Think of me as another brother. I'd hate to see your idealism crushed without warning."

*Think of me as another brother.*

Dear heavens. Another surge of embarrassment washed over her. Was she mistaken, then? Had she been reading more into his words and actions than was truly there? She'd harbored a *tendre* for him for the last four years. First, she had been too young. But now she was a lady grown, and while he was at least ten years her senior, she was far more mature than most ladies who were of an age with her. He was worldly, it was true, but he needn't treat her as if he were a kindly uncle and she a recalcitrant niece running about in skirts above her ankles.

"Once again, you're too kind," she managed past the disappointment lodged in her throat. "But as I already have a brother, I shan't need you to act as one."

"I wouldn't be so certain." He raised a brow. "I've seen the young bucks who are here looking to make matches, and as lovely as you are, I've no doubt you'll need more than one guardian to keep them in check."

She was not amused by his insistence she view him as a protector. Drat him, why couldn't he see her for the lady she'd become? She was not the same miss she'd been when he first met her, a shy girl who sat on her spectacles. "I'm more than capable of looking after myself, Mr. Whitney."

He offered her a half-bow. "Of course you are, my dear."

A strange thing happened to Bella then, to Bella who had to suffer the dowager on a daily basis, to Bella who had infinite amounts of tact and serenity. She lost her patience. "You need not placate me. I'm not a girl in the schoolroom even if you seem determined to treat me as such."

His expression changed, becoming part startled, part admiring. "I do apologize if I've been offensive."

She remained unmoved by his apology. "It is simply that I am one-and-twenty."

Jesse's smile returned, making him appear almost boyish. "I'm well aware of your age, but you're still naïve to the ways of the world. When I was your age, I'd already been through a war."

She longed to ask him about the black cloud that was always in the room with him, but she didn't dare. "I can hardly be faulted for my country's stability."

"It seems I'm not going to end this particular battle as the victor." He held up the books. "I think I'll take the fiction and the poetry both after all." He bowed again, and this time it was formal and stiff. "Enjoy your afternoon, Lady Bella."

"Thank you, Mr. Whitney." She watched him walk away, consternation mingling with regret. That had not gone as she'd hoped.

That sure as hell hadn't gone as he'd hoped. Jesse was still cursing himself for his conduct as he entered Lady Cosgrove's dining hall for dinner later that evening. Lady Arabella de Vere was, in a word, untouchable. That didn't preclude him from wanting to touch her, however. In truth, he didn't want to stop at a mere touch.

She was more than lovely as he'd said. She was exquisite,

with her glossy black curls framing her face and startling blue eyes. And as she'd said, she was a woman grown, which was precisely the problem. When he looked at her now, he saw the lush beauty she'd grown into and not the awkward girl she'd once been.

But he could not pursue her. It would be ruinous. He caught sight of her as he escorted his appointed dinner partner, the overeager widow Lady Boniface. Bella was striking in an elaborate pink evening gown that hinted at her décolletage. Lady Boniface, in stark contrast, was clothed in a gown cut so low he could almost see her nipples. Everything about her irked him, from her clinging touch to her rouged lips. Even her perfume was consternating. It smelled of a cloying combination of violets and powder. He seated her and narrowly avoided getting one of the feathers she wore in her hair up his nose.

By some turn of fortune's fickle wheel, or perhaps merely Lady Cosgrove's liberal sense of placement, Bella was seated opposite him at the table. He caught her eye. She looked away, unsmiling. He'd been rude to her earlier in an effort to hide his attraction. Now she likely thought him an arrogant ass.

"Lady Cosgrove is to be commended, wouldn't you agree, Mr. Whitney?" Lady Boniface murmured, interrupting the tide of his thoughts. "If I didn't know better, I should think we're seated in the midst of a seascape."

The effect their hostess had likely gone to great pains to create was lost on him. He briefly took note of seashells scattered about on the table. He'd never really given a damn for society the way the English did. In truth, all the trappings made him want to run as if a Union brigade were chasing him, bayonets drawn.

Jesse forced himself to tamp down a sigh and turn his attention back to Lady Boniface. "I certainly do agree, my lady."

The smile she sent him in response was predatory. "I'm

truly honored to be graced with your society, sir." Her tone was low, bedchamber style.

Jesse wasn't surprised. He'd already discovered she was husband hunting. Word traveled around at country house parties, Jesse well knew from experience. Men could be worse than a gaggle of females in such matters. Apparently, her widow's portion, while admirable at several thousand a year, was not enough to withstand her proclivity for fine dresses, baubles, and gambling. Regardless of her beauty, any man seeking to avoid becoming her next benefactor should maintain his distance.

And being any woman's husband was the very last role he wanted to play. Ever. After Lavinia, the entrapment had never called to him. He supposed he owed her his thanks for that much, if nothing else.

He was careful to remain only polite when he responded to his dinner partner. "I'm sure I'm the one who is honored, my lady."

He could swear he'd heard an unladylike snort from Lady Bella's side of the table, but when he cast her a discreet glance, she was focusing upon her mother, the dowager marchioness. He supposed he was mistaken. Certainly, he'd do best to pretend as if she weren't seated so near and keep his eyes trained on the handsome setting before him.

The last of the dinner party was seated at table, and Lord Cosgrove gave a booming pronouncement to officially begin the dinner. As the soup course went 'round, the dowager disrupted the peaceful silence.

"Lady Boniface, how charming to find you here." The expression of sour distaste on her lined visage belied her words. She looked as if she'd swallowed a forkful of spoiled mackerel.

Lady Boniface bestowed a pained smile upon the dowager. "Thank you, and I must say the same of course. I shall count myself doubly fortunate this evening to be surrounded by such fine company."

"Indeed." The dowager sniffed and sent a disparaging

look in Jesse's direction. "I must, however, confess I'm not accustomed to the liberal nature of assemblages these days. In my day, things were far more judicious, you know."

Jesse had long ago grown accustomed to the dowager's marked dislike of him. Far from allowing her barbs to cause him irritation, he found them entertaining. She was a lady who fancied herself a great wit but was in fact the opposite. She had an equal penchant for melodrama and mispronouncing words.

"I fear I misunderstand you, my lady," Lady Boniface offered in a hesitant tone. It was clear she neither wished to do injury to Jesse nor upset the august dowager.

The dowager resembled a determined bird of prey in her widow's weeds and lace cap."You've heard me quite right."

"Indeed," Lady Boniface offered weakly, "perhaps I have."

Jesse pitied the woman and decided to offer her a respite. "Let us avoid such strenuous subjects this evening, my dear ladies. Isn't there anything light to which we can commend our minds, Lady Bella?"

His question at last earned him her stare, and this time it teemed with lively irritation. Twin pats of color appeared on her otherwise perfectly pale cheeks. Christ, she was beautiful.

"Perhaps we could discuss poetry, Mr. Whitney," she suggested. "Do you care to honor us with a verse or two?"

The clever minx. She'd adroitly deflected attention back to him. "Why, I would be delighted," he said, enjoying the brief expression of disappointment on her lovely features. She'd thought to outwit him. "A lady friend of mine recently spoke to me of a poem by Matthew Arnold and it has been with me ever since. 'Ah, love, let us be true to one another! For the world, which seems to lie before us like a land of dreams, so various, so beautiful, so new, hath really neither joy, nor love, nor light.'"

She was shocked he had so quickly committed the verses to memory, he could see. But the truth of it was, the poem had for some time been a favorite of his as well, albeit for different reasons. He'd been surprised when she'd shared her admiration for it with him. He hardly expected a woman of her youth to be the possessor of the serious thoughts that apparently hid in her sharp mind.

"How exquisite, Mr. Whitney," Lady Boniface purred first. "You have such an agreeable voice that I swear I could listen to you recite poetry all day long although I've never been a great lover of the art."

"I'm afraid I have difficulty comprehending the words," the dowager interjected. "Forgive me, Mr. Whitney, but you Americans certainly have a troublesome treatment of vowels."

He flashed a wry smile. "I apologize for the rudeness of my speech."

"I've always thought the American accent most pleasing to the ears," Lady Bella offered, frowning, though he couldn't discern if her grimness of expression was for her mother or for him. Perhaps both.

"I'm sure you haven't," the dowager dismissed.

"Indeed, but I'm quite sure I have, *Maman*," Bella countered in a firm tone.

Her gaze met his. He went rigid as a walking stick beneath the table. He was an ass, truly. Lusting after his best friend's innocent sister was bound to earn him a place in hell if all the other disreputable acts of his lifetime hadn't already. Thank God Thornton was a few seats down the table.

"Lady Bella, I am most humbled by your championing," he offered, his admiration for her evident in his voice. Her daring warmed him. He could hardly believe she crossed swords with her dragon of a mother for him before everyone, and judging from the dubious expression on her face, neither could the dowager.

That fine lady was not amused. If her eyes had been equipped with daggers, they would have been slicing his neck. He grinned at her, enjoying himself at her expense. He was well aware that only the fortune he'd earned in New York real estate provided him entrée into the closely guarded ranks of English society. Of course, being friends with the Marquis of Thornton certainly didn't hurt his credentials.

"I'm sure you're very welcome," murmured Bella. The look she sent him was, he had no doubt, reserved for those she disliked most. Her upturned nose spoke volumes. "Pray think nothing of it, Mr. Whitney. There are any number of Americans such as yourself on our shores. I daresay I've met a goodly number, given my brother's propensity for touring."

He harbored a suspicion he was the only American Thornton had ever brought home, but the gentleman in him refused to allow him to point that out. "Indeed," he said simply, allowing his disbelieving tone to do the work for him.

Damn, but she was unbearably lovely. After casting her glance around to, he presumed, ascertain how closely she was being watched, she dared to send him a grin and wink.

He grinned right back, thinking with a bit of foreboding that very likely he was venturing into deep waters. If he knew what was best, he'd set sail in the opposite direction. But the hell of it was that he didn't want to.

Lady Boniface was perhaps feeling jilted in their conversation, for she chose that moment to reenter it. "I do so love a good aspic, don't you, Mr. Whitney?"

The mere thought of jellied meat made his stomach upend. "I'm afraid I cannot share your enthusiasm," he said honestly. "Aspics are one of your exceptional English customs I have been slow to take to."

The duchess sniffed and looked at him down her little beak of a nose as if his dislike of aspics rendered him beyond social redemption. "Aspics are one of the finest treasures of English cuisine."

He was somehow able to maintain a serious expression. Good Christ, if this was the dinner conversation he'd be forced to endure, he hoped the soup course was also the last one. "So I'm told." He decided to attempt another change of topic. "Lady Bella, what book did you ultimately choose for your edification, if I may ask?"

"Book?" The dowager raised an imperious brow. "My daughter does not particularly care for reading, Mr. Whittlesby. She is well-versed in the arts of dance, needlework, and watercolors, as all proper ladies should be."

"Nonsense," he scoffed before he could think better of it, choosing to ignore her deliberate mispronunciation of his surname. "I've rarely seen Lady Bella without a book."

The dowager flushed. "I'm sure you haven't seen her terribly often."

"We crossed paths earlier," Lady Bella admitted quietly, "in Lord Cosgrove's library. I was in search of a volume to distract me."

Her mother frowned but said nothing more, apparently thinking better of leading the conversation into even more dangerous territory. Lady Boniface once more entangled him in unwanted niceties. He spent the remainder of the dinner surreptitiously studying Bella. He had to admit that he wanted her very badly.

But trifling with one's friend's sister just wouldn't do. He'd do best to keep his distance for the remainder of the party. If he could.

Bella decided a turn in the gardens was in order. At least, that was the demure plan she conveyed to the dowager in her effort to escape the august lady's censorious gaze. Although she'd acquired the requisite accomplishments in finishing school, there was one skill above drawing and embroidery at which she excelled.

Duping her mother.

As she walked deeper into the elaborate gardens of Wilton House, book secured in a very useful little pocket she'd sewn into her walking dress, she didn't feel a bit guilty. After all, she *was* taking a turn in the garden. And then she was going to find a quiet spot to read for the duration of the afternoon. In her estimation, there was no part of the day more monotonous than teatime. Bella would far prefer to hide away and read a good book any day.

Thoughts firmly entrenched in what was about to happen in *The Eustace Diamonds*, she rounded a corner and promptly crashed into a masculine chest.

"Good heavens, I apologize," she blurted, looking up only to realize that, much to her dismay, she'd smashed into Mr. Whitney.

"Lady Bella." He grinned and she realized his large hands were on her elbows, steadying her. "Please think nothing of it. I'm afraid I wasn't paying proper attention to the path ahead of me."

She felt faint. Why did it have to be him? She was ever making an utter imbecile of herself in his presence. Little wonder he saw her as a younger sister. She was awkward. A goose in the presence of swans.

"I fear I must own my lack of grace," she said, trying to ignore the heat of him through the layers of her dress and wrap.

"To the contrary. I'm the oaf who ran into you." His dimple appeared. "Perhaps we shall put it down to being an American. Your mother would certainly concur."

Bella winced. "I apologize on her behalf. She can be quite the curmudgeon."

Jesse laughed. "She doesn't prefer my troublesome treatment of vowels."

Her wince turned into a grimace. "Unfortunately, I have no power over her uncanny ability to insult nearly everyone in her presence." Suddenly, the time of day occurred to her. The male members of the house party had left shortly after breakfast to indulge in a favorite country house activity, shooting. "I confess I'm startled to find you here. Do you not favor the hunt?"

His grin disappeared and he released her elbows at last. "I'm afraid not."

She felt him distancing himself from her. Clearly, something was amiss. She wanted to dig, discover what lay beneath his cool exterior, but was half fearful of what she would find. "It is an exceedingly English pursuit, I suppose," she commented, unsure of what, if anything, to say.

"Shooting makes me ill at ease," he surprised her by confiding.

It was difficult to imagine a man as strong and capable as he would have any qualms about firearms. "Is it because of the war?" she asked before thinking better of it.

His gaze grew shuttered. "I don't like to speak of the war."

More fool she for thinking he might trust her with his demons. "Of course." She inclined her head. "Pray forgive me my familiarity. If you'll excuse me, I shall continue my walk."

When she skirted around him, he startled her by once again gripping her elbow. "Wait, Lady Bella."

She turned to him in askance.

His complexion had paled and his jaw was set in a firm line. "I didn't mean to be discourteous. It's only that the war was a very long time ago."

Conscience pricked at her. She had no wish to pry, and yet she did. "You needn't explain yourself to me, Mr. Whitney. I understand the mere knowing of secrets does not necessitate the sharing of them."

A semblance of his former grin returned. "Then you are a rarity among the fairer sex."

She strove to match his levity, despite wondering just how much he'd suffered during the awful carnage she'd only read about. Had he been wounded? Had he wounded others, perhaps even killed? She shook the unwelcome notion from her mind. "What, sir? You have scads of ladies begging to be told your innermost thoughts and devils?"

He drew her closer to him. Her hem brushed his trousers. She could smell him. If she raised her hand a scant few inches, she could run it gently over his freshly shorn cheek. She rather liked that he didn't favor whiskers like so many English gentlemen did. Her eyes dropped to his mouth, wanting to feel it upon hers. What would it be like to be kissed?

Jesse's expression grew solemn. "And would you be jealous if I said I did?"

She nearly lost the ability to speak. Was he flirting with her? Again? He had her at sixes and sevens. "Should I be?"

"Ah, of course not." He guided her arm until it linked through his. "May I join your walk?"

He wasn't giving her much choice, but she didn't truly mind. Spending time with him was intoxicating. Not even escaping inside her books could compare. "You may indeed," she allowed, matching his slow, steady steps as they began wending about the garden.

"I'm surprised to find you here and not in the library," he commented lightly. "It is rare to see you *sans* book."

"If you must know the truth, I've a book in my pocket just now," she confessed. "I was thinking very hard on what shall happen next in *The Eustace Diamonds* when I collided with you."

"I take it Trollope is a favorite of yours? If I recall properly, you were reading Trollope in the library the first time we met."

He remembered. She nearly tripped over her own feet. Bella shot him a glance. "You do have a habit of remembering the oddest details."

"It's not every day one meets a lady with a proclivity for sitting on her spectacles." He sent her a sideways look. "Whatever became of your spectacles, my dear? They didn't meet a bloody end beneath a bustle, did they?"

She laughed at his daring for reminding her of how she'd clumsily attempted to hide them under her bottom that long-ago day. "*Maman* refuses to allow me to wear them in company, so I'm relegated to wearing them in my chamber." Unless she could sneak away to a quiet library where she didn't fear her mother would find her, of course.

Somehow, the mere mentioning of her chamber brought a level of intimacy to the conversation that had her flushing. She looked away, studying a statue of a classical god. The gardens here were rather magnificent, she had to admit. She'd heard Lord Cosgrove employed some forty staff beneath his head gardener.

"Contrary to your mother's opinion, I think your spectacles become you," he said lowly. "It's a shame of the worst order that if I want to ever see you wearing them again I shall have to sneak into your chamber."

Though said in jest, his words sent warmth pervading her body. Her stomach felt quite queer. "I'm afraid that would be rather indecent of you, Mr. Whitney."

"I'm rather an indecent fellow." He placed a hand over hers on his arm. "Let that be a warning to you. Never trust me."

He had a true knack for bringing out the minx in her. She stopped walking, forcing him to do the same. She turned to face him fully, searching his face. "Am I in danger now, then?"

He looked down at her—truly, he had an impressive height and cut quite a masculine figure with his strong muscles and lean legs—and the need to swoon came upon her. He was more than every romantic hero she'd read about in books. He was real. He was beautiful. And, with the sun shimmering around them in the quiet square of garden at Wilton House, he was hers.

Or was he? He had yet to answer. Before her better judgment forced her to reconsider, she reached up to cup his cheek. She had eschewed gloves, and his skin was vibrant, warm and just a bit scratchy beneath her fingers. The silence between them was heavy and full of so many things neither was willing to say. She may have been unschooled in the ways of men, but even she could feel the passion simmering. No man had ever looked at her in the way Mr. Whitney now was, as if he wanted to consume her.

"Well, Mr. Whitney?" she asked, unable to help herself. She never wanted this moment to end. The day, the greenery, the scent of early autumn about them, the man. They were all riveting. Better than a book. It was her Mr. Whitney, the man she'd longed after for years, looking at her as if she were a woman, as if she were more than a younger sister. "Am I in danger?"

Her fingers wandered from his jaw to his mouth, so manly yet firm. His breath was warm as it fanned against her skin. His eyes fastened upon hers. "Yes," he said simply, and then she was in his arms.

Perhaps she had played with the proverbial fire but now she didn't care. He crushed her against him, her breasts to his hard chest, her skirts smashed against his legs. Her corset cut into her sides from the force of his embrace, but she scarcely felt it. If this was danger, she wanted more of it.

As though he'd heard her utter the sentiment aloud, he obliged her by caressing her wasp silhouette with his hands. Even beneath the stiff boning and layers, his touch sent her heart madly tripping. But nothing could have prepared her for his mouth on hers.

Her first kiss.

His lips molded hers, gently at first, but then with greater ardency. She didn't know where to place her hands, how to move her mouth. She was still, relishing the moment, yet frozen in her untried innocence. She was terrified. What if she did something wrong? Good heavens.

He must have sensed her apprehension, for he pulled away. His face was still very close to hers. She could make out tiny flecks of green in his blue eyes. He was likely disappointed. She wanted to disappear.

"I'm sorry," she hurried to explain, "I have never before…that is to say, I'm not entirely certain of what I ought to be doing."

The admission was nearly as horrifying as being kissed

by the man she'd wanted for so long and being rendered incapable of movement. His hands tightened on her waist. He pressed his lips to hers again. "Bella," he whispered, his accent like honey rolling over her senses, "you've never been kissed?"

Goodness, her novels had left her with no notion of what to do in a man's embrace. Bella settled for doing what felt most comfortable. She hooked her arms around his neck and leaned into him. Her gaze never wavered from his. "Never," she confirmed.

"Then I count myself honored," he said in a soft tone that served to dispel some of her embarrassment.

He lowered his mouth to hers once more, and this time his kiss was slower, guiding. She moved her lips in time with his. Sensation buffeted her. The tingling began in her stomach and ended between her thighs and at the very tips of her breasts. It was new. His tongue slipped inside her mouth. He tasted of the richness of coffee. She wanted, oh, she didn't know. She wanted him. Her Mr. Whitney. Her tongue rubbed against his. *Angels in heaven.*

"Christ." Muttering the oath, he tore his mouth from hers as suddenly as he'd begun kissing her. His hands set her away from him.

They stared at one another, their breathing matched and harsh. He hadn't meant to kiss her. She could discern that much from his shocked expression. What's more, he hadn't meant to like it. And innocent though she was, she knew instinctively that he had.

"If that is danger," she said in hushed tones, "then I should like to be in danger more often."

"No." He shook his head. "You cannot. You should not. Damn it to hell, Bella, let this be a lesson. You must never let a suitor be so familiar."

She asked the question begging to be posed. "Are you a suitor, then?"

"I'm a friend," he corrected, regaining his composure. "Nothing more."

"Nothing more," she repeated, struggling to comprehend what had just occurred.

He cut an abrupt bow. "I'll leave you to your walk. Please forgive me for the interruption."

And just as hastily as he'd intruded upon her blissful afternoon, he vanished from it. Bella was left to watch his broad back rounding the bend, wondering how she could ever look at him again without imagining his kisses.

## Chapter Two

ELLA SAW PRECIOUS LITTLE OF MR. WHITNEY for days, which proved quite a feat given that they were attending a house party together and there were only so many places he could hide. She was confused by his apparent defection. Wounded too. Perhaps their shared kiss had not meant anything at all to him. It was a most deflating thought.

"Arabella, darling."

*Blast.* The dowager's voice trickled to her through the closed chamber door. Bella whipped off her spectacles and stuffed them beneath a pillow along with the book she'd been reading. She had just enough time to feign sleep before her mother swept the door open. When in doubt, Bella had learned over the years, pretend to nap. Typically, it fooled the dowager every time.

She heard the unmistakable swish of her mother's skirts, the steady and determined steps growing ever closer. *Drat and double drat.* It would seem she would not have such an easy escape.

"Arabella, do wake up, you sluggard." Her mother's edict was accompanied by an abrupt prodding of Bella's shoulder.

She suppressed a sigh and peeked from one eye. "*Maman*, I fear I am quite fatigued. Can you not speak with me later?"

"Nonsense," the dowager declared. "You will speak with me now, daughter. This is a matter of utmost importance."

*Oh dear.* She opened both her eyes in defeat. "Is something amiss?"

The dowager cleared her throat. "It has occurred to me that you've been quite Friday-faced for the past few days."

"I have not." She frowned, disturbed to realize even her mother, oblivious as she tended to be, had noticed the effect Mr. Whitney had upon her.

Her mother pinned her with an omniscient stare. "I should be very displeased indeed if your sour mood has been caused in any way by the society you've been keeping with that no-account American."

"I'm sure I don't know what you speak of," she lied.

"I'll not stand for prefecation, my dear," her mother countered.

Bella would have smiled at her mother's garbling of the King's English under ordinary circumstances, but she had the unsettling feeling the dowager had somehow been alerted to her interlude with Mr. Whitney. "I do believe you meant to say prevarication, *Maman*."

"Is that not what I said? I shall not tolerate insolence from you, young miss." The dowager sniffed as though she'd caught scent of something foul in a barnyard. "I have it from Hollins that there have been whispers that you favor Mr. Whitney when I have made it clear to you that you must be setting your cap for the Duke of Devonshire. What have you to say for yourself?"

Hollins was her mother's lady's maid and source of all manner of gossip, both true and false. It was not good for Hollins to be bringing untoward news to the dowager. Uncertainty trickled through Bella. No one had ever seen her alone with Mr. Whitney. Had they?

She sat up, wincing as her stays dug into her sides. "*Maman*, I do not favor Mr. Whitney at all. He was kind enough to help me fetch a book in the library, nothing more. You mustn't heed all the old gossips."

The dowager's expression remained pinched. "You must tread with care, Arabella. Romance is a petty notion better suited to books and schoolgirls than real life. You must ally yourself with a man with a family name and history suited to our own."

If she wished to avoid a lengthy diatribe, Bella knew it best to simply agree with her mother. In truth, the Duke of Devonshire was not a man who made her feel tingly with anticipation. He didn't memorize her favorite verses of Matthew Arnold. He wasn't handsome in a devilish, manly way. He wasn't Mr. Whitney.

Did she think she had a future with the no-account American, as the dowager called him? Her heart said yes, but her mind said no. His kisses had changed everything. She longed to be held in his strong arms again. Perhaps romance was a trifling thing, but Bella found she rather liked the way it upended her emotions. She wanted more.

But instead of voicing any of these dangerous sentiments to her mother, she nodded. "Yes, *Maman*. I shall endeavor to do honor to our family name."

"Good girl." Her mother patted her hand. "Remember, when you speak with the duke you must always agree with him. Pay attention in great detail to each word he speaks, as though it comes from the lips of the Lord Himself."

*Good heavens.* Bella gave her mother a saccharine smile. "Of course."

Despite the uncomfortable interview with her mother, Bella could think of nothing more than seeking out Mr. Whitney at the first possible opportunity. Days had passed without even a glance her way at the dinner table. She had to concede he was intentionally avoiding her. She was equally unwavering in her resolve to catch him unawares. How could he kiss her, alter her forever, and then act as if he didn't know her? It was vexing. Infuriating, even. She would not allow him to get away with it.

Growing ever more frustrated, she resorted to what she'd only read about in novels. She sent him a secret note with the help of her lady's maid Smith, asking him to meet her in the library once more. She very carefully chose a day when the house party was engaged in outdoor sport, knowing that like she, Mr. Whitney would eschew it.

It seemed to her that she waited a fortnight or more until he finally materialized in the library. She was pretending to read a book on a divan when he stalked into the chamber, looking unfairly handsome and, in that way he had, just a little bit uncivilized.

Bella rose, discarding her unwanted book without heed. "Mr. Whitney." Her voice sounded racked with nerves, even to her ears. "I feared you wouldn't come."

He gave her an abbreviated bow. "Lady Bella, I am, as ever, your servant."

She wished the words were true, but he was not and likely would never be hers. *Drat it all.* She had chosen her gown with care and fretted with it now, hoping he wouldn't realize how much thought she had given to her *toilette*. Smith had even taken extra time with her hair. Bella felt suddenly silly.

"You do not seek out sport as the other guests do?" she asked, though she already knew the answer.

"I have no need for weapons in my life." His voice was as solemn as his gorgeous face. "I shot the last gun I ever intended to shoot in the war."

"I'm sorry." She felt guilty for again dredging up such a delicate subject. "I didn't mean to pry."

"Not at all." He inclined his head. "I believe our kinship allows us a certain familiarity."

*Kinship.*

She frowned at him. "Mr. Whitney, we are not kin."

"I consider myself another older brother to you, my dear." He said this last mildly, as if he had never passionately taken her in his arms.

Her stubborn nature rose to the surface. She may have been a mild-mannered girl with no sins more alarming than a penchant for reading too many novels and outwitting her mother, but she was not about to let him try the same old road again.

"Do you put your tongue in all your sisters' mouths, Mr. Whitney?" She gave him a false smile. "I confess, Americans do have such odd customs."

"Lady Bella, you shock me."

Ordinarily, she would never be so forthright, so vulgar in her speech, but he had driven her beyond the brink of reason. That he could face her so calmly, as if they had never experienced the fire in one another's arms that they had, hurt her. She had thought of little other than him in the intervening days. Had he thought of her at all?

"Indeed? You will own that you did kiss me." Before she could keep the seam of her lips firmly sealed together, the words were out. Foolish, foolish girl. Had she not embarrassed herself enough before him already?

"Think nothing of it." He smiled at her, but it was not a lover's smile. Rather, it was that of a worldly man dismissing a green young lady.

She was not amused at his attempts to set her down, nor was she grateful for the tact he exhibited. Perhaps she was untried and had not much experience with men, but she was not an imbecile. She had emotions. She had a heart. He had to know what he did to her.

"Think nothing of it," she repeated his careless words, her tone grown cool. "You say it as though we were discussing nothing more than a speck of dust on the family silver. You kissed me, held me in your arms. Surely it is of more consequence to you than that."

His eyes flashed with dark emotion. For a moment, his

gentleman's mask slipped to reveal passion hidden beneath his imperturbable façade. "It was wrong of me, damn it. It cannot happen again."

"Why not?" Why did he insist on seeing her as a girl? She'd had her comeout years before. She hadn't even been this dizzied by curtsying before the queen in Buckinghamshire Palace and still the dratted man refused to treat her as his romantic equal.

"You are an innocent lady," he gritted, clearly growing frustrated by her determination.

She was unmoved. "Nonsense. So is every other unmarried miss."

He frowned at her. "You are my best friend's sister."

Ah, there was the true crux of it. Dash Thornton. Dash Mr. Whitney's cursed notion of loyalty. This simply wouldn't do. She decided to change tactics.

Bella met his gaze, searching. "Are you saying you could never love me?"

This time, he laughed. "My dear Lady Bella, love has very little to do with stolen kisses and romantic embraces. You show your naïveté."

Her breath left her. Before she could rein in her temper, she slapped him. The echo of her blow rang through the quiet of the cavernous library. They stared at one another. A faint trace of redness marred his cheek. She had done him violence. She almost could not believe it.

His lips quirked into a wry semblance of a smile. "The kitten has claws."

She wanted to apologize but her pride would not allow it. "I'm no kitten."

He raised a brow. "So I begin to see."

She was fast losing her composure, feeling as if she'd waded into the ocean and was caught up in its dangerous swells. But it was too late to turn back to shore. "Do you think that because I am younger than you I have no feelings?"

"Nothing of the sort. Rather, I think your youth leads

you to mistake your feelings."

Irritation nettled her. Of all the insufferable, arrogant notions she'd ever heard, it was the most maddening. "You think me too ignorant to understand my own feelings, then?"

He took her hands in his, an unwelcome gesture given the mercurial nature of her emotions. "Bella, you misunderstand me."

She stiffened and tugged away from his grasp. "Perhaps it's because I'm young and mindless."

"I meant nothing of the sort." He followed her steps when she would have escaped.

She pirouetted to face him, her emotions spilling over like a pot unattended by a scullery maid. "Pray explain precisely what it is you *did* mean, Mr. Whitney. For a few silly moments, I seem to have lost my head in your presence. I thought you were a gentleman, and instead you've proven yourself a cad capable of trifling with a young lady who has only ever held you in highest esteem."

His expression softened. "Forgive me. I fear I've paid you grave insult." He cupped her elbow, bringing her closer to him once again. "I never intended to hurt you."

She searched his gaze for an answer. "Then why did you kiss me?"

"Because I couldn't help myself." The admission seemed torn from him. "But Bella, I'm not worthy of an innocent like you. I'm not fit to lick your boots. That is why we must remain friends only. I'm sorry if I gave you cause to think otherwise."

*Oh dear.* This was not what she wanted to hear from his beautifully sculpted lips. Indeed, she'd rather they be engaged in the far more preferable business of kissing her instead.

She blinked at him, hopelessly confused, and decided to opt for levity to hide her embarrassment. "I daresay I should not want you to lick my boots, lest there be muck or far worse on them."

His mouth kicked into a semblance of a grin. "I shudder to think of what the 'far worse' could be. Where on earth have you been traipsing about, Lady Bella?"

"Only in gardens with you," she said with unmistakable meaning.

"And that will lead you nowhere but hopelessly astray."

She was curious once again and drawn to him as ever. "Why do you insist on acting as though you're unfit? You know as well as I that if you were a scoundrel, my brother would never have been your steadfast friend for all these years."

"Not a scoundrel, perhaps, but a man who has seen too much of life." His expression hardened, his eyes glittering like polished jet. "I've been through a war. It changes a body in ways you can't comprehend, in ways I don't want you to comprehend."

He seemed so alone in that moment her heart physically hurt inside her chest. She could only imagine what he'd seen in his lifetime. She knew the War Between the States had been devastating. It was too much for one man to bear alone. She yearned to reach out to him, give him solace.

She drew closer to Mr. Whitney, the hem of her dress brushing his trousers. Bella looked up at him, marveling at how handsome and elegant a figure he cut. "Did you ever think that perhaps I'm not so foolish and naïve as you suppose? You may confide in me."

He lowered his forehead to hers, breathing deeply. "You are too good. I could never burden your pretty head with the horrors I've seen."

"Nonsense." She traced his hard, bristled jaw. "You cannot forever be a man alone."

She didn't wait for his response. This time, she kissed him. She knew little still of what to do, only that she longed to feel his lips hot and insistent over hers. His mouth was at first immobile. She pressed her lips tentatively to his as he had done to her.

His arms suddenly came around her, crushing her frame

to his. To Bella, it seemed as if she had tipped over a kerosene lantern in a barn full of dry summer's hay. He was a passionate fire, ready to consume her. She came to life with his ardor, a steady ache building low in her belly. Their tongues tangled. He tasted once more of the coffee he must have consumed at breakfast and he smelled like himself, man and leather and something indefinably compelling.

The kiss deepened, his tongue sliding wetly into her mouth. She moaned, pressing herself into him, wanting more. His large hands settled first on her wasp waist and then slid upward to the swell of her bodice. He cupped her breasts through the barrier of her stiff, tight-laced corset. She was suddenly aware her dress fastened up the back with nearly thirty buttons. Drat her ninny-headed fashion.

Neither of them heard the library door click open and remained unaware of the surprised witness to their romantic tableau until a shocked gasp intruded on their passion.

"Oh, good heavens. I do apologize." The feminine voice that interrupted their fiery interlude was, unmistakably, that of Tia, Lady Stokey.

"Goddamn," Mr. Whitney cursed, his mouth still perilously near to hers.

Bella peered around his broad shoulder to find Lady Stokey standing in wide-eyed amazement, her hand at her throat. It simply wasn't done to be alone with a man, embracing him in the library. Her reputation would be ruined if her ladyship breathed a word.

"I beg you, my lady," she began, faltering when words would not rescue her scrambling mind.

"I think I shall go for a turn about the gardens," Lady Stokey announced with a forced sense of brightness. "Yes indeed. I do apologize." Flashing a strained smile, she disappeared as quickly as she had entered.

"Oh dear Lord." Fear replaced the luxurious desire that had been running through her. "I shall seek her out, Mr. Whitney. I feel quite certain she shall maintain her silence. We have no need to fear this will result in unwelcome complications."

"No." Mr. Whitney shook his head, looking up to her at last. "Please accept my most fervent apologies, Lady Bella. It has never been my intent to dishonor you. I will ask for your hand in marriage immediately."

"You must not," she rushed to deny. Goodness, she did not want a forced marriage. If he did not want her freely, then she did not want him at all. "I must apologize as well. This is certainly not what I had planned."

"Is it not?" He searched her gaze, his inscrutable. "Forgive me, but I have to wonder. First the note leading me here, then an interloper at just the right moment. Did you plan all this?"

"I beg your pardon?" Hurt flashed through her. "Of course I had no such plans in mind. How could you even suggest something so horrid? Do you not care for me at all? No, don't answer. Of course you must not or else you would never suggest something so detestable."

Now she was well and truly humiliated. What a fool she'd been. He was her senior by many years. She was unsophisticated, a mere girl by his standards. Of course he would want nothing to do with her, and yet she had sought him out, questioned and kissed him as though she had the right, fool that she was.

"Pray accept my apology," she murmured through nearly numb lips. "I never intended to distress you. I assure you from this point on, I'll take care to keep my distance from you."

"To hell with keeping a distance," he nearly growled, his American drawl becoming more pronounced in his ire. "The damage has already been done. I'll need to seek an audience with your brother."

The fiercely protective Thornton would murder him, Bella was certain of it. Had her heart been capable of leaping from her breast and leading her on a merry chase about the chamber, it surely would have in that moment.

In dawning horror, she pressed her hand over her

mouth. "You must not. Thornton shall trounce the both of us. And my mother would have an apoplectic fit. I'd be ruined."

"Bella, you're the innocent sister of my greatest friend. I don't have much choice."

"It was perfectly acceptable of you to kiss me when no one was watching," she pointed out. "But you've been caught out, and suddenly it's wrong?"

"Damn it." He raked a hand through his hair. "It's been wrong the whole time, but it's gone too far now."

"No," Bella rushed to deny. "No one need be the wiser. I don't want to be the cause of dissension between you and Thornton, nor do I relish the prospect of a rush to judgment."

She wanted pursuit and passion. She did not want her brother's misguided idea of sibling loyalty to destroy what dismal chance she had of impressing Mr. Whitney. She wanted to do things in the proper way.

The shifting expression on his handsome face said he was at war with himself, uncertain of how to proceed. While it was true that they had indeed gone too far, it was apparent he had no wish to hasten into a forced marriage either.

"Please," she pressed. "You cannot go to Thornton. Even if you don't care for me at all, I pray you'll grant me this boon."

"Very well, my dear." His voice was severe. "But you must in turn promise me you'll never again find yourself in a compromising position with a gentleman. Not all your suitors will be blessed with a conscience."

He was once again speaking down to her as though she were a pitiable and callow youth. She didn't appreciate it, especially given his particular lack of conscience. If he cared he'd upset her, it didn't show. Truth told, she was beginning to find him rather arrogant. She was fast realizing that not all life's choices were as simple as she would have them be.

It was time to put some distance between them. "I suppose I shall count myself fortunate that you have one then, Mr. Whitney." She dropped into a mocking curtsy. "I bid you good day."

Jesse felt like an utter bastard. He had always prided himself on his impeccable control. In the war, his life had been chaos, every day a battle against death, against the enemy, even against those he'd loved. For the past fifteen years, he'd taken care to avoid turmoil. He had lived a quiet life, poured his efforts into business, into travel abroad. Never had he accosted an innocent young lady with passion, not once and certainly not twice.

Perhaps he was descending into madness. Lord knew it had happened to some of his fellow soldiers. He'd thought he was beyond that dark time, beyond the nightmares he'd suffered intermittently ever since, but something in the last few days had brought it creeping back to him. He'd found it impossible to sleep for fear of the dreams that threatened to claim him.

How could he ever face Thornton again? Hellfire. He had promised not to reveal the truth to his best friend, and perhaps his motivation had been more selfish than selfless. He truly treasured the brotherly bonds he'd forged with Thornton. And if he were brutally honest, he didn't trust himself with an innocent heart like Bella's. He didn't have enough of himself left to give her. Certainly, he couldn't love her the way she deserved. The war had ruined him. Lavinia had ruined him. Bella was a kind soul who didn't know just how deep his wounds ran.

As he beat his hasty retreat from the library, he was so consumed by his tumultuous thoughts that he nearly collided with a set of enormous gray skirts. He was infinitely dismayed to realize the skirts belonged to the dowager marchioness. She sniffed the air as if she smelled something foul and sliced him with a glare.

"Do watch where you're walking, Mr. Whittlesby," she

took him to task.

"It's Whitney, my lady," he corrected although she'd been mispronouncing his name for years now. "Please accept my apology. I hope I didn't give you a start."

"That is precisely what I said." She looked down her nose at him, her expression one she might reserve for horse manure that had the effrontery to appear in her line of vision. "I daresay it would do to be more careful when traversing the halls, Whittlesby. Truly, I could have been injured."

The dowager was a formidable opponent. She couldn't be more different from her lovely daughter. Bella was beautiful and warm in nature, always ready to give. The dowager, on the other hand, had the appearance of a peregrine falcon, dark and sharp-beaked. A hunter.

"Once again, I offer my apologies." He gave her a bow. "May I escort you somewhere?"

Her eyes narrowed with what he supposed was either disgust or suspicion. "Why are you not the hunt?"

Ah, it was suspicion then. "I do not care for sport," he said simply.

"What sort of man doesn't care for sport?" She sniffed.

The sort of man who knew the scent of gunpowder and death, who still heard the cries of the wounded in his sleep. The sort of man who knew what it was like to be given a uniform and a musket as a naive young country boy and sent into battle, who had watched more than one soldier take his last breath. But she needn't know that much. "You may place the blame on my American sensibilities."

"Indeed. I have heard all manner of social atrocities committed at the hands of your countrymen. Why, I'm given to understand many of your people cannot even bother to dine with the use of cutlery. One can only hope your presence on our august shores will be improving upon your character."

He begged to differ. It rather seemed his character was going to the dogs.

"Indeed, my lady. One can only hope." He bowed again, anxious to be anywhere other than in her arrogant presence. "I bid you good day."

"One more thing, Whittlesby," she called out when he would have strode away.

He turned to her. "Madam?"

"You will do well to stay away from my daughter." Her expression hardened. "She is to have a coronet and nothing less when she marries. There is no place for you in her life and I'll not allow her to be ruined by some American jackanapes."

"I hold Lady Bella in highest esteem," he assured her honestly. "You have my word I will keep my distance."

He just hoped like hell he could keep it.

# Chapter Three

A GREAT DEAL OF SCANDAL WAS BREWING at Lady Cosgrove's country house party. Bella was kept entertained with the company's antics by her maid Smith as she prepared for dinner. There was all manner of belowstairs gossip, from Lady Aylesford spending far too much time with Lord Ribblesdale to Lady Grimsby falling asleep at the breakfast table.

Thankfully, none of it pertained to Bella. She'd been able to seek out the kind Lady Stokey, who had merely waved off Bella's concerns. She'd been very relieved at the woman's understanding. It had saved her from ruin and worse. After all, she had no wish to be a cause for resentment to Mr. Whitney.

Bella sat still before a mirror, watching Smith's animated reflection as she worked her hair into a sophisticated knot with sprays of curls framing her face. "My dear Smith, you do work wonders."

She wanted to look at her best advantage for the Elizabethan-themed dinner awaiting her. Bella had decided to try a different tactic in her battle with Mr. Whitney. She was determined to put on her loveliest evening dress and flirt madly with every man in sight. Every man, that was, except for Mr. Whitney.

"You have the most beautiful hair, my lady," Smith chattered happily. "I'm fortunate you were blessed with such thick, glossy locks. Miss Chilton's lady's maid says it takes mountains of false hair to accomplish even the simplest styles."

Miss Margot Chilton, also in attendance at the house party, was not a favorite of Bella's. "One must also wonder how much pearl powder her poor maid must apply to that horrendous nose of hers."

Smith laughed. "Oh, I shouldn't say aught as I've got quite a beak myself."

"But Miss Chilton makes it so easy to malign her." Bella wrinkled her nose. "I suppose I should exhibit more sympathy, but she is quite awful."

"Fret not, my lady. She was gossiping about Lord Thornton's row with Lord Ravenscroft, saying the two were fighting over Lady Scarbrough's affections."

Good heavens. Her brother, the supposedly staid politician, was currently losing his head over the married Lady Scarbrough, and it was causing the dowager no ends of distress. Apparently, he had actually come to blows with the Earl of Ravenscroft earlier in the day while a large audience watched in fascinated horror. Bella was aghast that her brother had sunk to such depravity. She had scarcely even seen him thus far at the house party, aside from his daily escort to the breakfast room and sitting at the same table as he during dinners. She couldn't make sense of the sudden distance he had put between himself and his family. The brother she knew had always been above reproach. It was the odious Lady Scarbrough who turned him into an utter lunatic, she had no doubt. But of course, love could do strange things to a person. She knew that all too well.

Bella sighed. "Oh dear. What did she say?"

"Forgive me, my lady, but she said your brother was fighting with the earl over Lady Scarbrough's affections. She swears she saw Lady Scarbrough in the thick of it."

"Thank you for telling me, Smith. Could you please do your best to blunt the talk belowstairs?" She frowned as she worried for her brother's once-sterling reputation. She feared he was on a course bearing no positive outcome.

"I will of course," Smith offered. "You know where my loyalty lies."

A thought occurred to her. Perhaps she was being overly cautious, but she wanted to make certain Lady Stokey was trustworthy. "Smith, have you caught wind of any other scandals?"

"Nothing more than the ordinary." Smith put the finishing touches on her coiffure. "There you are, my lady. Pretty as a picture."

Bella studied her reflection. She had to admit that Smith's dab hand had truly worked its magic this evening. "You've done a very fine job, Smith. I'm fortunate to have someone as talented as you to help me with my *toilette*."

Her maid flushed. "Thank you, Lady Bella. Is there aught else I can do for you?"

"That will be all, thank you." She cast a critical eye over her evening frock as Smith took her leave. It was a lush cream satin that had been designed by the great Worth. Her skirt was adorned with embroidered roses while French lace trimmed her perfectly fitted cuirass-style bodice. The dress was draped and tiered to perfection, molding her figure to advantage. And though the baleen stays supporting her cinched waist were a trifle uncomfortable, she wasn't about to complain. Worth was truly a master. If she couldn't impress Mr. Whitney this evening, she never would.

For reasons that perhaps had more to do with the meddling dowager's influence on Lady Cosgrove and less to do with their hostess's concern for social niceties, Bella was seated nearly an ocean away from Mr. Whitney. But the distance between them didn't serve to curtail her plans as her mother may have hoped. She used the opportunity to her advantage by plying the Duke of Devonshire with as much attention as was politely possible in hopes Mr. Whitney might notice.

Devonshire made for an agreeable dinner partner, but she couldn't seem to keep from casting surreptitious glances Mr. Whitney's way. Several times, she swore she felt his intense gaze on her only to find him laughing with the odious Margot Chilton. It seemed he was determined to make good on his word. Bella longed to fling a great glob of her dinner all over Miss Chilton's dress, but she suppressed the urge in favor of civility.

By the time the ladies took their leave of the men, Bella's hopes were quite dashed. She had turned herself out to tremendous effect, had sought to make him unbearably jealous. And she had failed.

Perhaps she was nothing more than the naïve girl he believed her to be after all. The ladies were shepherded to the drawing room for a series of parlor games that Bella found almost as loathsome as she did Margot Chilton. She wished she had a book to read.

Her mother presided over her like a hawk, her countenance grim.

"That Scarbrough woman will be the ruin of us all," the dowager lamented in a careful undertone.

Across the room, Margot Chilton volunteered herself for the first round of charades. Bella wanted to rip the false hair from her head. But she refused to allow her anger to show. "*Maman*, I do believe my brother is playing a most willing role in this scandal."

"Men are weak-willed," her mother declared. "Your father had the character of a bowl of aspic. I am decidedly disappointed that Thornton seems to be patterning himself in a similar vein. It's in the blood, I suppose."

Margot began gesticulating in the center of the chamber.

"You're a donkey," Bella guessed unkindly.

That earned her a narrow-eyed glared from her apparent

rival. Bella sent Margot a sweet smile in return.

"Parlor games," the dowager hissed, "are vulgar. I insist you cease playing immediately."

"Perhaps you are a cow," Bella called, ignoring her mother entirely.

Margot's glare turned frigid as Wenham Lake ice.

"A remarkably large sheep?" Bella suggested next.

"Arabella," her mother snapped. "Listen to your poor, suffering mother for once in your life. What did I do to deserve such unnatural children?"

"I am sorry, *Maman*," she fibbed. "I quite lost my head."

The dowager sighed. "It is bad enough Thornton has lowered himself to pugilism before the cream of society over some lightskirt."

"I daresay you ought to lower your voice." Bella was aware of the proximity of the notorious gossip Lady Grimsby even if her mother was not. The only time that lady was not listening for tidbits was when she was snoring over her eggs.

This time, the dowager sniffed. "Nonsense. Now how did you fare in conversation with the Duke of Devonshire? A worthy match there, I tell you."

"He's dull," Bella grumbled, quite forgetting to play her normal game of agreeable daughter. "All he did was natter on about rebuilding his country seat." In truth, he hadn't been a bad dinner partner, but he was simply not the man who occupied her every thought.

"You could do far worse than a gentleman like the duke," the dowager pointed out. "Thank the blessed angels that you've stopped speaking to that awful American. I was grateful indeed when Lady Cosgrove seated you nearer to someone more appropriate to your station as the daughter of a marchioness. If one doesn't stand on ceremony, one doesn't stand on anything at all."

"I was under the impression one stands on one's feet," she quipped, her irritation from Mr. Whitney's dismissal of her at dinner making her bold.

"Hold your tongue, Lady Arabella. When did you become possessed of such deplorable manners?" She pressed a dramatic hand to her brow. "The world has gone to the dogs, I tell you."

That rather gave her an idea. Margot Chilton was still pantomiming, no one having guessed her less than clever rendition of whatever she was pretending to be.

"You are a rabid dog," Bella guessed next.

"I give up!" Margot shouted in a most unladylike lack of decorum. "A baker. I was a baker." With a ferocious frown in Bella's direction, she all but stomped back to her seat.

Maybe it was small of her, but Bella felt a surge of satisfaction. If she'd had to suffer through extra whalebone crushing her all evening and hadn't earned so much as an appreciative look from Mr. Whitney, at least she could win one battle.

"Really, Bella," her mother clucked *sotto voce*. "I know the Chilton girl is dreadful, but that was cruel."

She shrugged. "I was simply exercising my creative liberties."

The dowager's eyes turned to slits of suspicion. "Has this anything to do with the attention a certain American blackleg paid her at dinner?"

"I hadn't noticed," she lied again.

"A liar is worse than a tradesman." Her mother sniffed with disdain.

"I haven't the slightest idea what you're talking about." Bella searched the assembled ladies for an escape route. "If you don't mind, I think I shall go have a word with Lady Stokey."

"She's the sister to that infernal Scarbrough woman," the dowager protested.

Bella once again chose to ignore her.

After the men rejoined the ladies following dinner, Jesse had a difficult time ignoring Bella. She was an ethereal beauty in a gown that made the lush woman's body hiding beneath the silken trappings all too apparent. And all too tempting. Dear God, he'd been hiding his arousal for most of the night, and no amount of staring at Miss Margot Chilton's sizeable nose could make it abate.

Of all the women in the world, why did he have to want Bella? The very last thing Thornton needed, in addition to the troubles he'd already created by brawling with Ravenscroft, was to worry about his innocent sister being ravished by his trusted friend. If fate had any sympathy, Jesse would never have met her. Why couldn't she be horse-faced and dim-witted?

She'd been gracing the Duke of Devonshire with an obvious amount of attention. Damn it if didn't bother him. Across the drawing room, she was at it again. Margot Chilton was an irritating presence at his side. He tried to pay attention to the girlish drivel she spouted.

"I do so love to draw, don't you, Mr. Whitney?" she asked coyly.

"I've never been particularly good at the arts," he admitted, trying to wrest his gaze from the stunning Bella.

"I have a fair hand for watercolors as well."

He forced himself to look at Miss Chilton. She was not a bad sort, but she didn't have much wit and she certainly lacked Bella's loveliness. "Indeed?"

"I confess I listened with much fascination to your stories of the American West the other evening at dinner." She smiled tentatively.

He didn't know much more about the Western world of outlaws and thieves than anyone else, but Bella had asked him to regale the party, he recalled. He knew what he read in the papers, and he'd known of Jesse James during his war days. The stories of the carnage wrought by James under Bloody Bill Anderson were legendary. But that was hardly a fit subject for a lady's ears.

"I'm delighted to have entertained you," he told Miss

Chilton, wondering when he could escape her clutches.

He heard Bella's sweet laughter joining with Devonshire's. It was akin to someone pouring ice water down his back. Jesse told himself to leave her to her comfortable fate with a man like the duke. He was an aristocrat, kind if not a bit staid, and would provide her with the life she deserved. Jesse, on the other hand, was all manners of wrong for her. He'd learned the painful way what havoc a relationship based upon lust could create. Hadn't he already caused enough damage with foolish decisions?

But Bella, it seemed, was willing to test fate though he might not be. She approached him, her hand on Devonshire's arm, a smile at the ready. He couldn't look away.

He bowed. "Lady Arabella, Your Grace, good evening to you both."

"The same to you, Mr. Whitney." Bella offered him her hand.

Jesse took it and kissed it, wanting with all the passion raging through him to yank her into his arms and take her away. Instead, he released her as though her touch didn't make him feel as if he'd just downed too much whiskey.

The duke took Miss Chilton's proffered hand, bussing the air above it. They all exchanged insipid pleasantries for a time. Jesse was hopelessly ensnared in Bella's gaze. Unless he was mistaken, he detected longing in her expression for just a brief moment. God help him, he didn't think he'd ever wanted a woman more in his entire existence.

"This evening was quite unique, wouldn't you concur?" Devonshire asked their small assemblage at large.

"It was lovely," Jesse agreed, but he didn't remove his enthralled gaze from Bella. If he had thought her beautiful before tonight, he thought her a goddess now.

"I did think some of the ladies were perhaps overdressed for the occasion," Miss Chilton said, wearing a sour pout. The dismissive glance she gave to Bella made it plain she spoke of Bella's elaborate gown.

"I too noticed an excessive amount of false hair," Bella snipped back at Miss Chilton. The smile on her lips was feline enough to show the kitten wasn't afraid to make use of her formidable claws.

There was a decided amount of feminine animosity in the air. Now that Bella mentioned it, Miss Chilton's hair did seem to possess an unnatural amount of volume to it. And dear Lord, was there a stuffed bird lurking in there? How had he failed to notice before? The thing looked positively evil.

The expression on poor Miss Chilton's face turned bilious. "Lady Bella, I can't imagine what you speak of. I've never heard of such a thing."

"Indeed." Bella's voice was sugar itself. "Pray forgive me if I misspoke."

And she was patently insincere. Who knew of the tigress lurking beneath her exquisite shell? Devonshire appeared flummoxed by the entire exchange, but Jesse couldn't tell if it was the references to fashion or the obvious venom spewing between the ladies.

He had to admit he was rather enjoying himself. It occurred to him that perhaps Bella was as jealous as he. To test his theory, he turned to Miss Chilton. "May I say that your coiffure is astoundingly pretty?"

"You may indeed." She flushed with pleasure. "Thank you, Mr. Whitney."

Bella's eyes were on him, hard as flint. He almost smiled.

"The weather has been spot on for hunting, wouldn't you agree?" Devonshire intoned, perhaps seeking to redirect their dialogue into safer channels.

"It certainly has," Jesse responded, merely agreeing out of a sense of politeness.

"I tell you, there's nothing finer than the scent of gunpowder and the crack of shots on an English country morning," Devonshire continued.

Jesse recalled all too well the scent of gunpowder, along

with the scent of rotting flesh in the July sun and the thunderous roar of cannon balls exploding, limbs flying through the air. It was as if a trigger had been pressed inside him. Suddenly, the war unleashed itself on him again. Whoever had said war was hell had been wrong. The real hell was what came afterward.

The last thing he needed was to appear a madman to the glittering lords and ladies around him. They needn't know the savagery lurking beneath his gentleman's exterior. The heavy dinner he'd consumed began churning in his stomach and his skin went hot. It was time to take his leave. He avoided all the gazes directed at him. "If you'll excuse me, I fear I'm weary."

Without waiting for their responses, he strode from the drawing room, hoping like hell he could make it back to his chamber without doing something foolish. Even after all the time that had passed, there were still moments when the horrors he'd witnessed assaulted him. It recurred with far less frequency now, but he knew the signs well enough. There was never any telling what caused it, but when the fires of Hades were at his heels, he knew when to run.

Something was wrong with Mr. Whitney, Bella knew instantly, and it wasn't as commonplace as the jealousy she'd hoped to stir within him. No indeed, it was something far more profound and far more dangerous. He'd looked as if he were about to cast up his accounts just before beating a hasty retreat, and she knew enough about him to realize it likely was related to the duke's unaware reference to hunting.

*I have no need for guns in my life*, he'd said.

But she suspected it was far more than a dislike of guns that kept him from a country grouse shoot. Thornton had hinted once that something very bad had happened to Mr. Whitney in the war. He'd been a young man then. She couldn't fathom the destruction and death he must have lived through. Her own life had been as easy as an afternoon tea by comparison.

"Do you suppose I said something amiss?" Devonshire wondered, his expression one of genuine puzzlement.

"I'm sure Mr. Whitney was merely fatigued," Bella hastened to dismiss his concern.

She didn't want anyone to deduce what she had about him. For some inexplicable reason, a fierce need to protect him rose within her. She knew then she had to go to him. *You cannot forever be a man alone*, she'd told him, and she meant those words. He'd given her no reason to have hopes he might one day grow to care for her. But she cared for him regardless of his emotions. There was no earthly way she could allow a man in such obvious pain to suffer on his own.

Bella had to escape the drawing room at the first opportunity.

Her course of action settled, she pretended to catch the dowager's eye. "Dear me, it looks as if my mother requires my assistance," she said in a light tone she didn't feel. "If you will both excuse me?"

She curtseyed and beat a path to her mother. It didn't escape her notice that for once, she was running toward her mother rather than away. Bella hoped the dowager wouldn't notice anything was wrong. Her mother could be rather canny in the most unwanted situations.

"Bella, darling." The dowager beamed at her as she took up her dutiful role at her mother's side once more. "I was just having a most improving discussion with Lady Cosgrove."

Their hostess appeared slightly aggrieved and it wouldn't surprise Bella to learn her mother had somehow insulted her. Lady Cosgrove was a mild-mannered and genial lady. Bella would have to mend fences. She sighed. "Lady Cosgrove, we must thank you for a wonderful house party. Truly, you have outdone yourself thus far."

"Thank you, my dear Lady Bella." Their hostess's frown

eased. "I was just telling your mother it is a shame indeed that we shan't be graced with your recitation for our Shakespearean theater."

Bella cut her mother with a glare. The dowager had forbade Bella's participation because she didn't deem the recitation of Shakespeare appropriate. Dealing with her mother truly could be vexing at times. "Please accept my apologies, my lady."

"Accepted, dear girl." Their hostess rose from the settee. "If you will excuse me, I must continue mingling."

When Lady Cosgrove flitted away, Bella turned to the dowager. "*Maman*, must you insist upon being so stringent with Shakespeare? It is only innocent fun, you know."

"Dramas are coarse and common self-indulgences better suited to the poor than anyone of consequence," the dowager stated in an august tone. "And as for Shakespeare, the man championed the eating of babies! Utterly preposterous."

"*Maman*," Bella was compelled to protest, aghast at her mother's lack of literary acumen. "We've been over this before. That was Mr. Swift, and it was satire."

"Tut." Her mother frowned with unparalleled vehemence. "I forbid you to speak of it again."

"Very well." Perhaps this was her opportunity to flee. "I find I'm quite done in, *Maman*. I think I shall make an early evening of it."

"What of the duke? I should think you'd want his ear for at least a bit longer. You can't leave him to suffer the company of that Chilton chit. Her father is a mere viscount and a pockets-to-let drunkard at that."

"I fear I must." She sighed, trying to sound her feeblest. "I truly am fatigued."

"Very well." Her mother gave in. "I shall accompany you."

*Drat.* She didn't want to arouse suspicion, but neither did she want to be encumbered by her mother's presence. "I wouldn't wish to curtail your enjoyment of the evening," she tried as nonchalantly as she could manage.

"Nonsense. I'm far too old for drawing room pleasantries. I daresay I don't care for most of the assemblage here anyway." Her mother announced this last loudly enough to be overheard as she rose and fluffed her ever-present gray skirts.

*Dear heavens.* The dowager certainly wasn't about to make this easy on her. With another suffering sigh, she played the dutiful daughter and followed her mother out of the chamber.

Once in the safe confines of her bedchamber, Bella rang for her maid and went to great lengths to uphold the pretense that she was planning an early slumber. She allowed Smith to undress her and take down her hair and dismissed her as usual. After Smith was gone, Bella hurried to put on her least fussy frock, a demure morning gown that she could manage to wear without the encumbrance of a corset. She bound her hair into a simple bun.

What she was about to attempt was extraordinarily ill-advised. If she were caught sneaking about in the halls as an unattached miss, her reputation would be reduced to ruins. But she'd seen the haunted expression on Mr. Whitney's handsome face. She knew he needed her.

Her mind firmly made, she peeked out into the hall. A servant bustled away from her in the dim light, turned a corner and disappeared down a back stair. Beyond that, there wasn't another soul in sight. She slipped from the chamber, holding her breath when the door emitted a rather obvious creak. She fervently hoped the remainder of the guests would be occupied in the drawing room for at least enough time for her to locate Mr. Whitney's chamber.

As quietly and quickly as she could, she started off down the hall, scanning each name placard. Every groan of a noisy floorboard sent her heart plummeting to her slipper-shod feet. She was acutely aware of the sound she made. It seemed hours passed as she traveled nearly the entire length of the Tudor wing. Just as she was beginning to despair, she found it.

Mr. Jesse Whitney's bedchamber. She had no business being there, but an overwhelming thrill skittered through her all the same. She cast frantic looks about her again before summoning the nerve to deliver a tentative rap on his door.

No answer.

She tried again. Still nothing could be heard on the other side. Her conscience warred with her heart before her heart won and she tried the knob. The door opened with a barely audible squeak.

"Who the hell's there?"

The otherworldly growl was almost unrecognizable as Mr. Whitney's. But there was his telltale drawl. She knew a moment of fear as she peered into the poorly lit chamber.

"It's Bella. May I enter?" She hovered at the threshold, praying no one would appear and catch her about to commit the unthinkable sin for an unwed lady.

"Bella?"

Her eyes adjusted to the darkness. He had lit a lone gas lamp on low. And dear heavens, he'd removed his jacket, waistcoat and shirt. He was bare-chested and magnificent, wearing only his trousers, leaning against the large oak bed. There was an intensity in his voice she'd never heard before.

"Are you unwell?" She took care to keep her voice no louder than a whisper.

"For the love of Christ, go back to your chamber, Lady Bella."

"No." Hoping she'd made the right choice, she stepped into his chamber and closed the door at her back.

"You don't know what you're doing," he warned, stalking toward her even though he had told her to leave.

She instinctively took a step in retreat. "I thought perhaps you needed a friend."

Bella couldn't help but notice how broad and muscular his chest was, dappled with whorls of blond hair. His stomach was taut as a drum. Her mouth went dry. He'd been stripped of his gentleman's airs. He seemed savage, filled with raw emotion. An answering heat burst into flame inside her. She rather liked the stranger in his place who looked at her as if he wanted to devour her.

A feral grin curved his lips. "It isn't a friend I'm in need of, Bella."

She knew she should not ask, but she had never been very good at doing as she ought. "What is it you need?"

He stopped inches from her. "You have by the time I count to fifteen to get out." Even as he spoke the words, he reached out to caress her waist with a possessiveness he'd never before shown.

Without her corset's rigid barrier, she could feel his large hands splaying over her, the power and heat so barely contained. Bella took a deep breath and cupped his face. "I won't leave you," she vowed.

"One," he muttered, already working at the double line of buttons on her bodice. "Two."

Her body was on fire with longing. She wanted very much to kiss him, to comfort him. To make him whole. "Jesse," she whispered, emboldened enough by the intimacy of the setting to use his given name. "You needn't exercise your knowledge of arithmetic on my behalf."

"Fifteen," he skipped ahead.

"I think you may have forgotten numbers three through fourteen," she offered needlessly.

"You don't know how much danger you're in right now," he warned.

"I don't care," she countered.

"You don't know me." He tore a whole series of buttons from their moorings. "You haven't the slightest clue as to the madness rotting my brain."

"I don't believe it's madness." Bella searched his gaze, seeing the stark pain, the anguish lurking in his eyes. "I believe you've been scarred by what you've seen."

"Goddamn it. You have no idea." He closed his eyes and pressed his forehead against hers. "Forgive me. I have no right to touch you with such familiarity. I'm an animal."

His profanity took her aback but failed to deter her. "I knew when I saw your face in the drawing room. I knew instantly that something had come loose inside you."

"I don't understand why." He buried his face in her neck, inhaling deeply as if he wanted to drink in her scent. "It's been fifteen years for God's sake. All it requires is one pompous prick in a drawing room mentioning guns, and I'm back to the beginning."

A shudder racked his strong body. She slid an arm around his lean waist, yearning to comfort him any way she could. Her heart hurt for him. With her free hand, she stroked the silken strands of his golden hair. "You mustn't punish yourself."

He pulled back to stare down at her, his expression severe. "Thank Christ you didn't come to me sooner. I was out of my head. I could have done you harm."

She was certain he needed to unleash the torment within him and that he unjustly punished himself. "I don't believe for one instant that you would have ever harmed me, Jesse. I do know you despite what you may think. You've revealed much of yourself to me, perhaps without even being aware."

"I pray to God you're right." He dropped his head again, resting it this time upon her breast. "I would never want to hurt you. It's merely that I don't trust myself when the storm comes upon me."

Bella rubbed his back in soothing motions. "I told you before that you cannot forever be a man alone, and I meant that."

"You are so sweet and innocent." Jesse—for he would always have to be Jesse to her from this point on—pressed a kiss to her neck. It was reverent. It was passionate.

It was the feather that pushed her off a cliff.

Bella was his forever. She knew it then with absolute

certainty. "Not so sweet and innocent," she murmured, her hands going to the fastening of his trousers.

It was bold indeed. Sinful definitely. But she wanted to see him naked. She was tired of being a quiet, bookish miss. She wanted to know the passion she'd only read about. She wanted to touch Jesse, to make love with him in every sense. She wanted him to take her.

He kissed a trail of fire up her neck to her mouth, lingering before trying to dissuade her once more. "One day you will find a man deserving of you. But I'm not that man."

"That is for me to decide," she told him, taking his lips for another kiss.

He groaned against her mouth, plunging his tongue inside to claim. His hands were all over her, caressing, demanding. Her senses careened out of control, runaway-carriage style. Nothing in her life could have prepared her for the onslaught of passion roiling through her. And she wanted more.

Jesse tore his lips from hers. "I cannot ruin you."

"I dislike that word immensely," she groused. "Ruin. I'm not a piece of fruit, by God." Blast society's honor. How was it proper that a man should be allowed, like her brother, to do as he pleased when a woman must not follow her heart? The unfairness of the situation hit her.

"You're an innocent. I won't spoil that."

His tone was suddenly quite determined. Bella decided some persuasion was in order. She started on the remaining buttons of her bodice. "I want to know you, Jesse."

His expression darkened and she swore she detected blatant hunger shining in his eyes. "You don't have an inkling as to what you're saying," he still denied.

"Nonsense. I'm fully possessed of my faculties." She finished with her bodice and pulled her arms from the sleeves. Bella had always been a no-nonsense sort. And if the dowager had taught her anything, it was to always be in firm possession of the reins. "Help me to pull this over my head, if you please."

# Chapter Four

ELLA WAS TAKING OFF HER DRESS. IN HIS chamber. *Oh hell.* How was he ever going to keep from doing to her what he so desperately wanted? All he could think of was sinking his cock deep inside her sweet, wet warmth until he forgot everything and everyone but the feeling of her tight little sheath sending him into heaven. But he couldn't do that, for God's sake. She was a virgin, a lady, the sister of his best friend. Untouchable.

*Damn it.*

His emotions were up and down like a whore's drawers on a miner's payday. He wanted to take what she offered and yet he didn't think she knew the ramifications of what she offered. He could marry her, yes, but he wasn't convinced Thornton would ever allow it. He wasn't Bella's social equal. That he'd amassed a real estate fortune mattered naught to these blue bloods in the end, Jesse had no doubt. They married for dynastic reasons. Not for love. Not for want. Not for any reason other than a title and a fortune.

He had a fortune but he'd never have a title. He had to

stop her.

"Sweetheart, you can't do this." He tried to halt her in the process of shucking off her dress.

"Of course I can. You're the least cooperative despoiler of innocents I've ever met," Bella complained.

He would have laughed had his nerves not been so tautly drawn. "I can't take you. You must return to your chamber."

Bella disappeared inside the voluminous folds of her dress. When she emerged, she tossed the dress to the floor behind her. She didn't wear a corset, only a thin chemise. He could see her pink nipples prodding the fine linen. He was already painfully hard.

"I believe we're beyond the point of polite society." With this pronouncement, she pulled her chemise up over her head as well. It landed with a barely audible swish of expensive fabric upon her already discarded gown.

She was naked and glorious.

He couldn't take his gaze from the sweet, lush curves of her body. She was every inch woman. Lust arrowed directly to his loins. He'd never wanted another woman more than he wanted Lady Bella de Vere in that moment, of that much he was certain. Her breasts were high, round and full, topped with pale-pink nipples that begged to be kissed and sucked. Her waist was narrow but luscious, her hips sweetly curved. Her limbs were as delicately formed as the rest of her.

"Bella," he managed to choke past the desire that threatened to render him incoherent. "Please, you must leave."

"I won't," she said simply.

She was like a siren now, clearly reveling in a power she'd never before realized. He was helpless. In the space of a mere few hours, he'd gone from the hells of war to the hells of unquenched desire. He didn't know what to do.

"Listen to me," he tried again. "You are lovely. I want nothing more than to take you to bed right now."

"Then take me," she challenged.

"And what then, Bella? I could get you with child." He was trying desperately to dissuade her. Because Lord knew he was old enough, wise enough, to know better. He'd been through more than enough. Her innocent young mind could never comprehend the horrors he'd seen, the depths to which seemingly good people could sink.

"I've never been afraid of taking chances." Her hands lingered at his waist, on the fastening of his trousers.

She wasn't wily enough to touch his arousal directly, and thank God she didn't because he'd be utterly lost if she did. He took her hands in his. "Taking chances can result in great penury at times," he cautioned her, knowing all too well the truth of the words he spoke.

"I love you, Jesse Whitney," she shocked the hell out of him by revealing. "I don't know what more I can tell you. What more could you need to know, really?"

Love.

He hadn't thought of love ever since he'd believed he'd last had it more than fifteen years ago. But the love he'd believed in had been false, and he was scared as hell to ever trust such a fleeting emotion again. The damage Lavinia's duplicity had wrought upon him had been true indeed. Lavinia had claimed love. She had left him for the first man who darkened her door thereafter, leaving him with a bullet wound to his back.

He didn't believe Bella. He couldn't believe her. Love was a child's fancy, nothing more. There he was, in the seductive low light of his personal chamber with an unbearably beautiful woman before him in a state of acute undress, and all he could do was stare.

"What more could you need to know from me, Jesse?" Bella asked again. "I love you."

"Are you old enough to understand what love is, darling?" He plainly didn't think she was. Hell, he didn't know what he believed at this point save that he couldn't ruin the delectable woman before him. Not without conscience.

*No, not at all, damn it.*

"How dare you suggest I'm too young to know my feelings?" Bella was truly insulted, it was apparent.

To him, she seemed a woman completely in control of her thoughts and wishes, and yet he had to wonder. She was so much younger than he. She was so much an innocent. He didn't want to take advantage of her, to unjustly influence her into something she would later regret. Because if there was anything he knew about all too well, it was the agony that regret could cause in life.

"How do you know you love me?" He was desperate to distract her, to dissuade her in any way he could conceive. He couldn't help but ask the foremost question plaguing his thoughts.

"I cannot explain it other than to say that if I were to wake up tomorrow morning and never see you again, I would be unbearably heartbroken." She threw up her hands in exasperation. "Must I prove myself to you before you 'ruin me', as you have so aptly phrased it?"

Hell. After what they'd shared the last few days, his world too would be a darker and lonelier place without her. He wanted her desperately, more than he'd even imagined possible. His cock was hard. His body was ready. But the thing that confounded him the most was his rotten old heart. His heart wanted her, cared for her as much as he could manage. She was too good and pure for him. He couldn't even begin to know how to love her.

But perhaps that was the problem. Of their own volition, his hands went to the fastenings of his trousers. He truly needed release, and he'd satisfied his sense of honor that what he wanted was exactly the same as what the lovely Lady Bella wanted. He knew without asking that she was an innocent. He hadn't wanted to rush into taking her, hadn't wanted to pressure her into lovemaking she didn't want. But it didn't matter now. She had made it apparent just how she felt about him, just how much she wanted. He was tempted as Adam, and yet his conscience reminded him of who she was yet again. Thornton's sister. Damn it all.

Jesse stared at her, lost. "No you needn't prove yourself. For the love of God, Bella, put your dress back on."

Disappointment warred with hurt. Bella's heart had never beat at such a mad pace. She wanted him. He wanted her. His kiss said as much. She was nude before a man when she'd never even so much as glanced at her own naked body in a mirror. And he was rejecting her.

Perhaps he did not find her adequately formed. Was she not attractive enough? Were her feet too large? Her breasts too small? Why did he insist upon holding onto his blasted notion of honor? It was all making her quite dizzy.

"Am I all a woman is supposed to be?" she asked, feeling very hesitant.

"Of course you are. You're perfect, sweetheart." His gaze once more lowered to her breasts, lingering there like a touch.

"Then why? Why won't you take me?" Frustration heated to a boil within her.

"Because I've lived with enough regrets in my life and I won't be yours."

"I could never regret loving you," she murmured with complete honesty.

He stared at her, clearly at odds with himself. Bella decided right then that the time for vocal persuasion was at an end. She closed the distance between them, linked her arms around his neck, and kissed him. He rewarded her boldness by kissing her back, crushing her against his powerful frame. She was unprepared for the first intimate feeling of her bare nipples brushing his manly chest. It was sinful, decadent, everything wonderful.

He groaned, fusing their mouths with a hunger that branded. Desire flowed through her like warm honey, making her breasts tingle, her stomach flutter. The apex of her thighs bloomed with heat and wetness. When he reached between them to caress her there, she moaned, arching into him, desperate for more of the intoxicating feeling.

Jesse slowly moved them across the room. Bella followed him step for step, never allowing the kiss to break. She knew their destination was the large bed she'd seen upon her initial entrance. She didn't know what to expect next, only that she desired very much for it to happen. Whatever the mysterious *it* was.

Bella sincerely hoped she was about to be edified.

He lifted her onto the mattress, depositing her with tender care. When she lay sprawled on the bed, mouth swollen with his kisses, he broke away from her. "I meant what I said about not ruining you," he told her, his voice as breathless as she felt.

Confusion warred with the sensual curtain that had descended over her senses. "What do you mean?"

"There are ways we can pleasure each other that don't require me to take your innocence," he explained, his fingers at work on the fastening of his trousers.

She lost her breath entirely when he whipped the last of his clothing away to reveal his large manhood jutting proudly at attention. She'd never seen the like. She was instantly fascinated. She wanted to touch him.

"Absolutely gorgeous," he murmured as his gaze roamed over her. His drawl had never been more pronounced.

She was pleased that he liked what he saw after all. Bella felt simultaneously powerful and alive. She took in his beautifully sculpted body as well, finding him to be absolute masculine perfection. Far better than any crusty old Greek marble, anyway. He was tall, muscled, golden.

"You are unbearably lovely, Bella," he whispered, joining her on the bed. He crouched over her, skimming his fingers up her thigh. Lowering his head, he dropped a kiss on the inside of her knee.

"You're unbearably handsome," she returned, watching his thick blond mane getting nearer to her most secret spot.

Oh dear heavens, what was he doing to her? She reached down to caress his broad shoulders, to toy with his soft hair. He glanced up at her, his gaze molten. "Will you open for me, darling?"

As he asked her, he softly guided her legs apart so that she was revealed to him in every way. "Beautiful," he said, his voice like velvet. "You're pink and lovely, just as I imagined you'd be."

He had thought of her before, then, and not as the brother he'd been claiming to be to her. *Thank the blessed angels.* Cool air sluiced over her heated flesh, making her ache. Surprisingly, she experienced no shame in showing him herself. Rather, she luxuriated in the freedom, in the intensity of his expression as he looked upon her. She shivered, aroused to be on display to him, to watch his eyes worship her.

And then he buried his face between her legs. The act was so utterly foreign and yet so unspeakably delicious, Bella didn't know whether she should faint or die of mortification. He pressed kisses against her starving flesh, his tongue working upon her until her legs quivered from the wondrousness of it all.

She grabbed at his hair, arching into his wicked mouth. She couldn't look away from the sight of his beautiful golden head bowed, caught in the pulsing vee of her legs. She was going to lose her mind soon, her entire body poised on the brink of something indefinable, something she desired so desperately she throbbed with the need. He looked up at her then, meeting her gaze.

"Dear heavens," she whispered, wondering if perhaps she had somehow died and was experiencing the marvels of heaven. Jesse Whitney, the man she'd longed after in secret for the last four years, was kissing her in the naughtiest and yet perhaps best way possible.

He continued torturing her with his mouth, working the sensitized nub within her folds. The sweet tension within her built to a frantic crescendo. She was powerless, slave to the pleasure he bestowed upon her.

She threw her head back, her eyes closing as she gave in completely, going where he would take her. It was decadent, delicious. Ripples of pleasure spiraled from between her legs as he continued to lave her. She never wanted it to end, and then suddenly, a rush of pure bliss hit her, making her entire body shake.

He kissed a path up over her belly, his large hands caressing her curves. With a wicked grin, he met her gaze and sucked one of her nipples deep into his mouth. She arched into him, running her fingers through his thick, fair hair. He was such a beautiful man.

Jesse kissed his way to her neck, flicking his tongue out in hot darts against her skin. And then, his mouth was on hers. She could taste herself on his lips, and it both fascinated and shocked her. Their tongues tangled. His knowing fingers dipped to her mound, stroking the wanton bud he'd already pleasured. Bella held onto him tightly, reveling in the power of his body, the smooth planes of his back.

He increased the pressure on her sex, his pace clipping into a gallop. She writhed beneath him, overcome yet again. The delicious madness sent her into a sudden series of spasms. The wonderful sensation of release saturated her body. As the waves of pleasure slowly ebbed, he broke their kiss, breathing as heavily as she.

Jesse rolled away from her onto his back, staring at the ceiling. Bella watched him, uncertain of what to do next. She couldn't help but to admire his naked form. The realization that she had been very intimate with him hit her, but she felt no guilt or shame, only delight and satisfaction. This was what she'd longed for without ever knowing.

This was everything.

His silence troubled her, however. She placed a tentative palm on his chest, feeling the rapid thrum of his heart. "Is something amiss?"

He sighed. "I shouldn't have done that."

Why did he insist upon clinging to some sort of misplaced chivalry? Frustration pricked her. She was weary of his insistence that he could never pursue her because he was friends with her brother. Never had another circumstance caused her more exasperation. "Can we not simply be a man and a woman?"

"There is no simplicity in lovemaking, Bella. Thornton would have my hide if he knew. Jesus, I wouldn't blame him. I should tan my own hide."

"I don't wish to be your regret either." An unaccountable wave of sadness replaced her pleasure.

He took her hand and raised it to his lips for a kiss that was as formal as it would have been had they been meeting in a ballroom. "I don't regret you, merely the circumstances in which we find ourselves. You deserve far more than a tawdry moment of pleasure."

She wanted to be free to love him, for him to be capable of freely loving her. But it sometimes seemed the obstacles between them were unsurpassable mountains. "Nor would I be a burden to your conscience. If you cannot see me as other than Thornton's sister, I fear I have no hope."

Jesse closed his eyes. "I cannot give you hope. You must go, Bella. I never should have touched you."

After the fiery passion they'd just shared, his abrupt declaration was a bucket of slop water to the face. Each time she thought they'd grown closer, he shoved her away once more. Hurt, she rose from the bed to gather her hastily discarded garments. He could not give her hope. Did it mean he could never love her? That he would never wed her? That he no longer wanted her?

"Are you saying you will never court me, Jesse?" She didn't want to ask because she was terrified of the answer, but she also couldn't refrain from posing the one question that had been plaguing her.

He rose from the bed. "Yes," he said plainly, whipping his trousers off the floor and up to cover his nudity. "I'm not the man for you, sweetheart. I'm sorry."

So he had been willing to propose to avoid a scandal before merely because Lady Stokey had caught them together. But he would commit far more sinful acts with her now and send her on her way. How dare he? She didn't want to hear apologies from him after the tenderness they'd just shared. She threw her dress over her head and struggled to pull the ample folds into their appropriate position. Giving up, she looked back to him, meeting his gaze. "I am sorry as well. Sorrier than you know."

"One day you'll thank me. You are still young and have much to learn of life."

His arrogance astounded her. There it was again, his perpetual and infuriating references to her youth. Why should she be punished for the circumstances of her birth? She made short work of her buttons, not caring that many of them had found the wrong moorings and others were missing entirely.

Bella drew herself up in the icy haughtiness she'd learned from the dowager. "Thank you? For tossing me aside as if I'm no better than a ruined handkerchief? I think I shall reserve my gratitude for those who deserve it. Next time, Mr. Whitney, you will come to me."

Then, with a bravado she certainly didn't feel, she stalked from his chamber, praying inwardly that no one would see her. And that she wouldn't start to cry until she'd reached the safety of her own room.

Bella awoke on the morning following her unseemly visit to Jesse's chamber with a heart full of awful guilt. What had she done? She had been intimate with a man who was not her husband, who was not, through inexplicable choices of his own making, even her suitor. She didn't think she would ever comprehend his reasons for keeping her at a distance, nor did she think she would fully recover from the humiliation his rejection produced. She felt dreadfully unwanted.

With a sigh, she rang for her maid, wondering what course she could next take. She had told him he would have to come to her. But she harbored no end of trepidation on that account. He was drawn to her, of that she had no doubt. She knew the passion between them was real as it was rare. Still, he was a determined man, one who it seemed wanted her physically but not emotionally.

After a discreet warning rap, Smith entered the chamber with her usual vigor and cheerful smile. "Good morning, Lady Bella."

"Good morning to you, Smith." Bella wished she could summon a smile, but she found little pleasure in the day. "I fear I've a case of the megrims."

"Shall I make you a poultice, my lady?"

"While your knowledge of herbs is unsurpassed, I feel quite certain no mere poultice can cure me at the moment." Bella sighed again and went to the window. "Pray tell me, Smith, have you ever been in love?"

"I'm sure I haven't the time for that," Smith answered amidst the familiar sounds of rustling linen and silk. "Shall you wear the violet morning gown with the lovely train or the cream with lace overlay?"

"Have I any morning gowns in gray?"

"The marchioness requested only colors, my lady," Smith reported. "I've always thought violet sets you to advantage if I may be bold enough to say so."

"You know we never stand on ceremony, Smith. If you suggest the violet, I shall wear the violet." Bella turned back to her dear maid, who had somehow become her only confidante. "What would you do if you'd confessed your heart to someone and he didn't seem to care?"

"I should think him hard indeed, Lady Bella." Smith busied herself in preparing Bella's *toilette*. "And then I would find myself a new suitor."

"A new suitor?" Bella didn't particularly relish the prospect. "That seems rather faithless, does it not?"

"Not a real suitor, mind you," Smith clarified with an elfin grin. "Perhaps there is a poultice to soothe your megrims after all. Jealousy."

"Do you suppose such a scheme would work, Smith?"

"Just so, my lady."

She'd attempted to make Jesse jealous only the day before and had failed miserably. But that had been before she'd lain naked with him. Bella's spirits rose a bit. "Turn me out as best you can, if you please. I would dearly love to look my finest today of all days."

"Of course," Smith agreed. "But we need be quick about it. The marchioness has requested an audience, and Lord Thornton also sent word this morning that Mr. Whitney will be escorting you to breakfast."

Jesse. Lord in heaven. What was she to do?

She wasn't prepared to face him so soon, and particularly not with her mother present. Blessed angels' sakes, she'd wither into a puddle of guilt. How typical it was of her brother to meddle at the most horrid of times. Every other morning, he had done his duty in escorting Bella and the dowager as was their mother's wont. Why had he chosen now to send a proxy?

Moreover, why had Jesse accepted the duty? Did it mean he regretted his treatment of her? Likely not, her head chided her heart, but that didn't douse the minute spark of hope that had begun burning in her breast. She'd told him he would come to her next, and it seemed she was right, whether or not it was of his own volition.

"Let us be quick, then," Bella told Smith.

Jesse appeared as promised at the appointed hour. The interview with her mother had proved nearly interminable, so much so that by the time he sketched a gallant bow, she felt little of the nervousness of earlier that morning. Instead, she was filled with relief. He was dressed to perfection, every bit as handsome as any English lord. It occurred to Bella that she had seen his naked body, had felt his skin upon hers. He had used his tongue upon her. The thought made her knees buckle. She pretended to rearrange her skirts and hoped with all her might that he hadn't noticed.

"You're late, Mr. Whittlesby," the dowager pronounced in her wintriest tone, unwittingly cracking the underlying tension of the moment. "I detest tardiness, especially at the breakfast hour. It is imperative that one break one's fast as early as possible."

Jesse's expression was unreadable. "It is Whitney, my lady," he corrected, refusing to even glance in Bella's direction.

"Precisely what I said. Goodness, I daresay you Americans have deplorable hearing." Her mother's eyes narrowed. "Puzzling, given the size of your ears."

Bella longed to hide somewhere, anywhere. Her mother was an utter bear. How she wished she had been blessed with the same grace most ladies of an age with her had. But she had not, and the dowager was determined to insult Jesse at every turn. It was most vexing.

"Please accept my sincere apologies for my unfortunate American hearing and large ears," Jesse said, his deep voice laden with sarcasm.

"Why has Thornton chosen not to meet his mother?" the dowager demanded next.

The question of what nonsense Thornton was about, disappearing on them in such unexpected fashion, had occurred to Bella as well. Her mother was terribly afraid he was ruining his political aspirations by dallying with the married Lady Scarbrough, and his absence suggested she wasn't mistaken in her suspicions. Why, Bella had still scarcely even seen him during the entirety of the house party, aside from when she had inadvertently happened upon him in a tête-à-tête with Lady Scarbrough herself. She hadn't been altogether certain of what she'd seen that day, but she was sure it didn't bode well for her brother.

"I understand he left for an early-morning ride," Jesse said smoothly. "It's my pleasure to be his substitute."

Bella nearly laughed. She was certain being her escort was anything but his pleasure. "Is it indeed, Mr. Whitney?" she could not help but ask.

He favored her with his gaze for the first time. The intensity of his eyes on hers gave her a physical jolt. "My dear Lady Bella, you must know it is."

She swallowed, wondering at the implication of his words. He seemed more himself this morning, the perfect gentleman rather than the passionate lover. He regretted their heated interlude. But had the pure wonder of it haunted him the way it had her? Perhaps just a little?

The dowager sniffed, effectively spoiling the moment. "I'm sure it's very improving to have the privilege of such elevated company, Whittlesby. Now if you don't mind, I am quite faint with hunger. My doctor says I must eat nearly at once upon waking in the morning or suffer biliousness."

Jesse's lips twitched in undoubted mirth. Bella shared a suffering look with him, longing to apologize for her mother's peculiar notion of conversation. However, she knew that to do so would only incite the dowager's wrath. Instead, she held her tongue as Jesse escorted them to the breakfast room with perfect care. He was once again every bit the civilized gentleman, his every word and gesture unimpeachable. Bella scarcely recognized the studious politeness. She rather favored the wildness in him.

But if she had hoped for any heated looks or subtle brushes of his hand against hers at the breakfast table, she was sorely disappointed. Jesse focused on his kippers and eggs with great care, consuming them as though his life and limb depended upon it. She wanted to stomp her feet, demand that he look at her, demand that he was aware of her presence.

She stabbed at her eggs with more vigor than necessary. It was maddening. How could he touch her with such passion and then treat her as if she were nothing more than a precocious younger sister? She didn't think she would ever, in all her years, understand the working of that man's mind. Love could be tiresome indeed.

The fortuitous appearance of the Duke of Devonshire lightened her mood. If she could only stir up some jealousy in Jesse's stubborn heart, he might not be so noble. Bella greeted him with her loveliest smile.

The duke bowed. "Good morning, Lady Thornton, Lady Bella."

Her mother brightened considerably. "A good morning it is, Your Grace. Have you been for a ride as yet?"

"I fear I have not," he murmured, meeting Bella's gaze. "But I did hope to take a walk in the gardens. I find the morning air in the countryside unparalleled."

"It is most invigorating," the dowager agreed, nearly choking on her breakfast in her eagerness to play the matchmaker. "Lady Bella so enjoys a morning promenade, do you not, my dear?"

"Yes, *Maman*," Bella hastened to answer, both to please her mother and upset Jesse, even if she despaired the latter was possible. She was beginning to feel as lost as if she'd been placed inside the famed Wilton House maze, blindfolded.

"May I be bold enough to hope you might join me for a small walk, my lady?" the duke asked as if on cue.

"I would dearly love to," she answered, with perhaps a bit more enthusiasm than necessary. She stole a sideways glance at Jesse.

He met her gaze and raised a brow. She tipped her chin up and looked away. If he didn't want her, then he shouldn't mind if another man did. The duke was a fine matrimonial catch. He was handsome, kind, and was rumored to have a fair income. He was a trifle too polite, true, but she wasn't going to allow that hindrance to deter her. Of course, there remained the small matter of her not actually caring for him romantically. Yes, there was that, bother it all.

Later that afternoon, Bella found herself in the drawing room of Wilton House, surrounded by the entire assemblage. The weather had turned grim, and the countryside had been enveloped by a battering storm. Now they were all cooped up together, awaiting the whims of their hostess and the parlor games she had prepared for them.

Bella had made an art of finding the quiet corners of rooms where no one else would bother her. If the entertainment was suitably dull, she was quite adept at daydreaming and preferred to do so without an audience.

Her walk with the duke had been delightful, though not intense or wonderful the way her exchanges with Jesse were. He was a knowledgeable man and pleasant company. True, he didn't allow much opportunity for her to speak, but he did seem to share her love of literature, and she had nearly enjoyed their interlude.

*Oh dear.* She had better try to strike Jesse from her mind, because compared to him, all future suitors were bound to fail. He hadn't seemed affected by her walk whatsoever. Indeed, he had ignored her following breakfast. She hadn't even seen him in the drawing room. Perhaps he was wise enough to eschew silly games.

"Did you enjoy your walk, my dear?"

The unexpected drawl in her ear gave her such a start that she jumped and let out an unbecoming squeak. Pressing a hand to her thumping heart, she turned to see the subject of her thoughts standing far too close to her for propriety. He smelled divine and looked so handsome she wanted to kiss him.

She had to exercise more control over her wayward thoughts. She would not think about the strong muscles hidden beneath his gentleman's threads. Nor would she think about the way his shoulders felt beneath her palms. Or the sight of his gorgeous mouth making love to her body.

*Good heavens.* Her face was flushed. She realized she was staring at him, having quite forgotten what it was he'd asked. "I beg your pardon?"

"Was it so unmemorable, then?" He sounded amused, pleased even.

She loathed that he had her at a disadvantage. "I'm afraid I don't know what you're speaking of, Mr. Whitney."

"Your walk with the Duke of Dullness," he clarified, wearing a smug grin.

"He most certainly isn't dull," she informed him sharply, despite having had the very same thought upon at least one occasion.

"Perhaps we're speaking of a different duke?"

"You're being decidedly unkind," Bella pointed out. She turned her attention back to the group of revelers. Lady Cosgrove had announced their entertainment was to be recitations of Shakespeare.

"I never claimed to be kind." His fingers traced the line of her arm from elbow to wrist. "I'm being quite charitable regarding the duke in question and you know it."

"He's very well versed in a number of intriguing subjects," she hissed. "Do be quiet. I'm trying to listen to our hostess's announcement."

"A number of subjects?" He leaned closer, his lips grazing the shell of her ear. "Do tell."

Oh dear. He'd rather called her bluff, hadn't he? "He knows an inordinate amount about birds," she defended hotly, trying not to notice the delicious heat of his breath on her neck.

"Birds," he scoffed, straightening to put an appropriate distance between them once more. "Is he an expert authority on butterflies and flowers and the cut of a lady's dress as well?"

The nerve of the man. "I haven't had the opportunity to enjoy further dialogue with him, but I daresay I shall soon."

"You don't care for him," Jesse growled, more statement

than question.

She turned to him again. "Why should you concern yourself with my romantic life when you've expressed such a vehement desire not to be a part of it?"

He stared at her for a heated moment's pause and she wanted him to say something wonderful, something life changing. Was it too much to ask for him to profess his undying love?

"I'm merely concerned for your future, as would be any caring friend," he said, banishing her tentative optimism.

"I have friends enough, Mr. Whitney," Bella told him pertly. "I don't require your interference."

He shrugged as if he hadn't a care. "As you wish it, my dear."

Of course it was how she wished it. Couldn't the dratted man see that she wanted him to be her lover and not her friend? "It is most certainly how I wish it." She was careful to keep her voice as icy as possible.

"I won't utter another word about His Dullness," he assured her.

"Thank you." She broke her gaze from his and looked back to the gathering of guests. Her brother and the Countess of Scarbrough had inexplicably been paired together for a recitation from *Love's Labour's Lost*. She did her best to listen to their spirited scene, trying not to think of how her heart was breaking.

"They make a lovely match, don't you think?" Jesse asked, sounding thoughtful.

"She is married to another." Bella cast him a stern glance. "How can they make a match when she is not a free woman?"

"It's a good question, is it not?"

She frowned, trying to discern the hidden meaning in his words. "Do you think he loves her?" She was nearly afraid to give voice to her misgivings. Her mother loved dramatics, but Bella thought this time the dowager was not wrong.

"Love can be a terrible affliction," he said instead of

answering her.

"How so?" Her interest was piqued. Mayhap there was a reason for his reticence.

He shrugged. "A mere observation, Lady Bella."

She didn't believe him. "Can it not be a boon as well?"

"Ever the romantic heart," he said with a faint trace of a smile. "I haven't known it to be."

She disliked the bent of their dialogue. "You never answered me," she changed the subject, "when I asked if you thought my brother harbors tender feelings for Lady Scarbrough."

"I would venture to say he does. Look at them."

Bella followed his gaze to her brother and the countess.

"See how his gaze never wavers from hers? They stand very near to one another, but it looks natural rather than scandalous. Look at how he touches her elbow, so gentle and yet possessive." As he finished his study, he drew closer to her again. His fingers tangled with hers, hidden in the voluminous drapery of her skirt.

Her heart ached. "Why must you torture me?" she whispered, tightening her fingers over his.

"I could ask you the same thing," he said, sounding bemused.

"You are correct in one aspect at least." Bella kept her eyes trained ahead. "Love is a terrible affliction."

"I'm sorry for that."

"Would I could believe you." She couldn't keep the bitterness from her voice. "True contrition is better expressed in deed rather than sentiment."

"Now you sound like the dowager, spouting tenets."

"Pray don't attempt to make light of me," she said lowly, "not in this."

"I truly am sorry," he said again. "If you can love the duke, you should welcome his courtship. I have no right to counsel you otherwise."

"You are correct again." She slanted him another look. "You do not have any rights at all when it comes to me."

"I want only your happiness, Bella." He gave her fingers a lingering squeeze.

Bella took a breath for fortitude before plunging forward. "Then you need but give it to me."

# Chapter Five

ER WORDS STRUCK HIM WITH THE FORCE OF a bullet. *Then you need but give it to me.* The idea that he was responsible for her happiness was more terrifying than facing a wall of enemy troops. Christ, if only it were that easy. If only he could give in to the madness of desire. If only he could be a suitable husband to her.

But she knew so little of him. He bore scars far uglier than those he wore on his skin. How could he be a proper husband to such a gentle, sweet innocent? He didn't think he could. Just the thought scared the hell out of him.

"Would it were that simple," he told her at last, releasing her fingers and putting a step's distance between them for his own sanity. "You must know I would do anything for you."

"Not anything," she denied with a hint of sadness.

The gathered assemblage began tittering at what he presumed was a particularly witty Shakespeare line. He cast a glance over the glittering ladies. Though they were all turned out to perfection, none could even compare to the woman standing before him. The word "lovely" didn't begin to do her justice. He wanted her badly.

But he could not have her.

"I only seek to protect you from yourself," he murmured. "One day, you'll thank me."

"So you have recently said," Bella snapped. "I grow weary of hearing such piffle."

He was as frustrated as she sounded. As much as he told himself to stay the hell away from her, he couldn't seem to resist. It had taken every speck of his conscience to keep from taking her innocence the night before. He had wanted to plunge inside her and lose himself, to make her his.

Unbidden, images of her lush, naked body rose in his mind. Their sinful interlude had been the most meaningful he'd ever experienced in his life, even unfulfilled. He knew how she tasted, knew the delicious moist heat between her thighs, knew how to bring her to her climax.

He stifled a groan. He could not continue like this, by God. He shifted his stance, praying his arousal wasn't noticeable thanks to the cut of his trousers. Christ, he had to distract himself or he would go mad.

Thornton saved him from making an ass of himself, approaching them with an affable smile.

"Bella," the marquis greeted. "Jesse. I trust you're enjoying our hostess's damnable parlor games?"

"Pray excuse me," Bella muttered, "but I fear I have a megrim. I should like to sit down."

Without waiting for their acknowledgment, she disappeared.

"Damn women," Thornton growled. "Why must they forever be having the megrims? A great lot of shite if you ask me, friend."

*Friend.* The sobriquet sent another wave of guilt crashing over him. If Thornton knew he'd been naked with his sister the night before, Jesse would be sporting a black eye and broken nose instead of a rigid cock.

He cleared his throat. "The fairer sex is more delicate than ours."

"You're being far too charitable, old boy." Thornton

grinned. "Fortunate man not to be plagued by the whims of women."

"If I had to hazard a guess, I'd reckon you are suffering the whim of one in particular," he observed.

"Am I that obvious?" Thornton shook his head. "I am, by Christ, and I know it. I know I should keep away from her, and yet I cannot seem to do so, even at the expense of my honor and reputation."

Jesse understood more than his friend knew. "I'm sure you aren't the first or the last man to be so bedeviled by love."

"Spoken like a man who knows." Thornton raised a brow.

Jesse nearly swallowed his tongue. Christ, was he that obvious? He hoped like hell Thornton hadn't noticed the inordinate amount of time he'd been spending in Bella's company. He decided not to answer his friend. They watched the remainder of the recitations in an uneasy silence.

Bella's mood turned quite dour over the next few days. Jesse didn't want her. Nothing she could do or say would alter his mind. No matter how she tried to throw kindling on the fires of his jealousy, she only wound up with a meager spark. He'd made it plain that he would prefer to marry her off to the Duke of Devonshire than to wed her.

She decided to cut him from her life, which proved more difficult than learning how to make a proper curtsy had been. And Bella had never been particularly graceful or adept at curtsying. Indeed, it wasn't long before her efforts were thwarted. He found her in the gardens, where she had taken to hiding in favor of the library for fear he'd discover her there again.

The crunching of footsteps on the path alerted her to the arrival of an unwanted intruder. She didn't even need to look up from her book to know it was him. His mere presence set her on edge. He stopped perilously near to her, so close his boots had come into her vision. She didn't want to see him.

"Lady Bella, you are precisely the woman I was looking for."

His pronouncement earned him a suspicious glance. Their gazes clashed as she looked up. Her breath faltered, her stomach suddenly nervous. She wished she hadn't met his gaze. "You were seeking me out, Mr. Whitney?" It was far better, she thought, to maintain a polite wall between them. But a swift dart of hope entered her imprudent heart nonetheless.

"I have something for you." He reached into his coat and fished out a handsomely bound volume that had been wrapped with a ribbon. "It's my way of crying truce."

Truce. Bella was quite certain she had no idea what truce meant from him. "Do you always dole out books by way of apology? If so, I suspect your library is quite empty."

He inclined his head. "Your barbs have the keenest knack for finding their mark."

She rose from the bench, weary of craning her neck to look up at him, and slipped the book she'd been reading into the hidden pocket on her gown. "I merely believe in honesty. There appears to be too little of it in this hard world of ours."

"I've tried my best to be honest with you," he said, his voice a low, buttery drawl.

Bella summoned a false smile. "I can only blame myself. Think nothing of it."

"That's the problem, Bella. I do think of it." His eyes held the same intensity as his voice. She couldn't look away.

How he confused her. She wanted him to kiss her. She didn't want a truce, a book, or an admission. She wanted him to remove the boundaries he'd created. "Why?"

"I'm not without a heart, Bella. I simply want what is best for you." He paused as if he were about to say more but didn't trust it. "Here you are." He held out the book for her.

She stared at the volume, at his strong hands so capable of being gentle, of bringing the most exquisite sensations to life within her. She almost didn't want to accept the gift from him. "You needn't have, Jesse."

"I know."

His frank concession had her glancing back up at him, startled. He grinned then, his devilish dimple once again in full show. "I wanted to, Bella. Please take it."

She would have preferred his heart, but she wisely kept that bit to herself. "I won't accept a gift, generous though it may be of you."

"It's not a selfless deed. I've missed your companionship and your eager wit. I find you have an unparalleled mind."

She couldn't resist a jibe. "For a girl of my years?"

"For a woman of your station and beauty. Many ladies are content to be a mere blossom in a vase, lovely to look upon and nothing more. But you are like the wild rose, growing up amongst the vines."

She tried in vain not to allow his compliment to start a warm glow seeping through her. "Thank you for your kind words, but I'm still afraid I cannot take the book."

"Of course you will."

He was certainly sure of himself. Bella was conflicted. She didn't wish for them to remain at odds. Indeed, even if he didn't return her feelings, she relished his company. "You're a stubborn man."

"More stubborn than you know, my dear."

His grin dissipated. There was a hidden meaning to his words, she had no doubt. But she could no sooner make him say what she longed to hear than take flight. She was convinced in that moment that he surely felt something for her. She accepted the book from him, her fingers brushing his.

"*Men and Women,*" she read aloud from the spine.

She glanced back up at him to find his familiar grin back

in place, façade restored. "I thought it seemed appropriate, somehow," he said easily.

Bella did not particularly appreciate his wit. The subject was a bitter one for her.

"Robert Browning poems." She studied the volume, wondering at the meaning behind his gift.

"I enjoy *Love Among the Ruins* in particular," he told her. "I suppose it reminds me of the war in a sense. Have you read it before?"

"I haven't," she admitted. "It seems you have finally bested me in my literary pursuits."

A hesitant smile reappeared on his lips. "I've read it often over the past few days. It's long been a favorite of mine, but something made me seek it out again."

He was exceptionally handsome this morning. Her heart hurt just looking at him. Perhaps she was foolish to think his cryptic words possessed a hidden lining like the book pockets she'd sewn into her dresses. Had she learned nothing from his repeated rejections of her?

It would seem she had not for she couldn't keep herself from asking him the question gnawing at her. "What has renewed your interest?"

He startled her again by reaching up to touch a curled tendril of hair that had intentionally been left out of her coiffure. "You," he said simply.

Bella inhaled on an unsteady breath. The heavy weight of the unspoken emotions between them was already enough to topple her. But the stark longing she saw in his eyes would surely make her lose her composure altogether.

She turned and pressed a kiss to his fingers, the gesture as ardent as it was reverent. "I'm honored to have been in your thoughts."

He caressed her cheek. "There has been little else."

The admission shook her. She wanted to throw herself into his arms and forget the world, the house party, propriety, everything. It was incredibly unfair of him to be hot as a scalding teakettle one moment and cold as Wenham

Lake ice the next. "Why must you torture me?"

"If it gives you any comfort, know that I torture myself as surely as I do you," he whispered. He bowed his head, his lips so near to hers she felt the warmth of his breath fanning over her mouth.

She gripped the book so tightly its edges cut into her hands. "Do you care for me, Jesse?"

He stilled. "You are the sister of my oldest friend. Of course I care for you."

"Not as Thornton's sister," she persisted. "Pray stop using him as a wall to be built between us."

Stiffening, he stepped away from her, dashing her hopes of another stolen kiss. "Answering your question will not do either of us a service."

"Forgive me if I disagree with you," she told him, her tone rife with pent-up emotion. "I should very much like to know where I stand."

His expression went carefully blank. "There can't be more than friendship for us, Bella."

Friend. Sister. Innocent. Bella wearied of the roles he would have her play. Sadness warred with anger within her. "Then why must you insist upon seeking me out? Why follow me into the gardens when I've been doing my best to stay away from you?"

"Because I can't stay away from you, goddamn it," he burst out, his polished veneer cracking to reveal the emotions he battled to hide.

Bella gaped at him. He sounded furious. She'd never seen him lose his self-possession so completely other than the night she'd gone to his chamber.

He raked a hand through his hair, leaving it askew. "I can't stay away," he said again. "I don't know why. You're too damn young and innocent for the likes of me."

"Surely not so innocent any longer," she reminded him. Their heated interlude in his chamber had been haunting her for days. She knew she'd never be the same girl she'd once been. She had tasted passion and she wanted more.

He sighed and passed a hand over his face. "You are as innocent as you need to be to go to your future husband without shame. That is all that matters."

Bella longed to grab him by his coat and shake him. How dare he be so obstinate? "Do you know what truly matters, Jesse?"

She waited for his answer, but he was silent as a stone, his expression equally hard.

"Being loved is what matters." She searched his eyes. "I pity you if you are determined to live the rest of your life without it."

He maintained his silence. Bella's frustration grew to a crashing crescendo.

"Have you nothing to say?" she demanded.

"You know it must always be thus," he told her at last. "My little romantic, I'm afraid I don't even believe in love."

His pronouncement took her by surprise. Such a dearth of passion had not even occurred to her. "It's not possible," she denied. "You cannot profess to be an admirer of poetry and great literature and not believe in love."

Jesse's sculpted mouth quirked into a self-deprecating smile. "I haven't seen much to convince me the kinder nature of man or woman exists."

She noted he had said man or woman. Perhaps she had finally hit upon the crux of the matter. "Has a woman hurt you?"

His gaze grew even more shuttered. "Let us say I was very unwise in my youth and have never forgotten the lessons taught me."

He'd suffered a broken heart at the hands of another woman. She was stunned, both that she'd never before thought of such a possibility and that he admitted it. Still, she supposed she shouldn't be so taken aback.

Of course he would have loved before. He was over ten years her senior. He had lived an entire life before meeting her. There would necessarily be ladies in his past. But even if her rational brain told her it was only natural, jealousy stirred within her. She hated to think another woman had experienced his heated embrace, his kisses. Perhaps another woman had even lain naked with him and experienced the pleasures to which she had been newly introduced.

The thought almost made her ill.

"Were you in love?" she asked, needing to satisfy her curiosity though it might well prove upsetting.

"I was a blind fool," he said lowly. "You'd be amazed how ruthless people can be to one another. Maybe it's war that brings out the monsters in us all. But I've seen the cruel side of human nature and I can't say I ever wish to see it again."

There was far more, she sensed, to what he was telling her. He must have loved the mysterious woman from his past. He must have loved her very much. There was still the pain of betrayal in his voice when he spoke, still a strong tide of bitterness.

Bella touched his coat sleeve. "Whoever she was, she certainly wasn't worthy of you."

"It was a long, long time ago."

But not so long ago that it didn't haunt him still. An unaccountable wave of sadness washed over her. "I wish I could rewrite your history."

He withdrew from her touch. The void between them was almost tangible. "Our histories make us who we are, the bad as much as the good."

Perhaps he had no regrets. She knew she had no right to feel possessive of him, but her stubborn heart refused to consider him a lost cause. "I suppose you're correct. But surely there's no harm in wanting to replace the bad with good."

"I'm afraid that's a Sisyphean feat."

"Do you think if we had met before," she began, only to allow the sentiment to trail away. Like so many things, it was likely best left unspoken.

"We cannot change who we are or what we've done. The book is yours to keep," he said in a tone devoid of emotion.

"Do with it what you will, Lady Bella. It's all I can give you."

He offered her a formal bow and turned away.

She watched him leave, feeling quite helpless. She wanted so much more from him than a mere spine and set of inked pages. But if he remained unwilling to overcome his misguided loyalty to her brother and the demons of his past, what choice did she truly have? He could have taken her that night in his chamber and he had not. Perhaps the time had come for her to put an end to the mad *tendre* of her youth at long last.

After his beloved figure had disappeared from view, she stood for a long time in the garden path with the great hedges towering over her. She glanced back down at the pretty volume in her hands, opening it to make a disquieting discovery.

Mr. Browning had dedicated the collection of poems to his wife.

As the second and final week of her house party neared its end, Lady Cosgrove crowned her success as a hostess with a Shakespeare-themed mask ball. It was generally considered to be the most important event of the entire fortnight. Ordinarily, Bella would have been aflutter with excitement. She'd chosen her costume with great care. But she couldn't summon up much enthusiasm given the doldrums that plagued her.

She danced with the Duke of Devonshire as if she were an automaton, listening to him with half a mind while she searched the throng of revelers for Jesse. He was the man in whose arms she longed to be. Meanwhile, the dowager preened like a happy little owl from a corner of the ballroom, secure in her hopes that Bella would finally snag herself a coronet as a matrimonial prize.

After she politely disengaged herself from Devonshire, time crept by for Bella with the speed of a century. Still no sign of Jesse, drat the man. She had to admit to herself he was the only person she longed to see even as she was approached by a series of gentlemen. She danced to pass the time. She flirted to cure her boredom. She kept a false smile on her lips and tried not to think too much about how dreadful and empty her life would be without Jesse in the coming months.

After the house party was over, he would be returning to London while Bella would be off to her brother's country seat, Marleigh Manor. She knew not when or if she would see him again. The mere thought left her feeling as if a gaping hole had been torn into her heart. It seemed impossible to think that only a fortnight had passed and yet her life had been so irrevocably altered.

As she completed yet another tiresome round of dancing, her eyes at last found him. She barely managed to mumble a few required pleasantries to her partner. She caught Jesse's gaze from across the ballroom and her knees nearly gave out. They hadn't spoken since the day he'd left her in the gardens. In the interim, she'd read the entire volume of Browning poems twice. Jesse never strayed from her thoughts.

A great rush of yearning swept over her. Bella wanted to close the distance between them. She wanted him to take her up in his arms, kiss her as if he might never have another chance to do so in his life. Heat pooled low in her belly. She wanted him to make love to her. Blessed angels, she'd never wanted anything more in her life. Their sinful encounter had only left her hungry for more.

But he was not meant to be hers, and she had better reconcile herself to that sad fact. She forced herself to turn away from him and give him the cut. There was no use in longing after a man who would not have her.

Tears threatened her vision. Hoping no one would see her, she escaped through a side door into the moonlit gardens. The night was unseasonably cool, but she almost didn't even feel the nip of the chill air on her skin. With a sigh, she made her way down a path, trying to admire the last of the lovely blooms Lord and Lady Cosgrove had cultivated. Trying to ignore the emptiness in her heart.

"'When I do come, she will speak not, she will stand, either hand on my shoulder, give her eyes the first embrace of my face.'"

It was a velvety drawl she'd never forget. She spun, heart in her throat. There he was, golden and beautiful on the gravel walk behind her, silver moonbeams catching in his glorious hair. He was unbearably gorgeous. Bella recognized the words he spoke. She'd read *Love Among the Ruins* at least a dozen times since he'd bestowed the Browning volume upon her.

"'Ere we rush, ere we extinguish sight and speech'," Bella quoted the next line of the stanza back to him.

"'Each on each'," he finished, his expression as somber as his tone. "You committed it to memory."

She studied him with equal solemnity even though she longed to rush into his arms. "A wise man told me the poem was a favorite of his."

"Not so wise, I'm afraid." He ran a hand through his already tousled blond locks. "More like a fool."

She couldn't help but to recall how smooth that golden hair of his had felt in her hands. She wanted to feel it again. She wanted the enchantment of his touch once more. The desire between them was almost palpable, simmering beneath their mutually polite exteriors.

"Why a fool?" she asked, seeking to delay the moment when they would need to return to the ball to stave off whispers. They would have to go back to being acquaintances, would have to dance with others, pretend they'd never shared anything more intimate than a Robert Browning poem. She tried to stop a swift stab of despair from cutting through her.

His stare was hot upon her. "Because of all the beautiful ladies in attendance tonight, I have eyes for only one."

Her stomach upended as if she were riding on a runaway

stagecoach. "Whom?"

"You know I speak of you, Bella." He paused and exhaled as if trying to maintain his composure. "Damn it, you are the loveliest Juliet I've ever seen."

She swallowed, suddenly nervous. "Thank you." She examined his costume in an effort to distract herself. He wore a black velvet coat and Elizabethan shirt beneath, but the effect was more pirate than sixteenth century. "And who do you pretend to be this evening, Mr. Whitney?"

He grinned in truth then, his deadly dimple reappearing. He was a wickedly handsome man. "Can you not tell? I am the bard himself." He dropped into a formal bow as Bella devoured him with her eyes. "Mr. William Shakespeare, at your service."

Bella laughed. "But you don't look in the least bit like him. He had dark hair, for one thing, and for another, you are far more fine-looking than he was."

The moment the unabashed observation left her lips, she regretted it. *Oh dear.* She ought not to have spoken so freely. She busied herself with readjusting the pleats on her voluminous skirts.

"Thank you," he said, his tone low and intimate.

Her senses were clouded by his nearness, by the faint but delicious scent of him on the wind. She had never wanted to rush headlong into sin more in her life. He made her into a true wanton. Images of what he had done to her flashed through her traitorous mind. It was time to steer her sailboat into safer harbors.

"What are you doing out here?" she asked suddenly, determined to distract herself.

She hadn't meant to be so abrupt, but neither could she help herself. It seemed as much as she tried to keep away from him, he was equally determined to cross her path. And yet he would not bend.

Jesse raised a brow. "I might ask you the same."

"I was in need of air," she lied, holding her breath as he closed the separation between them.

He stood so close her skirts brushed his legs. "I must admit I was surprised you had chosen Juliet this evening, knowing your proclivity for happy endings."

Why did he have to recall every conversation they'd ever shared with that pristine memory of his? It made her love him all the more. "Though she is a sad figure, I do admire the romance of her story," Bella admitted.

"Ever the romantic." He smiled, tipping up her chin. His hand lingered in a caress. "Sweet Bella, does your heart know no bounds?"

"I do not wish it to," she said, captivated by the intensity of his gaze. "I would ever be free to roam and love as I wish rather than be a captive in a gilded cage."

"Who would seek to cage you?" He drew even nearer, quite discomfiting her.

"I know not," she whispered, frozen as his fingers trailed a path of wickedness down her neck to her décolletage. "Only that I would never wish to be so confined."

"Speaking of cages, did you enjoy your dance with the Duke of Dullness?"

Bella was surprised to realize he had been in the crowd all along, watching her. "You noticed?"

"For the first time in my life, I envied another man." The admission was seemingly wrenched from him.

She absorbed that thrilling bit of knowledge. "To be candid, I wished he were you for the entire duration of the waltz."

He traced the line of her neck in a whisper of a caress, stopping to tilt up her chin. "You'll be the death of me, but the more I touch you the more I don't give a damn."

Bella pressed her eyes closed for a moment, fighting to keep the tentative grip she maintained on her fleeing composure. "It's the same for me."

Jesse lowered his lips to hers in a swift, possessive kiss. "I cannot have enough of you, Bella. No matter how hard I try to stay away, I'm always back at your side."

She cupped his beloved face, searching his gaze. "Why

must you stay away? I fear very much that we will soon be apart forever."

His hands swept down to grasp her waist, pulling her more firmly against his hard body. "Why? Surely you aren't planning on wedding the Duke of Dullness?"

Twin fires of jealousy burned in his eyes. Bella was pleased. It seemed he wasn't as immune to her as she had supposed. Unless she was mistaken, he didn't particularly relish the prospect of her nuptials with another man. *Good. Let him suffer as I have.* Perhaps he would bend after all.

"What if I were to marry the duke?" She wanted an admission from Jesse. A white flag of surrender. Anything was better than the aloof stranger who set her body aflame with one stolen embrace and then ignored her the next day.

His grip tightened on her. "You must do as you wish, Lady Bella."

She wanted to shake the truth out of him. Drat him for being so stubborn, so unwilling to show her the man beneath his marble exterior. "Shall I be another man's wife, then?"

Perhaps she was relentless, but she had discovered it was a necessary trait in any row with Jesse Whitney. He remained silent, looking down at her as if he weren't certain if he should push her away from him or hold her closer.

"Shall I, Jesse?"

"Damn you," he growled. "You know very well that I don't want any man to have you but me."

She exhaled the breath she hadn't realized she'd been holding. A warm sensation of victory stirred within her. "You want me?"

He caught her hand in his and pressed it between them, allowing her to feel the ridge of his cock. She gasped, stunned that he would be so bold with a ballroom of guests not far away but nonetheless eager. It was what she had wanted all along, to break the polite barriers between them. Something about this time was different. There was a heaviness in the air, passion and possibility sparking hot and heady between them.

"I want you as I have never wanted another woman in my life, Bella." His voice was pure velvet-laden desire.

She rose on her tiptoes to kiss him. "I want you too, Jesse. Very much."

He stilled. "You don't know what you're saying."

"I have always known." She pressed a kiss to his mouth again, winding her arms around his neck. "Always, from the first time I met you in the library at Marleigh Manor so long ago."

"Christ," he said on a groan. "You have no idea how many times I've thought of taking you since the night you came to my chamber. If the war wasn't enough to make me mad, surely you are."

They were interrupted by a lady's giggle and a low rumbling male voice. Jesse pulled her into the shadows, holding her against him. She buried her face in his coat and savored his scent. His heart thumped beneath her ear in a steady, reassuring rhythm. A hushed silence fell over them again as the couple wandered off into the gardens, clearly intent upon the same furtive coupling.

They remained in the shadows, embracing. Bella pulled his head down to hers for another lingering kiss. His tongue sank into her mouth, claiming. Desire uncoiled within her, leaving her entire body sensitive. Her breasts ached and tingled. Wetness pooled between her legs, along with a slow and steady yearning. His hands moved to cup her breasts through the layers of her dress, tightening her nipples into hard little pebbles. She moaned, wanting more.

He pulled away a bit to look down at her. "Bella, I have to stop or you'll be on the ground in the next breath."

"Stop?" There was disappointment in her tone. She didn't want to stop. Not in the least. "Why must we?"

"Because all I can think of is that you've never been more lovely aside from when you were naked in my arms." He dipped a finger inside her bodice, between the swells of her breasts. "And I very much want to be inside you right now."

She feared she would swoon. Her entire body was wound as tightly as a spring. "You mustn't say such things to me. It's vastly unfair."

"I can't seem to help myself."

"Nor can I."

"I don't want you to marry the Duke of Dullness," he said suddenly. "I don't even want you to dance with the son-of-a-bitch again."

"I shan't," she reassured him.

He cursed, pressing his forehead to hers. "I will come to you tonight, Bella. You have the next few hours to decide whether or not you will open the door to me."

She started to tell him that of course she would open the door, but he hushed her.

"No. We will not be hasty." He kissed her, hard and quick. "Think very carefully, darling."

Then he released her and stalked off into the night, leaving Bella to stare after him, her heart beating the staccato pace of a galloping horse. Blessed angels' sakes. Jesse Whitney was coming to her tonight. Nervousness blended with anticipation inside her. She didn't have to decide whether or not she would welcome him. She already knew.

Belatedly, it occurred to her that he had called her darling.

# Chapter Six

ONCE ALONE, JESSE REGAINED A SMALL MEASURE OF his sanity. He hadn't been thinking straight, possessed as he'd been by potent lust, when he'd told Bella he'd come to her. But now, his passion had cooled enough for guilt to begin seeping back into his consciousness.

He was faced with the most difficult decision he'd made in his life. Should he go to Bella's chamber or stay the hell away? He stalked around the gardens in the cool darkness, at war with himself. His rational mind, of course, knew the answer. But the rest of him was another matter. The rest of him wanted nothing more than to make her his in the most primitive sense. It didn't matter that he would ruin her innocence or betray his friendship.

Ah, his friendship with Thornton. *Hellfire.*

It was an uncomfortable nettle in his conscience. He had never known a better man and yet he repaid him by planning to deflower his sister. He felt like the worst sort of lecher.

Thornton had asked him to share a brandy and soda-water after the ball and he'd refused. In fact, he'd spent much of the house party avoiding the marquis. It was damn difficult to look a friend in the eye when lusting after the man's sister, particularly when he'd long since crossed the boundary of mere lusting and had lain naked with her.

The thought of her glorious curves was enough to make him hard, even in the chill of the evening. Images of their stolen encounters flitted through his brain. She was his already. He had caressed her, kissed her, tasted her on his lips. He'd given Bella her first kiss, her first initiation into lovemaking. But it wasn't enough. He still wanted more. Everything she had to give.

He raked a hand through his hair, nearing the exit to the maze. He'd halfheartedly hoped he'd get lost within its dark confines, making it impossible for him to go to her. No luck in that, it seemed. His feet were steadfast in taking him to her.

He couldn't define what had changed for him, but his defenses had been blown to bits. Watching her dance with the duke had done something to him, caused a shifting deep inside where he hadn't thought he'd had feeling anymore.

He was jealous of a man who was as interesting as a blade of grass. But it didn't matter how dull the duke was. It didn't matter if the man was Bella's social equal, a fine match approved by her cunning mother. All that mattered was that he didn't want to see another man trying to woo her. He couldn't bear it.

Nothing could have prepared him for the mad attraction he felt for her. In his life, he had known many women, some of them beautiful, some of them worthy mates. But since Lavinia, he had never longed for a woman as if she were his life breath. It had been enough to mutually slake passions and leave emotions to romantics and fools.

Maybe he was the worst sort of fool. He wouldn't say he was in love. He didn't think himself capable of it. The war had hollowed him out, but not completely, it would seem. There was something left yet of the ideal dreamer he'd been. He knew that if he went to her, it would not be the end but only the beginning, and that scared the hell out of him.

He also knew that he didn't give a damn.

She'd begun to fear he wouldn't come. It was hours past midnight. Bella had stayed up in her dressing gown, attempting to read *The Eustace Diamonds* but not meeting with much success. Then came an unmistakable tap at her door. She threw the book to the side and ran a frantic hand over her hair. She had allowed Smith to take down her elaborate coiffure, but she had taken great pains to make certain her tresses were properly curled. If Smith noticed the extra worry she'd taken with her evening *toilette*, she wisely hadn't spoken a word.

Bella didn't dare call out for him to enter lest someone overhear. She rose from her bed and nearly ran across the chamber. With great care, she opened the door slowly to avoid any unwanted squeaking.

He stood waiting in the shadows of the unlit corridor, his expression intense. Wordlessly, Bella stepped aside to allow him entrance. He followed and the door clicked closed behind him. Just like that, everything had changed. She watched him, suddenly unsure of herself. He had removed his jacket and wore only a loose white shirt and trousers. In the soft light of the gas lamp she'd left lit, he was sinfully handsome.

"You came to me," she said, still feeling somehow as if she'd wandered into a dream and that at any moment, she'd wake.

"I couldn't stay away." He closed the distance between them in two long strides. His hands went to her waist, anchoring her against his powerful body.

Bella slid her arms around his neck and pressed a kiss to his mouth. "I'm glad."

He kissed her back, a brief, passionate claiming. "It isn't too late to change your mind."

"I have never been more certain of anything in my life." She meant it, much as the words frightened her. The dowager had raised her to be intelligent in matters of romance, if not in many other subjects. From a young age, she knew her worth was based as much upon the skills a lady should possess as her chastity. A lady must, above, all, retain her innocence. But Bella was a woman in love, and she cared far less for her worth on the marriage mart than for the man in her arms.

She couldn't be certain of what would happen after this night. Perhaps he would gaze at her with the expression of an aloof stranger. Perhaps they never would touch again. After all, the house party was at an end. She had no way of knowing if she would ever chance to find herself in his handsome shadow once more. Bella didn't give a fig. She wanted him, always had, and always would.

He growled, pressing her body closer to his, and bestowed another hungry kiss upon her. "Do you think we should?"

She sighed, her hands in his hair. It was silken and wonderful to her seeking fingers. Molten heat pooled between her thighs. She felt for the first time in her life a surge of feminine power, and she found she rather relished it. Bella rubbed her lower lip against his, at once teasing and seductive. "Do you think we shouldn't?"

"Christ no." He kissed her, then stopped for a ragged breath. "I mean yes. Ah, hell, what you do to me, woman."

Passion sluiced over her like honey, slow and tantalizing, sweet and delicious. "What do I do to you, Jesse?" Feeling brave, she ran her tongue along the seam of his gorgeous mouth.

He opened, sucking her tongue. Another growl sounded low in his throat. Their kiss became wet, downright voracious. "My darling, I cannot stay away."

"I don't want you to stay away from me," she murmured, wrapping her bare leg around his trouser-clad one. She didn't care if she was a wanton. He brought it out in her, and she had ever been one to be open, honest and free. Despite what the dowager and finishing school had instilled in her.

"You don't?" He framed her face in his large, strong hands. His calloused fingertips were a welcome abrasion on her cheeks.

They were teasing one another, and Bella had to admit the prolonging heightened her desire. "No indeed, sir." She turned her head to kiss his fingers. "On the contrary, I want you to be very, very near."

"Mmm." He brushed his thumb over her lower lip once, twice. His handsome countenance was tantalizingly close. "How near?"

Ah, so he was encouraging her boldness in their lovemaking. Awareness swept through her. Did she dare? There was so much she wanted, so much for which she longed. She'd never before even considered it, but with Jesse, her desires seemed natural.

She reached for his hand and slid it, ever so slowly, inside the gaping vee of her dressing gown. His warm hand settled upon her bare breast. Her nipple tightened instantly into his palm. Their gazes clashed, his astoundingly blue. "Would this near do, Mr. Whitney?"

She found the pretense of formality added an element of excitement to their dangerous, sensual taunts. There was no mistaking this encounter. It wasn't an innocent garden maze in which they met. No, indeed. This was her bedchamber. His hand cupped her naked breast. His leg slid between hers, his muscular thigh creating an intense and pleasurable pressure upon her mound. She wanted him to make her his, to possess her. Their mouths were a kiss apart. The entire affair was naughty, forbidden, and utterly heavenly.

He swallowed, the only outward suggestion he was moved as much as she by their banter. "Perhaps nearer would do, my dear."

"Pray forgive me," she whispered. "What would you have me do, sir?"

"Do you love me?" His voice was nearly guttural, desire evident in the intensity of his blue gaze.

She kissed him. "And if I do?"

"I don't deserve it, my darling." With his free hand, he pulled her dressing gown away from her shoulders. It pooled at her waist, snagged by her belt, leaving both her breasts bared for his appreciative gaze. He cupped her with his hands, sending a wave of sensation skittering through her. She adored the feeling of his skin upon hers.

"But if I do love you," she persisted, knowing somehow that they were not so much playing as revealing. She was not well-versed in the art of seduction, but neither was she an insipid miss. After all, she prided herself upon the knowledge she'd collected through the many novels she'd read. Though she was a neophyte, she was not entirely ignorant, thanks to him. "What then?"

His gaze darkened upon hers, his intent clear. "Then I am at your mercy. What would you have me do, my lady?"

*Oh dear.* She very much wanted to tantalize him as he did her, but she hadn't an inkling what to say next. Best, she reckoned through her passion-addled mind, to allow him to be the one to direct. "What would you like, sir?" As she asked him, her fingers sought the belt at her waist. She undid the knot and pulled the sash free. Her dressing gown fell to the carpeted floor in a whisper of fabric.

She was completely naked.

"I would very much like if you kissed me," he said, his voice soft. "I have been looking upon you all evening, wishing you were mine. I should like nothing more than to believe you are."

"I *am* yours," she confirmed. "I have been, from the moment you caught me in the library at Marleigh Manor with my spectacles beneath my bustle." She smiled, reveling in the wonder of how quickly, yet how imperceptibly, life could alter. She had never dared to dream Jesse Whitney would ever come to her like this, hold her in his arms, make love to her.

"You are more beautiful than I deserve."

"Never," she denied, bestowing another kiss upon his

lips. "By far, sir, you are the most handsome suitor upon whom I have ever laid eyes." And she wanted him as naked as she. Her hands went to his shirt, undoing the line of buttons.

"Bella, are you utterly certain, my darling girl? I fear this is the last time I can ask you with any hope of putting an end to this madness."

"I am completely certain in every way. I love you so very much." She kissed his neck, inhaling deeply of his scent. How she wanted him. She felt it possible that he loved her, even if he couldn't put words to the emotions he felt. She was certain she knew Jesse well enough to know he would never be familiar with his best friend's sister unless theirs was an inescapable attraction. He was, after all, an honorable man. Was he not?

She hadn't long to consider the question her dowager-forged conscience asked, for in the next instant, he had whisked away his shirt. Her fingers went to the fastening of his trousers. Nudity was a lonesome state.

"Is it love?" He kissed her again, his tongue going inside her mouth to tease and taste, to own. "How can you be certain?"

"I've never known anything comparing to the emotions I feel for you." She kissed him back with all the fervor in her soul. Their tongues tangled. Desire was a heated thing snaking through her body. How she needed this man. Perhaps she still didn't know entirely what that meant since he had not fully taken her before, but she needed him regardless, whatever may come.

He nipped her full lower lip and simultaneously rubbed his thumbs over her hard nipples. "Do you want me, darling?"

Did she want him? Good heavens, did she want to breathe in the air that gave her life? She sighed again, arching into his strong body. He wore only his trousers now. "Oh yes."

He dropped a path of kisses beginning from her mouth

and trailing down her neck, to her collarbone. Then lower still. He kissed his way to her breasts. "I have wanted you ever since the first moment I saw you in the library at Marleigh Manor. But I knew I could never have you."

She was fascinated to know he too had wanted her even then. She'd thought herself too young, too awkward. He had been older, wiser, unbearably handsome. How could he have ever been attracted to her quiet self?

Bella couldn't quite squelch a moan when he sucked a nipple into his knowing mouth. "Why did you think you could not have me?" she asked, almost unable to string a proper sentence with the naughty things he was doing to her.

Jesse raked the sensitive bud with his teeth before releasing it and looking up to meet her gaze. "You are far too good for the likes of me. I've seen too much of the world. Be certain you want me, Bella, with your mind and not just your pretty body."

"Of course I want you." She finally opened his trousers. Perhaps she wasn't thinking with her reasonable mind, but even when she wasn't in his arms, she always longed for him. "It is only your honor that says I don't."

Bella took him into her palm, loving the velvety, warm feel of him. She had very much wanted to touch him before, but he had separated himself from her before it was possible. He was rigid and long, and holding him made the ache in her all the more potent. She wanted to feel him inside her. Now.

His breath hissed from his lungs as she tightened her fingers around his arousal. She didn't care that he was older than she, that there had been other women he had loved before her. All that mattered was that she had found in him a heart to answer hers. She wasn't about to let him to turn away from her again this night as he had before. No indeed, this night, he was to make her his in every sense.

"You must be very sure," he urged again, his voice sounding strained. He cupped her face in his large, rough hands. His golden beauty awed her. "There can be no reversal."

She knew he was giving her every opportunity to save her innocence. He had done so once before, introducing her to pleasure without ruining her. But there was no other man for whom she would save herself. He almost appeared vulnerable, naked and towering over her. She had never loved him more.

"I know my own mind, Jesse." She reached up and wound her arms around his neck. "I love you."

"Christ." He lowered his mouth to hers for a crushing kiss. His tongue slid against hers, dipping in to taste and tantalize. "I can't wait any longer," he whispered before taking her up in his arms.

Startled, she let out a squeak, tightening her grip on him. "No one has ever carried me before."

He strode across the chamber with her and then deposited her upon the bed. His eyes were dark with desire as he joined her, his strong, naked body equally hot at her side. "Then this is a night of many firsts." He dragged one hand gently through her unbound black curls and caressed her cheek with the other, kissing her again.

It began slowly, almost tentatively, as he molded his lips to hers. Bella turned into him, wanting to feel him against her. Her breasts grazed his chest, his arousal pressing into the soft swell of her stomach. She rested her palms on his brawny shoulders, arching into him. Everything felt right. Perfect. She never wanted the evening to end.

He dragged his sinful mouth down over her throat to her breasts, leaving behind a trail of fire on her sensitive skin. The slight roughness of his golden stubble scraped her in the most delicious way. When he took her nipple into his mouth, she moaned again, unhinged by the sensation on the tight bud.

"Hush, darling," he murmured, pressing a kiss to the side of her breast. He looked up at her and grinned, his dimple flashing for a moment. "You must be as quiet as you can or else we'll have the dowager storming in to rescue you from this horrid American."

He was gorgeous, her horrid American, and she almost couldn't fathom he was lying with her. "I don't need rescuing," she told him with an answering smile at his levity. "I shall endeavor to be as quiet as possible."

"Good." He took her other nipple in his mouth, delivering the same bold torture to it. "Because I'm about to do this." Jesse kissed a path down over her belly, pulling her legs apart as he did so.

She was open to him once more, but this time she wasn't embarrassed. She knew all too well the pleasure awaiting her. Her heart kicking into a gallop, she ran her fingers through his thick golden hair. He kissed her slowly, his tongue darting out against her. She pressed the back of her right hand to her mouth, stifling another moan as best she could. Dear heavens, it was the most glorious feeling, entirely scandalous, completely sinful. And she loved every second.

He sucked and toyed with his tongue, bringing her the same powerful ecstasy she'd felt before. She moaned, closing her eyes to relish the powerful desire rocking through her. He teased her with a maddening rhythm, using his thumb on the nub of her sex until she was shuddering against him. She reached her pinnacle, twisting against him as she felt herself coming, the pleasure so intense she didn't know if she wanted to push him away or keep him there forever. He held her still against him, absorbing the ripples of her pleasure against his mouth.

Her breath left her in heaving gasps. Somehow, it was even more intense this time than the last. She realized through the haze of passion fogging her mind that she had forever crossed the line from girlhood to womanhood. There was no reversal, as he'd said, and neither did she want one.

He looked up at her and pressed a kiss to the inside of her thigh. "Do you like my mouth on you, Bella?"

She swallowed as another wave of desire crashed over her. There was more to this heady dance, and she wanted to know it. "You know I do."

With a groan, he rose, pressing his big body over hers. Her legs fell apart easily, welcoming him as if it were the most natural position in the world. His cock was between them, prodding her hungry entrance. She wanted him inside her so badly. Longing swept through her. Bella wriggled beneath him, restless with the wait. She had waited so very long for him to make her his.

He kissed her, again, propping himself up with his large hands splayed on either side of her head. "Be still, darling. I want to go slowly."

"I can't help it." Bella ran her hands down the sleek planes of his shoulders, feeling the corded muscle beneath. "I need you, Jesse."

He nipped her lower lip and reached down to position himself at her throbbing sheath. "I don't want to hurt you. There will be pain the first time."

She wasn't afraid. Indeed, she was quite certain she would explode if he didn't soon ease the ache building within her. She wanted to say as much, but she couldn't speak beyond one monosyllabic word. "Please."

Jesse's hips moved as he claimed her mouth, his tongue teasing hers. Her body stretched to accommodate him. She felt at once pleasure and a bit of discomfort, almost like a bee sting. Until he thrust into her again, and the sheer size of him sent a raw shot of pain through her. She stiffened, startled. For some reason, she hadn't expected it to hurt this much.

He stopped moving, tearing his mouth from hers to meet her gaze, his expression one of concern. "Have I hurt you?"

"A bit," she admitted, trying to stanch the tears threatening her vision.

"Do you want me to stop, darling?"

"No," she denied quickly. It was too late now, and she

had no regrets.

"I'm sorry, sweetheart. After you grow accustomed to me, the pleasure will return." He thrust a little farther inside her.

She tilted her hips up, easing the entry. One more thrust, and he was buried deep within her. The pain remained, a dull, burning ache, but as he gradually slid almost completely out of her again, the pleasure began to return just as he'd promised. He lowered his mouth to hers, giving her a soothing kiss that said more than mere words could. Jesse thrust inside her again, then out, then in again, starting up a rhythm that she did her best to match. With each stroke, the pain lessened, until she was once more caught up in the throes of passion.

Their kisses grew more intense, tongues tangling as he made love to her in truth. Her body was already on edge, ready to come undone again. Small, breathy sounds of bliss escaped her. Jesse continued pumping into her, his pace increasing until the frenzy he'd built within her reached yet another crescendo. She tightened around him, spasms racking her body as extreme pleasure washed over her again.

Suddenly, he tore his mouth from hers and pushed into her again, grinding their hips together. He threw his head back and moaned as she felt him change. A hot spurt shot inside her, giving her another sharp spear of pleasure. Bella held him against her tightly, loving the feeling of him atop her, within her. Finally, he collapsed against her, breathing heavily.

He lay that way for a few heartbeats before rolling to his side, his body slipping away from hers. "My God," he said at last.

She turned to admire him, committing to memory every line of his beautiful body. She feared she'd lost her ability to speak entirely. Her body throbbed in odd places, but she had never been happier. She dropped a kiss on his chest and rested her head there.

"Are you in pain, darling?" He stroked her hair.

She shook her head, still incapable of intelligent conversation.

He kissed the top of her head as an easy silence descended. He had been right. There was no turning back now. Jesse had made her into a woman in the ancient sense. Perhaps she would pay for her sins later, but she relished them for the moment. Some time passed without either of them speaking. Bella was content to listen to his breathing, tucked to his beloved side.

She must have fallen asleep, for Bella woke to realize she was alone in the bed, the covers pulled carefully around her. Startled, she sat up, scanning the chamber for Jesse. He was in the middle of the room, collecting his garments, his back to her.

"Where are you going?" she asked, disappointed that he would disappear on her without saying goodbye.

He spun about at her voice with a start, clearly thinking her still asleep. "I cannot remain here, Bella. We risk your reputation."

"The servants won't be about for hours yet." She disliked the idea that their idyll must be over so soon. "You needn't leave so soon."

"I don't want to fall asleep, my dear."

"I'm a dreadfully light sleeper," she countered. "I'll wake you long before Smith comes in with my chocolate and no one will ever be the wiser."

"I cannot."

His tone was suddenly distant. Bella didn't like it, not one bit. She watched him beginning to dress before rising also. She was keenly aware of her nudity now that the flaming intensity of their lovemaking had died to a low fire in the grate.

She placed a palm on his strong shoulder, troubled when he flinched away from her. "Jesse? What is it?"

"It's nothing. It is merely time to return to my own chamber. I wouldn't have you hurt for the world, Bella." He fastened his trousers around his lean hips.

Bella wasn't having it. "There's something you don't want to tell me," she guessed. "Pray be honest with me. What can be the matter? Have I disappointed you? Do you regret making love to me?"

"Never that. You could never disappoint me, darling." He sighed and raked a hand through his already mussed hair. His expression hardened. "Since the war, I've been plagued by nightmares. I wake sometimes screaming in the night, convinced I'm in the midst of battle. I cannot take the chance of someone hearing me here in your chamber. Nor would I want to burden you with my demons."

She ached for him. How unspeakable the war must have been to still have a pronounced effect on such a strong man all these years later. She closed the distance between them, drawing him into an embrace. Bella laid her head against the steady thrum of his heart, savoring the familiar scent of him for a few moments. She never wanted to let him go. It seemed terribly unfair that in the morning they must go through their day as strangers once more. It seemed even more unfair that perhaps she would never see him again. The very idea broke her heart.

"You could never be a burden to me," she told him, stroking his back. "I only wish I could slay your demons for you."

He caressed her hair, bestowing a kiss upon her head. "Dear girl. I know you would if you could. What did I do to deserve you?"

She smiled and pressed an answering kiss to his lightly haired chest. "You found a reserved miss in the library and didn't mind that she wore spectacles and talked far too much about books."

"Not to mention that the miss in question crushed her spectacles beneath her sweet bottom." He tipped up her chin and grinned down at her, the heaviness that had settled between them dissipating.

She wrinkled her nose at him. "It is exceedingly unfair of you to keep reminding me about my appalling lack of grace."

Jesse gave a soft chuckle. "I expect I'll be reminding you of it for years to come."

Bella's heart leapt at his words. Did he mean to say he would be in her life for years to come? She was afraid to ask, afraid to hope for too much. Instead, she asked him the question that had been haunting her. "Where are you off to after the house party's end? Surely not back to America?"

"I'm afraid you'll not be rid of me so easily," he teased. "I haven't been back to America in years and don't feel much of a need to return."

As answers went, it wasn't a commitment, but it was still promising. A spear of hope went through her. "Does that mean I shall see you again?"

His dimple reappeared. "Of course, darling. I'll need to give you a proper courtship now."

She blinked at him, utterly confounded. "You will?"

"You didn't think I would compromise the innocent sister of my best friend and simply walk away?" He raised a brow. "Bella?"

Bella pursed her lips, searching for an answer that wouldn't offend him. She wasn't certain what she'd imagined. But she certainly hadn't anticipated a proposal. Not that he had proposed, but he'd implied as much.

"You *did* think I'd compromise you and then leave," he said, but there was no heat in his voice. "You won't be rid of me that easily. I'm honored, my darling, that you chose me." He kissed her soundly. "Now I must go."

She nodded, rising to her toes to give him another kiss. She truly didn't want him to leave, not after sharing the most incredible experience of her life. But she knew he was right. "Shall I see you in the morning?"

"You shall." His dimple was in full force as he shrugged into his shirt and coat before slipping quietly out the door.

After he had gone, his words of the other day returned to her. *My little romantic, I'm afraid I don't even believe in love.* For Bella, it was an ominous pronouncement indeed. Perhaps he had changed his mind. A troubling inner voice warned her that it was likely he had not. Could she marry a man who didn't believe in love? Would their passion be enough?

Mind weighed down with heavy thoughts, Bella gave up trying to go to sleep. She spent the remainder of the night attempting to read her book, her mind wandering from the plot with each turn of the page.

# Chapter Seven

Y NOON THE NEXT DAY, BELLA WAS MISERABLY gazing out the same carriage window as a fortnight earlier, watching the countryside trickle by her. She was certain the young lady who had been en route to the house party would scarce recognize the woman leaving it. She had hoped to see Jesse Whitney from afar. Instead, she had shared his bed. He had taken her innocence. It seemed almost like a dream, except for the soreness between her legs. She could still smell the faint traces of his body on hers, and she savored it, couldn't help herself.

She looked to her mother, guilt skewering her. She wondered if *Maman* could tell what she'd done. Likely not, she decided. Drat her conscience. She couldn't help but feel badly to know that she had been circumventing her mother's plans for her in such a bold way. If the proud lady had an inkling that Bella had been so much as seeing Jesse Whitney or speaking with him in private, there would be a most severe reckoning. But Bella had done far worse than that, and she was certain that if the dowager ever uncovered the depths of her sins, it would be her mother's undoing.

Of course, she wasn't the only de Vere who had been engaging in questionable behavior. Her brother had been openly courting scandal during the house party, and he showed no sign of returning to his former, respectable self. The dowager's face was knotted up in a ferocious frown. *Maman* had discovered that he planned to take his paramour to Marleigh Manor and to jilt his proper fiancée. It spelled the end of his political aspirations as Prime Minister Gladstone's protégé. However, where Bella had initially been unable to comprehend her brother's defection, she now understood completely. Love changed everything.

"My son shall be the death of me," her mother declared, breaking up Bella's thoughts as she fanned herself.

"All will be well, Mother," Bella reassured, even if she wasn't entirely certain of the veracity of her own words. "Thornton will not bring us to ruin."

The dowager took her by complete surprise, leaning across the tiny space of the carriage to slap Bella across the cheek with her kid glove. Despite the lack of muscle behind the gesture, it surely stung.

"How dare you?"

Bella pondered her next words with great care. Never before had she experienced violence at the hands of her mother. "Pray accept my apologies, *Maman*," she said at length.

"Your brother had highest hopes," her mother nearly spat at her. "Some years ago, he fancied himself in love with that slattern Lady Scarbrough, as she now calls herself. She wed the earl, rotten scoundrel though he may be, and now she has no claim upon my dear, innocent son." The dowager shook her head in her passion, resembling nothing so much as an enraged sparrow. "She has no claim upon him!"

Bella stared at her mother, nearly aghast. She knew that Thornton's less-than-circumspect flirtation with the married countess was setting the dowager at sixes and sevens. But she supposed she'd been far too concerned with the secret scandal she'd been brewing on her own to have a care.

Guilt threatened anew to swallow her. If Thornton's actions caused her mother so much distress, there was no telling what havoc Bella's would wreak upon her. She poked at the pleats of her traveling skirts. "Just so. I feel quite certain that my brother will see the error of his ways."

Truly, Bella hadn't the crumb of an idea as to what Thornton had in mind. She knew from her mother that he intended to bring the married countess to their home. Beyond that, her brother had not confided in her. They had shared heated words about Lady Scarbrough on more than one occasion, and it hurt her that they seemed forever at odds. Once, they had been quite close. Now it seemed years and experience had come between them.

"I do pray so every evening," the dowager announced with a fervent air that was nearly disturbing. "I must say I am endlessly relieved to have invited Miss Cuthbert to be joining us at Marleigh Manor. Yes, I daresay she is possessed of just the winning winds we need to blow through this most difficult life of ours. Do you not think so, Bella dearest? Say you adore Miss Cuthbert as much as I do. You know her father is such a well-respected pillar of our society." The dowager stomped her foot, her face screwed again into displeasure. "It is not right that the marquis should have been so close to glory, darling Arabella. It is most unfair indeed that we shall never see your brother reach his true aspirations if this awful person is to continue on in his life. Surely you must see the indisparity of it all?"

Bella cleared her throat. "I do believe you mean to say disparity, madam."

"Precisely what I said." The dowager sniffed and then rested her head against the bobbing carriage, closing her eyes. "Now it is merely time that we must rest. Do go to sleep, my dear girl. I find I am desperately fatigued."

"Sleep well, *Maman.*"Bella looked at her mother, already near to snoring state. It was just as well, she reasoned. Better her mother never find out the truth of what she had done, which was far more unforgivable than what her brother had done before her.

She gulped, pressing her face against the glass. All she could hope was that Jesse would do as he promised and meet her at Marleigh Manor. If he didn't, Bella knew not what she would do.

Back in Marleigh Manor, Bella stretched from the familiar comforts of her old bed. It had been some time since she'd been enveloped in its confines. Odd indeed, she supposed, but somehow welcome nonetheless. She was actually pleased to be back in her home, romping about the estate in which she'd grown up. But she was having difficulty truly enjoying it, her mind too preoccupied with thoughts of Jesse.

An entire day had come to pass since her arrival at the manor and yet she still hadn't heard if he had arrived. She yawned and reached for the bell pull, hoping that Smith would answer the question she'd been longing to have answered without her having to ask it. Was Jesse here as he'd promised? Nearly two days had passed since they had made love. She had been left with no one to ask if he'd arrived save Smith. But while she adored Smith, she'd been terrified that her dear maid might suspect something untoward had happened. She had to admit that it was most likely that he had followed her to Marleigh Manor as promised, but she was terribly afraid that he hadn't.

In truth, Bella didn't know what she would do, how she would react, if he had disappeared. It was her greatest fear. After all, back at Wilton House, she hadn't been able to have a private word with him as they had planned. Although they'd seen one another at breakfast, the time for the party to disperse had been upon them. Her mother was in fine dudgeon, determined to return to Marleigh Manor as soon as possible. Bella had been left with no choice save to follow the dowager. To have attempted to remain would have been utter foolishness.

Smith burst into her chamber then, all smiles and bustle as was her wont. "Good morning to you, my lady, and what a glorious day it appears to be, back here in Marleigh Manor. I can't say as for you, but I've missed it dearly. I do so love the lake and the trees. Wilton House was dashing indeed, but Marleigh Manor is where I shall always consider home."

Her brand of enthusiasm was quite infectious.

Bella smiled. "Good morning to you as well." She paused for a moment, trying her best to avoid being transparent. "I do so miss the excitement of having a house party all about us. Tell me, Smith, do we have any guests?"

"Yes, my lady," Smith concurred, busying herself with preparing Bella's morning *toilette*. "We have Lady Scarbrough and her sisters fresh from the house party, along with the American Mr. Whitney and your cousin, Lord Fordham. We also have Miss Honoria Cuthbert and her maiden aunt as visitors of the dowager."

She nearly sighed with relief. Jesse was here. Blast the rest of them. She couldn't care for their scandals and troubles now. The man she loved was here. He had followed her, coming just as he'd promised. Her heart was reassured. All would fall into place. It had to now. Didn't it?

The dowager was most displeased. Nothing ruined her disposition more than the failure of someone in her coterie to live up to her exacting standards. First, her only son— once the light of the Liberal Party—had lost his head over a trollop. Now it appeared to her that her only daughter was going similarly mad.

She sighed from her very bones, unbearably weary for a woman of her years. "Hollins," she called out to her maid who was across the chamber readying her *toilette*. "Do come here at once."

Her loyal lady's maid hastily appeared at her side. Truly, the woman was a godsend, servant or no, and she'd been a retainer for twenty years. No maids had ever lasted as long in her employ, and she dared say they never would again. She hoped Hollins outlived her, else she'd be lost.

"How may I be of service to you, my lady?" her maid queried, ever eager to perform her duties.

She frowned, phrasing her question with delicacy. "What do you know of that American fellow, Mr. Whitney? I'm sure you must have overheard some belowstairs tales by now."

"I know only that he doesn't keep his own man," Hollins replied. "Aside from that, I suppose no one has said aught."

"He hasn't his own manservant?" The dowager sniffed. "How positively horrid. We shall have to put it down to those beastly American customs, no doubt."

An idea began forming in her mind then, one that was so wicked she almost thought she couldn't manage the carrying out of it. But then she thought again of the way her silly chit of a daughter seemed to forever be finding mischief. She was meant to have a coronet. The Duke of Devonshire was the man the dowager had hand-picked for Bella. No tawdry American devoid of manners was going to usurp the duke's place as her husband. Why, the man had no knowledge of the proper way of things. It was an outrage to be sure.

"Hollins," she began again, her tone contemplative, "your cousin is a footman here at Marleigh Manor, is he not? What is the fellow's name? Palmer?"

"Yes, my lady. His name is Patterson, madam."

"Just so." She waved her hand at the difference in surname, slight as she saw it. "There is something I must have done, and no one must ever know. Do you understand?"

Comprehension dawned in Hollins' rabbit-brown eyes. She was an intelligent woman or the dowager would not have stood for a moment of her company. She couldn't abide by hen-witted servants.

"Of course, Lady Thornton."

"I should think it would be a delightful opportunity for young Patterson to act as Mr. Whitney's manservant. Naturally, I shall be requiring some assistance from Patterson. He must be very circumspect. You will make that clear to him, no doubt."

Hollins nodded. "Yes, of course, my lady. I'll be certain to make him aware of your requirements. I've no doubt he'll be pleased by the change in circumstance."

"Good." The dowager smiled, quite happy with herself. "Bring me the housekeeper. I'll let her know I've hand-chosen a manservant for Mr. Whitney. It's the least I can do for our guest."

What the hell had he done?

It was the question that had been banging about his mind like a cow trapped in a burning barn ever since he'd risen the morning after making love to Bella. Jesse paced a length of the intricate Marleigh Manor gardens as he waited for Bella to appear, wondering for the hundredth time how he'd come to deflower his best friend's sister. Whatever the inexplicable answer, he'd done the deed and now he needed to set the situation to rights, even if it meant saddling Bella with his demons forever.

He wished to God he'd thought more about her future than about how badly he wanted to sink inside her sweet body. She deserved far better than a drifting ex-soldier who couldn't bear the mentioning of guns without turning into a frenzied lunatic. There was a reason he'd never settled with one woman in the last fifteen years. He was thirty-six years old, for Christ's sake, and he still couldn't face what he'd done as a young lad. He looked down at his hands, hands he'd used to club a man to death in Petersburg, hands he'd used to pull triggers and to raise a bayonet against his fellow countrymen at Gettysburg, at Sharpsburg and countless other places. Time traveled on, the guilt following steadily along.

Ah, Christ. His sweet, innocent Bella couldn't begin to imagine the evil things he'd seen and done. He'd tried to rebuild himself, forge a new identity from the ashes. But the truth was he couldn't escape the war completely, no matter how hard he tried. She was young and untouched by the vast cruelties life loved to deal. She said she loved him, but she didn't know the sins he was capable of committing. Never had he been more ashamed of himself.

Yes, he was a selfish bastard of the highest degree. He wanted to bask in her love, lie in her tender embrace, to lose himself in her over and over again and pray she could make him whole once more. Part of him wanted to save her from himself, but he was keenly aware it was too late. Already, his child could have taken hold within her womb. The die was cast, as they said, and there was no help for it now. He had to wed her and somehow keep her from his madness as best he could.

He heaved a sigh and forced his mind to the matter at hand. Bella ought to be appearing any moment and it wouldn't do for her to see him in such a state. He'd sent her a message at his earliest opportunity, needing to speak with her in private without being tempted to further ruin her. Not that the temptation didn't remain, but he didn't wish to dishonor her more than he already had by taking her without the bonds of marriage. She wasn't the sort of woman to be trifled with, that much was certain. He couldn't afford to make love to her again.

He suppressed a groan as he turned on his heel to crunch back in the direction he'd just come from. The thought of making love to Bella had him stiffer than the statue of Poseidon he'd passed on his way into the gardens. A mere day had intervened since he'd seen her the previous morning, but already it seemed a chasm of time separated them. They had to decide upon a mutually agreeable course of action.

Guilt skewered him yet again.

He was having a devil of a time figuring out precisely how he was going to tell his old friend that he wanted to court his sister. One thing was certain. There would be no more late-night visits to her chamber until they were wed, regardless of how tempting the prospect may be. He could not—nay, would not—run the risk.

She was an innocent. Had been an innocent, at any rate. His gut couldn't have been swirling with more anxiety if he'd been about to face a wall of Federal sharpshooters. He wouldn't be surprised if Thornton wanted to beat him to a pulp. Very likely, he deserved to be beaten. He was no gentleman, though he'd endeavored to hide himself in business and properties, money and parties, and women who didn't ask questions about the times he woke sweating and screaming out into the night.

A flurry of skirts and color caught his attention. Bella rounded the bend in a hurry, her beautiful face flushed with unabashed delight. She was, in a simple word, ravishing. He had scarcely enough time to note she wore a navy-and-cream-striped dress with a fall of hand-dyed ecru lace at her décolletage. Her black curls had been piled into an artful arrangement beneath a dashing chipped-straw hat that knocked him in the nose as she threw herself into his arms. He caught her around her tiny waist, holding her petite body against his for a few moments longer than necessary before returning her to the ground. He recalled every creamy expanse of her lush body beneath the layers of her walking dress, undergarments, and stiff corset.

She reached up to press a hand to his cheek. "I've missed you. I confess I feared you wouldn't come."

Very likely, he shouldn't have. She deserved far better than a broken man for a husband. But he'd ruined her, and now there was no hope for either of them. He pressed a kiss to her blessedly bare palm, wanting her even more than he had the night he'd taken her. She made him feel as if he'd hurtled himself from the roof of the hotel he'd invested in with Thornton in New York, completely out of his skin, falling helplessly from a great height. "I made a promise to you, Bella."

A frown marred her expression. She was not pleased, it would appear. "I hope you aren't suffering misgivings?"

Was he? Hell yes. He was an utter jackass, taking advantage of her. She fancied herself in love with him. Christ, she didn't even know the real man hiding behind his gentleman's exterior. He shook himself from the grim thoughts that had been plaguing him with ceaseless persistence. "Of course not," he said, taking care to keep his voice mild. He didn't want to alarm her or cause her sweet face to crumple any more than it already had.

She smiled, and a dart of heat shot directly to his groin. Why did she have to be so beautiful, so tempting, so charmingly bereft of feminine artifice? She was the opposite of every woman he'd known. Where others had been manipulative and self-serving, eager for the better man who came along, she was steadfast and earnest. She'd chosen her path and remained true. He wanted to gather her into his arms, carry her off into a secluded corner and make love to her all over again. Perhaps meeting her in secret hadn't been the best course of action. It seemed his honorable self was at war with his lascivious self once more.

"I've thought of little else but you," she murmured, her voice soft and sweet.

He wanted to love her, Christ he did. He just didn't think he could. He closed his eyes for a moment against the onslaught of her loveliness. She was an angel. He wasn't fit to even kiss the ribbon-trimmed train of her dress. Attempting to collect himself, he opened his eyes once more to find her gaze fixed upon him, her tender feelings evident in the openness of her expression. She wore her heart upon her silken, lace-bedecked sleeve.

"It's been the same for me," he said, meaning his words but not in the way she likely thought. He couldn't help but feel the traitor. She was open and loving. She ought to have better than the likes of him.

"When can we be alone?"she asked. "Truly alone? Will you come to me tonight?"

Dear God, he couldn't bear to make love to her again, much as he longed to lie with her once more. He had to maintain his honor, to maintain her honor. Didn't he? Ah, the temptation was ripe and strong as a magnolia in the Southern sun. Guilt assailed him anew. "I can't, my dear. I wouldn't risk your honor for the world."

She raised a brow, her face drawing into a quizzical knot. "But haven't you already done so?" Bella paused, more inherently gorgeous than any woman had a right to be. He longed for her with a desperation that frightened him.

He set her apart from him at an arm's length, trying to maintain propriety. He was too old for this game, surely. He took a deep, exacting breath and found that he had utterly nothing to say to save himself.

She frowned again, her full mouth tautening from a bow into a straight line. "Have you not already taken me as a husband would take a wife?"

"Dear God, yes," he hastened to answer. "Of course you must know I have. It's simply that I will not sully you again."

Bella stepped forward, making him feel for the first time as if he, as a man grown, should retreat lest he devour her on the spot. She pursed her lips, looking a bit as if she'd taken a bite of a dinner she wasn't convinced she liked. "Whatever do you mean?"

Christ, he was making a mess of this. Everything had changed between them. He knew what she tasted like. He'd taken her maidenhead. He had spent himself inside her. He was responsible for her now in a way he hadn't imagined he could be, duty-bound to become her husband. He'd been an orphan living with his maiden aunt in Richmond before running off to war, effectively having no family. Nothing in his life had prepared him for the magnitude of his sudden duties, not even the brief romance he'd shared with Lavinia.

"I will come to you as your husband," he endeavored to explain. "I am, from this point hence, yours."

She smiled again to rival the cheeriness of the soft autumn's day, her air becoming teasing. "I should certainly hope so, Mr. Whitney. I daresay I was beginning to wonder."

He was abashed. "Naturally, I must ask your brother for his blessing."

She worried her full lower lip, her concern evident. "What do you think he shall say?"

Jesse was well aware that he would have to be honest with his friend and reveal the full extent of his betrayal. He would not, however, tell Bella as much. No need to give her further cause to fret. "I expect he will be surprised, but given our long friendship, I hope he'll give me his blessing to take you as my wife."

"Wife." She cast him another beaming grin. "I find I rather like that title."

If he'd been in need of more lessons in humility, he wasn't any longer. She was an aristocrat, the daughter of a marquis, happy to be wedding a Virginia boy who hadn't called any place home in more than a decade. Naturally, he didn't expect her to relinquish her title. It would all be a part of the settlement he reached with Thornton. "You will be welcome to keep your title, of course," he hastened to say. "Mrs. Whitney certainly isn't as illustrious a name as Lady Arabella."

"But I cannot think of any title I would wear with greater pride," she told him, reaching up to cup his jaw in her fine-boned hand. "I don't wish to be known as Lady Arabella after we wed. I wish only to be Mrs. Jesse Whitney."

He had to forcibly restrain himself from snatching her up in his arms then in a show of primitive ownership. He hadn't been prepared for her to throw over her old life in favor of beginning anew with him. In his experience with the English nobility, it simply wasn't done. He swallowed, his throat suddenly gone thick with emotions he chose not to examine. "Are you sure, my dear? You may want to rethink your remarkable loyalty."

She traced a path down his throat, her touch marking him as permanently as any brand. Her eyes were a vivid and gorgeous blue, pinning him to the spot. "I shall never have cause to rethink my loyalty to you, Jesse. I hope you always know how very much I love you."

If he hadn't been drowning in a sea of shame before, he was now. He wanted to tell her he loved her in return. But he still wasn't certain he ever could. He took her wandering hand in his and raised it to his mouth for a kiss. Once he caught a whiff of her glorious scent, he couldn't stop at one and kissed a trail that nearly went to her elbow. He bunched up her walking dress and under sleeves as best as he could, desperate for her creamy skin.

"You are too good for me," he whispered against her, his head bowed. He couldn't bear to look at her just now, not when she had him all but on his knees. He was powerless in the onslaught of her innate goodness, her sweet disposition. Their war was most certainly not a fair one.

"Nonsense," she was quick to say, her free hand raking through his hair. "I shall never be too good for my husband. It's far more likely that you are too good for me."

Her touch sent a sluice of desire down his spine. He wanted to stay in the golden, enchanted day forever, with Bella loving him without hesitation. In her eyes, he was a good man, a man worthy of her affections. He couldn't bear to ever see her look at him with contempt, or perhaps with fear. She'd seen him in the grips of his madness only once, but the spell had been a mild one. He shuddered to think what would happen, what he was capable of doing, should a more violent episode attack him.

"My darling," he said lowly, the words torn from him, "You will always be too good for me." He raised his head to meet her gaze once more. "You'd do well to never forget that."

"You are a far better man than you think, Jesse Whitney." She drew him to her, and he allowed himself to be moved. She pressed her petite form to his, her heart beating fast against his chest even through her thick corset and the layers of her dress and undergarments.

He hugged her to him tightly, keeping himself from kissing her with every shred of self-control he possessed. He lowered his mouth to her ear, sneaking his way beneath her monstrosity of a hat. "I will go to Thornton as soon as I can. Do you have a preferred month for a wedding?"

"You won't—" she paused, seemingly collecting herself. "You won't tell Thornton that we've been...that is to say, you won't tell him we've been as husband and wife already, will you? I couldn't bear to face him if you did."

He pulled back, looking sternly down upon her. "Bella, I must go to him as a man and reveal that I have not treated you with honor. I fear our friendship depends upon it."

Concern marred her pretty features. "But what he doesn't know surely cannot hurt him."

"My conscience will not allow any less," he clarified. He owed that much to Thornton and to Bella. If his friend chose to send him on his way, then he would respect his wishes. He knew that if the situations had been reversed, Thornton would have shown him the selfsame consideration.

"But surely you agree nothing can be gained by his knowledge?" she persisted, obviously distressed.

"Don't worry, my dear. The fault is purely mine, as a man of experience and age. You'll not suffer."

She closed her eyes for a moment before fluttering them back open again, her expression resigned. "I suppose you will do as you must. But I beg you, wait for a sennight or two. My brother is already beset as it is by our mother, his fiancée Miss Cuthbert, and Lady Scarbrough. He has trouble enough."

In this instance, he reasoned, delay couldn't hurt. He didn't want to rush Bella if she wasn't ready to face her brother. It was he who deserved punishment, not she. Perhaps given a few days to mull it over, he'd be able to muster up the proper words to bring to his friend. Likely not. Christ, he was doomed, and so was poor, lovely Bella.

He bowed anyway. "It will be as you wish."

Dinner that evening was an awkward affair indeed. The dowager was determined to disparage Americans at every possibly opportunity. Bella's irascible cousin Lord Fordham seemed to have been over-imbibing, the result of which led to rambling soliloquies punctuated with sweeping motions of his food-filled fork. Thornton was preoccupied with his fiancée and a tedious discussion of the Lambeth Street floods. Lady Scarbrough tittered with her two sisters. Bella was left attempting to hold a polite conversation with Jesse, which was exceedingly difficult given that he was seated rather far away and they were subject to an unwanted audience. She found it almost impossible to conduct bloodless discourse as though they hadn't been in one another's arms, as though he hadn't promised to make her his wife.

In the end, it was nearly a relief to retire to the drawing room and leave the gentlemen to their own devices. Bella seated herself, surprised when Lady Scarbrough and her sisters, Lady Stokey and Lady Helen, followed suit next to her. She didn't know any of the ladies particularly well. All she did know was that the dowager was terribly distressed by Thornton's sudden obsession with Lady Scarbrough. She thought she ought not to treat any of them with too much familiarity.

For her part, the dowager settled herself with Miss Cuthbert and the girl's mother and aunt. Bella wasn't certain why her mother was so determined to see Thornton wedded to Miss Cuthbert. She well understood, of course, that he could not marry Lady Scarbrough as she was already married to the odious earl. But if Thornton loved the countess and she loved him, what was the harm? Bella sighed. Perhaps finding love of her own had altered the way she looked upon the world, for it hadn't been long ago that she too despaired of her brother's sudden defection from the moral path.

Lady Stokey tipped her head in Bella's direction and spoke *sotto voce*. "I don't know about you, Lady Bella, but I daresay Lord Fordham ought not to be partaking of any more spirits."

Bella nearly laughed aloud at the woman's daring, but the dowager was pinning her to the settee with a formidable, slit-eyed glare. She dared not. "I beg your pardon, my lady?" she asked, hoping to deflect Lady Stokey's attention in another direction. While she remained appreciative that the older woman had been true to her word and kept Bella's tryst with Jesse a secret, she still didn't wish to earn her mother's fury.

"You may beg my pardon all you like," she whispered, patting her elaborate blonde coiffure. "I know you aren't as angelic as you pretend, my dear. Your cousin was drunk as a sailor on leave. I confess I was quite terrified he'd slop béchamel all over my silk."

Bella couldn't help but giggle before stifling it with a hand pressed to her mouth. The woman had temerity. "I understand he favors whiskey," she murmured back, shrugging.

"Ah yes," Lady Stokey responded. "Lord Fordham and a host of other men, of course. They all seem to favor whiskey, don't they? Good Lord, my own husband was inordinately appreciative. Of whiskey, that is. And large quantities of food." She sighed, appearing lost in her thoughts for a moment. "I do suppose it's what ultimately did him in, the old reprobate."

Bella was taken aback by such open discussion of one's husband, particularly a husband who was now deceased. "I shouldn't think to question your husband's spare activities, my lady," she offered, feeling awkward indeed. "Although I daresay no end of men have been possessed of similar sentiments."

"Think nothing of it, my dear," offered her ladyship with a careless wave of her dainty hand. "You must understand I've been a widow for some years now."

Being a widow didn't seem to upset Lady Stokey in the least. To the contrary, it appeared to be a mantle she wore with great pleasure. Bella had never met his lordship, but she was privy to a host of gossip concerning him. It was said that Lady Stokey had married the old baron after having her heart broken by the Earl of Denbigh, who had broken their betrothal to wed another woman. Lord Stokey had been as wealthy as he was given to excess, and it was rumored he'd sired a dozen bastards by various opera singers over the years. Lady Stokey had not provided issue, but that didn't seem to displease her either. She was known for lavish parties and keeping company with great artists and writers of the day.

Bella actually found her terribly fascinating. She tossed a glance her mother's way to find the dowager happily ensconced in conversation with Miss Cuthbert and her chaperones once again. How delightful it was to have plentiful distraction. Ordinarily, she couldn't escape her mother's censorious gaze unless she feigned sleep.

"Tia," Lady Helen inserted herself into the conversation, "do stop boring Lady Bella with tiresome talk of men and their moral failings. I daresay it's a subject which could go on all evening."

"And well into the morning," added Lady Scarbrough, speaking at last.

She was an inherently lovely woman, small yet beautiful enough to draw attention wherever she went. It was little wonder Thornton was so drawn to her. There was also the matter of their history, of course. Bella knew her brother had been madly in love with Lady Scarbrough before she'd married the earl. What had happened between them to cause such a rift remained unknown to her. She supposed the dowager knew but withheld the knowledge.

Bella wanted to dislike Lady Scarbrough, truly she did. But she and her sisters made for a charming trio. She'd never had a sister, and she envied them their obviously close relationship.

"I admire your dress, Lady Scarbrough," she ventured, tentatively seeking to forge a truce. If her brother had brought the woman here to Marleigh Manor, he was serious about her indeed. She hadn't the slightest inkling as to what he planned to do with his fiancée, poor Miss Cuthbert.

Lady Scarbrough sent her a cautious but warm smile. "Thank you, Lady Bella. You're most kind."

The dowager's head snapped up then, her eyes sharp as a hawk's. Apparently, she'd discovered Bella was consorting with the enemy. And it was plain from the pinched expression she wore that she did not approve.

"My dear daughter," she said with a signature harrumph. "I was just having the most delightful discussion with Miss Cuthbert about embroidery."

Bella stifled a groan. She detested needlework of all sorts. But perhaps not as much as she detested being the object of her mother's ire. She pinned a falsely bright smile to her lips. "Indeed? I do so love embroidery."

Best, she reasoned, to stay on the dowager's good side. After all, she'd soon be making her mother angry enough when she made it known that she wished to marry Jesse. No doubt the dowager would not react to the news with aplomb. Truly, she dreaded it, but it was a necessity. Nothing would stop her from becoming Mrs. Jesse Whitney, she vowed.

Nothing.

# Chapter Eight

OVER A MONTH HAD PASSED SINCE JESSE HAD MET Bella in the garden, and they still weren't any closer to being betrothed. He and Bella had both decided to wait a fortnight, given that Thornton had been under a great deal of stress from all directions. After confiding in Jesse that he was in love with the married Lady Scarbrough, Thornton had sent Miss Cuthbert and her companions on their merry way. Thornton was living openly with Lady Scarbrough as his mistress, and while the storms of gossip had yet to completely weather his reputation, it was all just beginning. To Jesse, the securing of his future with Bella was far too precious to embark upon with haste, and while he wanted nothing more than to call her his—selfish though it was of him—he also wanted to win his friend over as best he could. He owed that much at least to Bella, to make the process as easy for her as possible.

But now the moment had at long last come to plead his case. He was enjoying a glass of fine whiskey with Thornton in his study, biding his time, when the butler interrupted their solidarity with a discreet knock. They'd been in the midst of having a laugh over some of their old antics. Jesse had just determined he would petition his friend for Bella's hand that evening, but he still hadn't a clue as to how he'd manage such a feat without earning himself a broken nose in the process. The disturbance was almost a welcome one. But not quite.

Levingood entered at Thornton's bidding, a small packet in his hands. He bowed, ever formal, and Jesse was shocked to find himself the object of the butler's speech. "Mr. Whitney, some correspondence came up for you from London."

Thornton quirked a brow. "At this time of the evening?"

The usually imperturbable butler appeared sheepish. "Patterson was to have delivered it, but regretfully it escaped his notice. Pray accept my apologies, Mr. Whitney."

"No matter, Levingood," Jesse dismissed easily, accepting the surprisingly thick packet.

He turned it over in his hands, noting it appeared to have already been opened and then resealed. Puzzling, that. Ordinarily, he would have waited to read the message until in the quiet of his chamber, but he rarely received correspondence unless it was absolutely imperative he be reached. He'd begun selling most of his remaining business ventures in preparation for living in England.

"Thank you, Levingood. That will be all," Thornton dismissed, taking another draught of his spirits. The door clicked quietly closed. "What the devil is it, Jesse?"

He opened the packet to find another envelope, along with an accompanying note from his man of business in New York. He quickly scanned the contents of the first letter. "Jesus Christ," he muttered aloud, completely shocked.

It couldn't be. Could it? Of all the ghosts in his past to resurrect themselves, he'd least expected this one. Fifteen years had passed and yet the mere thought of her still had the power to shake him. He recognized the pinched scrawl on the second missive. It belonged to her.

Lavinia.

Her name alone took him back to war, to the screams of the wounded, thunder of cannon, the horrific stench of battle, of death. Hands shaking, he unfolded the paper only to run headlong into a vast chasm of bewilderment. One word stood out in stark relief amongst all others. Daughter. He wouldn't have been more surprised if a Union soldier appeared before him, bayonet fixed on his heart, ready to take him to hell.

"Good God, man, you look as if you're about to expire. What is it?"

He looked up to find his friend watching him with a curious expression. What could he say? Dear God, if what Lavinia had written him was true, it changed everything. Of course, the possibility she was lying existed. But why now, fifteen years later? She'd said she was dying, that their daughter was to be without a guardian. Was it possible he'd had a child all these years without ever even being aware of her existence?

Yes, he had to admit, it was. He hadn't seen Lavinia since the war, hadn't been to Virginia in as many years. Like so many aspects of his time as a soldier, he'd chosen to tuck her existence away in his mind. It had been either that or go mad. But she'd somehow found him again, and the pain was as real and vivid now as it had been then. Damn her. He'd come such a long way toward healing, only to fall back into the abyss.

"Well? Is it your family?" Thornton persisted, concern coloring his voice.

He had no family. At least, he hadn't until this moment. But he couldn't tell Thornton about his daughter—if she indeed was his—for it could very well jeopardize his relationship with Bella. Already, he had to convince his friend that despite the age difference between he and Bella, and despite his lack of blue blood, he would make a good husband for her.

"Yes," he managed at last past the guilt threatening to clog his throat. "It's a family matter."

"Then you must go home," Thornton said in a tone that allowed for no argument. "I'll have the carriage readied to take you straightaway to London. The trains won't be going at this time of night."

He supposed he should go. The letter was dated two months prior. Lavinia could well already be dead, his daughter left entirely alone in the world. But how could he leave Bella now, of all times? And yet, how could he knowingly abandon his daughter? The decision was gut-wrenching, but he was left with little choice. Bella was safe here and would await his return. However, his daughter could be in danger.

Regardless, he knew he had to tell Thornton the truth before he left. His conscience wouldn't allow him to remain silent. The guilt had been eating away at him ever since Lady Cosgrove's country house party.

He stood, mentally preparing himself for what he would say. "Thornton, I've got to tell you something before I go."

His friend stood as well. "How grave is the matter?"

"Very grave," he said, thinking of how he had taken Bella's innocence.

"Good Christ, if someone is dying, you can't tarry here a moment longer," Thornton responded, clearly mistaking him. "Whatever it is you've got to tell me can wait."

Jesse reached for his glass of whiskey and tossed the remainder back in one burning gulp. It stung like hell, but he needed the fortification. Maybe Thornton was right in this instance. Maybe revealing the depth of his depravity could wait. Feeling like the worst sort of coward, he followed his friend from the study in silence.

God in heaven, what was he going to do with a daughter he'd never met?

With the help of Patterson, the man who'd been assigned to him at Marleigh Manor, Jesse's entire life since he'd been in

England was packed in just under an hour. He'd never entirely grown accustomed to the English aristocracy's penchant for valets, but for the first time he didn't mind the assistance. He stared at the trunks neatly stacked and awaiting their trip to the carriage Thornton had sent around for him. It was damned difficult to believe his worldly possessions fit so neatly into a handful of valises. Yet tidy as it all looked, he couldn't escape the crushing anguish within his chest. There was one part of him that he would be forced to leave behind.

Bella.

While he wanted nothing more than to carry her away with him, he could never treat her with such callous disregard for her reputation. How the hell was he going to explain this to her? Would she even want him if he'd fathered a bastard child by another woman? Christ, he couldn't ask her to take on his sins. He raked a hand through his hair and paced the chamber, a tumult of emotions roiling through him.

He had to try to see her, tell her why he needed to leave, let her know he'd return for her. He couldn't bear to lose her now. His mind settled, he stalked from his chamber, hell-bent on finding her chamber in the labyrinth of Marleigh Manor's halls. It didn't take long for him to realize seeking her out wasn't exactly wise. The conveniently labeled chambers of Wilton House weren't in existence here. He hadn't a clue where to find her.

To make matters worse, he nearly crashed into the dowager as he rounded a corner.

Her hand fluttered to her heart, her expression one of weary dismay. She wore a fluttering cap and her customary, severe gray gown. "Good heavens, Mr. Whittlesby." Her eyes narrowed into suspicious slits. "Whatever can you be doing skulking about in the halls at this time of the evening?"

He knew where her thoughts were headed. She didn't trust him, and she wasn't to be blamed. But little did she know the damage had already been done. He wondered if the curmudgeon would ever deign to refer to him by his true surname. "Forgive me, madam. I fear I've lost my way in the corridors of your lovely home."

If possible, her expression grew even more dubious. "Indeed, I confess I find it altogether baffling that a grown man might lose himself in a simple hallway."

"Nevertheless, it's true," he lied. He'd never imagined he would resort to deceiving a young lady's mother so he could slip into her chamber unnoticed. Hell, he was a man grown and yet he was playing the part of a stripling.

The dowager made a dismissive gesture, obviously not believing a word of it. "Haven't you any houses in America, Whittlesby?"

He nearly laughed aloud at her daring. "None of such great majesty as Marleigh Manor," he said, opting for gallantry.

"Of that I have no doubt." Her face relaxed ever so slightly. "May I be of service to you, sir? What was it you were doing wandering about in my home?"

Christ, he had to leave. He didn't have time to argue with an old harridan. "I'm preparing for departure," he answered in half-truth. "While I thank you for your inordinate hospitality, I must return to my homeland."

Her silver eyebrows shot upward. "Indeed? You're leaving, are you?"

He didn't miss the note of glee in her voice. "I regret that there's a matter of some importance that has arisen."

A daughter. He still could scarcely believe it even though the notion had already had some time to acquaint itself with his rattled mind. In fact, given that it was Lavinia who'd written, he wasn't entirely certain he ought to believe it. But he did, for he didn't think that even she could be that demented and cruel. He had been young, stupid and eager for love once. She'd cured him of that disease well. Still, he couldn't even comprehend that all these years he'd walked about the earth without ever knowing he had a flesh-and-blood child.

"A matter of importance?" the dowager repeated, her tone turning smug. "I'm sure it must be something immensely imperative, else you wouldn't be taking your leave in the midst of the night."

She was prying, but he wasn't about to give her what she wanted. He nodded. "Indeed it is, my lady."

"Well then," she announced with a sniff, looking at him as if he were a street beggar, "I daresay you ought not to be tarrying by getting lost in halls. Your chamber, sir, is to be found in the direction from whence you've come."

Damn. She'd painted him into a corner quite neatly, the shrewd dragon. He bowed. "I'm much indebted to you."

"I most certainly hope you are not, Mr. Whittlesby." With that pronouncement, she harrumphed once more.

He gave her another abbreviated bow and took his leave of her, aware of her sharp eyes on his back with each step he took. There would be no finding Bella after all. Not only would it be virtually impossible to find her chamber on his own, but now her mother was acting the sentinel. As much as he longed to see her and hold her again and to explain the entire sordid affair to her in person, he was left without a choice. He didn't dare linger another night. His daughter could be alone in the world, helpless and terrified, perhaps even on the streets of Richmond. He had no idea what financial straits Lavinia had been left in following the war, and he had never been one to rely upon Fortune's fickle wheel. He had to somehow set matters to right, if there even was a way to do so.

Bella would understand his need to see his daughter safe. He would return for Bella as soon as he possibly could. Their wedding could wait. It would have to, because short of dragging her across the Atlantic without benefit of marriage, he had no other option. Mind firmly made, he stalked back to his chamber, sat at his desk, and penned the most difficult letter he'd ever written in his life. He hoped like hell she'd still love him after she read it.

Bella paused at the threshold to the breakfast room. Jesse, a perpetually early riser, was missing. It seemed odd indeed that he wouldn't be breaking his fast with them as he had done each day since his arrival. She wanted to ask the reason for his absence, but the dowager would likely find suspicion in it. Instead, she greeted everyone as if nothing was amiss and sat at her mother's elbow.

The dowager sniffed. "Really, Arabella, you have been such a sluggard these last few days. You must try to rise earlier. I do so despise tardiness at the breakfast table. It simply should not be done."

She'd been dreadfully tired of late, but it was unkind of her mother to bemoan it before company. Bella's patience was growing thin as a threadbare petticoat. "I apologize, *Maman*. Pray forgive me my tardiness."

Her mother's mouth knotted up into a severe frown despite Bella's apology. "Quite." She turned her attention back to her kippers.

Worry tangled with fear in her stomach. Where was Jesse? Everyone was present, from Lady Tia to Lady Scarbrough. Even her no-account cousin Lord Fordham was cheerfully stabbing his eggs despite the sallow tinge to his complexion that bespoke another evening of over-imbibing. Yet there was no Jesse to be found. She missed his teasing smile, his honeyed drawl, the way his eyes tended to secretly meet hers across the table. For over a month, he'd been a constant presence in her life as they bided their time, waiting for the right moment to announce their desire to wed. That he was missing couldn't be good. Something was very wrong. She hoped he hadn't suffered another of his episodes.

She was seated and served by Levingood, who always knew how she took her eggs. But the mere sight and smell of food had her feeling ill. She pressed a subtle hand to her swirling stomach. Beneath the layers of her dress, undergarments and stiff corset, it rumbled with an ominous portent. Breakfast continued with the soft clinking of cutlery until finally Bella could no longer stand to wait for an answer. She looked to her brother.

"Thornton, where is Mr. Whitney this morning?"

"He departed last night," Thornton commented lightly as he speared a bite of sausage with his fork. "He received word from America, some sort of family matter, I gather."

He had left? Bella's heart felt as if it had plummeted to her slippers. It couldn't be true. "Where was he off to?" she asked with great care to keep any emotion from coloring her voice. Above all, she could not draw suspicion to herself.

*I haven't been back to America in years and don't feel much of a need to return*, he had said to her at Wilton House. The rotten, lying cad. He'd certainly never made mention of a family either. Because he never spoke of them, she'd assumed his parents had long since passed on, and that he had no siblings.

Thornton stabbed another bite of sausage. "I daresay that if he received a summons from America, then that is where he's gone."

America. It was an entire ocean away. He may have gone to the moon instead for she would be just as unable to reach him there. He had left her without a word. What of his plans to wed her? Dear God, it was all becoming too awful for her to contemplate.

She swallowed. "Had he said when he would return?"

"No, he didn't." Thornton looked at her, a questioning expression upon his face. "One can never tell with Jesse."

Perhaps he would never return. The mere thought filled her with fear. She averted her face to her breakfast plate, not wanting her brother to see what she was so desperate to hide. The last thing she needed now was to be caught out.

It seemed surreal.

She nearly couldn't believe it. Jesse was gone. Truly gone. Dear heavens, how could he have left without even telling her? Her face must have blanched then, for she'd never felt more ill in her life. She knew her mother's shrewd eyes were upon her, so she forced herself to bring her fork to her lips for a tasteless mouthful of poached eggs.

"I can't say I shall miss his odd patterns of speech," the dowager remarked to the table at large. "Americans have the most appalling way of butchering our dear language. Don't you agree?"

Bella could not speak. She stared at the snowy table linens, unseeing. She longed to rage and shout, mount her horse and follow him to wherever he'd gone. How could he have done this to her, to them? He'd promised to court her, to make her his wife.

Of course, he had also told her he didn't believe in love. What a fool she'd been for believing in him, for believing her love could be enough to hold him.

"Are you feeling well, Lady Bella?" Lady Scarbrough's concerned voice interrupted the misery of her thoughts.

Bella swallowed, looking to the woman who was likely her brother's mistress. "I fear I have a touch of the megrims," she lied. "Perhaps I shall return to my chamber for a spot of rest."

The need to escape was insistent within her. It was either hide herself away or humiliate herself by bursting into tears before the entire assemblage. Questions would be asked, questions she couldn't bear to answer.

"You do look positively bilious," the dowager rather unkindly observed. "I daresay ladies were made of sterner stuff in my day."

"Of course," Bella mumbled, not even caring to argue with her mother in her current state. She rose from the table. "Excuse me. I find I cannot endure breakfast today. I've quite lost my appetite."

She hoped fervently that no one could hear the tears in her voice. Without waiting for a response, she marched from the room with as much haste as she could manage. Her mind was in such a state of shock that she was like an automaton, desperate to return to the safe confines of her chamber. There, she could cry as she pleased without any shame. Her slipper-shod feet hit the polished floor in a maddening beat as she picked up her pace. Each muted step and swish of her skirts seemed to mock her, magnified by the silence of the remainder of the house. It seemed almost a dream, too horrible to be real.

How dare he? How could Jesse have left her with no warning or reason why? A sob caught in her throat and she began crying in earnest. She dashed at her tears with angry swipes as she passed a chambermaid who was discreet enough to avert her gaze as though she didn't see Bella at all.

A thought occurred to her then, so suddenly that it gave her pause.

Perhaps he had written her a letter. It was certainly possible. Afraid to hope, she picked up her skirts and jogged down the remaining length of the hall to her chamber. She burst inside, breathless and tear-streaked, to find Smith still within. She looked up in startled surprise, in the midst of putting away a stack of embroidered corset covers.

"My lady." Smith bobbed into a curtsy. "I thought you were at breakfast."

Bella closed the door at her back and then crossed the room. "Smith, I must know if I have any correspondence."

Her lady's maid frowned. "I believe there was a letter from your aunt in the Lake District. Would you like it now?"

"No." She shook her head and reached out to grip Smith's elbows. "Please think. Did anyone attempt to pass you a note this morning, perhaps belowstairs?"

"Why, no, my lady. I haven't anything for you except for the post. Is something amiss? Have I forgotten something?"

"No," Bella whispered, desperate once more with a combination of anger and sadness. "It isn't you who's forgotten. It's someone else."

"I beg your pardon, Lady Bella." Her maid considered her with a grave expression, her tone one of concern. "What can I get for you, my lady? You look a mite pale."

"Are you absolutely certain there was nothing for me?" she asked again, needing to hear the truth once more.

"I'm that sorry, my lady, but there was nothing but the letter from Lady Featherston."

There was nothing. Bella released Smith, assailed by an abrupt weakness. After all the time they'd shared, Jesse had run off without even saying goodbye. Not even a letter. Not a word. Simply nothing. He was gone, possibly never to return. She swayed, her corset feeling too tight with her choppy, upset breathing. Black flecks swam before her, the world tunneling into a narrow slice of only Smith's concerned face.

"My lady? Is something amiss?"

Smith's words reached her as if they traveled a long distance. She became aware that her skin was tingling, her face flushed and dappled with perspiration. Bella had never known betrayal until that moment. It was as though all the clouds had unleashed their thunder and lightning on a sunny day, violent and without warning. She felt physically ill. Had he ever even cared for her? Had his every word, every touch, merely been a carefully calculated lie? Had he been planning to leave her all along?

Maybe he'd never meant any of it. Her heart ached with the pain of it all. She thought of the book he'd given her, the conversations they'd shared, of his nude body pressed to hers, of the way he tasted, of the indescribable sensation of him spilling his seed deep inside her body. He'd made love to her, brought her to life, and tossed her over as if she were no better than a soiled waistcoat.

"My lady, please let me help you to sit. I'm very worried about you," came Smith's voice again through the cacophony of her frantically beating heart and madly churning mind.

Her knees completely gave out then, sending her spilling to the floor. A wave of nausea assailed her with so much violence that she couldn't keep herself from casting up what little breakfast she'd eaten all over the flowered carpet.

"Oh dear heavens!" Smith exclaimed, dropping to her knees at Bella's side with a washbasin and a cloth in hand.

Bella embarrassed herself by heaving again, doubling over until it seemed that nothing remained in her body. When the feeling of sickness at last subsided, she passed the back of her hand over her clammy forehead. Dear heavens, what had overtaken her? She'd never, in all her life, emptied her stomach in the middle of her chamber.

"Here now." Smith wrung out a strip of linen and used it to wash Bella's face. "How are you feeling, my lady?"

"Horrid," she admitted, attempting to muster up a smile and failing. "Smith, could you be a darling and help me out of my dress? I think I need to lie in bed for a bit."

With the way she felt, perhaps she needed to lie in bed for a week, she thought to herself as her lady's maid helped her to her feet. "I'm so sorry, Smith," she apologized. "I did not mean to—"

"Nonsense," her maid interrupted her in that staunch way she had that belied her tender years. "I will take care of the mess, my lady. Do you feel strong enough to stand?"

"Yes." She held still while Smith began to hastily undo the long row of buttons on the back of her morning dress. Her mind was reeling with what she'd learned, but the mysterious sickness that had overtaken her had distracted her for a moment. Now the ugly reality returned and with it came the harsh pain of his duplicity. She pulled her arms from her gown and untied her under sleeves, pulling them off.

"Lady Bella," Smith began, her tone hesitant, "have you been feeling ill often?"

Bella frowned. "For the last few mornings, my stomach has been most upset. I can't think why."

Smith came to stand before her, finishing the removal of her dress and undergarments before undoing the fastenings of Bella's corset. "Forgive me, my lady," she paused, looking as if she were afraid to continue, "but I've noticed you

138

haven't had your courses when you ought to have."

She inhaled deeply as the corset was whisked away. Thank the blessed angels. She needed that air. Her stomach already felt more settled. She mulled over her maid's words. "I suppose I haven't. What of it, Smith?"

"You've only felt ill in the mornings?"

Bella was confused by her maid's swift round of questions. "Smith, what do these queries of yours mean? Pray tell me and cease hinting. I haven't the strength for playing games just now."

"My lady." Smith's expressive face was lined with worry. "I fear it means you're with child."

# Chapter Nine

OH DEAR GOD. IT COULDN'T BE. COULD IT? SHE'D only lain with Jesse once. She knew precious little of such delicate matters, but it stood to reason that once would be enough, particularly with a man as virile as Jesse Whitney. Her hand crept over her midriff. She had been feeling ill fairly often, but had merely put it down to worry that Thornton would accept Jesse's suit for her hand. She'd never once imagined she could be carrying a babe.

Jesse's babe.

Stricken, she stared at Smith. "If ever you possessed even a shred of loyalty to me, I beg of you…" She stopped and closed her eyes, trying to gather the words up from her numbed mind. First Jesse had left her in the night as if he were no better than a common outlaw, and now she was carrying his child out of wedlock. It was all too dreadful to be true.

"You needn't utter another word, my lady," Smith hastened to say. "My first loyalty is of course to you. Forgive me for my plain speaking. It is merely that I noticed the bedclothes at Wilton House. I've also noticed a difference in you ever since."

The bedclothes. She had bled after losing her maidenhead. How foolish she'd been to think she could keep her sins a secret. "Pray don't apologize, Smith," she said wearily. "You were right, of course. I fear I'm carrying Mr. Whitney's babe."

"Oh Lady Bella." Her maid's voice was as pitying as her gaze. "He left last night. I heard it this morning from Patterson, who was acting as his man while he was here at Marleigh Manor. He said he's going back to America."

"I know." Tears pricked her eyes anew as the devastating truth of her plight sank into her bones. "He's gone, and I don't know where or if he'll ever return. America is a vast country, Smith, and I've no hope of finding him." She pressed the back of her hand to her mouth, sobbing. "And I love him so terribly much. The pain is almost too much to bear."

Very likely, she ought not to be sharing all her secrets with a servant, but Bella had come to think of Smith as a confidante more than a mere underling. She had proven her mettle and allegiance again and again. Her lady's maid had become her friend. They'd grown up together, after all.

"My lady, pardon me if I speak out of turn, but there are ways a woman can rid herself of that which is unwanted." Smith's expression grew pained. "I've known of some servants who have taken herbs to remove the babe early so as to keep their positions, without anyone being the wiser. I tell you in confidence only so that you may know you have a choice."

*There are ways a woman can rid herself of that which is unwanted.*

Bella shuddered. Smith spoke of somehow harming the babe, of forcing it from her womb. She couldn't bear the thought of hurting the child she'd created with Jesse, if indeed that was the mysterious affliction ailing her. For much as she hated Jesse in that moment, she had to admit that his child would never be unwanted. Her love for him hadn't altered. He was her first love, would be her last. No, she could never willingly rid herself of the babe, as Smith had suggested.

"Thank you for your kind offer, Smith, but I think I must bear my shame," she murmured, swallowing against another onslaught of tears.

Dear God. If she was truly with child, she was doomed. She wasn't completely naïve to the ways of the world. She wasn't the only lady in society to have found herself in such dire straits. She'd heard that unwed ladies were often bundled off to the Continent where they were forced to give up their babes and return as if nothing untoward had occurred. But she couldn't do that. She hadn't the strength. No, she needed time to think and formulate a battle plan.

"Pray don't tell a soul what you know," she begged her maid.

"You have my word, my lady," Smith vowed. "Now let me help you into bed if you please. You're looking wan as death, you are."

Bella allowed herself to be handed up into her bed, feeling incredibly weary. "Send a message to the dowager. Let her know I am ill and merely need rest."

"Of course." Her lady's maid turned to leave.

"Smith?"

The maid stopped, looking back. Bella wished for the first time that they could trade places. How freeing it must be to have one's independence. To not have the shadow of a demanding mother whose fondest fancy was for her to marry a duke. To not have suffered the pain of loss.

"Thank you," she said simply, meaning the words more than she ever had.

The heavy dread that had taken up steadfast residence in his gut couldn't be shaken. Jesse had arrived in London at first light and immediately arranged for passage across the Atlantic. His course was set. He was going home to Virginia for the first time in years. The fact didn't bring him anticipation or joy. In truth, when he'd left his home state after the war, he had never wanted to return. The lush fields and hills of his youth had been forever tainted for him.

He took a gulp of the whiskey he'd ordered at a questionable-looking tavern by the docks. It singed a fire straight to his soul, but it didn't numb him as it once had. His mind went, for the hundredth time since leaving Marleigh Manor, to Bella. She would have risen this morning to his absence. He couldn't help but feel the letter was a mistake. Unable to explain the complexities of his situation to her, he'd merely written that unforeseen circumstances had forced him to return to America, but that he would hasten back to England and explain all to her. Now it seemed foolish by the light of morning. Christ, he should have searched every chamber in the east wing for her. He should have found her, thrown her over his shoulder, and brought her with him.

He missed her already.

He was a grown man who had lived through the fiery hell of war. He'd been a lone wolf for fifteen years, content with keeping to himself, traveling, expanding his wealth. He had never known such depth of feeling for a woman. What he'd felt for Lavinia had been a youthful passion, fueled by the fear of never knowing if he'd live to see another day. What he felt for Bella was so much more vivid, complex, frightening. He meant what he'd said to her. He didn't believe in love. But he did believe there would never be another woman for him now that he'd found her. It didn't matter that she was the sister of his great friend. It didn't matter that she was far too gentle and sweet for the likes of him. She was his, damn it.

He certainly didn't deserve her. Guilt was a stone in his stomach. He tossed back some more whiskey. Hell, maybe by going away he was doing her a favor. She'd have time to be firm in her decision to wed him. Lord knew she ought to run as fast as she could in the opposite direction. She'd been born to nobility, groomed to wear a duchess's coronet. She hadn't been raised to fall in love with a mutt of a Southerner who didn't even call any place home. A man who had a daughter he'd never known.

He didn't take his responsibilities lightly, and suddenly the man who'd prided himself on never growing any roots into the ground had two immensely important responsibilities pulling him east and west. It was ironic, he supposed, but at the moment he couldn't find the humor in it. He hadn't expected to go back to Virginia or to hear from Lavinia again. He had to admit her letter had stunned him, taking him back to the darkest of times he'd vowed never to revisit. He had traveled straight through the night, afraid to sleep for what demons slumber would bring him.

Jesse finished his whiskey and stood, looking at his pocket watch. The time had come. He had to face the ghosts of his past, find his daughter, and bring her back to the home he wanted to create in England. He knew what he needed to do. He only prayed he'd find his way through it all with his sanity firmly intact. And he prayed that when he returned, Bella would be awaiting him with open arms.

The days collected with a morose tedium for Bella. She pressed her heated forehead to the cool glass of the library window, staring out into the gray early-winter afternoon. She still adored the quiet comfort of the library, but she no longer found solace in its familiar walls of books. She hadn't been able to strike up enough enthusiasm to read in a very long time. Her heart simply wasn't in it.

Much had changed at Marleigh Manor since Jesse's departure. Lady Scarbrough's husband had unexpectedly met an early demise, leaving her free to wed Thornton. Forgoing propriety and mourning periods, they had wed as soon as possible because the countess—now the marchioness—was *enceinte*. But while her brother's wife's condition was a cause for celebration, Bella's was not. Only Smith knew.

She sighed, watching her breath fog the pane and obscure the view of the gardens below. Soon, she would no longer be able to hide her secret from her family. Her hand traveled to her midriff. She'd convinced Smith to continue tightlacing her into her corset despite the weight she'd gained. It was imperative that she keep her condition from the dowager for as long as possible.

Two months had passed. Still no word from Jesse. Still no battle plan. She was bereft, knowing now that she'd likely never hear from the man she loved or see him again, and that she was left with the herculean task of somehow raising his child. She was determined to keep the babe, for he or she was all she had left to give her hope.

"Darling daughter," the dowager trilled from behind her, her voice tinged with uncharacteristic delight.

Bella turned to find her mother sweeping into the library, the ribbons of her cap flying about her head. Her ever-present gray silk skirts swished and frothed about her. To Bella's eye, the effect was all quite silly. She'd never know why the dowager insisted upon remaining in half-mourning for the marquis when it seemed to Bella that she'd never even harbored the slightest bit of fondness toward him in his lifetime.

She sighed again, feeling quite dismal to have had her musings interrupted. "Yes, *Maman*?"

"I have correspondence for you from the Duke of Devonshire." She held out a small missive bearing the duke's seal, waving it as if it were a royal banner. "That's three times in the last fortnight. I daresay he's smitten!"

Bella accepted the letter without even a frisson of excitement. The duke was a dear man and had begun writing to her with increasing frequency. He was kind, steadfast, and everything Jesse Whitney was not. While the tone of his letters was always above reproach, he had begun hinting that his feelings for her were no longer platonic.

"I'm sure he's no more smitten with me than I am with him," she murmured, tucking the letter into the pocket of her day dress.

"What stuff." The dowager waved her hand in the air dismissively. "I've asked Thornton to extend an invitation to Marleigh Manor. We have no way of knowing if he'll choose to court you, given your brother's disastrous decision to wed *that woman*. But I have every hope that he shall take into account our extensive familial history and your infinite suitability as his future duchess."

Blessed angels. She didn't want to wed the duke. Even if she did, there was no way she could go to him as his bride while carrying another man's child. She hadn't the heart for deceit, and soon she would no longer be able to cinch away her problems.

"I'll not marry the Duke of Devonshire," she told the dowager. "And you must cease referring to Cleo as 'that woman'. She is Thornton's wife and the Marchioness."

*Maman* shuddered, her disgust for her son's choice of wife evident. "Do not dare take me to task, Lady Arabella de Vere. Whilst your brother has taken leave of his faculties, I have not. You are the sole hope of this family. Marrying the duke will go a long way toward repairing our reputation in the eyes of society."

Bella frowned, most uncomfortable with the idea of herself as the de Vere family savior. If anything, she was bound to bring more shame and ruin upon the family than her brother had. They would forever be scandalous now. Her poor mother would have an apoplectic fit when she discovered the truth.

"The duke has hardly been courting me thus far," she reminded her mother, attempting to blunt her expectations. "He's merely become a friend, nothing more."

Her mother sniffed. "Men and woman are not meant to be friends, daughter. He's already written that he will come for a visit. Mark my words, he would never come to Marleigh Manor in the midst of the dreadful scandal in which we now find ourselves unless he could find it in his heart to desire you for his wife."

The Duke of Devonshire was coming to see her? The mere thought rendered her weak. How was she to possibly smile and make merry as if she hadn't a care? "When will he come?"

The dowager smiled, evidently pleased with her clandestine machinations. "He arrives in a fortnight, and he will stay until the following Saturday. More than enough time, I should think, to court you and ask your brother for your hand."

"No." Bella shook her head, distraught. "I won't marry him, *Maman*, and I do not wish for him to travel to Marleigh Manor. You should not have orchestrated this on my behalf."

"I am seeing to your well-being and securing your future. You will treat His Grace with all the welcome and kindness he deserves, my lady, and that is final."

With that parting directive, the dowager took her regal leave of the room.

The trip from Buckinghamshire to London had proved monotonous but not nearly as much as the passage over the Atlantic. It was difficult to believe he was almost home. Of course, home had become something more of a murky dream and something less of a reality in the last fifteen years. Jesse winced. It was an irony indeed that a man who never put down his valise had made his fortune in the buying of property.

Then again, perhaps not. It was the selling of it that had earned his way in the world. He could never abide to stay in one place for very long. He was a nomad by circumstance, and he had to admit there was no pleasure in his return. The hired conveyance swayed over familiar roads. This was no great homecoming. He had been summoned for a purpose, and it was a grim one indeed.

His mind traveled again to Bella. God, how he missed her with a desperation that frightened him. She would have read his letter by now. She probably detested him after the way he'd disappeared. He wouldn't blame her in the slightest. He'd been in a dark place the night he'd gone. His letter, he had no doubt, would not serve to ameliorate the confusion his abrupt departure would have caused her. What could he say for himself? What the hell had he been thinking? Perhaps that was the crux of it. He hadn't been thinking at all. He had compromised his best friend's sister and then walked away from her to chase old demons.

If he could relive the night he'd received word from Lavinia, he would tear down every hall of Marleigh Manor until he found Bella. He should have simply tossed her over his shoulder and taken her with him. She hadn't deserved his callous treatment of her. But he'd wanted to protect her, love her, keep her as sweet and innocent as ever. He hadn't wanted to drag her into the labyrinth of his past. Ah, his past. Just the thought of seeing Lavinia again was enough to make his entire body feel like a tightly wound pocket watch.

The carriage slowed outside a modest-looking townhouse. Richmond showed fewer signs now of the rampage that had reduced it to ruins. He could still recall the ravaged shells of grand buildings after the city fell in flames. The process of resurrection was, he suspected, as ongoing for the South as it was for the war's soldiers.

With a weary sigh for the upcoming interview, he stepped down from the carriage. After he thanked and paid the driver, he stood on the walk, remembering. It had been a long time. Suddenly, the onslaught of memories hit him with the precision of a *minié* ball. Though time could pass, the nightmares of battle would never fade.

Nor would what had come after.

But now was not the time for dwelling in the past's heavy muck. He strode up the walk, uncertain of what he would find waiting for him inside. A servant greeted him at the door. He was expected. The home was furnished in a surprisingly elegant style. It appeared Lavinia had done well for herself despite the war's toll.

The servant led him up a staircase in complete silence. The only sound to be heard was their carpet-muffled footfalls and ticking clocks. All the drapes were drawn over the windows. It seemed to be a home in mourning, as if Lavinia had already passed.

She had not. He entered an equally darkened chamber to find the youthful beauty he recalled had withered into a wan, pale creature. There was only the meager light of a gas lamp to illuminate the room. Lavinia lay in bed, her frail body propped up with what seemed to be dozens of pillows. Her once glossy black hair was dull, her skin ashen, her eyes flat. She looked like a corpse.

"Jesse." Even her voice sounded brittle. "You've come to me."

He stopped a few feet from her sickbed to look down upon her. "You knew I would. I'm amazed you were able to find me."

"I tracked you down by your man of business in New York, and from there, it was not terribly difficult at all." A faint semblance of a smile curved her mouth. "It is your daughter you've come for, not me. I may be dying but I'm no fool."

"I've always credited you with being sly as a coyote." He couldn't hide the bitterness he felt toward her. It didn't matter that she had been lowered to a husk of her former beautiful self. Her death wouldn't expiate her sins. He suspected she knew as much.

"You won't grant me forgiveness? Not even now?" A racking cough punctuated her questions. She held a lace handkerchief to her mouth and when she pulled it away, blood bloomed over the pristine white of the fabric.

If she wanted his pity, she would not receive it. Nor would she receive his mercy. He felt nothing for her except disdain. "Does it matter, Lavinia?"

She fidgeted with the handkerchief. "Perhaps it does. I don't wish to die with a burdened soul."

Jesse raised a brow. "I would swear you didn't have a soul."

"I suppose I deserve your harsh words." She closed her eyes.

"You deserve worse, but I will leave you to the suffering God has imposed upon you."

"I didn't know he was trying to send you to prison camp, Jesse."

The breath fled from his lungs. The mere words were enough to cause a visceral reaction in him. For the last decade and a half, he had done his damndest to forget the horrors of his final months of battle. He'd been shot by his fellow soldier, nearly killed in the process, and had just barely avoided being captured that day. Only luck had saved him. In her desperation to run away with her lover, Lavinia had proven herself the ultimate Judas. Her actions had cured him of any notion he'd ever loved her, nor she him.

"Forgive me if I don't believe a word you say," he bit out. "I haven't returned to reminisce. I've come to collect my daughter. Where is she?"

She coughed again, this time more violently than the last. "Maybe I shall change my mind. If you insist on being nasty, you won't have her."

It was to be a power struggle with her to the last. He wanted to throttle her. He clenched his fists and desperately fought to maintain a shred of calm. "Where the hell is she?"

Lavinia, it seemed, wasn't about to relinquish her control over him. She tilted her head, giving the impression of a drab sparrow when once she had been a vivid canary. "Have you ever thought of me, Jesse?"

"Never," he lied. The truth was, she had lived in his nightmares for some time. But he had never intentionally allowed his mind to stray to either her or her betrayal. Some things were best left buried in the past.

"I never wanted you to be harmed, you know."

He suspected she suffered from a guilty conscience, but for him it was too little, too late. "You seem to think I can absolve your sins but you're sadly mistaken."

"I don't want an absolution." She coughed again and dabbed at her mouth before proceeding, as though she were doing nothing more than holding afternoon tea. "I am sorry for your suffering, whether you believe it or not."

"Your contrition is suspect at this point." He didn't bother to hide his disgust for her. "I was almost killed."

There it was, the brutal reality. He'd taken a bullet to his back. The mere recollection brought the taste of blood to his mouth.

"I didn't want you dead."

"Lavinia, I'd sooner believe you could sprout wings and fly."

"I see you're determined to be unpleasant." She closed her eyes and her weariness was almost palpable. He knew she would soon pass. He'd seen death many times before. That she would no longer walk the earth didn't give him as much pleasure as he'd thought it would.

He grew tired of their verbal sparring. "Let's place our cards on the table. I didn't travel across an ocean to have a match of words with you. I came because you had my child fifteen years ago and denied me the right to ever know her."

The fact that he had a daughter somewhere, beneath the same roof, seemed surreal. His daughter. He hadn't allowed himself to contemplate her. What if Lavinia was lying? What if she were as cold a bitch as Lavinia? Far too many questions lingered, questions he'd come very far to answer.

"James wouldn't allow it of course," Lavinia said matter-of-factly. "But he never loved her as a father. He always knew Clara wasn't his."

Clara. His daughter had a name. An odd sensation trickled through his chest, slow and sticky as treacle. "Does the girl know?"

"I told her after James died." She paused. "It seemed right, but she didn't take the news well."

"And what of now?" For God's sake, he didn't know what to do with a daughter, let alone a daughter who didn't appreciate a new father in her life.

"She's had some time to acquaint herself with it."

An ugly thought occurred to him. He wouldn't be surprised if Lavinia was guilty of it and worse. "Does she know I've come for her?"

"Of course she does. I'm not entirely a monster. I do this for the good of our daughter. I haven't any living family worthy of protecting her, and James' family is little better." She began another brutal series of coughing. "Would you please get me my laudanum?"

He strode to the table where a collection of bottles was strewn about and took up the one she'd indicated. "I want to see her now." He needed to be satisfied that Clara was truly his. It would have been like Lavinia to lie solely to gain a more comfortable existence for her daughter.

"You don't believe she's yours," Lavinia noted shrewdly. "I have no reason for prevarication. You were my only lover until I wed James."

Jesse was shocked as hell to hear that. The scheming seductress he'd known had not come to him as an innocent. "I will judge for myself."

"Very well." She called for her servant, who had been hovering at the threshold. "Daisy, please fetch Miss Clara."

It seemed an eternity before the servant returned with a diminutive blonde girl. Her hair was worn in sweet ringlets around her angelic face. Her dress was a demure pale pink, its hem halfway up her calves as proper for a girl her age. She wore a locket at her neck but no other adornment. She met his gaze as she curtseyed. It was like looking into his own eyes.

"Mama," she greeted in a girlish voice. "Mr. Whitney."

Of course she did not call him "father" as he'd foolishly imagined she would. She was breathtaking, having the perfect combination of his blond features and her mother's dark beauty. "Clara," he offered in return, his voice hoarse with pent-up emotion. "It is a great pleasure to meet you at last."

She was his daughter. There was no question of it in his mind.

"I wish I could say the same," she murmured, startling him.

Not that he had expected she would treat him like her father, but he had not anticipated disdain. "I regret that our first meeting is due to the unfortunate circumstance of your mother's ill health, but I certainly do not regret our meeting. Had I known of your existence, I surely would have hastened here before now."

"My mother is dying," she pronounced baldly.

"I am sorry for that," he told her, at a loss.

"No you're not," she countered. "Mama says you hate her."

He looked to Lavinia, who was nodding off under the influence of her laudanum. She would be no help. "That isn't precisely true," he fibbed.

"She said Papa nearly sent you to prison during the war."

"Clara," Lavinia at last snapped. "You were taught comportment. Please show it."

It occurred to Jesse that he didn't know the slightest thing about young girls. He had somehow envisioned a sweet, biddable girl overcome with happiness at finding her father. What an ass he'd been. The girl before him was as soft as the butt end of a carbine.

His daughter clasped her hands together at her waist and studied him the way a young child studies strangers while clinging to her mother's dress. She remained silent. Judgmental, he supposed. She had deemed him unworthy of her. She blamed him for his absence. He could see that much. The road ahead was undoubtedly fraught with treacherous terrain.

"Apologize to your father, miss," Lavinia commanded weakly. "At once."

Clara's expression remained stubborn. "With utmost respect, Mama, I will not."

Yes indeed, it was going to be one hell of a road.

# Chapter Ten

$\mathcal{B}$ELLA HAD A KNACK FOR EAVESDROPPING ON conversations. As a girl, she'd caught more than her share of the naughty gossip adults only indulged in when they thought no small ears could hear. It was another thing entirely, however, to find herself the topic of the overheard conversation.

"I'm afraid the blood loss was quite severe, my lady." The masculine voice, low and mellow with age, unmistakably belonged to Dr. Redding, the country doctor her brother favored.

"Oh dear heavens, I feared that was the case." There was a pause in the feminine speech that garnered Bella enough time to discern the voice belonged to her sister-in-law, Cleo. "There was a frightful amount of it everywhere. I cannot fathom all that blood from the small gash on her head."

Blood. Gash on her head? Blessed angels' sakes, what had occurred?

Foggy images flitted through her mind. Her body was in as much pain as if it had been flattened by a locomotive. Remembrance surged over her in waves. The storm. She'd saddled her mare, needing to escape the falsehood she'd been living, determined to ride away the awful hurt despite the portent of a deluge on the horizon. She recalled the sensation of launching through the air, her bone-crunching landing in the mud.

"Lady Thornton," came Dr. Redding's familiar voice once more, "I'm afraid this is a delicate matter."

"Blows to the head are, no doubt," agreed Cleo. "What shall we do for her whilst she recovers?"

The doctor cleared his throat. "You mistake me, my lady. The source of the blood was indeed, as you suggested, not Lady Bella's head."

"Has she other wounds, then?"

"Lady Bella was with child," Dr. Redding explained, his tone hushed. "It was very early on, and the force of her fall was too much. I do, however, expect an eventual recovery. She will need to remain abed for a time."

"With child?" Cleo's voice was incredulous. "Surely you must be mistaken."

"I fear I am not, Lady Thornton."

She had lost everything. Her fall from grace was complete, as was her devastation. Bella's heart physically hurt in her breast. How could she have been so foolish, so careless? In her childish anger, she had only served to spite herself.

Her sister-in-law's voice grew hushed. "May I request your discretion, Doctor?"

The doctor's response was equally quiet and grave. "You need not ask."

Bella remained still while muffled sounds reached her ears, suggesting the doctor was taking his leave. She didn't want to wake. She wanted to sleep again, sleep until all was well. If ever it could be.

The thud of a closing door echoed in the silence of the chamber, then the steady return of footfalls. "Bella, my dear."

She weighed the prospect of feigning sleep. Truly, she did not want to see a soul at the moment. Her mind was a jumble of thoughts, her body a jumble of bumps and bruises. She wanted quiet and peace. She wanted to be left alone. She had never felt more miserable in her entire existence.

"Bella, I know you're awake so you may as well face me now."

Bella opened her eyes at Cleo's stern directive, expecting to see a censorious expression upon her sister-in-law's face. Instead, she saw concern.

"I suppose you expect an apology," she murmured.

"Nothing of the sort," Cleo countered, worry tucking the corners of her mouth down. "You know as well as I that I'm no stranger to scandal. I can hardly hold the rest of the world to higher standards than those to which I held myself."

She knew Cleo spoke of the unconventional circumstances surrounding her marriage to Thornton. But her sister-in-law's generosity of spirit was little comfort to her now. Her mind swirled with the awful truth of what she'd done and just how much she'd lost. Everything. Not only had Jesse left her, but now the babe as well. A wave of dizziness assailed her, but she forced herself to speak, attempt to make sense of what had happened.

"I should say I am ashamed of myself, but the truth is I am not. I don't regret any of my actions save riding my mare when I was not clearheaded enough to do so." Bella closed her eyes for a moment as the sting of anguish renewed. "I will ever regret causing this until the day I die." Sobs threatened to slip past her lips, but she did not want to show weakness now.

"Are you in very much pain, my dear?" Cleo took her hand and gave it a gentle squeeze.

"Not nearly as much pain as my heart is in." Her bones ached from her jarring spill from her horse. Her abdomen was very sore as well, the result, she suspected, of her miscarriage. But her body had fared much better than her mind.

"In time, you shall make your peace with it. God's plan is unfathomable at times, but it is always good."

Bella didn't share Cleo's opinion on that score. Losing first the man she loved and then his child was nearly enough to break her spirit completely. She would grieve both forever. "Forgive me if it does not seem so at this particular juncture."

"You're far stronger than you think." Cleo's eyes reflected both pity and compassion. "Dr. Redding says you must rest and afterward you shall be your old self once more."

"No," Bella denied. "I shall never return to the naïve girl I was. She is quite gone, I fear."

"It may seem so at the moment, but given time I'm sure your opinion will alter. I too have suffered the loss of a babe, Bella. I know the pain you feel." There was the hint of a tremble in Cleo's voice. "Please know I am here to offer counsel should you need it."

"Thank you, Cleo." Bella faltered, guilt clashing with self-loathing. "I'm a horrid person. I've been lying to all of you for weeks, and now I've killed the one life I was meant to protect."

"None of us is without sin." Cleo paused. "You must try not to punish yourself for this, Bella. But in the meantime, I think it best if you inform Thornton of the nature of your illness. I cannot in good faith keep this secret from him."

There was a limit to her sister-in-law's understanding, it would seem. Bella knew she was right even if she'd rather throw herself in front of an omnibus than confess her shame to her brother. "Do you think it might wait until I've had a rest? I shouldn't think I could face him just now."

"Rest is precisely what you need to help heal," Cleo agreed. "Fortunately, your mother has yet to return from her visit with Cousin Clothilde. It will be your brother's decision as to whether or not she is ever to know the full extent of this."

"I understand." Tiredness assailed her. "I am at his

mercy, as I should be."

"You must prepare yourself to answer questions you may not like," her sister-in-law cautioned. "He will want to know the babe's father, my dear."

That much Bella was not willing to give. It would be her undoing. "He'll not have it from me."

"Bella, it's Mr. Whitney, isn't it?"

"It's no one, for there is no longer a babe." Bella closed her eyes again. "Now, if you don't mind, I wish to sleep."

Jesse listened with only half a heart as the clergyman before him droned on about the rewards of heaven. Heaven was a long, long way from Richmond, Virginia. Of that much, he was certain. The land where he'd grown from boy to man was much changed, but not enough that his return didn't bring an onslaught of pain. He'd spent a great deal of time in Richmond, having been raised there by his maiden aunt Hortense, who'd been such an awful harpy he'd gleefully run off to what he'd naively believed to be his great adventure in the war. Ultimately, the fight had brought him back when the city was under siege, and he'd been forced to watch the wholesale destruction of the buildings and people he'd come to know so well. Even now, he could still smell the smoke of cannons and burning houses, hear the cries of the wounded and dying.

He sighed heavily as the weight of his past came barreling into him yet again. Nothing could have prepared him for the return to the place that had once been hell on earth for him. The years didn't ameliorate the sting, didn't stanch the flow of memories. His nightmares had grown markedly worse, keeping him up through the early hours of the morning. Death, he supposed, had a way of turning a man inside out.

It had taken weeks after his initial arrival, but at last, Lavinia had gone to meet her maker. Beyond the small chapel where only two mourners had gathered, a freshly dug grave was the last remaining sign Lavinia Jones had ever walked the earth. Aside, that was, from the petite blonde girl standing stiffly at his side.

Clara.

He glanced to her, noting her pale, tear-stained cheeks. She had his blue eyes, his long nose, his thick golden hair, and the signature beauty Lavinia had possessed before it faded away, obliterated by illness. There was no doubt Clara was his daughter. It mattered little if she despised him. She was his flesh and blood, and he was sworn to protect her. Of course, she was every bit as hardheaded and determined as he was. When he'd been her age, he was off fighting in a war he'd had no business partaking in. She hadn't spoken more than a handful of sentences to him since his arrival. She'd made it known to him that she didn't care for him and that the last place in the world she wished to go was anywhere he would be. She wanted to stay in the land she loved. He couldn't blame her for her constancy—in truth, it was an admirable trait.

Out of respect for her, he had allowed her to remain in Virginia until her mother's passing. But he was itching to return to England and the life he found himself longing for from afar. England with its cold snaps and dreary rains had become his new home. He didn't fool himself as to the reason why. It was Bella.

Ah, Bella. He glanced back to the head of the chapel, his eyes resting briefly on Lavinia's coffin before rising to the stained-glass windows above. Bella hadn't answered a single one of the many letters he'd sent her, and it troubled him greatly. He couldn't be certain if his correspondence wasn't finding its way to her, or if hers wasn't reaching him, or if something worse was afoot. Perhaps she had elected not to write him. If she were angry with him, he truly couldn't blame her one whit.

He missed her. Dear God, how he missed her. It was as if he had lost a part of himself, the very best part of himself.

In the empty stretch of weeks he'd spent in Virginia, he'd made a terrifying realization. He didn't simply admire her for her sweet concern for him, for her lovely face, or her tempting curves. He didn't merely adore her keen mind and outspoken love of literature. He didn't just miss her. He loved her.

He loved Bella de Vere, the woman he'd met when she was but a schoolroom girl, sitting on her spectacles in the library at Marleigh Manor. Perhaps he'd loved her since that day four years ago. He didn't know. Love had a way of appearing in a man's life and rendering it impossible to recall what had come before it. He regretted his rushed departure, for he had come to see that Lavinia had exaggerated the extent of her illness in an effort to make him hasten to her side. Oh, she had been taken very sick with consumption, but she had been cunning to the end, knowing full well that he would arrive before her death.

While he was glad to have his daughter's well-being secured, he wished to God he had the same confidence when it came to Bella. He'd thought, perhaps foolishly, that she would at least write him once. After all, she'd professed her love for him on many occasions. They were all but betrothed. Some word from her would have been appreciated, and would have gone a long way toward providing him the peace of mind he wanted most.

The minister finished his piece and bowed his head in prayer. Jesse followed suit, his heart constricting as his daughter's sobs became more pronounced. Lavinia, despite the multitude of sins she'd committed, had apparently been a beloved mother to Clara. He put an arm around his daughter's thin shoulders, awkwardly offering her support she likely didn't want. She shocked him by turning into his embrace, pressing her cheek to his chest, and breaking into body-racking cries.

Humbled, he held her tightly to him. As the minister droned on with his prayer, Jesse was overcome by an inexplicable feeling of absolution. The anger he'd kept for years dimmed like a lamp running out of oil. In her death, it was far easier to think that perhaps Lavinia, like he, had somehow been a victim of the savagery war wrought upon the land. He liked to think, at least, that she was sorry for enabling him to nearly be captured. In the end, he'd mercifully escaped with his freedom and his life both intact. And if he hadn't lived through the hell of battle, he would never have moved to New York, never would have traveled on to England, and never would have met the woman he loved.

His mind drifted again to Bella. He could finally be back on his way to her.

"Amen," he whispered.

"Who is he?"

The question emerged as a rather violent growl. Bella winced as she watched her brother stalking around her chamber as if he were a bull about to charge. She'd managed to escape his wrath for a blessed three days, but now the time had come. Oh how she dreaded the interview about to unfold.

"Or perhaps," Thornton continued through clenched teeth, "I should ask you who the bloody bastard was, because I'm going to murder him when I have his name."

"I don't know," she lied, utterly terrified of what his reaction would be should he discover her lover's identity.

"You don't know," he repeated, nearly spitting the words like little darts. "Do you mean to say there is more than one possibility?"

"Yes," she lied again. "Please accept my apology, Thornton. I am deeply ashamed for the scandal I have brought upon myself. But surely you must see that your attacking anyone would not enhance the circumstances."

"The hell it wouldn't. Nothing would delight me more than to thrash whoever's done this to you." He stalked closer, cutting quite a menacing figure in his fury. "Protecting him will not serve you, Bella."

Regardless of what he said, she wouldn't be swayed. She knew her secret was best kept, not revealed. "Thornton, your brotherly loyalty is admirable, but I shall not countenance violence."

"Arabella, the only sin worse than a lack of loyalty is the sin of misplaced loyalty." He glared at her, every inch the formidable politician he was.

His philosophical pronouncement had her at a loss. She felt certain she'd read it somewhere before, but couldn't place it in her overburdened mind. "Who said that?"

"The goddamn Marquis of Thornton said it to his wrong-headed minx of a sister," he exploded. "As your brother and the head of this family, I demand you tell me who has compromised you."

"I'm afraid I cannot as doing so will accomplish naught." Bella refused to waver in her decision.

"On the contrary, it will accomplish a great deal, including the unmerciful trouncing of the man you're about to name."

He was stubborn, her brother. But she was born from the same stock, and she was equally determined to thwart him. "I don't want contretemps. The plain truth of it is that I'm not going to tell you so you may as well give up."

Thornton raised a brow, his expression becoming imperious. "Would you prefer to involve our mother in this tête-à-tête?"

Dear Lord, the dowager was the very last person in the world she wanted to face. The dowager in high dudgeon was not an experience to be relished. "Cleo promised me secrecy."

"How very nice for her. I, on the other hand, did no such thing."

The cad. "Thornton, I've just gone through the worst few days of my life. I'm finally regaining my strength and a bit of my sanity. Could you not be benevolent just this once and allow me the dignity of putting my mistakes behind me?"

"If benevolence is allowing some blackleg to abuse my innocent sister without consequence, then I want nothing of it." He was hollering and very likely the entire servants' wing could hear him.

Her head throbbed. "Please have a heart. I do not wish to make a row of it with you, but I remain firm in my unwillingness to speak of any more than I already have done."

"I cannot accept your decision." He ran a hand through his black hair. "Your honor is at stake, Bella. I couldn't live with myself were I to allow this man to continue on with his life as though he hasn't caused you such anguish. If our father were alive, he would do the same."

Their father was but a shadowy memory to her. He'd passed away when she was very young. Thornton had stepped in and been the reliable and honorable male figure she'd needed as a young girl. She loved him very much, so much that she could never tell him what she'd done. The truth would devastate him.

"Is it the Earl of Ravenscroft? By God, if that whoreson touched you, I truly will kill him this time," her brother snarled.

The earl in question had also been a guest at Lady Cosgrove's country house party. He was a notorious lothario and an easy conclusion. Bella thought briefly of settling on Ravenscroft but her conscience wouldn't allow her to bring an innocent man into her web of shame.

She shook her head, looking away from her irate brother to toy with the book in her lap. "I have told you all I'm willing to tell you."

"Please tell me it isn't that mutton-headed Duke of Devonshire."

"Thornton," she protested, growing weary of his interrogation.

"Bella," he countered, "if you don't tell me, there will be

penalty for you."

"Surely no more penalty than that which I've already paid."

"No more books," he said, seizing the unopened tome from her lap. "You are hereby barred from the library indefinitely."

"Are you to send me to the guillotine as well, then?" She knew she was exhibiting cheek, particularly given her circumstances, but she couldn't help herself.

"Insolent minx." He frowned at her. "Count yourself fortunate I don't have one at my disposal, else I'd be using it on whatever blighter has done this to you. And you are to have nothing. No fripperies or hundred-pound Worth gowns until I deem your time of punishment to be over."

Her time of punishment. Really, after all the scandal he'd recently brewed, this was rich indeed. "Am I to wear a scarlet letter of shame?"

"It is a miracle that I once considered you a quiet, biddable girl who would settle down with some bookish earl and never so much as sneeze at the wrong time of day."

"I am not sure if I should be insulted or pleased."

"Insulted, by God. I never would have thought you had the devil in you."

She'd had the devil in her all right, but not in the way her brother would like to think. She wisely kept silent on that particular gem of wisdom. "Perhaps I waited until now to show my hand." She shrugged. "Take what you want from me. Bury me away in the countryside forever. I will never tell you anything more."

"We shall see," he vowed, his tone deadly. "We shall see."

# Chapter Eleven

"**I**T'S A GLORIOUS DAY," MURMURED THE DUKE of Devonshire to Bella as they walked slowly through the Marleigh Manor gardens. "I must say, the countryside is particularly refreshing."

Stones crunched beneath their heels. The day in question was rather cold but sunny enough to warrant a jaunt away from the dowager's chaperoning ears. She looked to him, thinking him handsome enough. He was tall, blond-haired like Jesse, and yet so different. Where Jesse had been bold and passionate, Devonshire was cool and composed, quick to offer praise and yet always above reproach. He had wooed her mother as well as wooing Bella, for he was clearly a man who knew the way of the world.

She pulled her dolman more tightly around her walking dress to stave off the chill. "It is indeed quite bright and pretty for this time of year."

It was odd indeed, she thought, to be walking and talking as if all were right with the world. But everything was wrong. The smile she donned was false. The silk Worth gown she wore had been hand-picked for the occasion by her mother. Bella couldn't be bothered with such trivial details any longer after her life had been altered in such an awful, irrefutable way.

Her babe was gone now, forever lost because she'd been stupid enough to take out her mare in a storm. She would never forgive herself. The pain was an awful, gaping chasm inside her. Thank the blessed angels her mother didn't know. Her brother and Cleo had been true to their word and kept her secret, and although Thornton had done his utmost to learn the identity of the babe's father, she had maintained her silence. She supposed he'd quite given up on her.

So it was that she'd been paraded before the poor, unsuspecting duke like a mare trotted out for the consideration of prospective buyers. She shivered, as much from the December air as from the dreadful feeling of emptiness within her. It all seemed so much like it had been a nightmare now, and she was dressed to her best yet still just a husk of her former self.

"I wonder, my dear Lady Bella," the duke began, interrupting her morose thoughts, "if you've enjoyed my time here at Marleigh Manor as much as I have."

Bella's gaze snapped to his, searching. Was it possible that he was more perceptive than she'd given him credit for being? Had he sensed her detachment? She pursed her lips, crafting her response with care. "You must know I find your company most delightful, Your Grace," she murmured at last.

Truly, the duke was a kind man. If she needed to be married off to anyone—which her brother assured her she must, given her ruined state—it may as well be someone as quiet and compassionate as he. Of course, she hated being dishonest with him. He deserved a wife who could love him with a whole heart. Bella's had been so badly bruised and battered that she wasn't even certain it could ever recover.

"I'm honored by your compliment," he said, giving her a warm smile. "I must say that I treasured the brief opportunities we had for conversation at Lady Cosgrove's house party. Afterward, your letters sustained me. Your knowledge of literature, particularly the works of Anthony Trollope, is to be admired."

If she were honest with herself, she'd acknowledge that she too had enjoyed corresponding with the duke. He shared her love of novels. But exchanging letters with him had nevertheless been a pleasant task, even if she'd done it mostly to appease her insufferable mother.

Guilt skewered her at the expression of frank admiration on the duke's face. "I look forward to discussing *The Eustace Diamonds* with you, sir, should I ever have the opportunity to finish reading it."

"My lady." He stopped abruptly, turning to face her and take her hands in his. "Forgive me if I'm being too forward, but I must tell you that over the last few months, I have come to think of you with great fondness."

Oh dear. She swallowed, the guilt blooming more and more within her stomach with each word he spoke. "I am fond of you as well, Your Grace." For the first time, she realized he had neatly diverted her so that they were no longer visible from the windows of the drawing room where the dowager waited. He wasn't immune to the ways of men, it would seem.

Slowly, he lowered his head and pressed his lips to hers. The kiss was warm and firm, closed-mouthed and surprisingly passionless. She supposed she had come to expect kisses that devoured. Jesse's kisses had been hot, hungry and demanding. They had not been tepid and polite. Before she could further compare, it was over as quickly as it had begun.

She blinked, looking up at him, feeling none of the sensations Jesse's kisses had evoked within her. She felt instead a curious ambivalence. Apparently, the duke mistook her puzzlement for pleasure, because he dipped his head again. This time, he kissed her with more insistence, opening his mouth slightly over hers.

Bella pulled back abruptly, overcome. She'd just been

through the most difficult time of her life. She most certainly wasn't ready to be exchanging kisses in the gardens with a new suitor as though she hadn't anything more important to worry about than whether or not her hat matched her slippers.

The duke appeared contrite. "I'm sorry," he said on a rush. "I didn't mean to insult you, my dear. I quite lost my head."

If his cool, quick kisses were the result of losing his head, she was a mermaid. And the last she'd checked, she had feet, not fins. Blessed angels, Bella thought they were hopelessly mismatched. She felt utterly horrid, leading him down a path from which there was no return. He didn't even know who she was. For that matter, Bella didn't even know who she was any longer. She'd certainly lost every last crumb of her idealism.

"It is I who must apologize, Your Grace," she told him, her voice laden with guilt. She wanted very much to like him. Perhaps she could like him, given time, but she was too broken now to care for anyone. "You see, my heart has been broken, and while I count you to be a cherished friend, I'm not able to feel for you as I ought. You are a perfect gentleman and have been most kind to me this last week. The truth is that you deserve much more than I can give you."

He brought her hands, still linked with his, to his lips for a kiss. "You are to be commended for your honesty. I shall treat you to the same. I very much believe in taking on a wife who is my equal in every way. You are intelligent, well-versed in the arts of society, the daughter of a noble family. If I were to tell you I loved you, I would be lying. But I think I can grow to love you, and I hope that you might also grow to love me in return."

She frowned, considering his surprising soliloquy. "But Your Grace—"

"Pray," he interrupted gently, "think over what I've said to you. Hearts, like crumbling castle walls, can always be mended."

He still wanted her as his wife. She hadn't been prepared for such a reaction. She had to admit his reasoning seemed sound, his logic quite pragmatic. She already respected him. Feelings of tenderness for him could surely follow in time. Love, however, was another matter entirely. She needed to tell him as much.

"Your Grace, I am confident that I have lost the only man I shall ever love."

"And I'm equally confident that I can rival any man for your affections." He smiled, lowering their entwined hands. "You are yet young, my dear, and young love always hurts the most."

"With utmost respect, Your Grace, I beg to differ," she countered. "Love is not ruled by age but by passions and unruly hearts. Besides, you aren't a great deal older than I."

The duke raised a brow. "I'm old enough. But let's call a truce, shall we? I too have been in your most unenvied shoes. I know all too well that a broken heart smarts worse than any broken bone ever could."

His understanding only increased her sadness. He was almost too good, really. Why did he have to be so understanding? The weariness in her made her want to trust him. She tilted her head, considering him. He didn't seem especially capable of a grand passion. "I hadn't realized," she said simply. "You appear so stalwart."

The duke's expression grew shuttered. "Outward appearances hide a multitude of things, Lady Bella. The sooner in life you learn that lesson, the less disappointed you'll be."

Unexpectedly, her mind turned to Jesse. He had hidden much from her, it seemed, including his true nature. Otherwise, he never would have disappeared from her life with nary a goodbye. He'd left her alone to face the consequences of their glorious night of passion, alone to face the horrible anguish of losing their babe. He hadn't even known of its existence. He likely never would. Nor, she supposed, would he care about the tiny life she'd carried within her for almost three months before having it ripped from her body. Their precious babe had been snuffed out as effectively as a timid fire in the grate. To nearly everyone else, the babe had never been real. To her, the babe had been everything. Yes, the duke was right. Outward appearances could hide a vast amount of secrets, some of which would never be made known. Tears stung her eyes.

"Don't cry, darling Bella." The duke startled her by taking her in his arms for a comforting embrace.

He smelled rather nice, she thought, a musky blend of man and leather. His coat was fine and soft against her cheek. If only she had loved him instead of Jesse Whitney. Life would have been more bearable, surely. She never would have been alone and stupid, riding her horse in a storm. She never would have lost her babe or the man she loved. The tears unleashed themselves steadily upon her, racking her body with sobs. Had she been herself, she would have been dreadfully embarrassed. But she was a ghost wandering about in the skin of the woman she'd been, and the ghost didn't give a fig for keeping up appearances.

He comforted her, patting her back as though having a woman crying her eyes out in his arms were the most natural position in the world. "Everything hurts less with time, Lady Bella. You shall see."

She fervently hoped he was correct in his assertion. She nodded miserably against his lapel, unable to formulate a reply. Perhaps one day she would be capable of functioning as a normal person again. Lately, it seemed she fluctuated wildly from emotion to emotion. The worst was the sadness. It never left her.

"I must return to my estate today, my dear," he murmured, still stroking her back. "But I should like to return in a fortnight. While I'm away, pray mull over all I've said to you. I believe quite firmly that we can make a remarkable match. But I shall leave the decision to you. If you write me, I shall come to ask the marquis for your hand."

Bella looked up at the duke, tears making her vision blurry. "I w-will think on it, Your Grace. I th-th-thank you for the honor you pay me."

"Very good, my dear." He pressed a brotherly kiss to her forehead. "Now dry your eyes. I fear if we tarry a moment longer, your lovely mother will come barreling around the bend to demand I marry you at once."

She managed a small laugh at the image of the dowager coming upon them in full dudgeon. "Thank you, Your Grace."

"Any time, Lady Bella," he said kindly. "Any time."

*Acrid gun smoke stung his lungs. The clash of hand-to-hand combat rattled around him. Bayonets collided with swords and daggers, minié balls whistling through the air as angry hornets. Men screamed. Canisters were emptied into human flesh. Horses whinnied and fell. Fear gripped his heart like a giant's unrelenting fist. Before him, the bodies of his comrades stretched out, faces twisted into death masks, stomachs and heads blown open, oozing life's blood as if it were no more precious than water in a stream. The devilish bellow of a cannon blast roared through the din of battle. The howitzer cut down a swath of men to his right. Heads and limbs were torn from bodies.*

*Jesse fumbled to reload his gun. A Yankee officer rose from the heavy cloud surrounding him, sword poised to run him through. He tried to scream, move, shoot the bastard, but somehow his hands had been rendered powerless. No sound emerged from his throat. The blade arced toward him, dripping in the red blood of the wounded, ready to plunge into his gut. This was it, he thought, his final moment before death. He felt the sword skewer him, the ripping pain unlike any earthly sensation he'd ever felt before…*

Jesse returned to consciousness with a start. He stood in utter darkness, and for a moment he wasn't sure where he was or how he'd gotten there. He was sweating, his breathing heavy, fists clenched and aching. Christ, he must have been caught up in one of his nightmares again. Taking a deep breath, he tried to shake the remnants of the dream from his sleep-fogged mind. Gradually, reality returned to him. After traveling across the Atlantic on a tossing, hellish ride, he had at long last arrived in England with Clara. Now he was in London, in his own chamber.

*Thank God.*

Slowly, he took a few steps in the direction of what he fancied was the gas lamps. He'd only been here for one night and he'd been sleeping in so many different places that it took him some pause to gather his sense of just where the hell he was. He had arranged for the purchase of a house in Belgravia during his stay in America. It had been dear in price but necessary if he wanted to begin a life with Bella. And he wanted that life more than he wanted breath in his lungs.

The house itself was grand, as befitted a woman of her position in society. He was glad, for he'd bought it sight unseen. While he'd stayed in many fine establishments over the years, he had to admit that there was something about this edifice that had felt different for him the instant he'd walked in the door. This was not merely a shelter but a home, the place where he'd at long last plant his roots.

Blindly, he felt before him until his fingers discovered the ridge of his oak bed. He followed its sturdy lines to the gas lamp and lit it. The room illuminated in a subtle orange glow. He gulped in air, trying to calm his jagged nerves.

The nightmares were getting worse, damn it. They'd been plaguing him with a relentless persistence ever since he'd gone back to Virginia. Hell. In the flickering light, he caught sight of his fists. They were cracked open, oozing scarlet blood. Jesse lit another lamp and made his way through the chamber, searching for what he'd damaged. It wouldn't be a surprise to learn he'd destroyed something with his fists. For some inexplicable reason, his fits were worse than they'd ever been before.

He stopped dead when he saw the wall.

Damn it all. There was a series of deep, bloody craters in the damask wallpaper. Christ. This wasn't the first time he'd damaged his surroundings. It had been occurring with alarming frequency of late. What the hell was wrong with him? He looked down at his hands in the faint light, flexing his fingers. They ached with each motion but he didn't think they were broken.

Jesse went to the washstand and poured fresh water into the waiting bowl. While the house was relatively modern, the bathing chambers still weren't plumbed. He would have to work on that. Heaving a sigh, he plunged his hands into the bowl and scrubbed as if the act could rid him of the wounds he'd inflicted upon himself. The journey back to England had been a long and arduous one. He hadn't lingered in Virginia a breath longer than necessary, but still he had been gone for far too long as it was. After Lavinia's passing, he had needed to see through the selling of her home with the profits to be held in trust for Clara. Afterward, he'd left as if the hounds of hell were on his heels.

And indeed, perhaps they had been.

A hesitant knock at his door interrupted the bout of self-hatred overtaking him. Christ. He looked down to realize he was nude. With a curse, he stalked to his wardrobe and withdrew a thick, quilted dressing gown.

"Enter," he called, suspecting he knew all too well who was on the other end of the rapping.

True to form, Clara stepped inside his chamber, the door creaking loudly in her wake as she snapped it closed behind her. "Mr. Whitney?"

Ah, no matter how many times he heard her refer to him as though they had no familial connection at all, it still stung. She refused to refer to him as her father. While he did his utmost to uphold the pretense that her insistence didn't affect him, the plain truth was that he was hurt by her denial of him. He knew she'd been through a great deal of upheaval, and he could only hold out hope that she would accept him in time.

"Yes, daughter," he murmured, the word still feeling somewhat foreign upon his tongue. "Whatever is causing you distress?"

. "I heard a commotion," she said, sounding hesitant.

She wore a billowing lacy nightdress that he supposed had followed her from home. Lord knew he hadn't bought her a stitch of dress since he'd met her. He didn't know how. Indeed, it was his fondest wish that Bella would take over with the girl who had his face but remained a stranger to him. It seemed she wanted to hate him, regardless of whether or not he'd had any control over his presence in her life. She knew he had not, but he could only guess that she suspected there was a hidden motive for Lavinia's secretive nature. While his daughter had said upon their first meeting that she knew the tale of his relationship with her mother, he'd begun to realize that the naïve girl really hadn't been given the full story by Lavinia.

"Is anything amiss, Mr. Whitney?" she probed, disrupting his thoughts.

He cleared his throat, at a loss. He couldn't tell her the truth, that he'd been treating the wall like an enemy soldier. She'd think him mad. "Not at all," he lied. "I apologize for the disturbance."

"I feared you were being attacked."

Jesse stared at the girl who was his daughter. She'd never before shown a hint of concern for his well-being. Her words sent a warm surge through his chest. Was it possible that she cared for him just a bit? He couldn't be certain.

"I had a dream" he said, deciding to be at least partially honest with her. He little knew how to treat a daughter, but she wasn't a child. She was old enough to nearly have her first ball. The mere thought of Clara being trussed up in the finest fashion and paraded before a gathering of randy males set his blood to boiling. He knew men. He was one, after all, and he didn't want his innocent daughter falling prey to any of them.

"What sort of dream?" Clara frowned, her small yet expressive face pinched with what he swore was concern. "I know you suffered similarly on the ship here. Are you well?"

Ah, he thought he understood. She had already lost her mother to a prolonged illness. Now he was all she had remaining. She didn't want to lose the last bit of permanence she clung to in her life, whether or not she despised him.

"I'm as well as can be expected," he answered, wiping his clammy palms upon his robe.

She blinked at him, looking for all the world like a little forlorn owl. Her curls were trapped in a lacy cap, her feet shod in embroidered slippers. "Is it the war that's disturbing you?"

His knuckles ached. "The war has never been far from my side in all these years."

"Mama had nightmares," she startled him by revealing. "For many years, she called out in her sleep, even after Papa died. I heard her asking for you by name, particularly after she took ill."

Her disclosure shocked him. He wouldn't have expected Lavinia, selfish woman that she was, would have ever thought of him even once. Perhaps she'd possessed some small shred of conscience after all. "I imagine the war had the same effect upon us all," he offered.

Clara crossed the chamber to him, looking small and incredibly innocent. "Mr. Whitney, I don't like England very much."

"You'll grow accustomed to it," he assured her. Christ, but he didn't know how to be responsible for a young girl. He'd been a bachelor his entire life. It was damn difficult to grow accustomed to being a father, especially to a girl who was nearly grown. "I have embraced it as my second homeland, and I have no reason to think you won't be able to do the same."

She crossed her arms and sent him a ferocious frown. "But it's insufferably cold here."

He shrugged. "It's winter, my dear."

"And it always rains," she continued.

"I lived here for some time before coming to you in Virginia, and I can assure you that it doesn't always precipitate here," he said firmly.

Clara fixed a look upon him that was akin to hatred. "The fog is deplorable. It covers everything. Virginia was always bright and sunny."

"Clara," he said at length, "I have a suspicion that you wouldn't care to be in England even if it was declared heaven upon earth. I understand it hasn't been easy to adjust to the notion of living in another country, but adjust you shall."

"I hate it in London," she persisted, her tone stubborn. "I told you I had no wish to come here."

He inclined his head. "So you did, Clara. But you are now my ward, and as such, you must travel where I go."

"I don't want to be your ward." Tears slipped down her pale cheeks. "I never wanted you."

Well, sweet Christ, he certainly hadn't wanted her either. He'd been living a perfectly glorious life, about to marry the woman he loved, when he'd first learned of her existence. By God, he had uprooted his entire life for his daughter, only to have her disparage him with every other sentence she uttered.

Jesse sighed. He didn't think he would ever become familiar with the rapidly altering moods of a young girl. He well understood that she missed Lavinia, that it was a difficult task indeed to weather a mother's passing. But he had never once raised his voice to her. He had only been all too solicitous in meeting her every demand. He had paid for hundreds of books, dozens of her old dresses, and even a few pieces of—to his mind, anyway—hideous furniture to be transported to their new home in London in an effort to ease the transition for her.

And still she remained despondent. He was beginning to suspect that there was no way he could ever make his daughter happy. "While I understand that you never wanted me in your life, I am nevertheless the only family you have. Like it or not, Clara, I'm your father. I've sworn to protect you and take care of you as best as I am able, and I don't take that vow lightly."

"Not as lightly, I suppose, as your vow to love Mama," she hissed, her face twisted with anger. "She told me how you asked to wed her and then ran off with another woman. Thank heavens she found Papa, who was man enough to try to make up for your sins."

Oh hell. He didn't even know how to deal with such an unreasonable person. He crossed the room and took his daughter's arm firmly in his grasp. "While I know it isn't advised to speak ill of the dead, what I'm about to say to you is nothing but honesty." He paused, gathering his thoughts. "Your mother lied to you. She claimed to love me, and then she secretly met your stepfather without my knowledge. It was she who betrayed me, and I'm the one who ended up with a bullet in my back."

Clara shook her head, her blue eyes wounded. "No. I don't believe you."

"It's true," he pressed on, tired of having to pretend that Lavinia was someone she had never been. "Your mother made certain that her lover, Mr. Jones, would shoot me. While he meant to kill me, his aim was off. He shot me in the back, but I survived. He didn't know it then. He believed that if he wounded me, I would either be dead or be captured. I was nearly both, but I escaped."

"That isn't the story my mother told me," his daughter denied, her tone still upset as ever. "She wouldn't lie to me about that. I know she would never have encouraged Papa to shoot you."

Each time she persisted in referring to Mr. Jones as "Papa" sent a dart of pain directly to Jesse's heart. He was Clara's father, not Lavinia's no-account husband. As awful as his tribulations had been at the time, he'd never once imagined that they would result in his almost-murderer raising his child as his own. The agony of it was unspeakable.

Talking about what had happened all those years ago took him back to a dark place in his mind. Once again, he could hear the rumble of the cannon, the drums. He could smell the awful scent of decaying flesh. He'd lain in a field all night long, listening to the war raging around him. His only accompaniment had been the dying and the dead bodies strewn about the outskirts of Richmond. It had been torture.

He wanted to hit something. How dare that bastard take his daughter from him? How dare he try to kill him and then take Jesse's flesh and blood as his own? "That man," he said slowly, "was not your father. I am your father, Clara."

"He was the only father I knew," she argued, lips pursed in resentment.

He took her arm in his and began guiding her from the chamber before he completely lost his mind. "I have a new rule for you, Clara. I don't care who raised you. I don't care what man your mother married after she betrayed me. But I will never have you refer to that bastard as your father ever again. Are we understood?"

"But he was my Papa," she protested, stubborn to the end.

"I don't give a goddamn," he all but hollered at her, not proud of raising his voice but unable to help himself. She pushed him further than anyone had ever done in his life. "From this point forward, you may call me your father, or you will not call me anything. That is an order."

She flinched, her arm stiffening beneath his touch. "As you wish, Father," she said.

He swore she was mocking him still. But he didn't have the heart to address it. "Thank you. Now go to bed. We're rising early tomorrow to travel to the country."

At long last, he was returning to Marleigh Manor. The time had come to see Bella and find out why in God's name she hadn't answered a single one of his letters. He could only pray the reason wasn't what he suspected. If he lost her, he didn't know what the hell he'd do.

## Chapter Twelve

"**B**ELLA?"

She paused in the act of penning her response letter to the Duke of Devonshire and looked to her chamber door. It was highly unusual for her brother's wife to seek her out. While they weren't precisely enemies, they weren't yet friends either. She frowned, wondering what Cleo could want from her, and put down her pen.

"You may enter," she called.

Cleo rushed into the room, her cheeks flushed. Beneath her navy silk morning dress, the evidence of the reason for her hasty marriage with Thornton was becoming increasingly pronounced. Bella jerked her gaze back up to her sister-in-law's face, trying to tamp down the rise of envy within her. Sometimes, it hardly seemed fair that she should have to watch Cleo's happiness with her brother when she remained alone and miserable.

"Bella, my dear, you must prepare yourself," Cleo said, wringing her small hands in distress as she crossed the chamber.

She'd never seen her sister-in-law in such a frenzied state. Worry crept to life within her. "What on earth can be the matter? Has something happened to Thornton?"

"No," Cleo hastened to assure her, her expression still strained. "Your brother is fine. It's Mr. Whitney, Bella."

Pain slammed into her at Jesse's name, followed by fear. "Mr. Whitney? Has something befallen him?"

"Quite the contrary." She placed a calming hand on Bella's arm. "He's alive and well, and he's here at Marleigh Manor."

*Oh dear God.*

The air fled from her lungs in one big rush. She couldn't breathe, couldn't think. Jesse had returned? What could it mean? And why now, just when she'd begun to slowly regain her sense of self? He'd had months to come for her.

"Bella, are you well? You look frightfully pale."

Cleo's concerned voice tore her from her wildly vacillating thoughts. "I don't know," she murmured. "Has he said why he's come?"

"I haven't any idea. Your brother told me just this morning that he'd written ahead and he was expecting him today. I didn't want to press the matter and give him cause for suspicion." Cleo gave her a quick hug about the shoulders. "You needn't worry. He still doesn't know about you and Mr. Whitney. I would never betray your confidence."

She nodded, her mind digesting what her sister-in-law had told her. "There is that, at least. Thank you, Cleo, for being such a good sister to me. I know I haven't always been a good sister to you in return."

"Nonsense. I'll not hear another word of it. The past is precisely where it belongs, in the past." She paused, worrying her lip. "But I'm afraid there is something more you ought to know, my dear."

While she was grateful for Cleo's understanding, her sister-in-law's words had caused another arrow of dread to shoot her directly in the heart. "Whatever can it be?"

"He has brought a female companion with him."

Blessed angels' sakes. She hadn't been prepared for such

an awful, heartbreaking possibility. A female companion. Perhaps she was someone from his past, his reason for leaving in the first place. A horrid thought occurred to her. She closed her eyes, fighting a sudden wave of nausea. "Is she his wife?"

"I don't know, my dear. You mustn't read too much into this. I'm sure she's a relative of some sort. She appeared awfully young to my eyes." Cleo paused. "It is merely that I wanted you to be prepared."

"Of course. Thank you, Cleo." She opened her eyes and gave her sister-in-law a tremulous smile. "I do appreciate your kindness."

"I know how very difficult the last few months have been for you. Don't forget there was a reason you loved him. No one understands how destructive basing your life on a misunderstanding can be better than I."

She smiled sadly and Bella knew she was speaking of the years she'd spent apart from Thornton. Watching the two of them together had proven to her that their love was true. It had given her a measure of comfort to know that love was possible after all.

"Misunderstandings are a different matter entirely." She stood, deciding her letter to the duke would have to wait. She couldn't spare a thought for him now. She was brimming with a complex blend of anxiety and excitement. "I cannot think of a reason why he would disappear for months without a word, leaving me when I needed him most."

"I can't either, my dear. It doesn't sound like the Mr. Whitney we know, does it?"

"No," she whispered, helplessness threatening to overtake her, "but I've begun to think I never knew him at all."

Jesse was beginning to feel like a caged monkey at the zoo.

He'd been back at Marleigh Manor for two hours already, and he hadn't seen a sign of Bella anywhere. With the way news traveled in big country houses, he hadn't a doubt she would already know of his arrival. But she was nowhere to be found. The silence was ominous. He'd seen Clara settled in her rooms and gone in search of Thornton. Instead, he nearly collided with his friend's wife in one of the many halls of the east wing.

"Lady Thornton," he greeted, genuinely happy to see a familiar face that didn't belong to a servant. "I understand my felicitations are in order on your recent nuptials." He couldn't say he was shocked to hear that his friend had wed the woman he'd loved for years, and he was genuinely happy for Thornton to have finally found contentment.

She inclined her head, beautifully regal. "Thank you, Mr. Whitney. Welcome back to Marleigh Manor. I'm sure my husband would have greeted you himself, but unfortunately he's away this afternoon on business. I do expect him to return before dinner, however."

While her words were purely convivial, he couldn't shake the impression that her voice lacked warmth. Something was odd here. It was just his rotten brand of luck that his friend wasn't at home for his arrival. Dinner loomed hours away, and now that he was under the same roof as Bella, he didn't want to see her for the first time while the dowager scowled at him over the soup course.

"I wonder if you might assist me, my lady," he began, thinking that perhaps she was his best ally in this odd game he played of attempting to reunite with the woman he loved. Cooling his heels in his chamber simply wouldn't do. It was Bella who he longed to see, Bella who had haunted his every waking hour for the last few months, and he wanted nothing more than to touch her again, reassure himself that she hadn't somehow disappeared from the earth before he had returned to claim her.

She raised a brow, her expression turning cautious. "Indeed, Mr. Whitney? How may I be of service to you?"

He hesitated, unsure of how much he could reveal to her. "I'm merely wondering after the welfare of Lady Bella."

Lady Thornton's Cupid's bow mouth thinned into a frown. "She is as well as can be expected."

Her response brought a wave of alarm crashing over him. "Is something amiss? She hasn't taken ill, has she?"

"She isn't ill any longer," she said, casting a look about the hall, he reckoned, to ascertain that they were yet alone.

"Any longer?" Her lengthy silence began to make sense. "Dear God, what was it? Has she recovered?"

"I daresay I ought not speak for Lady Bella." Lady Thornton clasped her hands together at her waist, looking as if she were about to say more before thinking better of it.

"Where is she?" he asked, desperate to go to her.

She sighed, seemingly struggling inwardly. "Mr. Whitney, the particular illness that ailed Lady Bella was of a most personal nature. No one other than myself and Lord Thornton were aware of her…condition."

He stared at her. "I'm afraid I don't understand." But in truth, he was all too afraid that he did. A personal nature of illness, kept secret from the household, could only mean one thing. And there was one reason why Lady Thornton was divulging the information to him now.

"You understand my meaning perfectly," she said, her voice low. "I know, Mr. Whitney. My husband does not, else you would likely be a bruised and bloody carcass in the drive instead of a respected guest in his household."

She knew. Dear God. The hints she'd been giving him came together to at last form an ugly picture. Bella had not suffered from an illness. She'd been carrying his child. Christ, he hadn't thought it even a possibility, hadn't for a moment believed that their one night of passion could have led her to such a fate even though he'd warned her of the selfsame outcome. His emotions roiled within him, shock mingling with self-loathing. He'd left her alone when she'd needed him most. Little wonder she hadn't written.

And then, like the end of a carbine crashing into his gut,

the full meaning of Lady Thornton's words struck him. She had spoken of Bella's illness as if it were a thing of the past. There hadn't been enough months for her to carry a child.

"Jesus," he hissed, his voice hoarse. "Are you saying what I think you are, my lady?"

"I am," she confirmed. "Her condition is a thing of the past."

The affirmation hit him with the force of a physical blow. Dear God, no. Bella had carried and lost his child, and he had not been there to help her through it all. "Where is she?" he demanded, not willing to waste another minute without going to her side.

"I'm not sure it's wise for you to see her just now, Mr. Whitney."

"Forgive me, but I don't give a damn about wisdom at the moment." There was a clear note of desperation in his voice, but he didn't bother to disguise it. "I need to see her at once."

Lady Thornton remained silent for several beats. "I just left her in her chamber," she said at last. "It's eight doors down, to your left. But make haste. You'll not want to be seen. You've already done enough damage to her as it is."

Eight doors down. He nodded, already striding in the direction she'd indicated. "Thank you, my lady. I'm forever in your debt."

"I'll not be far, Mr. Whitney," she called after him in warning tones.

He didn't bother to respond. He was too busy racing hell for leather to Bella's chamber. He had to see her, make certain she was well, beg for her mercy. Christ, he had grossly mistreated her, leaving her to suffer a horrible loss. She must have been frightened and angry. He could only hope she didn't despise him.

Bella was pacing her chamber, wondering how in the name

of all the heavens she was to face Jesse Whitney again, when her chamber door flew open once more. She spun about, expecting to see Cleo, and nearly dropped to the floor in shock.

He had come to her chamber, stalking inside and slamming the door at his back as if he belonged there, and perhaps, she acknowledged in the far recesses of her mind, he still did. She drank him in with her gaze, not caring how betrayed her heart now felt by him. He was handsome as ever, his tall form perhaps leaner than it had been when she'd last seen him, his golden hair wild about his cleanly shaven face. He looked every inch the English gentleman in light trousers and a jacket, with a simple waistcoat worn over a white shirt. She wanted to fly across the chamber and into his arms.

Instead, she took three steps in retreat. "Stop where you are," she ordered him, her voice as badly shaken as she felt. "Don't come near me or I shall scream."

He ignored her, stopping only when he was close enough to touch, close enough for his familiar scent to find its way to her like an old friend. "Bella, my love," he said in the honeyed drawl she knew and had loved so well. "I have missed you more than you know."

The urge to cry was strong, but she forced it to subside, not about to appear weak before him. "If I believed that, I daresay I would also believe that pigs shall sprout wings and take flight."

"I deserve your anger," he murmured, reaching out to place a hand upon her arm.

She flinched and pulled away, hating that even now his touch made her long for him. "I'm truly not certain why you've bothered to come into my chamber," Bella told him, her voice as cold as she felt. "You are not wanted here, nor do you belong here."

She must not allow her foolish feelings for him to get the best of her. No, better to cling instead to the hurt and pain he'd given her. How could he have left her as abruptly as he had, leaving her to her fate and her foolish mistakes, if he'd cared? Merely the sight of him was enough to give a tremor to her hands. Upset warred with fury inside her, until she wasn't certain if she would shame herself by crying or raging before him.

"I've come because Lady Thornton shared a confidence with me." His expression was inscrutable. "I couldn't stay away another moment. I had to see you."

Cleo. Bella might have known. She had not been certain that she would tell him about the babe. What use was it to tell him of something that would never be? "What did she tell you?"

He stood utterly rigid, very soldierly. "Is there anything you would tell me yourself?"

Why did he feel the need to cross verbal swords with her? Hadn't he caused enough pain? She gave him her back and paced to the window, deciding how to proceed.

"You have nothing to say to me, then?"

She started, realizing he had followed and stood in very close proximity to her. She closed her eyes, steeling herself. Above all, she knew she must not lean back into the comforting strength of his chest as she wanted.

"If she told you I lost a child, and that the child was yours, she was correct," Bella revealed, her tone as devoid of emotion as she could keep it.

"My God." The words seemed torn from him.

She could tell he was shocked. He hadn't suspected, then. That knowledge made her marginally less hurt by his sudden defection. It wasn't much, but it was something.

"I'm glad to hear that you didn't leave because you thought I was with child," she murmured, opening her eyes back up to the harsh light streaming in the window.

"Of course I didn't. Christ, what do you take me for, a monster?"

"Not a monster," she murmured. "But certainly not a gentleman either."

"I deserve your anger. I am so very sorry for the pain

you've gone through. You must know that I never would have left you had I any inkling you were carrying my babe." Jesse sighed. "I owe you a great deal, the least of which is a full explanation." He placed a hand on the small of her back.

She shrugged away from his touch and spun to face him. "You owe me far more than a simple explanation. You should count yourself fortunate I have not yet cried out for the servants."

He bowed his head ever so slightly. "Agreed. But since you haven't, perhaps you will allow me to try to assuage your anger."

"I don't truly think you can assuage it." She pondered the temerity of such a request from him. "Indeed, I daresay if all the angels in heaven appeared in this room right now, pleading your case, I should still be quite angry with you."

"Bella, there are some things you don't understand about me." He passed a hand over his face, looking weary. "I cannot blame you as I haven't been entirely forthcoming. When I was very young, I met a woman I believed myself in love with."

There it was, finally spoken aloud, his reason for leaving. The other woman he'd loved. Bella's stomach churned at the mere thought. She hated that he had known and loved others before her. Was that wrong? Was it childish of her to feel jealousy toward a faceless, nameless creature long in his past? She didn't honestly know. But it was also a fact that if the woman held enough power over him to make him leave Bella, she could not truly be long in his past.

"Is she the woman you've brought to Marleigh Manor?" she asked, silently praying that it wasn't so. She couldn't bear it if the woman were his wife.

"No she is not," he continued. "She wrote me, and told me we'd had a child together whose existence I'd never known of. She'd raised her as her husband's child for the last fifteen years. Bella, the girl I brought with me here to Marleigh Manor is my daughter."

The revelation stunned her. He already had a daughter,

one old enough to nearly be of an age to have her comeout. Suddenly, the connection she'd had with him seemed paltry by comparison. How could she compete with a woman who had borne his child, who had raised her into near adulthood?

"Are you still in love with her?" Bella had to ask, even if she didn't want to know the answer. She couldn't bear to hear him confirm her worst fears.

"Of course not. I would never have become romantically involved with you had I still loved another."

"I wish I could believe you."

His gaze was impenetrable. "I've never been dishonest. I swear it."

"Why would she tell you now?" she wondered. "What could she possibly stand to gain?"

"Her husband is dead and she was dying. She needed a guardian for the girl."

Perhaps she'd grown jaded, but she found the woman's claim too convenient. "How nice for her to belatedly find her conscience. Have you proof the child is yours?"

"She looks very much like me." His tone grew soft and affectionate. "I have reason to believe Lavinia wasn't lying."

Lavinia.

The specter of his past had a name. Ugly name for an ugly woman, Bella thought unkindly. She hated that Lavinia had chosen to reemerge in his life, that she had such a claim upon him to have taken him from Bella's side as if she were of no more importance to him than an old boot. "Is she still alive?" She had to know.

"No." His voice was once again devoid of emotion.

"Is that why you've returned, then?"

"I returned for you," he said.

She shook her head. "You returned far too late. Why have you come now with this daughter of yours, invading my life once more as you've invaded my chamber? You don't belong here, Mr. Whitney, and you never did."

"I would like for you to meet Clara. I've come for you

as I promised, as quickly as I was able. I'm sorry I had to remain in America so long. Had I known of what you were enduring here, I would have been back at your side in a heartbeat."

She had no intention of meeting his daughter or of ever seeing him again after this dreadfully uncomfortable interview. She hadn't the strength. The fight in her had long since fled.

"What promise?" She didn't bother to conceal her bitterness. "You made me no promise." At least, not any that he'd intended to keep.

"Of course I did. But I was also obliged to see to the welfare of my daughter. I was torn in two very different directions, Bella, and if I'd known then what I know now, I would have done everything differently."

"I see. You abandoned one child for another." If her statement was harsh, that didn't render it any less true. It was all beginning to make sad sense. He'd been so swept up in finding his child that he'd forgotten about her. It was her fault for being reckless and losing the babe, but nevertheless, his absence had been abrupt and unfair.

"Bella, I didn't know you were with child," he said flatly. "You chose not to confide in me."

"How dare you try to put all the blame upon me? You disappeared without so much as a goodbye. How was I supposed to have confided in you when you weren't anywhere to be found?"

He raked a hand through his hair, leaving it standing on end. "I apologize for the hasty manner in which I left."

Bella stared at him. "You act as if you left for a picnic lunch. Jesse, you disappeared from the country."

"I cannot explain myself other than to say I never intended to hurt you." Jesse closed the distance between them. "All I can do now is beg for your forgiveness."

She wasn't about to give it to him. "Regardless of your intentions, you did hurt me. How do you think it feels to know you went running back to your mistress the moment she asked it of you? To know that you think so little of me that you haven't written once, not in all these months? For all I knew, you were dead."

"I've written you dozens of letters."

Did his daring know no bounds? Did he think her a complete imbecile? She hadn't heard a word from him in months. It had been the most crushing part of his betrayal. "I received no letters from you. Not a single one. How dare you stand before me, after all you've done, and lie?"

His brow furrowed. "It's no lie, Bella. I wrote you an abbreviated explanation before I left and gave it to my manservant. I would have gone to you, but it was late and I'd run into your mother in the corridor. I didn't want to risk your reputation any more than I already had."

She didn't believe him. She had no reason to do so. "Why do you insist upon prevarication? It won't do you a bit of good."

"Christ." He pressed a hand to his temple as if it throbbed. "What of the other letters I wrote you?"

She couldn't contain the bitter laugh that escaped her at his posturing. "If you expect me to believe that you wrote me a gaggle of lovesick letters and they were somehow all lost in the post, you're more foolish than I thought."

Jesse shook his head, his expression one of consternation. "I wrote you letters, damn you. Three dozen, perhaps. I wrote you explaining that I was clearing up matters with as much haste as I could manage, that I hoped you would do me the honor of waiting until I could return for you and ask your brother for your hand."

She searched his gaze, looking for any hint of deception. She found none. But he had already proven himself most untrustworthy. She didn't think she could bear to believe in him again. "It is cruel indeed of you to pretend now as if you cared for me. You can see how much I've suffered already."

He grimaced. "I deserve all you've said and more. I've been the worst sort of scoundrel to you. But you must know

I wouldn't lie to you, and I would never willingly hurt you."

"Yes, you have and you would. I'm sorry, Jesse, but no matter how hard I try, I don't think I can believe you or forgive you. I certainly cannot forget what you've done. To me, you have committed an unpardonable sin."

"It wouldn't be the first, likely not the last," he said, his tone bitter. "I warned you a long time ago that you were far too good for the likes of me."

Bella felt as if she'd been dragged beneath a runaway carriage. Her emotions were overwhelmed, her mind tired of attempting to process all the information he'd laid upon her. More than anything, she wanted to be alone. To have time to muddle through her thoughts without his haunting face before her.

She sighed, overwhelmingly weary. "I think it best if you leave now."

"Perhaps before I go, it would be wise to discuss my real reason for coming here to Marleigh Manor."

She raised a brow, her suspicions heightened, hackles raised. "Real reason?"

His expression hardened. "I would like to finally speak with your brother regarding the truth of what has come to pass between us. I thought you should be made aware of it so that you may prepare yourself."

Prepare herself for her brother's wrath and scorn. Dear God. He couldn't possibly be serious. Too much time and distance had intervened, and now it seemed altogether irrelevant. She had no wish to face Thornton should he learn the truth. Very likely, he would kill them both. Or lock her in her chamber for the rest of her life and attempt to beat Jesse to a bloody carcass. She felt suddenly dizzied.

Bella pressed a hand to her throbbing temple. "You cannot mean to do something so utterly foolish and senseless. Not now. What good could it possibly serve?"

"As we discussed before I left, I find my honor requires it," he returned. "I cannot in good faith be a friend to him while knowing I have dishonored his sister. Before we go any further, the truth ought to be made known, at least to him."

His dratted honor confounded her. It made no sense. "You astound me, sir. Is this the same honor that led you to abandon me while I suffered a miscarriage on my own? Do you not think it the least you can do to keep your silence?"

"I need to rectify my own scruples. I understand from Lady Thornton that he was aware you carried a child, but not that I sired it. I have not been a friend to either you or your brother in quite some time, and for that I must pay the price."

"But in doing so, I will pay the greatest price of all. I'm nearly engaged, Jesse. If word of our relationship is spread, my chances will be ruined."

"Nearly engaged?" Surprise was evident in his voice. "Who is he?"

The part of her that was still aching from his leaving hoped he was hurt by the prospect of her marrying another man. "The Duke of Devonshire."

"The damn Duke of Dullness? Christ, Bella, you cannot be seriously considering marrying him."

"He's not the slightest bit dull," she defended, even though she had once shared Jesse's opinion of her suitor. "He has a wonderful sense of humor, and he knows all there is to be known about nearly all matters."

Which was a beastly lie, but she didn't care. She wanted him to think she was completely content without him. More than anything, she wanted it to be true. Still, if she were brutally honest with herself, she had to admit she didn't know if there would ever come a day when she didn't long for Jesse.

"Strange," Jesse said, his tone gone icy, "I only recall listening to him drone on about his crumbling country seat and the merits of sheep farming."

Bella sniffed, doing her best dowager impression. "I'm sure he's never spoken of sheep farming. He is a gentleman from an old and well-respected lineage. He doesn't dabble in farming at all."

"You want to be buried in some tumbledown country house for the rest of your life with a man who's about as interesting as treacle?" He all but sneered.

"As long as he loves me, I do," Bella snapped.

"And does he love you?"

"Of course." It didn't matter that he'd never spoken the words. She wanted Jesse to think it more than she even wanted to hear them herself. "He and I have grown quite smitten with one another over the last few months." Another beastly lie, but she was feeling rather beastly.

"Indeed? Do you think he would like to know that I took your innocence?"

She gasped, the blood draining from her face. "You wouldn't do something so dastardly."

"Try me." He smiled, but it was an ugly smile without mirth.

How she wanted to make him hurt as she had. That he would return to her life now, after so long, and just when she had come to accept her fate, was nearly unthinkable. "Do you not think you've already brought enough torment to my life?"

"I'll do what I must," he said tightly. "You are mine, Bella, not the duke's or any other man's."

"Then you should not have left me," she cried out, unable to contain the hurt a moment longer. "If you had been here, I never would have gone riding in the storm that day. I never would have lost the babe. Don't you dare ruin what small chance I have for happiness. Don't you dare!"

The tears she'd been restraining streamed down her face in earnest, and she was too proud to dash them away. Let him see what he'd done to her. She had only ever loved him, and he'd led her straight to ruin.

"I don't want to hurt you, Bella," he said slowly, "but I'll not allow you to become another man's wife."

"You don't have the right to keep me from him." She took a deep breath. "Now leave me, if you please. Take your daughter and leave Marleigh Manor forever. I never want to see you again."

He bowed, his jaw clenched with obvious anger. "I'll go now, but I'm not leaving Marleigh Manor unless it's with you as my wife. Consider yourself warned, Bella."

With that parting shot, he stalked away, slamming her chamber door at his back.

# Chapter Thirteen

ESSE DIDN'T WANT TO DO WHAT HE WAS ABOUT to do. It would change everything, perhaps ruin all that he'd worked so hard to build. At the very least, Thornton would beat the hell out of him. Worse, Jesse knew he deserved it. He had betrayed his friend's trust and brought dishonor and suffering upon an innocent lady. He hated that she'd been alone when she'd needed him most. He didn't deserve Bella, of that he was more than certain.

If he had a shred of honor left in him, he'd leave her to her staid existence as a duchess. She'd never want for anything, financially or socially. But he was a selfish bastard through and through, and he wanted her for himself. There was fight in him yet.

Even so, it didn't stop his conscience from launching a final charge on him as he waited for the butler's announcement. He could walk out the door and never return. He could take his daughter back to America as Bella had asked, spend the rest of his life trying to forget her. Instead, he entered Thornton's study.

His friend stood with a welcoming smile. "Jesse, it's good to see you. I trust America treated you well?"

If he'd felt like a bastard before, it was nothing compared to now. "Not as well as I may have hoped."

"I'm sorry to hear that. Is something amiss? You look as if you've just seen the ghost of your grandmother."

"I'm afraid my visit here is not a mere social one." He hesitated, wondering how to proceed. "I need to discuss a rather grave matter."

Thornton's smile faded. "Well, what the devil is it, Jesse? Has our hotel in New York burned down?"

"The hotel is safe," he assured him. "But I fear our friendship may not be."

Thornton's expression hardened. "Indeed? Why?"

Jesse took a breath before plunging headlong into the hurricane. "I'm in love with your sister."

"The deuce. Bella? You're in love with Bella?"

He nodded. "I have been for some time."

"Hell." Thornton raked a hand through his black hair, leaving it standing on end. "I don't know what to think about that particular pronouncement."

"That isn't the worst of it."

The marquis stiffened, and Jesse had the distinct impression that the severity of the meeting was becoming apparent to him. His voice was grave when he spoke again. "Jesse, tell me you aren't the son-of-a-bitch who compromised Bella and got her with child."

Jesse met his gaze, knowing he needed to put himself at Thornton's mercy. "I cannot."

"You bastard," Thornton growled. With lightning quickness, he grabbed Jesse's coat, shaking him. "Do you have any inkling as to the suffering you've brought upon her in the last few months? I should kill you for what you've done to her."

That he had caused her any pain at all would always haunt him. He'd never wanted to hurt her. If he could rewrite their history, he would. Leaving her in the night as he'd done had been selfish and thoughtless and no one knew it better than he. He should have married her and carried her away with him. If he had done so, maybe their babe would not now be a mere memory. He had to face the consequences of his actions. He owed Bella and the babe they'd lost that much at least.

Jesse braced himself for the bout of fisticuffs that was surely to come. "While I realize this is hardly a defense, I was not aware she was with child at the time I left. Had it been made known to me, I would have married her immediately."

"How generous of you." Thornton's jaw clenched. "What makes you think I would have allowed you to wed my sister?"

"Not a blessed thing. I acknowledge she is my better in every way." He meant what he was saying, had never meant anything more in his life. "I wouldn't have blamed you if you had denied me."

"Damn right she's your better. You miserable prick. I counted you a friend."

"I'm deeply sorry for betraying your trust in me," he said, knowing it was little consolation, offered too late. "I accept whatever punishment you would give me."

"I don't need your approval to beat you to a bloody pulp, Whitney." Thornton gave him another shake.

"Hit me then," he said simply. It was what he deserved and more. He waited for the coming blow.

And waited.

"You're not worth the damage to my fist," Thornton sneered, every inch the marquis.

"Likely not," he agreed.

"Have you nothing to say for yourself?"

"An apologia wouldn't be enough to explain the depths to which I've sunk."

"I don't want an apologia, damn you. I want a reason why. Why would you trifle with my sister? She was an innocent."

He remained unflinching in the face of his friend's wrath. If nothing else, he was a man who stood his ground.

"I have no reason, other than to say I allowed my heart to rule my head. I should never have done so, and I know it well. But the die has been cast. I found no recourse other than to unburden myself to you."

"Tell me something." Thornton's eyes narrowed. "Why have you chosen to reveal this to me now when Bella is on the brink of making a match with the duke? I might never have known."

"Conscience," he lied. "I needed to for the sake of our friendship."

He couldn't bear to see her wed to a dull fish like the duke. Or any man else for that matter. True, Jesse didn't deserve her. But she had loved him once. He had to hope she could one day find herself capable of loving him again. Damn it, his letters had been his ruin. If he could but prove to Bella he'd sent her word and hadn't simply abandoned her, maybe she could forgive him. He had to believe that she was being guided by her anger and not by her heart. He had to believe it, or he had nothing left.

Thornton finally released him, but his gaze was still flinty, skewering him with the effect of a bayonet. "I wish I could believe you."

"I don't expect you to. I haven't proven myself a trustworthy ally."

"You sure as hell haven't, sir." Thornton paused before he continued, voice colored by suspicion. "You say you love her."

"I do." That much was true, though it seemed he certainly hadn't done a thing to show it.

"Then why not let her go to the duke? She's no longer with child. Your obligations are at an end. Let her find her happiness where she will."

"I compromised her, Thornton. Do you not think the duke would take issue with an unchaste bride?"

"I daresay she wouldn't be the first in the history of our esteemed empire," his friend snapped. "Certainly not the last."

He knew his ability to marry Bella was in Thornton's hands. He didn't want to push him too far and lose everything, so he chose to retreat just a bit. "I've done my duty in informing you of my sins. You have my word that I would marry her tomorrow if you but ask it. In fact, I would consider it my life's greatest honor."

"Christ." Thornton raked another hand through his hair. "Marry her?"

His reaction suggested Jesse marrying Bella was akin to flying an omnibus to the moon. He wasn't that bad of a matrimonial catch, damn it. "I could provide her with the life to which she is accustomed. You know I've plenty of wealth at my disposal. I would not take her from England or her family. I've purchased a more than adequate house in Belgravia, and I think she would like it well. I may not be a perfect man, but I am responsible for what I've done."

"What makes you think she would have you?"

"Nothing," he admitted. "I've had an interview with her and it didn't unfold particularly well."

"I expect not. She was quite cut up over what happened and with good reason."

Jesse inclined his head in acknowledgment. "I've begged her forgiveness, but I do understand it's not owed to me."

His friend stalked across the room, exhaling a great rush of air. "Damn you. I should be pummeling your face right now, not considering your offer of marriage to my sister."

"If the roles were reversed, I cannot honestly say I would have shown your restraint."

"I'm not certain if it's restraint I have or utter stupidity." Thornton turned back to him. "I suspected something of this nature, but I hadn't wanted to believe it. I suppose I've had some time to acquaint myself with the notion of my best friend ruining my only sister."

Jesse winced. He considered Thornton to be the brother he'd never had. But he had committed an act of treason. He doubted whether Thornton would ever forgive him. Indeed, he wouldn't blame him one whit if he didn't.

"I never intended to ruin her. Hell, I never intended to even look her way."

"If I hadn't gone through what I did with Cleo, you'd be bleeding profusely just now. Sad to say, but I know what you're speaking of." He stopped his frantic pacing. "That doesn't mean, however, that I sympathize with you. Quite the opposite as Bella is still my sister. She's naïve and idealistic, and she didn't stand a chance against a man like you."

A man like him. Jesus, Thornton didn't even know the half of it. They'd never spoken much about his time in the war. Jesse didn't suppose they ever would. Strange, but Bella knew more about him than any other soul in the world.

"I can't explain it. All I can say is I wish to hell I had courted her properly."

"But you didn't."

"No." He sighed. "There's one more revelation I must make."

"I shudder to think what it could be," Thornton drawled.

Jesse ignored his sarcasm. "I have a daughter. She's the reason I left so abruptly."

"Christ in heaven, what other secrets have you been keeping? Are you a spy? A bloody pirate? Have you murdered any innocent children lately?"

"I've earned that response," he agreed. "But this was not a secret I willingly kept. My daughter was unknown to me until I received a message at Marleigh Manor the evening you and I were in your study. When I was in the war, there was a lady to whom I gave my heart. She married another but unbeknownst to me carried my child. She chose to wait until she was on her deathbed to tell me the truth. I had no choice other than to go to my daughter, fearing that her mother was already dead and she was alone in the world. It was never my intention to abandon Lady Bella."

"That's one hell of a muddle," Thornton said, showing a surprising amount of compassion. "I won't condone the way in which you left, or the straits in which you left my sister, nor will I forget your conduct with her. However, I can see that you were a man torn."

Jesse nodded. "I thank you for your generosity."

"Where is this mysterious daughter of yours, Whitney?"

"Clara has traveled here to Marleigh Manor with me."

"I suppose it's natural for you to be seeking a maternal figure for the girl, but surely you can't believe Bella is of an age where she can act the part of mother. How old is the child?"

"She is fifteen years." Jesse paused, choosing his next words with care. "Don't think I haven't considered Bella in my altered circumstances. I would never expect her to play the mother to Clara. I assure you that I take very seriously my obligations to both Clara and your sister. If it was merely a replacement mother I sought, I never would have crossed an ocean."

"You must appreciate this isn't the sort of alliance I would ever want for her. As the sister to a marquis, she deserves a coronet at the very least. She's been bred to know her place in society."

"I'm aware I'm nothing more than a Southerner with questionable lineage. I wasn't raised in a grand country house. I will never be a duke," he conceded before proceeding with the intensity of the fire burning inside him. "But I can be the man who looks after her, the man who provides her with the greatest comforts in life. And I can be the man who will love her until my last breath."

He had no recourse other than to put himself at the mercy of Thornton, but he'd be damned if he'd give up Bella without one hell of a fight. He knew what it was like to battle nearly to the death, and he wasn't afraid to do what he must for the woman he loved. He knew the scent of gun smoke the way he knew the scent of Bella's hair. He was no stranger to combat, whether of the body or the heart.

"You say you love her and yet love commands such a paltry price in our glittering world," Thornton murmured.

"We marry for far less noble reasons here. Dowries and lineages and such."

"Yet you yourself did not," Jesse pointed out. "Moreover, I have no need of any dowry Bella may have. Keep it in your coffers, Thornton."

"It isn't her dowry I'm concerned with keeping." His friend's expression turned grim. "Besides, I'm a rare exception. Don't think it gives you an advantage. I need time to consider your proposal."

"How much time?" With each day that passed, he feared Bella drifted further out of his already tenuous reach.

"You overstep your bounds, Whitney. I can take as much time as I damn well like and you'll know my conclusion when I decide you shall. It would be best, in the meantime, if you and the girl keep to your rooms." Thornton offered him an abbreviated bow. "I find I'm late for an appointment. If you'll excuse me?"

For the first time in his years-long friendship with Thornton, Jesse was being dismissed. He returned the bow and took his leave, his gut more riddled with worry than it had been before he'd first entered the marquis' study. More than anything, he didn't want to lose Bella. But he greatly feared he would.

Bella received a summons from her brother. Since he'd largely ignored her following her refusal to reveal the name of her child's father, it came as a surprise. A most unwanted surprise. She suspected she knew the reason for the sparsely worded message she received just before dinner.

Jesse had carried out his threat.

She went to Thornton in his study as he had requested. She didn't bother with the formality of being announced, merely entered. Perhaps, she reasoned, it would be in her favor to catch him unawares. He glanced up from a sheaf of papers at her entrance, seeming quite imposing.

He stood and offered her an abbreviated bow. "Arabella, I trust you are well?"

Oh dear, she was being treated to her full name. He was still most displeased, it seemed. "As well as can be expected, thank you." Warily, she crossed the length of the chamber and seated herself before him. "Pray, enlighten me as to the meaning of this interview so that I may no longer wait on tenterhooks."

Thornton sat and skewered her with a most withering stare. "I daresay you already know the meaning."

She said nothing, not wanting to implicate herself.

"Jesse came to see me a short while ago," he continued. "He has told me everything."

Bella tensed. She truly did not relish the prospect of facing her brother's wrath. Perhaps she could stall him. "What is this 'everything' he has told you?"

Her brother raised an imperious brow, looking every inch the marquis. "Need I elaborate?"

She lowered her gaze. "What has he gained in humiliating me before you?"

"The return of his honor, I suspect." Thornton cleared his throat. "He wants to do right by you, Bella."

"Indeed?" She gave a bitter laugh. "What is his concept of doing right by me at this particular juncture?"

"He has asked for your hand in marriage."

Disbelief sliced through her. He wanted to wed her? He'd never hinted in the slightest during their heated meeting that he still sought her hand. An overwhelming rush of sadness hit her next. Months ago, she would have loved nothing more than to marry Jesse. Now the prospect simply made her numb. She didn't know what to think.

"Surely you wouldn't consider such a foolish request," she protested at last.

"Is it foolish? I've had some time to think about all that I've learned, and I realized I'm a complete duffer for failing to notice what was right before me. He was always at your elbow during the entirety of the house party. *Maman* complained quite loudly that you were always disappearing or napping. I should have known better, but I suppose my head was otherwise engaged at the time." He paused. "Bella, I know you well enough to know you must love him."

Did she still love him? She didn't know. She'd forced herself to bury that part of her along with the grief. She was certain of so little these days. "I loved him," she admitted with great deliberation. "But I know not what I feel for him now."

"Look at me, sister."

Bella took a breath and forced herself to meet his gaze. The censure she'd been afraid she'd see was absent. There was only warmth, compassion. She wanted to weep.

"He claims to love you."

Bella shook her head. "He does not."

"How can you be sure? He has not much reason for prevarication."

"He could not love me or he wouldn't have acted as he did," she said, determined not to allow her heart to soften. "He abandoned me when I needed him the most."

"Nevertheless, he is willing to atone for his sins," Thornton countered. "He admits he was wrong in his actions."

"Are you taking up the cudgels for him now?" she asked, aghast. "I know he is your old friend, but I am your sister. I should have expected more loyalty from you, Thornton."

"It is you I fight for." Thornton rose from his desk and began pacing in atypical fashion. He was more distraught than he appeared, then. "It is merely that no one knows better than I how great the price is when hearts are stubborn. It is best to speak openly and without deception in matters of the heart. You must tell me how you feel for him, Bella. I cannot make this decision blindly."

"You mean to say you haven't refused him outright?" An acute combination of horror and elation soared through her. She would have anticipated outrage from her brother at Jesse's confession, not sincere contemplation of giving her to the man in wedlock.

"I desire time to deliberate," her brother informed her curtly. "This is a matter I face with a heavy mind. You are my only sister, and there is nothing I want more than to protect you and see you happy."

"The Duke of Devonshire can make me happy," Bella lied. In truth, she didn't know if she was cut from the cloth of a duchess. Her mind and heart were hopelessly muddled by Jesse's return. Why hadn't he stayed gone?

"In affairs such as these, there is more to consider than mere happiness," he continued, stalking back to the desk once more. He appeared like a thundercloud, menacing in his concern. "I'm afraid there is the fact that Jesse ruined you. I cannot in good conscience allow you to go to Devonshire without letting him know his future bride is not chaste."

She had no doubt that the duke would throw her over if he knew she was not an innocent. If her brother revealed the truth to him, Bella would be ruined in social circles as well as in deed. She would be a pariah.

"You would condemn me for the sake of your conscience?"

"My honor demands it," he confirmed, not without a hint of remorse.

Drat men and their deuced, tardy senses of honor. He had built all his political aspirations upon his sterling reputation, so she supposed she ought not to be shocked by the revelation. But she was terribly disappointed. It seemed her options were limited by first Jesse and now her brother as well.

"Then I am either to wed Jesse or face social ruin," she observed aloud.

"I'm afraid the decisions you made have achieved such an end," her brother said.

An awful thought occurred to her. "Have you spoken with *Maman?*"

"I have not. You know as well as I that she will not take

news of her daughter wedding an American with much grace."

"She'll have an apoplectic fit." Bella heaved a sigh as the reality of her situation gradually dawned upon her. She would have to marry Jesse. There was no other path for her to take. She didn't know how to feel. He was as much a stranger to her as he was a familiar lover. He had a daughter more than half Bella's own age. It was all horridly worrying. "I will wed him if I must."

"You do know that Jesse has a daughter, I am given to understand?"

"I do. I expect she will hate me." She rose from her chair. "How much time have I until you speak with him?"

"Given the circumstances, I should like to speak with him at once. You will have an appropriate length of courtship. No need to set tongues wagging more than they're already bound to do. But I do wish to see you settled as soon as possible." Her brother came to her then and took her in his arms as he had not done in years.

She returned his embrace, taking strength in the comfort he provided. She'd thought he would be enraged upon learning the truth and was most relieved he was relatively calm. Perhaps love had settled his restless spirit. She had to admit that she admired Cleo very much and thought her an excellent match for her sometimes austere brother.

Thornton kissed her on the forehead and Bella reached up to press a hand to his cheek. "I'm sorry for disappointing you, Thornton," she murmured.

"You haven't disappointed me at all, Bella." He smiled slightly. "Not a whit. I would expect nothing less than for you to follow your heart. It is the example I set for you, after all."

*Follow your heart.* She returned his smile as best she could muster. Tears pricked her eyes. "Thank you for your kindness. You are a true brother."

He tipped up her chin, answering tears gleaming in his eyes. "If he hurts you again, I shall kill him. He will understand it to be so."

How she wished for her life to be different. How she wished she could go back to the carefree girl she'd been at Wilton House. Catching a sob in her throat, she spun and took her leave from the room before she embarrassed herself.

Jesse came to her the next morning. He'd been notably absent from dinner, but she had gathered it was by design. The de Vere family had shared one final meal with one another before everything was to change.

She was in the library, doing her utmost to concentrate on *The Eustace Diamonds*, a volume she'd been unable to thoroughly enjoy ever since the country house party. He entered without ceremony, without being announced. But she sensed him the moment he entered the cavernous room. She was attuned to him. That much she could not deny.

Knowing she would face him that day, she had dressed with care. She wore a morning gown of cream satin designed by Worth. It was simple in its beauty, with one long pleated bustle, a line of pearl buttons down the bodice, and lace trim with a cutaway skirt. Smith had braided her hair into a loose coronet with a few dreamy tendrils released to frame her face. She knew she was handsome, but that knowledge did little to bolster her flagging spirits.

He stopped halfway across the chamber, taking her in. Their gazes clashed. Had she not already been seated, she feared her knees would have quite buckled. He looked very fine indeed, dressed in an elegant black coat with matching trousers. His hair had grown rather long, she noted for the first time, scraping his collar. Goodness, he was still the most striking man she'd ever seen.

"Lady Bella," he said at last, offering a deep bow.

"Mr. Whitney," she greeted, finding her voice, breathless though it inexplicably was. "Good morning, sir."

"Good morning, my dear." He rose and favored her with a smile that unleashed his elusive dimple. "May I approach?"

His formality struck her as almost absurd and yet she sensed that he was trying his best to make what was about to unfold as appropriate as possible. "You may," she said, equally formal. She closed her book and put it to the side as he crossed the carpets.

Her mind went back to the other, far more carefree times when they'd met in libraries. Her heart gave a pang. How she wished they could somehow return to those times. She simply wasn't certain it would ever be possible. Nothing could erase the pain of his betrayal. Nothing could alter the course upon which they'd already set sail.

When he reached her, he sank to his knees like a knight paying homage to a fair maiden. She would have appreciated the sweetness of his gesture had not the circumstances been so very grave.

"Lady Arabella de Vere, I have wronged you and for that I am endlessly sorry. I will not insult you by begging your forgiveness because I understand you owe me nothing."

"Why play the role of dutiful suitor?" Her heart and mind were at a loss. He knew well how to charm her, but she was determined not to allow him to woo her this time. She wanted a lucid mind. Goodness, she needed time to process what had befallen her in the last day. "Surely it will not serve you now."

"I've earned your cynicism," he surprised her by saying. "I told you once that I'm not fit to lick your boots, and it is not any less true today than it was then. You are my better in every way. I do not deserve you as my wife, and yet fate has decreed I must ask your hand."

"Fate has not decreed," she corrected him, not willing to abandon her defenses. "You have decreed it."

"As have you," Jesse pointed out to her.

It was true. She had done her best to win his heart, all but throwing herself at him. "I own my part in this farce of ours. But I never sought to entrap you."

As he had done to her. The accusation hung unspoken between them.

His eyes hardened. "If you can tell me with honesty that you love the duke and wish to pursue him, tell me now."

She stared at him, knowing she could not.

"Say the words, Bella. I will not have a wife who loves another."

"I cannot," she admitted softly.

He took her hands in his. "Will you be my wife?"

She closed her eyes for a moment. "It seems I have no choice."

"You may decline if you like." His voice was harsh, even bitter perhaps.

Of course she could deny him. But what would doing so accomplish? Only more foolish ruin and misery for her. "You know as well as I that I cannot," she argued. "You've rendered any path other than marriage with you impossible for me."

"Hate me if you must. I know all too well I have earned your scorn, but I still require a definitive answer from you. Will you or will you not wed me?"

She did not hate him, not at all. She was still hurt by his defection and the months of silence that lay between them. She was confused by his assertion that he'd left a letter with his manservant and had written her dozens more. It made no sense, but then, neither did his sudden reappearance in her life.

All in all, she didn't know precisely what it was she did feel for him, which was the crux of the matter. She supposed that perhaps she shouldn't care since the white flag had already been raised. "Yes," she said simply, surrendering.

He brought her hands to his lips for a kiss. "I will be true to you, Bella. I promise to do my utmost to make amends for what I've done."

Bella wasn't certain he could make amends, but there was some comfort in knowing he intended to try. "As will I be true to you," she returned.

Jesse leaned into her skirts, and she could clearly tell his intent was to kiss her. Even as her heart tripped over itself in excitement, she turned her cheek, leaving him with no option other than pressing a chaste kiss there instead. But he lingered, his breath fanning in a hot wave over her face, down her neck. He kissed her again, his palms coming between them to cup her jaw. With a gentle deliberation, he turned her face until their gazes met and their lips nearly touched.

"You have no idea how badly I've missed you," he whispered.

His admission shook her. How she wanted to believe there was more to his hasty actions than misplaced honor. How she longed to believe he harbored tender feelings for her, mayhap even loved her as he'd claimed to her brother. And she had missed him as well, she realized, allowing herself to feel some of the emotions her stubborn heart had locked away. She still wanted him with an ache that was as physical as it was intangible. She was startled to realize that while she'd thought so much had changed for her in his absence, in actuality, it had not.

Bella couldn't seem to keep her hands from caressing his beloved face. She searched his gaze, unable to determine what she found in the sky-blue depths. "Jesse." When she would have said more, the words were lost to a sob she hadn't known she'd been withholding. Truth be told, she'd been utterly lost without him.

"Don't cry, my darling," he murmured.

She couldn't seem to stop the tears that began streaming down her cheeks. Her entire body shook with the power of her confused emotions. He crushed her to him and kissed her at last. Being in the secure strength of his arms was like a homecoming. His mouth slanted over hers and she opened to him. The familiar taste of him mingled with the salt of her tears. He kissed her as he'd never before kissed her, at once tender and yet hungry, with a newfound possessiveness.

He pulled back, breathing as heavily as she. He brushed a runaway tendril of hair from her face. "Bella, my love. You have made me a happy man."

The term of endearment was not lost on her. Against the stern misgivings in her mind, she leaned into him, taking his lips for her own this time. Their tongues tangled. She inhaled deeply, filling herself with the scent that was uniquely his and uniquely divine. The kiss turned voracious. Her fingers sank into his thick golden hair. God, how she had missed him.

How she loved him still.

The horrible realization sent her reeling. Suddenly, it was all too much for her. She shoved him away and retreated back into the upholstery of the settee. Gasping for breath, she pressed a hand to her swollen mouth. What had she been thinking to allow such liberties between them? She could not afford to blindly trust in him again. When he'd left it had nearly killed her.

"I shall need time, Jesse," she said at last. "I am sorry."

"I understand. Forgive me. I didn't intend for that to happen."

She believed him. The sudden combustion between them had been as mutual as it had been unexpected. She lowered her head to gaze at her hands, tightly laced in her lap lest she be tempted to touch him again.

"I have a ring for you," Jesse said, reaching into his coat. "Christ, I'd almost forgotten. I hope you find it to your liking."

He took her hand again, slipping a ruby ring upon her finger. The stone itself was breathtaking, quite large and deep in color. It nestled in an elaborate setting of filigree. The fit was perfect. Their betrothal was sealed.

"It is lovely, thank you." She hadn't thought about a ring, and now everything seemed much more final.

"It belonged to my mother," he told her, his tone turning wistful. "Though I never knew her, I was told she was a strong and beautiful woman, just as you are."

Despite her best attempts to harden her heart, she was secretly thrilled that he would entrust his mother's ring to her. "I shall treasure it always."

He raised her hand to his lips for another kiss. "Thank you, Bella. I love you more than I can say, my darling."

His pronouncement produced a visceral reaction in her. He had never told her he loved her before, and the weakest part of her was overjoyed. He had nothing to gain now. She had already acquiesced. But that didn't mean she trusted him. Or should trust him, for that matter. She had to keep a clear head.

She did not wish for their conversation to become too sentimental. Exercising prudence, she turned her mind to another topic. "There is still much for us to discuss if we are to form an alliance. I should like to make the acquaintance of your daughter."

He smiled, his dimple becoming pronounced once more. "I would dearly love for you to meet Clara. She is a victim in all of this mayhem too."

For the first time, the fact that he had a daughter became real to her. She hadn't wanted to think of her, not even by name. Her existence had been too painful to contemplate. "I look forward to meeting her." Surprisingly, she did. After all, the girl would be a part of her married life. She could not help the frustrating circumstances of her birth and life.

"Your brother wishes a socially acceptable length of courtship, so I expect we shall have time aplenty to spend together." He kissed her hand again. "I will make this up to you, Bella. I vow it."

As he took his leave of her, she hoped he was right.

# Chapter Fourteen

"I WILL NOT ALLOW IT!" THE DOWAGER punctuated her proclamation with an uncharacteristically childish stomp of her foot. "Absolutely not, Thornton. She. May. Not."

Bella winced as her brother sighed and closed his eyes, clearly trying to gather his patience as much as his wits. The deed was done. Bella was officially to become Mrs. Jesse Whitney. They had reserved the most troublesome portion of the process for last. Informing the dowager that her daughter was to be given in marriage to an American was not exactly unfolding with the grace Bella and Thornton would have preferred. To say their mother was in high dudgeon was a vast understatement.

The dowager was positively livid. "An American, of all things. She was within reach of a coronet. She was to have been a duchess!" She let out a low, funereal moan. "Have you any idea how close she's come to getting what she deserves? I've been reading his letters, and I tell you that he was about to propose!"

"You read my letters from the duke?" Bella stared at her mother in shock. The dowager had been rummaging

215

through her private correspondence? The letters had always been sealed. Bella hadn't suspected for a moment. How dare she? Her indignation was lost, however, as her brother took the reins of the conversation.

"Mother, cease your howling at once," Thornton ordered. "Bella, her ladyship is deplorably calculating and you ought to have known that by now. Both of you, I have made my decision, and that is final."

"Decision? You dare to suggest you have deliberated upon this, this farce? Why, it is insupportable. I fear your alliance with that woman has rendered you quite mad." The dowager's expression was as intense as her tone. Never mind the presence of "that woman" in the chamber in which they all sat. "Perhaps you have fallen into drink as I often feared you would. Next I shall be visiting you as you die of delirium tremens in a hospital for the poor."

Bella cast her sister-in-law an apologetic glance. Cleo shrugged and gamely rolled her eyes, well accustomed to the dowager's antics.

"Spare me your temperance society ramblings and theatrics," Thornton bit out. "Apologize to my wife, if you please."

"Thornton," the dowager protested, her chin actually trembling as if she might burst into a fit of hysterical tears at any moment.

"Apologize."

"Very well." She sniffed, her chin instantly ceasing to tremble. "I am sorry, Lady Thornton, for abusing you in the heated thrall of my soliloquy."

"No insult taken, madam," Cleo murmured, giving Bella a quick wink.

Bella was grateful for Cleo's calming presence. Her mind was still whirling with the sudden changes the last few hours had wrought upon the rest of her life. She had been dreading her mother's reaction to the news with a ferocity that was unmatched.

"You cannot want to wed him, Bella?" Her mother

turned on her with a look of expectation. "You cannot want to live in a land of rabid kangaroos and insects the size of horses. Why, they have monstrous creatures there. I've heard they possess horrid diseases that make men lose their ears. I daresay the Lord will see fit to sink the entire island into the sea."

"*Maman*," Bella said, not knowing where to begin, "America is not an island."

"It is unseemly to contradict one's mother." The dowager harrumphed. "I asked you a question, daughter. Do you truly wish to wed that man?"

Would that the answer was uncomplicated and unencumbered by weighty emotions and doubt. But she knew what she must do. She could not marry the duke, and the plain truth of it was that she'd been writing him as much the day before when Cleo had rushed into her chambers. Jesse Whitney had not changed her heart, even if he had forced her into being his wife. "I do wish it, *Maman*. If it causes you distress, I apologize, but I must do what is right."

"But it cannot be what is right." The dowager began fanning herself. "Indeed, it is altogether wrong."

"The facts are plain," Thornton said, stepping back into the verbal fray. "Mr. Whitney cares for Bella. He has a more generous income than most men in our social circle could even dream of calling their own. He has promised to look after her, and I take him at his word. As for Bella going to America, he has assured me that he and Bella will take up residence in London upon their nuptials."

Bella hadn't expected he would want to remain in England. She was startled to realize the question of their living arrangements had never even occurred to her. She had been so caught up in the web of haunting emotions and yearning that she had entirely overlooked the more practical facets of their future life together.

"Has he a home in London, then?" Although the dowager still seemed rather overset by the news of Bella's engagement, she showed signs of softening. Bella was certain it was Thornton's talk of a generous income that had proved the cure to her upset spirits.

"I am to understand he has taken one in Belgravia," Thornton affirmed. "It is surely more than suitable to a woman of Bella's means and station. Moreover, he has refused to take her dowry. He hasn't any need of it."

Good heavens. Her life had been decided already, without her ever having been the wiser. It was awfully arrogant of Jesse to assume he would win her. He'd purchased a home, had arranged every last detail as if she would be his.

The dowager appeared somewhat placated, perhaps by the news of the dowry more than anything else. "I will have to commission a trousseau."

"Naturally, Mother." Thornton bowed. "You have carte blanche."

"Just so." Their mother sniffed. "I would expect nothing less, Thornton."

Their courtship began without fanfare. The same afternoon as the dowager's reluctant capitulation, Jesse was to bring his daughter to the drawing room for her official presentation. The dowager was to preside over their afternoon visit in the interest of both propriety and familial harmony. The dowager was not yet ready to relinquish her position as de Vere family matriarch, and Cleo was, to her credit, willing to entertain the dowager's demands and politely bow out in this instance. Meanwhile, Thornton was taking no chances with Bella's reputation after the way the situation had played out already. She was thankful for that much at least, even if it meant suffering an uncomfortable interview with her dragon mother.

But perhaps the dowager would lend a calming air to the affair. Bella was unaccountably nervous to make the girl's acquaintance. After all, she was to become her stepmother.

She wished to make as an advantageous impression as possible. Their circumstances would not be ideal, it was true, for she knew the girl had only recently lost her mother. But she hoped to be a true companion to Clara. She hadn't the slightest notion of what to expect from a young girl. She could only hope that Clara would be kind and gentle, willing to make friends with a woman she'd never met.

"Are you very certain this is what you wish, daughter?" the dowager asked of Bella as they waited for their guests to be announced. "You'll recall that even now, the Duke of Devonshire thinks it may be his great earthly joy to call you his duchess."

"As certain as I may be of anything," Bella returned with bare honesty. "While the duke has been a faithful correspondent to me and a most appreciated friend, I fear that we are not suited after all."

The truth was that she wasn't precisely certain of her alliance with Jesse. After all, there remained a host of questions that needed answering. He had left in the midst of the night only to return months later with a grown daughter in tow. There was also the matter of his claiming to have written her dozens of letters she'd never received. Bella was quite confused by his assertion. He had never lied to her in the past, but his abrupt departure did not exactly engender a sense of trust. In fact, she was quite hopelessly confused. But she did know that Jesse had made it impossible for her to wed the duke any longer, and that furthermore, she hadn't wanted to wed Devonshire anyway. It was all rather a mess.

There wasn't, however, time for her to dwell on the questions swirling in her mind. The drawing room was set for tea. It was all to be quite properly done. There was no reason for her to feel as if her heart were about to pop inside her chest. None at all. She swallowed and picked at an imaginary wrinkle in the overskirt of her gown. She very much hoped this first meeting would go well.

She had the opportunity to take a deep breath for

composure's sake as Levingood appeared, formally announcing Jesse and his daughter.

Her eyes went to Jesse first. Their gazes clashed and he sent her a tentative smile. He was as nervous as she, it seemed. His daughter was a petite creature indeed, standing at his side with a stiffness of posture that suggested either uncertainty or disdain. Bella was not certain which. Dressed in austere mourning weeds, she was an ethereal blonde and rather lovely. Even Bella had to admit she very much took after Jesse, though she had initially questioned the girl's lineage.

"Miss Whitney," Bella greeted with as much warmth as she could muster with worry swirling through her. Her stays seemed suddenly tighter. It was surreal meeting Jesse's daughter.

The girl gave her a haughty stare. "My surname is Jones, miss, if you please."

The correction would undoubtedly provoke questions from the dowager, who had not been made privy to the exact circumstances of the girl's birth. Thornton had deemed it best to avoid complete disclosure, given their mother's disapproval of the union in the first place. Now Jesse's daughter had quite ruined their chance to keep the truth a secret.

Bella had to admit too that she was taken aback by the frosty reception. So was her mother who, bless her heart, could never hold her tongue.

"My dear girl," the dowager clucked, looking appalled. "If you are to remain on in England, you must learn how to address your betters."

Jesse bowed, his expression one of embarrassment. "I apologize, my ladies, for my daughter. As a newcomer to this country, she is still acquainting herself with your customs."

Miss Jones, as she would be called, appeared unmoved. Her face was a stiff mask of feigned politeness. She seated herself on a settee opposite Bella, holding herself with a regal air that belied her youth. Bella had to give her credit for her gumption, if nothing else. Jesse seated himself at her side and the interview commenced with an awkward silence.

Bella decided she would have to try her hardest to avoid further insults from the dowager. She began pouring the tea and looked to the girl. "Miss Jones, I'm delighted to finally be meeting you. Tell us, how do you find England?"

"I think it dreary and cold," the girl responded, her drawl rather pronounced. "I told Mr. Whitney I desire to return to Virginia as soon as possible."

Jesse exchanged a meaningful glance with Bella as he accepted a teacup and saucer from her. "I informed Clara she would be well advised to avoid making hasty decisions."

"Indeed," the dowager drawled in a wintry accent. "In this matter, I would defer to your father, Miss Whittlesby. England will, I feel quite certain, be incredibly improving upon your character."

Oh dear. *Maman* was still insisting upon mispronouncing Jesse's surname, never mind that Jesse's daughter was determined to go by a different name entirely. She feared her mother would call her Mrs. Whittlesby after the wedding, so stubborn was the old bird. Bella cleared her throat, wondering if the awful heaviness of the interview weighing down upon her would break her back.

"Miss Jones, we must take you shopping," she tried. "I'm certain you shall find our shops and dressmakers to your liking. I would very much enjoy showing you the finer aspects of London, once we return there."

"You are kind," Miss Jones said, her tone rather disingenuous, even to Bella's ears.

"Indeed." Bella grew impatient with pretense and decided upon a different tactic entirely. "Miss Jones, would you like to take a turn in the gardens with me?" She sent Jesse a sympathetic glance, hoping he wouldn't be too displeased to be left at the mercy of her mother. "Mr. Whitney, I should like to have a moment alone with your daughter, if you don't mind."

Jesse didn't appear pleased, nor did the dowager, but both politely accepted her sudden change in plans. Miss Jones looked as if she'd swallowed a bite of rancid mutton but she allowed Bella to lead her away nonetheless. Outside, it was a gray day, the weather having turned damp and oppressing. They collected their wraps before venturing out into the cool afternoon.

Bella waited until they were beyond earshot of servants to begin her conversation. She still wasn't entirely certain what she wished to say. She knew frighteningly little about girls of an age with Miss Jones other than having been one herself. She decided tact was in order.

"Miss Jones, I do admire your dolman," she said of the fashionable cloak, noting that it was finer than the dress Miss Jones wore. "The trim is especially lovely."

"Thank you," said Jesse's daughter with obvious reluctance. "It is arctic fox, I believe. It belonged to my mother. I wouldn't wear it now, but Mr. Whitney has not seen fit to procure me a proper mourning wardrobe."

It was likely that Jesse didn't have the slightest idea what to do with a fifteen-year-old girl who required mourning dress. But Miss Jones was not precisely accommodating, either. Indeed, if she'd thought she and the girl would readily develop a relationship, she was rapidly rethinking her supposition. Miss Jones was neither kind nor gentle.

"Let us be candid with one another." Bella slowly led her deeper into the formal gardens. "I am very sorry for your loss, my dear. I feel it quite important for you to know that I don't wish to ever take your mother's place in your affections."

"That is best, for you never could," the girl said coolly.

"Just so," she agreed. "But you are now your father's ward, and I am to become his wife. We shall be forever linked inextricably. I understand you've seen a great deal of change in the past few weeks, but that is no reason to be ill-mannered to those who only wish to help you."

Miss Jones looked taken aback by her bluntness. She

opened her mouth, then closed it, twice, before finally speaking. "I haven't been ill-mannered."

"Yes you have." Bella patted her arm, if not affectionately, then with a consoling air. "There is to be no nonsense between us. As you've seen, my mother is quite the dragon and I am made in her mold."

The girl stiffened. "I'm not afraid of your mother or you, my lady."

In her ire, her Virginia drawl was all the more pronounced. She very much looked like Jesse in that moment, all stubborn fire. She was so much his image that it gave Bella pause. No, there was no doubt the girl was his daughter.

Bella stopped and considered Miss Jones more fully. "My dear, you ought to fear both of us. We are in possession of your future. With our aid, you will see the proper dressmakers, meet the right members of society, and make a fine match one day. But if we are to be enemies…" She shrugged, allowing the girl to make her own inference.

"Do you dare to threaten me, my lady?" Miss Jones adopted a perplexed tone.

"I am not governed by spoiled children," she informed her. "I have no patience for insolence and nor does your father, I expect. As I said, I sympathize with your plight, but that doesn't mean I'll allow you to treat me with disrespect."

Miss Jones, it seemed, was not ready to bend. Her face darkened. "I am his daughter. You are not even yet his wife. You cannot dictate to me. I don't care if you're the queen."

The little imp certainly possessed a great deal of foolish bravery. Bella pinned her with a hard stare. "You mistake me, Miss Jones. I am not allowing you the opportunity to plead your case. I'm telling you how it will be between us from this day on. I will very soon be your father's wife, and you will be beneath my rule every bit as much as if I were Queen Victoria herself."

They eyed one another warily, each testing the other's mettle. Bella wasn't concerned. She was every bit as determined as a spiteful fifteen-year-old. She was well aware who would win this particular war, and it wasn't the blonde spitfire before her.

"I don't like you," Miss Jones growled.

"To be perfectly frank, my dear Miss Jones, the sentiment is mutual." Bella raised a brow.

Miss Jones tightened her lips, looking quite sour. It would seem she realized she'd happened upon a well-matched opponent. Poor Jesse, tasked with raising this minx on his own. He never would have stood a chance.

"Now then," Bella said brightly, confident the matter had been mostly settled. "Why don't we join your father and the dowager to enjoy the remainder of tea?"

Bella didn't have much time to savor her minor triumph. Before the drawing room door had even closed upon Miss Jones' black skirts, the dowager turned on her, demanding answers.

"Is she the product of a divorce or is she a bastard?" Either prospect, it appeared, suited the dowager as well as a dinner of spoiled mackerel.

"The girl has chosen to take her mother's surname," Bella tried to evade. She disliked such labels very much. After all, her own babe, had she not lost it, very well could have been born a bastard. Of course, she didn't know whether or not Miss Jones' mother had been married to Mr. Jones or not at the time of her birth. Oh heavens, life could be incredibly complicated.

"Nonsense." The dowager's gaze narrowed. "Do I have the look about me of someone who was born yesterday?"

"*Maman.*" Bella frowned.

"Quite so." Her mother's tone was triumphant. "The girl is a bastard, isn't she?"

She faltered, not wanting to dissemble but not wanting her mother to go into high dudgeon just the same. "Miss

Jones is his daughter, and that can be all that truly matters."

"Oh, my poor heart." The dowager's hands fluttered over her breast as if she were experiencing difficulty breathing. "I knew no good could come of this match. Surely Thornton was influenced by drink when he gave that dreadful American permission to wed you. We cannot introduce the girl to society as his bastard. Blessed angels' sakes, we'll be ruined."

Bella hadn't contemplated the matter in that way. She'd been too preoccupied with becoming a maternal figure to the girl. Her mother did have a valid argument on that score. Questions would be asked, whether behind fans or drawing room doors, and they would need to present the answers in the most advantageous light possible.

"Perhaps she must be introduced merely as his ward," she suggested.

"Dear me. I daresay we shall be inundated with all manner of ugly insinuations. Tell me something, Bella." She pierced Bella with an intense, searching glare. "Have I utterly failed as a mother?"

She hadn't many soft feelings toward the dowager, but the termagant was still her mother, after all. Empathy flitted through her. "Of course not, *Maman*. Why would you ask such a silly thing?"

"I suppose I was so absorbed with the commotion your brother caused at that cursed house party, I never knew you'd fallen in love until it was too late." She startled Bella by reaching out and patting her hand in a rare show of affection. "You do imagine yourself in love with him, do you not? Ah, how I wish now to never have attended Lady Cosgrove's country house party."

She contemplated her mother's words. "You cannot fault Lady Cosgrove for hosting a country house party."

"I most certainly can." The dowager sniffed. "That woman is proof that society is going to the dogs."

"I hardly think so." She paused, still concerned by the potential storm of scandal on the horizon. "Will you agree that we must call Miss Jones a ward? The truth is that she was raised by her mother's husband and her existence was only recently made known to Mr. Whitney."

"Oh pish." The dowager swatted the air as if a persistent fly were buzzing around her head. "I know Mr. Whittlesby's sordid tale of the discovery of his daughter's existence already. You know how I deplore provocation."

Bella raised a brow. "I believe you meant to say prevarication, *Maman*. And you must cease referring to Mr. Whitney by the incorrect surname. It shall soon be my own."

Her mother pressed her lips into a ferocious frown. "Just so, precisely what I said. You are forever mishearing me."

"Indeed." She summoned her patience, knowing that today had cost her mother dearly. "Will you prevaricate for the greater good of the family? If we all stand together in this, no questions shall be asked."

"I suppose I may try," the dowager conceded. "But I'll not escort her about London if she can't be bothered to learn how to address her betters with proper care."

"Thank you." Something occurred to her then. "*Maman*, you said you already knew Mr. Whitney just learned of his daughter's existence recently. How could you have known, when I only discovered the news yesterday?"

"I said no such thing." The dowager rose from her chair. "Now if you'll excuse me, all this nonsense has made me positively bilious. I daresay I require a nap."

Bella watched her mother disappear from the drawing room with uncharacteristic speed. She couldn't shake the sudden suspicion that something was not quite right. She and Thornton had mutually agreed that the less their mother knew, the better off they'd all collectively be. How then would the dowager have known about Miss Jones? It was a question she was determined to answer.

The answer to Bella's question, as it turned out, was procured fairly easily. With a little help from Smith, she'd discovered that the manservant assigned to Jesse during his original stay at Marleigh Manor was none other than a cousin of Hollins, the dowager's lady's maid. This suspicious information, coupled with the dowager's recent admission that she'd read Bella's private correspondence with the duke, was enough to have Bella marching into her mother's chamber.

The dowager was being helped out of her gown by Hollins. She cast a horrified look in Bella's direction as the door closed soundly behind her.

"Arabella, good heavens! You cannot simply go barging about my chamber. This is unheard of. Can't you see I'm preparing for a nap?" The dowager's expression was startled, and unless Bella was mistaken, just a trifle guilty.

"*Maman*, I should like a word alone with you," Bella announced, her tone one of steel.

Hollins stopped in her ministrations, leaving the dowager's bodice hanging around her waist, her arms still bedecked in lacy white undersleeves. "My lady?"

"Whatever you'd like to discuss can wait, my dear." The dowager harrumphed, but the result was rather comical given that she was half-dressed.

"It cannot." Bella crossed her arms over her bosom and stared down her mother. "I require a dialogue with you, and I don't want an audience." She pinned the dowager's lady's maid with a meaningful glare. "Hollins, you may go."

But the dowager was ever stubborn. "Hollins, you may stay. I have no wish to speak just now as I am extraordinarily fatigued."

"I suppose she may as well stay," Bella said at last, losing her tenuous grasp on her patience, "seeing as how she aided you in your hideous campaign of stealing my correspondence."

The dowager's brows snapped together. "I am not a thief. I merely read a few of your letters from the duke to ascertain his intentions. Who can blame a mother for being protective of her daughter?"

"It isn't those letters I'm speaking of, and you know it," she countered, unmoved. "Mr. Whitney told me that he left a letter with his manservant for me explaining his abrupt departure. He also claims he sent me dozens of letters during his time in Virginia, and yet I never received a single line from him."

Her mother's face went pale. "If that no-account American is deceiving you regarding correspondence he didn't bother to write you, I fail to see how I may be involved."

"He isn't deceiving me. You are."

The dowager sniffed. "I am horridly offended by your unfair accusation. Apologize at once."

"It is you who owes me an apology." Bella shook her head, still shocked that her mother could stoop to such a cruel level of interference in her life. "You also owe one to Mr. Whitney, as your tampering with his letters has led to a grave misunderstanding between us."

"I didn't tamper with a single letter," the dowager declared. "I won't offer an apology where none is due."

But Bella wasn't about to be swayed. "His manservant at Marleigh Manor happens to be a cousin to Hollins. He told me he gave the man a letter for me, a letter that I never received. It doesn't require much thought to draw a conclusion as to why he would withhold the letter. You gave yourself away in the drawing room."

At last, the dowager's façade cracked, giving way to a hint of worry beneath. "What business did Whittlesby have sending you secret messages? I was merely doing my duty as your mother and trying to protect you from making the greatest mistake of your life. Don't you see how disastrous a match this is for you?"

Bella's shoulders sagged. She had wanted, despite her conviction that her mother was at the heart of the missing letters, to be wrong. "What you have done is disastrous," she said, the fight seeping out of her. "I don't know if I can forgive you for this."

"I have done nothing which requires forgiveness," the dowager insisted, appearing incredibly ridiculous in her undergarments and skirts. "You could have been a duchess, but you, like your brother, refused to be governed by your head. I had to do something. If that wretched American hadn't returned when he did, I daresay you would be betrothed to the duke now instead."

While she understood that her mother thought her actions had been justified, Bella couldn't absolve her so easily. She had suffered for months, not knowing if Jesse would return, thinking he'd abandoned her without a word, and all that time, the dowager had been secreting his letters. All that time, all that pain and anguish, and the dowager had known.

"I suppose I ought not to be surprised by what you've done," she murmured at last. "But I am thoroughly disappointed in you."

"You're my only daughter," the dowager snapped back, her gray eyes flashing with anger. "A mother must know what is right when her daughter does not."

"It was not for you to decide." Sadness overtook her then. "I'm going to speak with Thornton. I would like Cleo to oversee my trousseau instead. I can't bear to look at you just now."

Her mother became red as a beet root. "You cannot! I'll not have that woman taking my place!"

Bella inclined her head. "I'm afraid I can. It seems you're fated to hate both of the spouses your children have chosen. I can only hope that in time, you will soften and see reason."

With that, she quit the chamber, leaving the dowager to sputter behind her.

## Chapter Fifteen

*J*ESSE CAME TO HER IN THE GARDENS. SHE'D SENT a note to him via Levingood, making certain to eschew his manservant, lest any more of their correspondence go hopelessly astray. The day was cold and gray, but she knew a surge of warmth when she saw him striding toward her on the path. She couldn't help but think of how much they'd been through together, how much he had come to mean to her over the years. What she'd felt for him had initially been a girlish fancy. She'd been too inexperienced and immature to know the difference. But the love that had grown inside her for him was real. It still beat within her racing heart. It had always been there though her hurt had forced her to tamp it down.

He stopped as he reached her, taking her cold hands in his. "What is it, Bella? I came to you as quickly as I could." His Virginia drawl sent a frisson of desire snaking through her.

She met his vivid gaze. "It would seem I owe you an apology."

"Indeed?" He raised a golden brow. "I thought it was I who owed you an apology after Clara's meeting with you. I know she was rather rude to you and your mother both. I have no excuses for her other than that she's going through a difficult time, having lost her mother and now being so far from the only home she's known."

She smiled. That was a rather politic way of putting the girl's behavior, to her mind. "I think Miss Jones and I have reached an understanding of sorts. We shall get on just fine. I have no doubt of it."

"I hope so." He squeezed her hands and raised them to his lips for a lingering kiss. "I wish I didn't come to you with a wagon full of valises."

Bella pulled a hand free and pressed it to his whisker-stippled cheek. He hadn't shaved this morning, she noted, savoring this small intimacy between them. Much had come to pass, but she believed they could mend the cracks between them. She had to hope.

She took a deep breath. "I have some valises of my own in the form of my mother. She took the letters you'd written for me. Every one of them."

"I see." He paused, appearing to mull over her revelation. "Your mother likes me about as much as she likes tradesmen, Americans in general, and tardiness."

His words stole a laugh from her. "I suppose you know her well."

Jesse searched her gaze. "She merely knows, as I do, that you are far too good for the likes of this ragtag Virginia boy."

She cast a deliberate glance over the fine, gentlemanly figure he cut. "You're hardly ragtag," she pointed out. "I am sorry for believing the worst of you. I never thought my mother would have stooped to such awful meddling."

"You needn't apologize, my dear." His expression grew serious. "I deserved it, leaving you as I did. I'll never forgive myself for that."

She pressed a finger over his sensual lips. "Pray, don't speak of it again."

He kissed the digit. "I must. I've been able to think of

precious else since I learned what you'd been through. I would give anything to go back in time and right the wrong I've done you. I would never have left you knowing that you were carrying our babe."

That he had left her so abruptly still hurt, as did the loss of the babe they would never know. But she could empathize with his struggle. She knew the war had taken a toll upon him, and that he likely hadn't been in a normal state of mind when his past had once again come calling. She also well understood that his honor would demand he return to care for his daughter. And as Cleo had so recently said to her, she knew that if they ever wanted to move forward, their past would have to remain where it was. In the past.

However, before they put their mistakes and misunderstandings behind them, she needed to let him know that she was responsible for the miscarriage. The guilt of her foolish actions weighed her down heavily. Had she never gone riding that day, everything would be different now. She wanted him to know she was at fault.

"I very much regret losing the babe." The words were difficult to say. "I wish I could change what happened, but I suppose the world is not always ours to command." She paused, not wanting to reveal the rest to him, but knowing she must. "There is something I must tell you, Jesse."

Seeming to sense the turbulent emotions churning through her, he put an arm around her waist, drawing her against the comfort of his big, lean body. His hands spread over her back, stroking and soothing as his eyes searched hers. "What is it, my love?"

"I caused the miscarriage." Bella took a deep, steadying breath. "I was out riding before a storm, and I lingered too long when I ought not to have. My mare startled, I was tossed to the ground, and when I woke, the babe was already gone."

In the span of days and weeks since that dreadful day, she had purposefully kept thoughts of the babe at bay as best as she could manage. But in the safety of Jesse's arms, the reality of it crashed over her. She'd never been able to grieve. Not truly, for almost no one had known. The tears came slowly at first, her sobs soul-deep.

"Don't cry," he whispered. "You mustn't punish yourself for what's happened. You weren't at fault, darling. We are just beginning, and we have a lifetime waiting for us."

He pressed a kiss to her cheek and she wept all the more for the gentleness he showed her. Jesse took a handkerchief out of his pocket and used it to wipe at her tears, drying her face. She allowed him to perform the tender ministrations, her heart swelling even more within her breast. He was a good man, scarred on the inside and imperfect as anyone, but a very good man nonetheless.

"Do you forgive me, Jesse?" she asked, wanting to hear it from him. It felt like heaven to be back in his arms. It was where she most longed to be. It was where she belonged.

He was her home, she thought simply. Jesse Whitney was her home, her heart, and the man she would always love more than life itself. Not time, not distance, not her mother, nor anyone else, could come between them again. She vowed it to herself as much as to him.

"There isn't anything to forgive." He caught her face, tipping it up to his. "Nothing can take away the pain of loss. I know it well. But together, we can go on, discover the happiness we've always been meant to share."

"Together," she repeated. "I like the sound of that."

"As do I," he said, a slow, knowing smile spreading over the lips she'd grown to love so much. He lowered his head and sealed their mouths in a passionate kiss.

Bella's arms went around his neck. It had been so long since she'd shared a true embrace with him. She opened to him, moaning when his tongue slid past her lips to taste and claim. Bella kissed him back with every bit of pent-up longing that had been simmering within her for the past few months. Her hat got in the way and she knocked it from her head, not having the patience for any encumbrance, however fashionable it may be. Their kisses turned voracious, as though they could somehow consume one another.

He pulled away, dragging his lips down over her neck, his breath hot and wet upon her eager skin. "Ah, Bella. I've missed you so desperately."

"Not as much as I've missed you," she murmured, holding him tightly against her. She wished she were not trussed up in so many layers that kept her from feeling him as she wanted. As it was, she was impeded by her dolman, walking dress, petticoats and miscellaneous undergarments, and her hated corset. It seemed to be tightening upon her ribcage by the moment.

He sighed, disappointing her by setting her away from him. "Much as I would like nothing better than to take you in my arms and carry you directly to your chamber, I'm afraid your brother will murder me for good this time. And if I have you in my arms for one moment more, I'll be tossing you over my shoulder and looking for the nearest spot to have my wicked way with you."

Desire sluiced over her, heady and potent. She hadn't forgotten what it felt like to make love with him, and now that they were betrothed, their differences mended, she couldn't wait to share his bed again. Perhaps it was wanton and wrong of her, but she didn't give a fig. Jesse had taught her how to be a woman in form as well as name, and she wouldn't return to the naïve girl she'd been for all the gold in the world.

"While I don't want Thornton to do you harm, I'd like nothing more than for you to carry me away right now," she said, meaning the words. Since her path in life had been decided, she was eager to plunge headlong down it rather than linger at her brother's country estate like a young girl waiting for her comeout ball.

He grinned. "You tempt me sorely, but I dare not until we're properly wed. Come, let us find our way back inside before we're missed and you're left with a suitor sporting a broken nose."

"Very well." With a sigh, she allowed him to retrieve her hat before following him back to the main house. She could only pray that the weeks until their wedding would fly quickly by, for she didn't think she could wait a moment longer.

Bella stared at herself in the enormous gilt-framed mirror in her new bedchamber. She wore a nightdress that had been crafted just for the occasion. Her wedding night. Constructed of finest linen and handmade lace, the nightdress was thin to the point of being sheer. Long, white and diaphanous, its sole embellishment was an embroidered set of initials upon her breast that she'd sewn herself, a J and a B. Jesse and Bella. She hoped he would notice before he peeled the garment from her.

The days of proper courtship had slipped by like the scenery outside a train window, torpidly until they at last reached their destination. Thornton had determined the wedding ought to occur before the start of the Season, and Bella had concurred. She hadn't desired a massive affair. They were married in the chapel at Marleigh Manor, attended by Jesse's daughter, the disapproving dowager, and Thornton and Cleo. Immediately after their vows, they left for their new home and new beginning in London.

And now, here she was, Mrs. Jesse Whitney at last. A smile curved her lips as she stared at her reflection. Finally, she was Jesse's wife, and she had to admit that it was wonderful, more wonderful even than she'd supposed it would be. He was her husband. The gold band on her finger, along with the ruby she'd only just become accustomed to wearing, made her feel complete. She was married, and she couldn't be happier. To be sure, they faced some obstacles. Clara wouldn't be easy to win over. There would always be his war demons. But Bella felt certain that in time, the rest of their lives would fall into place.

Now all she needed was her groom. The door joining their chambers clicked open, and as if she'd conjured him, there he was. Jesse's eyes met hers, sending a jolt of awareness through her. A fierce possessiveness surged through her. He was hers.

At last.

He flashed her a wicked grin that brought his dimple out of hiding. Blessed angels' sakes, he was a handsome man. The mere sight of him, tall and lean, clad in only a masculine dressing gown, was enough to send a pulse of need straight to her core. She was at once eager and nervous for what was to come. She knew now the mechanics of it, the sweeping feelings lovemaking evoked. But she still felt very much a novice, uncertain of what she ought to do.

He surprised her by offering her an elegant drawing room bow as if they were courting in mixed company and not husband and wife, disrobed and alone. "Mrs. Whitney, you are astoundingly lovely."

"Thank you, sir," she said, taking up his game with equal formality. She dipped into a curtsy, which felt odd indeed without the proper encumbrance of her skirts and petticoat.

His gaze roamed hungrily down over her. "I surely hope your husband doesn't know I'm in your chamber."

She smiled, glad for the levity as it lessened her anxiousness. "If you're very nice, I shan't tell him."

"He's one hell of a lucky man, that husband of yours," he drawled, his accent sliding over her as if it were a caress. "And I have a feeling he won't want to share you."

She raised a brow, feigning innocence. "Not even with the Duke of Dullness?"

"Most definitely not with the damn Duke of Dullness or anyone else." He closed the distance between them, striding across the chamber to slide his arms around her waist and anchor her to him. "You're mine now, Bella."

"And you're mine," she returned, reaching up to run her

hand over his beloved jaw.

"May that be a blessing and not a burden to you." He kissed her palm. "I will do my damnedest to make you happy."

"You've already made me quite happy," she said quietly, meaning the words. They'd begun their betrothal on uncertain grounds, but she felt confident that they could more than recover. Their love had already withstood loss, distance, and hurt.

"Happiness is a fleeting thing sometimes." His expression hardened, his tone growing serious. "I know."

His ghosts continued chasing him about, even now. Her heart ached for him. How she wished he would unburden himself to her completely, for she sensed he still withheld his deepest pain from her. He tucked it away in a box in his mind, but like old letters from someone loved and lost, it remained, a haunting reminder.

"It doesn't have to be fleeting," she pointed out, "if we but strive to make it last."

He caressed her cheek, his gaze hot upon hers. "Spoken like the romantic heart you are. I reckon I ought to be grateful for your sweet disposition, or else you would never have chased this jaded old hide of mine down."

"I'm certain I didn't precisely chase you, as if I were a hound and you a hare. I seem to recall you seeking me out in the gardens at Wilton House." Bella smiled, feeling a surge of love for him all over again. She traced a light path around his sensual mouth with the tip of her finger. "Perhaps you are jaded, but hardly old."

"Old enough," he countered. "Christ, I honestly never thought I'd be a married man."

She raised a brow. "Regrets already, Mr. Whitney?"

"Not a single one, Mrs. Whitney." He groaned, lowering his head to press his forehead against hers. "I wanted to go slowly this evening, but you make it difficult indeed."

The temptation proved too strong. She couldn't resist closing the distance between their mouths for a kiss. He angled his lips over hers, quickly taking control. Bella ceded to him, her arms going around his neck, opening beneath the onslaught of his claiming kiss. She'd quite forgotten how delicious it was to be in his arms. His hands slid down the curve of her back to cup her bottom, pressing her intimately to him until she could feel his hardness against her. An answering ache pulsed between her thighs. She wanted him with a ferocity that almost frightened her. Nothing in her life had ever been so real and consuming, and she knew instinctively that now that they were joined forever, nothing ever would match the way he made her feel.

He tore his lips from hers to kiss down her neck, his hot breath and mouth sending another stab of desire directly to her core. She moaned, tipping her head back to allow him better access. He kissed and sucked his way down to the hollow of her neck before gently scraping the stubble of his whiskers back over the sensitive skin. Bella moaned, clutching at his shoulders and writhing against him. His mouth upon her was sweet, sweet torture. She never wanted it to end.

One of his hands came between them to cup her breast. He pulled away to gaze down at her body, his blue eyes utterly searing as they homed in on their initials. His fingers lingered over the letters she'd stitched, tracing them. "Did you do this for me, sweetheart?" he asked, his voice gruff with emotion.

"Yes," she managed to say past her madly beating heart. "I've never been terribly adept at needlework, but I thought perhaps you'd like it."

"I love it." He rubbed over her responsive nipple, working it into a hard peak. "I'm honored to be your husband."

She gasped as he caught her nipple between his thumb and forefinger, giving it a delightful pinch. "I'm honored to be your wife," she returned, her breath nearly a pant now. He was working her into a fine frenzy indeed.

"But as lovely as your nightdress is, I want you naked,

darling."

His pronouncement made another stab of desire pierce through her. He was looking at her as if he could consume her with his stare alone. Though she hadn't thought it possible, the passion between them was even more heightened, more powerful than it had been before. Her entire body felt as if it were aflame. She was hungry for more, for the ultimate consummation she knew was to come, and yet she never wanted the night to give way to morning. Bella took the skirt of her slip in her hands and began to drag it up over her body until he stopped her, his hands catching hers.

"Allow me," he said, turning her so that he was presented with her back and the small row of shell buttons there. Ever so gently, he pushed the heavy curls of her hair aside, allowing them to trail down over her shoulder. He kissed the nape of her neck.

She shuddered, closing her eyes as she gave in to his slow seduction. Her buttons began slipping from their moorings. He kissed her throat, the shell of her ear, then lower, creating a trail of heat over the skin he revealed.

"Tonight, I'm going to worship you, Bella," he said lowly, his tongue flicking out to taste the smooth plane between her shoulders.

She sighed, an answering blossom of warmth spreading in her belly and lower, to the apex of her thighs. The anticipation he was building within her rivaled the heady pleasure of each touch, kiss and lick. His idea of worship was wicked and wonderful, and she loved every moment of it.

Her nightdress continued gaping, cool evening air caressing her back as her husband's mouth worked a delicious path in its wake. "Jesse," she protested, his name almost a whisper. "You're making me mad with this torment."

"Torment?" He opened another button, pressing a moist kiss to her lower back. "Whatever do you mean?"

He was being coy, the rotten man, enjoying the crescendo he was working her into. How unfair for him to be the only one doling out his breathtaking brand of lovemaking. With a surge of confidence, she spun about. He was crouched, a sinful smile on his lips, utterly still as he awaited her move in their chess game. She couldn't help but to run her fingers through his hair, loving its silken strands. She had never loved him more than she did in that moment, he on his knees before her. Her very own husband.

Bella shrugged, allowing her nightdress to fall down to her waist. She took her hands from his hair to remove her arms from the capped sleeves. Jesse sucked in a breath, his glittering gaze upon her naked breasts. Her nipples tightened under his scrutiny. She knew a feeling of womanly power she'd never before experienced. It was time for him to be at her mercy. With a smile, she tugged the garment down over her hips until it fell to the floor.

"Do I meet with your approval?" she asked innocently.

"Christ yes," he said on a groan, rising to his feet and surging toward her.

She stopped him with a staying hand on his chest. "No you don't. It's my turn now." Her fingers went to the knot in his dressing gown, giving it a hearty tug until it came undone. She slid her palms up over his bare chest, loving the heat and strength of him, until she reached his shoulders. He was magnificent, her warrior come to conquer her. From the looks of him, he was barely reining himself in. Licking her lips, she trailed her right hand down over his sculpted chest and taut abdomen to where his cock proudly jutted. She took him in her hand.

His breath escaped from his lungs. "Bella, damn you, if you keep this up, I won't last longer than five minutes."

Bella was well pleased by the effect she had upon him. "I don't understand," she murmured, feigning artlessness. "What do you mean, Jesse?" She squeezed and began a rhythm upon his thick shaft that mimicked their lovemaking.

He gritted his teeth. "If you want me to come inside your hand rather than inside you, you're doing a brilliant job of it."

"Not in my hand." She hadn't realized she possessed such a depraved side, but she did. For there was nothing that was going to stop her from making him as wild as he did her this night. "But perhaps in my mouth."

With that, she dropped to her knees and took his cock deep into her mouth. She didn't know what she was doing, merely that he had done as much for her and given her immense pleasure. Now she wished to do the same for him. She heard him moan and felt his hands sink into her hair, resting lightly on her head. Acting on impulse, she sucked and was rewarded with another groan. Her entire body came alive to his cues, listening for his increased breath, his groans, feeling the way his hips thrust into her. She used her mouth the same as she had her hand, moving up and down the length of his increasingly rigid manhood.

"Enough," he bit out, gripping her arms and raising her to her feet once more. His expression was slack with passion, his eyes glazed. "Where the hell did you learn that?"

"From you," she admitted, feeling slightly shy. She hoped she hadn't mistaken his body's response to what she'd done, for she had certainly enjoyed every moment of it. "I wanted to worship you as well."

"I'm the most fortunate man on this earth," he breathed, pulling her against him. "I truly don't deserve you."

"Nonsense," she denied. "We are neither of us without our flaws, but together we become better than we ever could be apart."

He kissed her then, melding their mouths in a powerful kiss that gave as much as it claimed. She matched his ardor, opening her mouth, her tongue mating with his. Her hands went to his shoulders and pushed the dressing gown off him until he was as fully nude as she. It landed at their feet along with her discarded nightdress. Jesse startled her by catching her up in his arms, their kiss still somehow continuing. She threw her arms around his neck for purchase, running her tongue along his as their kiss went on. She wanted him so desperately now she almost couldn't bear it.

He laid her upon the bed with great care before joining her. Jesse lowered his body over hers, kissing her again and then turning his attention to her throbbing breasts. He bent down to suck a nipple into his hot mouth, alternating between sucks and light abrasion with his teeth. Bella arched into him as his fingers slipped between their bodies. He rubbed her tender button, working it quickly and with just enough pressure to have her pumping into him, a moan escaping her lips.

"Do you like this, sweetheart?" he asked, glancing up at her. He pushed a finger inside her, probing her readiness.

"Ah," was all she could manage.

"I'm afraid that's not a response." He took her other nipple in his mouth, laving it with his tongue, tugging with his teeth.

"Mmm," she said next, nearly delirious with pleasure.

He sank another finger into her already wet and pulsing passage. The sight of him pleasuring her body was enough to make her come undone. As he worked the nub of her sex with his thumb, she shattered. Her desire reached body-racking limits before breaking over her like the waves on the beach during a bitter storm.

"I reckon you do like this, if your reaction is anything to judge by," he murmured, his voice a sinful, velvety drawl.

And then he replaced his fingers with his cock, thrusting into her. There was no pain this time, only the wonderfully new sensation of a different sort of pleasure entirely. She wrapped her limbs around his waist, bucking up against him in an effort to feel him deeper inside her body. He groaned and claimed her lips with another mind-hazing kiss. He pumped deeply and quickly into her, his pace just fast enough to make her body feel as if it were about to melt and just slow enough to bring her near to the point of climax without pushing her over the edge.

"Please," she whispered, moving in time with him.

"Please what, my love?" He rested his forehead against hers as he thrust into her again and again.

She moaned, completely overwhelmed by the intensity of their passion. "I don't know," she moaned. In truth, her overwhelmed mind was no longer capable of ordinary thinking. Waves of pleasure ricocheted through her, from her breasts as they grazed his chest, to her core as he claimed her in the most primal way a man could. She was mindless, intoxicated by desire. There was nothing but Jesse, over her, inside her, his scent in her nostrils, his taste on her lips, his muscled shoulders beneath her questing fingertips.

She still couldn't believe he was hers. She couldn't believe they were finally making love as husband and wife, or that her body was capable of such awe-inspiring sensations. Blessed angels' sakes, she didn't think she'd ever be able to move or speak again.

"I'm going to fill you with my seed," he told her. "Do you want that, Bella?"

An answering surge of yearning went through her. "Yes." She wanted nothing more than for him to find his fulfillment as she had done. The mere thought had her tightening on his thrusting shaft until she too climaxed again, welcoming the molten spurt of his seed into her body.

He rocked into her, his head back, eyes closed in pleasure until the aftermath of their lovemaking finally left him and he rolled to his side, taking her with him. Feeling as if she were trapped inside a dream, she pressed her head against his beloved chest, listening to the rapid thrumming of his heart.

How she loved him. Dear God, how she loved this man.

An indeterminate amount of time trickled by, neither one of them able to speak after the life-changing experience of their first union as husband and wife.

"Jesse," she murmured into the peaceful quiet of their contented breathing.

He kissed her head. "Yes, sweetheart?"

She thought of how he'd left her in the middle of the night at Wilton House. "Stay with me? Please? I know it's silly, but I don't want to be alone."

He was silent, stroking her hair. "Of course," he said. "Sleep well, Bella."

"I love you," she said on a pleased sigh. She nestled into his comforting warmth and drifted off into an easy slumber.

Jesse waited until his wife's breathing was even and steady enough to indicate she'd fallen asleep. While their joining had been wondrous, the cold truth of reality was once more prodding him like a carbine pressed straight to his head. He'd wanted to tell her about the alarming frequency of his nightmares. After all, she already knew he suffered some old war devils, having witnessed them at Wilton House. But they had changed. The night he'd awoke to holes punched in his bedchamber walls rose strong in his mind, an ugly reminder. He couldn't bear to unwittingly do Bella bodily harm. He'd sworn to protect her for the rest of her life, and he'd meant those vows.

He wouldn't be sleeping in her chamber, not this night or any other. Nor would he be sleeping in the adjoining chamber as he'd done before their marriage. He'd had a chamber arranged down the hall for his use. It was the only way to protect her. He would be too far away to stumble back to her in the grips of his madness, and too far away, he hoped, for her to hear him crying out.

Gradually, he eased away from her embrace and stood from the bed. In the shadows, he could faintly detect the lines of her beautiful form. She slept on her side, hair spun over the pillow like finest silk. Yes, he'd wanted to confide in her when he'd first entered her chamber. But then, he'd seen her looking so innocent and trusting, gazing upon him with such unadulterated love in her eyes, and he'd turned complete coward. He didn't want to see pity in her eyes.

He'd been afraid she would insist on putting herself in danger anyway, or that, even worse, she would look upon him with fear. He didn't want his own wife to be afraid of him. He strode across the chamber, snatching up his dressing gown from the floor and stabbing his arms into the sleeves. Damn his nighttime demons to hell. Why, after all these years, did the war have to choose now to return from its grave, trying to pull him back into its fiery depths?

He tied the belt at his waist with more force than was necessary. Maybe it had been seeing Lavinia, or the shock of learning he had a daughter. Perhaps it had been caused by his return to Virginia, a land steeped in memories as visceral as they were vicious. He didn't know. But what he did know was that he'd do anything to keep Bella safe from him. With one last look back at his sleeping wife, he quietly took his leave of the room.

# Chapter Sixteen

ELLA WOKE SOME TIME AFTER SHE'D FIRST fallen asleep, staring into the unfamiliar darkness of her new chamber. For a few breaths, she thought she was in her old bed at Marleigh Manor until she recalled the whirlwind of the day. She was Jesse's wife, in name as well as deed. Bella smiled and stretched, reaching for her husband.

And felt only bed linen instead.

She was once again alone. Jesse had left her to return to his own chamber, despite her having asked him to stay. Her smile dissipated instantly into a frown. She fumbled about in the murk to light a gas lamp. It sputtered to life, bathing her chamber in a soft glow. There was no Jesse to be found. Even his dressing gown was gone. The sole evidence of their lovemaking was her nightdress, still lying crumpled and alone upon the carpet. Indeed, looking upon the room now, she'd swear Jesse had never even been there with her.

Worry gnawed at her. Why would he have left? Was something amiss? She threw back the bedclothes and rose from the bed, seeking out her robe. A growing alarm settled like a rock in her stomach. With shaking hands, she donned it and crept toward the door joining their chambers. She almost felt as if she were intruding, which was silly because Jesse was her husband.

It was silly, wasn't it?

She hesitated, her hand on the knob, uncertain of how to proceed. She'd only been a wife for one day, after all, and the recommendations she'd received from the dowager for conducting herself in her marriage had been wholly unhelpful. Her mother had yet to accept Jesse as her son-in-law, and Bella wasn't certain if she ever would. But that didn't affect her current predicament.

Concern won out, and she opened the door, crossing the threshold. Jesse's chamber too was shrouded in darkness. She peered inside, having difficulty seeing. She hovered at the perimeter of the room, listening for his breathing in the silence. She heard nothing.

"Jesse?" she called, quietly at first, and then with greater insistence. "Jesse?"

No answer. Her fears mounting, she crossed the chamber, taking care to avoid furniture as best she could. It was almost as if Jesse wasn't there. Surely he wasn't that sound a sleeper?

"Jesse?" Her hands fluttered about in the darkness until they met at last with a lamp. She lit it, effectively dispersing the inkiness of the night.

The reason for his lack of response was at last revealed before her. His bed was empty, carefully dressed and tucked with nary a wrinkle upon it. To her, it seemed as if he'd never even been inside the large high tester at all. He had disappeared yet again, leaving her no inkling as to where he'd gone. Her heart weighed down as heavily as ever, she doused the lamp and returned to her chamber, at a complete loss. She had no recourse to find him, save waking the servants and causing a great deal of gossip belowstairs.

She'd simply have to wait until the morning for her answer, if indeed there was one. For a long time, she lay in the quiet emptiness of her bed, smelling Jesse on her sheets, praying he hadn't left her forever this time. The tears, when they came, slid down her cheeks. The violent sobs claimed her just as surely as her husband's possessive lovemaking had done.

The next morning, Bella's heart was galloping faster than a racehorse when she entered the breakfast room. She hadn't dared to confide in even Smith about Jesse's disappearance the night before. Her maid had simply chatted happily away and styled her in a jaunty silk morning gown of striped ivory and navy. Bella hadn't even paid any attention to her *toilette*, she'd been so preoccupied with wondering whether or not her husband would be waiting for her at the breakfast table.

But now, her fears were answered as she crossed over the threshold of the small yet brightly lit room to discover Jesse was already seated with a filled plate before him. He was perusing a newspaper as if he hadn't a care. The breath she hadn't realized she'd been holding slowly released. He was still here. Thank the blessed angels.

He looked up and stood at her entrance. "Mrs. Whitney, you're looking exquisite as ever this morning. I trust you slept well?"

In truth, she was quite fatigued, so tired her eyes hurt. Of course, perhaps the crying she'd done had contributed to that. Heavens, she hoped her eyes weren't puffed. She wanted to tell him that she hadn't slept at all. She wanted to demand to know where he'd gone. She'd heard of husbands keeping mistresses. It was a common enough practice in the Marlborough House set. But she hadn't believed Jesse would ever be such a man. Theirs had been a love match. Hadn't it?

She faltered on her way to the table as her emotions clamored to be released, but she was ever aware of the presence of the butler presiding over the sideboard. A footman seated her and she kept her silence, afraid she would say something utterly foolish and opting instead not to say anything at all.

"Lady Bella?" Jesse persisted, his tone marked with unease. "Is something amiss?"

She met his gaze across the table. "I'm not certain."

His brows snapped together in a frown. "I see." He turned to the servants attending them. "Jackson, would you be kind enough to allow me a moment of privacy with Mrs. Whitney?"

The butler bowed. "Of course, sir."

Bella watched the servants leave them in respectful haste before turning back to her husband. "You must simply dismiss them, Jesse, not offer explanation." She wasn't certain why she was chiding him now, except that it was a childish way of lashing out when he'd hurt her the night before.

He stared at her, his expression indecipherable. "I will endeavor to take that into account. I wouldn't wish to offend your English sensibilities."

Her words had hit their mark, but she felt no satisfaction. "It is simply that you must never become too familiar with them." Of course, she considered Smith a confidante, but that was neither here nor there. She was punishing Jesse the only way she could. Every bit of her was desperate to know where he'd gone, why he'd left her.

"Thank you, Bella." His tone was polite, but she detected an undercurrent of impatience. "Shall I make a plate for you?" He rose and strode to the sideboard without waiting for her response.

"Yes," she said quietly, still hopelessly confused.

He brought a plate laden with eggs and sausages to her. As he placed it upon the table, he leaned into her and kissed her neck. "This is how I prefer to wish my wife a good morning," he said lowly.

She couldn't repress the shiver of desire his kiss and nearness sent through her. Bella turned to him, trying to steel herself against the sight of his handsome face and tempting lips so close to her. "I woke last night, and you were gone," she began hesitantly, "when I had asked you to stay."

"Ah, is that what's distressing you, sweetheart?" He smiled, his dimple appearing. "I wondered what had you looking so cross."

"It is merely that I asked you to stay," she said again, feeling a bit foolish in the face of his charm.

"I'm sorry." He dropped a kiss on her nose. "I simply returned to my chamber. I didn't want to disturb you if I had a nightmare."

"You returned to your chamber?" She searched his gaze for any sign of dishonesty. "When?"

"Just as soon as you were fast sleep." He winked. "Don't worry. I won't tell a soul that you snore."

He was lying. The heavy stone of dread was back in Bella's stomach. She opened her mouth, about to ask him where he'd truly been, why he was prevaricating, but she was afraid she wouldn't want to hear the answer. Her grip on happiness was yet so new, so tentative. She trusted him with her heart. He wouldn't betray her, not the man she'd come to know and love. Perhaps he had simply gone to his study for a drink, she reasoned, before returning to his chamber. He'd told her at Wilton House that he sometimes suffered from nightmares. It all made sense.

She relaxed, the tension in her body easing. "I don't snore," she protested, at last realizing what he'd said.

Jesse just grinned before kissing her. It didn't take long for the kiss to deepen, their mouths opening. The desire he'd brought raging to life the previous night sluiced back over her like hot bath water. She rested her hands on his shoulders, angling her head to allow him better access.

He groaned, breaking the seal of their mouths. "You're every bit as tempting in the morning as you are in the evening. If I don't get my arse back over into that chair, I'll be taking you right here on the breakfast table."

"Good heavens," she murmured, catching her lower lip

between her teeth. In truth, she wouldn't mind if he did. But she supposed that would be rather depraved of them indeed. "You'd better return to your chair, in that case. What if Clara happens upon us?"

"Ah, I fear you're right." He pressed a chaste kiss to her cheek before straightening. "It's a damn good thing I have you to keep me in order from this point forward."

"It is indeed," she agreed, deciding the matter of his disappearance was firmly resolved. Surely it was simply a misunderstanding. She loved her husband, and that was all that mattered. Yet there remained a lingering speck of doubt in her mind, unwilling to be entirely banished.

Bella closed her volume of *The Eustace Diamonds* with a snap and a sigh. At long last she'd finished reading the novel that had been her constant companion over the last few months of upheaval and change. How she dearly loved a good book, and now that her life had finally calmed down, she could once more set her mind to the pleasant pursuit of great literature.

She'd settled into a comfortable, if somewhat unfulfilling role as Jesse's wife. She had been raised to manage a large household, but she found she was scarcely needed at her new home in Belgravia. The housekeeper Jesse had hired, Mrs. Beeton, was well-versed in the art of directing the servants and keeping the house running smoothly. Monsieur Billard was a talented chef from the Continent, capable of wooing their palates each evening with wonderful sauces and roasts. Everything was perfect. Or so it seemed.

The worldly trappings of her life hid the loneliness that had begun plaguing her with increasing insistence in the time since she'd become Mrs. Jesse Whitney. Jesse had found a sure footing in London. He was consumed by devoting himself to his business, so much so that she often didn't see him until the evenings over dinner. She hardly even knew what he was about during the days, but she supposed it wasn't her right to ask if he didn't deign to offer up the information on his own. Each night, he visited her chamber and made love to her, bringing her incredible pleasure, before slipping away to his chamber.

She'd discovered a new loathing for being left alone, and she couldn't shake the fear that beneath his charming smile and knowing hands there lay a deeply wounded man. He was keeping something from her. She could sense it the same way she could smell rain on the air. But just what that was, she feared she'd never know.

The door to the library opened, disrupting her morose turn of thoughts. She took off her spectacles, startled to find Clara entering the room. Though she wore her customary drab black dress, her expression was less guarded than was ordinary. Bella noted that her stepdaughter had finally chosen to heed her advice, eschewing the severe hairstyle she'd been wearing for a loose, more feminine coiffure. Her hair had been curled at her forehead, and the bulk of her long locks were tied at her nape, sweeping down her back in another series of corkscrews. Perhaps it was a sign of progress, small though the concession was.

"Clara," she greeted. "What brings you to this moldy old corner of the house?"

The girl faltered. "Have I interrupted your day, my lady?"

"Don't be a featherhead," she said with a dismissive wave of her hand. "Do come in and sit down. I'm in need of company. I'm merely surprised to find you in the library, is all. I thought you said you hated books."

Clara's cheeks went pink. Though she crossed the room as Bella had directed, she remained standing, her hands clasped behind her back as if she were a penitent awaiting punishment. "Perhaps hate was a strong word."

Her accent was much more pronounced than Jesse's but just as lovely to the ears. They'd been spending quite a bit of time together during Jesse's absences, and unless she was mistaken, Clara was slowly warming to her. "Your hair looks very handsome, my dear."

"Thank you, ma'am."

"You're welcome." She considered the girl, thinking that she was softening toward her as well. Although their initial meeting had been frosty, the cold between them had gradually begun to thaw. "Won't you sit? You're giving my neck a beastly cramp."

"I don't wish to impose," she said hesitantly, swaying slightly as if tempted to sit but not sure if she ought.

Bella suppressed a smile. "Clara, sit down. You're not imposing in the least."

Clara at last did as she was instructed, seating herself primly. She possessed polished manners, which was most fortunate. "It's merely that I wanted to tell you I've reconsidered your offer."

"Ah." Though she was pleased, she didn't dare show it. Clara was still naturally stubborn, after all, and there was no need to tempt her. "I suppose you're speaking of my suggestion that we outfit you in a new wardrobe and you take finishing lessons?"

Her stepdaughter's golden brows snapped into a ferocious frown. "With respect, my lady, I don't feel that I need finishing lessons."

She well understood Clara's sentiments, as she hadn't wanted them herself. But to blend and mingle in society, particularly for a young girl who had been raised in an entirely different manner, Bella deemed it an absolute necessity. "I sympathize with you, but you truly must. Pray recall that your circumstances are now vastly altered. You have my promise that I shan't find anyone as horrid as my mother did for me when I was your age. Indeed, you'd shudder to think of the governesses I suffered before finishing school."

Her candor won a reluctant smile from Clara. "It isn't as if I were raised in the wild. Richmond is a wonderful city, and I long to return one day. I don't think England is for me."

"Nevertheless, you are the responsibility of your father and me until you're wed." Heavens, she was beginning to feel decidedly motherly toward the girl. When had that happened? "England isn't all bad, is it?"

Clara primly adjusted her skirts. "I shall always love Virginia."

Bella couldn't blame her. "No one ever said that you cannot, my dear," she reassured her.

Before Clara could respond, a rap at the library door stole their attention. Jackson, their butler, was looking customarily formidable. Bella had already discovered the man was formal almost to a fault and nearly incapable of offering a smile. She was equally determined to make him crack. Perhaps it was the child in her that had never quite become a woman entirely grown. But she was enjoying the freedom running her own household afforded her. Escaping the dowager's wingspan had been a boon in more ways than she'd envisioned.

"Lady Stokey," intoned Jackson, stepping aside to reveal their unexpected guest.

Tia, Lady Stokey, breezed into the room like a beautiful little butterfly. She was dressed to utter perfection in a vibrant shade of purple silk only she would have the courage to wear. Her skirts were gathered in an elaborate waterfall of lace and bows. Bella hadn't seen her new, albeit unlikely, friend since her time at Marleigh Manor, and she was pleased to see her again now.

Lady Stokey wrinkled her nose in a fashion that was somehow still patently ladylike. "Dear me, whatever can you be doing in the library of all places? I daresay it smells of must and old boots in here."

Her words earned a chortle out of Clara. Bella cast a halfheartedly censorious stare in her stepdaughter's direction before offering their guest a welcoming smile. "Lady Stokey, how lovely to see you again. I'm afraid you've caught us in the one room of the house I love best."

"Gads." Lady Stokey seated herself on a *Louis Quinze* chaise with dainty care. "Libraries are dreadfully boring. I can't think why you'd harbor such a *tendre* for them."

"Books aren't boring," Bella countered, unabashed. She knew she wasn't conventional by any means. Ladies were meant to paint watercolors and embroider the family linen. But she'd never done what was expected of her, and her marriage to Jesse had amply proven that.

Lady Stokey winked. "I suppose it depends what books you're reading, Lady Bella."

"I prefer Trollope myself." Bella cast a glance toward the rapt audience they had in Clara. Lady Stokey was a trifle too fast for a girl of Clara's years, but she couldn't help but to like the woman. She had a charm that was as naughty as it was irresistible, as though she were privy to a secret joke that everyone else ought to know as well. Bella cleared her throat and then immediately hoped she wasn't turning into her mother. Oh dear. At least she'd always have a far better understanding of the English language than that august lady.

"I haven't an inkling who the fellow is, nor do I care." Lady Stokey laughed. "I suppose you'll think me dreadfully small-minded, but I've never been a reader. I dearly love dresses, however, which is why I've interrupted your little library *soiree*."

Bella was curious. While she hadn't invited Lady Stokey, as Cleo's sister and an acquaintance, she was always welcome to call. "Indeed?"

"My dear sister has told me you've written with the plight of our wonderful Miss Jones." Lady Stokey turned her attention to Jesse's daughter. "I understand that you're in need of schooling in our barbaric English customs, and that you'll shortly be in need of a new wardrobe when your time of mourning is over. Lady Thornton has deemed me a worthy ally in your quest. What do you think, Lady Bella?" She turned her attention back to Bella as she asked the last question.

She thought that Lady Stokey would make an excellent guide to Clara, as long as she didn't encourage her natural inclination toward being a minx. But she didn't dare say as much in front of her charge. Instead, she nodded. "I think that would be more than generous of you, and a great help to Clara. We were just now speaking of her future plans, so it's quite fortuitous that you have come to us."

"Indeed? I can't say I've often been blessed with good timing. It's what rendered me a widow, you see. Although, having known Lord Stokey, I must say that perhaps it was good timing I possessed after all." Lady Stokey beamed, clearly in a role that suited her. "This is going to be quite fun. My life has been deadly dull for the last little while, and I'm in desperate need of enlivening company."

Bella couldn't resist a grin. "Our dear Clara can more than amply provide you with that."

Her stepdaughter's eyes widened with what appeared to be surprise. "I hope I haven't caused you a great deal of trouble, my lady," Clara offered, sounding sincere. "I know I have not always treated you with kindness."

It wasn't an apology, but Bella wasn't certain she'd ever get one from her. They were, after all, two women who'd been thrown together by the oddest whims of fate. Bella never would have imagined she'd one day have a stepdaughter from Virginia, just as she suspected Clara had never thought she'd leave the land of her girlhood. But time could heal all wounds. Well, nearly all wounds, she rethought grimly. It seemed that Jesse's wounds would never completely mend.

"Of course you haven't," she returned, opting for honesty. "But in fairness, you've experienced no ends of upheaval, and I shan't blame you."

Lady Stokey clapped her hands. "Enough with the maudlin sentiments. We've a wardrobe and a comeout to plan. I do hope Mr. Whitney's pockets are deep."

And with that, the three ladies set about planning Clara's unexpected future.

A few days later, Bella was once again left to her own devices for the afternoon. Clara was busy with finishing lessons and Jesse was away on business. He'd left her with a kiss and a smile that morning, setting off to inspect some buildings he said he intended to purchase. Real estate was how he'd made his fortune, and Bella respected his determination. He was a quintessential American self-made man, and although the old society matrons still frowned upon such an unthinkable role, she was proud of him.

But she still missed her husband. She'd seen more of him during their time at the house party than she did now that they lived in the same edifice. With a heavy sigh, she turned her attention back to the volume of poetry she'd been attempting to read. As happy as she was, as much as she loved her husband, there remained a niggling feeling within her that something was wrong. He was not giving his entire self to her, and his withholding was beginning to wear upon her.

Jackson appeared in the door then, giving her a start. Blessed angels' sakes, the man had a way of creeping about stealthily. She almost never heard his footfalls. His face was dour as ever.

"The Duke of Devonshire requests to pay a call to you, my lady."

Devonshire? Bella couldn't have been more surprised if the butler had announced Saint Peter was in the front hall. After she had politely declined his suit, she'd never received another letter from him. She snatched her spectacles from her nose and dropped them into the open page of her book.

"Do show him in, Jackson," she instructed.

The butler bowed, returning forthwith to present the duke. Devonshire smiled when he saw her. He was dressed in gray and looked quite dapper sporting a new goatee. She offered him a matching smile, genuinely happy to see him.

Although she'd never harbored romantic feelings for him, he had become something of a friend. She'd missed his letters.

"Your Grace," she greeted when Jackson had once more discreetly disappeared. "What brings you here to my humble little piece of London?"

He bowed and crossed the room to take her offered hand and bring it to his lips for a quick buss. "Your piece of London is hardly humble, as you must know, nor is it little. I expect your husband is putting his American millions to good use here. As for why I've come, surely you must know, my lady."

She studied him, perplexed. "Must I?"

"Yes." He seated himself on a divan. "It is you, of course."

Good heavens. He didn't mean to continue pursuing her, did he? Why, she was a married woman now. "Me?" she nearly squeaked.

He raised a brow. "You needn't look so concerned, my dear. I come as a friend, nothing more."

"Of course," she said, feeling foolish. "I didn't mean to suggest otherwise."

"I merely wished to offer my felicitations on your nuptials."

"Thank you." Belatedly, she recalled her role as hostess. "Would you care for some tea?"

"I can't abide the stuff myself," he said easily. "I suppose it's against the grain, but there you have it."

"Something stronger? Spirits, perhaps?"

"None for me, thank you. I never partake before dinner." His smile faded at last. "It's been some time since I've seen you, and I must say the time has done well by you." He paused, seeming to choose his next words with delicacy. "When last we met, you confided in me that your heart already belonged to another. I trust Mr. Whitney is the man to whom you'd already given your heart?"

"He is," she confirmed, feeling awkward at discussing

the man she loved with the man who had once desired to marry her. She wondered again why he had come. He'd said she was the reason, but she could not offer him anything in that regard. "I hope you know how very much I enjoyed your friendship, Your Grace. I was honored that you wanted me as your wife."

"Honored." His tone was wry. "That's never the sort of thing a man wants to hear, even if it's too late for him to press his suit either way."

"I'm sorry." She meant the words. The duke was a very different man than she'd initially supposed, and he would make a fine husband to a woman one day.

"You needn't be, my dear. Fortune has a way of spinning her wheel in the direction things are meant to be." He paused. "Are you happy now, Lady Bella?"

Not entirely. In truth, she was quite conflicted. She loved Jesse. She knew he loved her. But yet for all that they were husband and wife, somehow they still remained two halves instead of one whole. The underlying suspicion that he was keeping something from her simply wouldn't be dashed away.

"You haven't answered my question," the duke persisted. "Are you happy?"

"Yes." She hesitated. "I am quite happy. Of course I am."

"Then I must be content." His tone held a tinge of sadness. "I wish you nothing but the best, Lady Bella."

She felt for him. He was a kind man and a gentle soul. "And I wish the same for you, Your Grace."

"I appreciate your generosity, my lady." He inclined his head. "I wonder if we may continue our correspondence. I find I miss your lively banter and keen insight. Your knowledge of Trollope is unsurpassed."

Bella pondered his request. While she hated to sever the ties of their friendship, it would undoubtedly be best. She didn't wish for him to think she was the sort of lady who would indulge in love outside the marital bed. "I'm not sure that would be very wise," she said finally.

"I understand. Pray, forgive me for even asking. It is merely that I found a kindred soul in you, and it is such a rare thing in these times of ours that I hated to think of losing it." He stood, looking awkward. "I'll take my leave of you. I apologize for the intrusion."

"Yours was not an intrusion, truly," she hastened to assure him as she too stood. "You've been a good friend to me, Your Grace. For that, I will always be most grateful."

He closed the distance between them and took her hands in his, his intense gaze meeting hers. "If ever your circumstance should alter, I am, as ever, yours. I admire you very much, Lady Bella. While I still think we could have made a brilliant match, I am willing to concede defeat. I pray your husband knows what a fortunate man he is."

His kind words touched her. Acting on impulse, she gave him a quick embrace. "Thank you, Your Grace. You must know that I admire you also, and shall always remember you fondly."

He returned her embrace for a moment before breaking away to drop a chaste kiss upon her forehead. "Just as I shall always remember you, my dear. I wish you happy."

"Duke, to what do we owe the honor of your visit?"

With a start, Bella stepped away from the duke to see her husband stalking into the drawing room. The expression upon his handsome face was hard indeed. He didn't appear pleased to find Devonshire in his drawing room. Bella felt guilty even though she knew she had no reason to do so.

"Mr. Whitney," the duke greeted, sounding as shaken as Bella felt. "It's a pleasure to see you again. I merely called to pay my respects to Lady Bella."

Jesse's jaw was as rigid as his expression. "I'm sure Mrs. Whitney was pleased to see you again."

The emphasis he placed upon her new surname was not lost upon Bella. Her husband was marking her, reminding Devonshire that she now belonged to him and always would. And he notably refrained from saying he was pleased to see the duke again. The temperature in the drawing room had become decidedly frosty. Oh dear.

"Her ladyship has been a cherished friend and correspondent to me these last few months," the duke said, seemingly unruffled by Jesse's menacing stance. "I sought to offer my congratulations on your marriage. I'm glad to see her well settled."

"Yes, she's very well settled now," Jesse gritted.

The two men were eying one another like a pair of bears about to tear each other to pieces. Bella decided it was imperative for her to step into the fray lest it become a melee. She stepped between them with a bright smile pinned to her lips that she didn't quite feel. "His Grace was just leaving, but it was so lovely of him to drop by, wasn't it?"

She met her husband's gaze, sending him a clear message with her eyes. She saw the moment he relented but knew he still wasn't exactly delighted with her. Very likely, he'd witnessed her embrace with Devonshire, and although her feelings for the duke were purely platonic, the expression on Jesse's face said he wasn't convinced.

"Indeed, we appreciate the call, Your Grace," he offered finally, his tone dismissive.

Devonshire bowed. "Take good care of her, Whitney. If you don't, there will be repercussions."

"I don't take threats kindly, and I have no intention of doing anything other than taking good care of my wife, Devonshire," Jesse returned evenly, the leash on his anger looking shorter by the minute. "If I ever hurt her, I'll be the first to kick my own arse."

The duke bowed again, cutting a somber, lonely figure. "Good day, Mr. Whitney, Lady Bella."

With that, he took his leave of the drawing room. Bella was left to face her agitated husband alone. "I'm sorry, Jesse. I didn't know he would be calling on me."

His face remained impassive. "Forgive me if I don't like my wife's old suitors appearing uninvited in my drawing room."

"He's not an old suitor," she denied. "He was a friend, nothing more."

He raised a brow, looking every inch the arrogant nobleman he'd made himself. "A friend you were preparing to wed, Bella. A friend I just now saw you embracing."

So he had seen after all. Bella's face flushed. "It was not romantic in nature."

"Precisely what was it, then?"

She stared, the complex emotions that had blossomed to life within her suddenly crashing over her like a waterfall. He was scarcely even a presence in her life beyond the bedchamber and the breakfast table, and yet he dared to suspect her of wrongdoing? "Why do you even care?" she demanded, unbearably frustrated with him.

"Why do I care?" His voice was cold, laced with fury. "You're my wife, damn you, and I don't want to come home to the Duke of Dullness attempting to make love to you."

"He was doing no such thing." Bella's patience snapped. "How dare you accuse me when you're the one who is never at home?"

He frowned. "I'm at home every day."

"For how long?" The hurt she'd been attempting to keep tucked away at last surfaced. "A few hours in the evening? Sometimes I scarcely even get to see you at breakfast. I swear I saw more of you at Wilton House than I've done in all the weeks of our marriage."

"I cannot be forever stitched to your side, Bella," he countered, raking a hand through his hair. "Wilton House was a brief idyll away from the world, but I've businesses to run. I trust I didn't mislead you in that respect. This house and all its upkeep must be bought somehow, and I've no ancient English estate to rely upon."

He made her sound like a spoiled lady of privilege, something she'd taken great pride in believing she was not. "Of course I know that you must tend to your business. I well understand you have responsibilities, but you also have a responsibility to me and to Clara. I've grown terribly lonely."

His eyes darkened. "Is that why you had the duke come calling?"

She hadn't wanted to make a row of it with him, but it would appear as if she must. Feeling weary, Bella sighed. "I didn't invite the duke here. He came of his own volition. But I was glad for the company. Sometimes I feel as if I've married an utter stranger. I never imagined our married life would be governed by business and absences."

"What are you saying, Bella?" His expression was a hard mask appearing as if it were about to crack. His voice was as tight as a cinched corset. "I want to be perfectly clear."

She paused, taking great pains to carefully phrase the tumult of emotions swirling within her. She very much did not want to hurt him, but neither could she deny the restlessness and deep unhappiness that threatened to envelop her. "You're keeping something from me, Jesse. I know it."

"Where the hell is all this coming from?" he asked, crossing the carpet until he stood before her. "You seemed happy enough this morning. What did that bastard say to you?"

"This has nothing to do with the duke. I've been feeling this way for some time, but I've been trying to make the best of our situation," she admitted. "You've almost grown more distant since we wed. It's simply not right between us. Surely you know it as well as I do, Jesse. For some reason, you insist on keeping yourself apart from me."

"Like hell I do." He raked a hand through his already-disheveled hair yet again. "I'm trying to build you the life you deserve."

"You're so distant. I—" she faltered, searching for the proper words. "I've grown most discontented. I don't wish to feel that way any longer."

"Ah, and there's the crux of it." The smile he gave her held little warmth. "Perhaps now that the adventures of courtship are over, you've decided you're weary with real life. You want the excitement and romance of your books. You want your escape."

Did she want escape? Her heart kicked into a frantic pace at the mere thought. Did she truly want to live separate lives as many of the Marlborough House set? Of course not. She loved Jesse. She only wanted him to be open with her, to hold her through the night if she asked it of him, to turn back into the devoted lover he'd been. Although she had known marriage would be different than courtship, somehow the intimacy they'd shared during that time had dissipated. She wanted to regain what they'd lost.

He tipped up her chin, his touch firm, almost punishing. "Do you know what I think, my dear?"

She swallowed, barely able to shake her head. She was trapped in the stormy depths of his eyes. Never had she seen her husband this angered, his entire being nearly vibrating with fury. She knew a moment of fear, not of his physical strength but of what her words could do to them. Once spoken, they couldn't be taken back. She didn't want to damage their love. She couldn't bear to lose him.

"I think that for all you raged at me about our age difference, you are, in the end, just a spoiled girl. You wanted something you couldn't have, and now that you've gotten it, you don't want it," he accused, sounding bitter.

"That's not true," she denied, anger kicking back up within her. How dare he call her a spoiled girl? Before she could rethink the wisdom of what she was about to say, she plowed onward, seeking to harm him as he had wounded her. "Everything changed when you left me. Maybe you should not have come back. I begin to fear I would have been happier with the duke."

He released her, visibly recoiling from the shock of her words. "If that is how you feel, perhaps you should take him as a lover."

"Maybe I shall. It certainly seems as if you cannot stand the sight of me," she tossed back at him in anger. "You can't even remain in the same chamber as I for longer than an hour."

The moment the words left her lips, she wished she could recall them. Of course she didn't mean them, not one whit. But he had pushed her to the cliffs of her patience and then she'd fallen over the edge. How easy it could be to wound the people one loved the most. Love should have been easy, but instead it was proving the most difficult part of her life. Still, she knew it could also be the most rewarding.

"You'll do no such thing." He caught her elbows in his grasp and pulled her into his chest. "You're my wife, damn you."

"Then why are you so insistent upon pushing me away?" she demanded, nearing desperation.

"You're doing the pushing, Bella, not I."

She was determined to pursue her course now that the die was cast. "Where do you go when you leave my bed?"

He stilled, seemingly startled by her question. "To my chamber. I've already told you."

"That's a lie," she countered. "I've checked. You're never there."

"Sometimes I have a brandy and soda-water before bed," he said, but there was an air of dishonesty to his explanation.

Suddenly, it occurred to her that he'd been doing an excellent job of avoiding her since their marriage had begun. Why? Was he hiding something far more sinister than old secrets? She searched his face for some hint of the truth. Dear heavens, she couldn't bear it if everything she'd held true was actually a lie.

"Do you have a paramour?" she asked, afraid to ask but afraid not to.

"Jesus. Of course not, Bella. What do you take me for?"

"I'm sorry," she hastened to say, guilt lacing through her for even doubting him for a moment.

Suddenly, his gaze strayed to a point over her shoulder. Heart in her slippers, she turned to find Clara hovering on the threshold. Her face was pinched, and Bella knew she'd been listening to their row for far longer than she should've been. Blessed angels, the last thing she needed was her stepdaughter as an audience to her folly.

"Clara," she managed to say in a cheerful voice even if she couldn't quite shake the tremor in her voice. "Please do come in."

"I finished my lessons early," the girl murmured.

"How wonderful." Bella pasted a smile to her lips that she didn't feel. "You are just in time for tea. I believe your father will be joining us. Won't you, Jesse?"

He shook his head, looking lost, his expression tighter than ever. "I'm afraid I can't stay. I've business to attend to."

Business once more. She stiffened. "I see. Then it shall be only Clara and I for tea."

Again. The unspoken word lay heavy between them. Jesse caught her gaze, seemingly torn, before he bowed and left the room. She wished she hadn't accused him of having a mistress. She knew very well he was bound to her alone. But even so, their ship couldn't sail in two different directions, she thought grimly as she watched him go. There could only be one captain, one course. Something would have to give, and she certainly hoped it wouldn't be their hull.

Bella sipped her tea in Lady Stokey's drawing room. It was a rare respite from the tedium of her days spent overseeing finishing lessons for Clara and approving menus with Mrs. Beeton. She'd grown quite close to Tia, as she was more familiarly known to her intimate circle, and she was grateful for her friendship now more than ever. With her sister-in-law Cleo still in the countryside and no other close friends, Tia had become her sole confidante.

"Your stepdaughter is rather a spitfire," Tia said, taking

a dainty sip of her tea.

"I should have warned you." Bella smiled, replacing her cup in its saucer with a delicate rattle. "She can be a handful at times, but believe it or not, her demeanor has greatly improved since our first meeting."

"I shudder to think what she was like then," Tia quipped. "But I do like the girl. She reminds me of myself when I was her age." She paused, considering Bella. "You're looking rather Friday-faced today. Why?"

Bella bit her lip. She hadn't realized she was that obvious. More than a sennight had passed since her angry confrontation with Jesse in the drawing room, and he hadn't come to her in the evening. Not even once. If she'd felt a chasm between them before, there was now an entire river valley. Perhaps even a vast ocean. She knew she was partly to blame for it, but she wasn't willing to claim complete responsibility.

"I had a row with my husband." She took another sip of her tea. "He saw the Duke of Devonshire in the drawing room, and I'm afraid we had an awful exchange."

"The Duke of Dullness?" Tia wrinkled her nose in obvious distaste. "Why on earth should he be jealous of such a boring fellow? I don't suppose he was doing anything more wicked than regaling you with tales about the country and such drivel."

Bella couldn't help but laugh at her friend's dismissal of the duke. Apparently, Jesse wasn't the only one who had applied the sobriquet to Devonshire. "In his defense, he's an avid reader. He's a bit shy, but when you earn his confidence, he's a lovely man. We enjoyed discussing the novels we've read with one another."

"Drivel, just as I said." Tia sniffed. "It isn't as if he was undoing your bodice in the drawing room. Indeed, I daresay he wouldn't even know how to find the fastenings on a woman's bodice. What caused the row?"

Bella flushed at Tia's frank language. "The duke and I were saying goodbye, and I embraced him."

"Oh dear. I begin to see. I thought perhaps you were going to say Mr. Whitney had received the bills for Clara's dresses and that was the cause."

"Hardly that." Bella grimaced. "It was impulsive and foolish of me to embrace the duke, and it meant nothing."

"But not to your husband," Tia wisely guessed. "I think I understand. Men are horridly jealous creatures at heart. I hope you assured him nothing untoward had occurred?"

"Of course I did. But to make matters worse, Mr. Whitney has been very distant since our marriage. I see precious little of him, and I'm afraid I didn't react well to his anger. I accused him of being inattentive, and I'm sure I insulted him grievously."

"Never fear, my dear." Tia leaned forward to give her hand a comforting pat. "Marriage is fraught with misunderstandings and rows. I'm certain I fought nearly every day with Lord Stokey. In my defense, he was an utter blighter, of course. But in the end, all shall wash out for you. I'm certain of it."

Bella wished she shared her friend's confidence. "I've never had a row with him like this before."

"Pish." Tia waved a dismissive hand. "Yours is a love match, yes?"

"Yes," she said without hesitation. It was the only fact she knew for certain.

"Then you haven't a thing to worry about, my dear, as long as you never forget what drew you together in the first place. But pray don't tarry. Life can be over quite abruptly. If I had known Lord Stokey was about to meet his end, I would have had no shortage of things to say to him." She frowned, seemingly mired in a long-ago place deep within her thoughts. "I daresay not all of them would have been nice."

"I've done my best to speak plainly with my husband, but I'm afraid I'm a failure as a wife. I don't know what to say or do," she admitted, feeling rather small in that moment.

"No one does, my dear." Tia flashed her a supportive smile. "We all merely act as if we do."

Bella had never considered that, and it imbued a fragile sense of possibility in her. "But I'm sure he could have found a better wife than I."

"And I'm equally certain that he could not have, for you're obviously the perfect wife for him. I can clearly see the love you feel for him on your face whenever you mention his name." She tilted her head, considering Bella. "I envy you, Lady Bella. Love is dear but worth the price."

Bella knew her friend was right. Love was indeed worth the price. At least, that was what she'd always believed. She'd loved Jesse for years from afar, and now that he was hers, she couldn't afford to allow him to slip through her grasp.

"Do you think the price is ever too dear?" she asked, wondering despite herself.

"The price for a multitude of things is too dear, Bella." Tia returned her teacup to its saucer with a clatter. "But never love, for that is a rare animal indeed."

Bella stood at the threshold of the door joining her chamber to Jesse's. He hadn't come to her tonight, and he'd been polite but distant at dinner. She'd lain in bed for some time, holding her breath, hoping to hear his familiar footfalls approaching her bed. Instead, there had only been silence and the same aching loneliness that had been building within her for weeks.

It seemed that if she wanted their lives to return to normal, it would be up to her. Her friend's suggestion was vivid in her thoughts. She was determined to put an end to their stalemate. Mind made up, she turned the knob and pushed her way inside. She felt her way across the carpet until she reached the gas lamps. As the light flared to life, she discovered that, once more, his chamber was completely empty.

Her heart felt as if it had plummeted to her toes. Where had he gone again? His bed was neatly pressed, the coverlet undisturbed. She was beginning to think her husband was a ghost. Until she heard it, a low, keening cry from somewhere down the hall.

Worried, she secured her dressing gown at her waist, took up a candle, and stepped out into the hall, trying to determine the direction of the sound. The cry came again. She moved along the corridor in the darkness, following the unmistakable sound of someone hollering as if the hounds of hell were upon his heels. Unless she was wrong, the voice belonged to Jesse.

At last, she stopped outside the chamber where she thought the noises were emanating from. Thumps sounded from within, along with another cry. She didn't waste a moment in sweeping open the door. In the dim glow of the flickering candlelight, she could make out a form in the bed. Some books and other items littered the floor, presumably knocked from their perch atop a nearby washstand.

"Jesse, is that you?" She tentatively entered the room.

He cried out again, twisting in the bed. Fear skittered through her. What if he was ill? She rushed to his side, placing the candle on the washstand before giving him a shake. Hands gripped her arms with painful force, dragging her against the bed and nearly atop it. She saw Jesse's face then, illuminated in the light, his expression so twisted and rage-filled she almost didn't recognize him.

"Jesse?" she managed, understanding he was still half-asleep, trapped in whatever nightmare had been plaguing him. "Wake up. It's me, Bella."

"Bella?" He blinked, the lines of his face gradually softening, his gaze lucid once more. "Christ, what are you doing in here?"

"I heard someone in distress and followed the sounds to this chamber," she said, relieved when he eased his punishing hold on her.

"Have I hurt you?" He sat up, his gaze searching her face. "Please tell me I haven't hurt you."

"I'm perfectly fine," she murmured, rubbing her arms, still reeling with shock. "But what about you, Jesse? Blessed angels' sakes, I thought you were being murdered in your bed."

His expression was as grim as his voice. "So did I."

Bella frowned, searching his gaze as she tried to make sense of it all. She recalled his reaction to the mere mentioning of shooting at Lady Cosgrove's party. He had told her then that he suffered nightmares sometimes. But this, it seemed, was far worse than she had supposed. Dear God, he had looked like a marauding warrior prepared to do bloody battle. "Is this why you haven't been sleeping in your chamber? Is this why you've hidden yourself away in this far-off room all this time?"

He closed his eyes and passed a hand over his drawn face, appearing suddenly weak. "They've gotten worse again," he admitted finally, as if the truth had been torn from him.

Dear God. And she'd once thought he had a mistress. All this time, he'd been alone and in pain, hiding his agony from her so that she wouldn't see, wouldn't worry. He needed her, she realized. This was where he'd been all along, hiding in another chamber just out of earshot from her. Why hadn't he simply told her the truth? Sadness swept over her, that he had been suffering in silence, that he had to bear the burden of his demons alone. How had they come to be two rather than one as they ought to have been? Somehow, it had all gone terribly astray.

"Move to the side, if you please," she instructed him primly. She was keenly aware that he was perhaps nude beneath his bedclothes but she remained unwilling to allow him to endure alone in his torment. Their ugly argument and the hurt she'd been holding onto vanished. She was getting into bed with her husband for the first time in a week. She shucked her dressing gown, leaving the only

271

barrier between them her nightdress.

He watched her, his eyes burning into hers with the smoldering intensity she remembered. After apparently mulling over her request, he decided to do as she asked. The coverlet slipped down as he slid to the side, exposing his chest and a slice of his lean hip. She wanted to divert her gaze but found she could not. She was hungry for him, and there was no denying it.

Bella climbed into bed next to him beneath the bedclothes. His body radiated heat. She caught his scent and a wave of longing slammed over her before she could stop it. Tentatively, she placed her palm on the smooth and muscled plane of his shoulder. For the first time, she felt a round scar low on his back. Before she could even think twice, she traced a gentle path over the old injury.

He flinched and caught her wrist in a punishing grip. "Don't."

The strength of his grasp sent a twinge of pain shooting up her arm, but she ignored it. "You were wounded."

Jesse clenched his jaw, clearly fighting to regain his composure. "Yes," he hissed.

One-word responses. Perhaps she ought not to push him, but she couldn't help herself. She had known him as her brother's friend for years, had known him as her lover and now her husband, and yet he still kept so much of himself from her. She had never before seen a hint of his physical injuries, nor had he mentioned them to her. But the wound was obviously from the past, long-ago healed. On the outside, at least.

"What happened to you, Jesse?" she pressed, wanting to know. The night was heavy with the unspoken.

"I don't want to talk about the war," he ground out, his tone as hard as the intricately carved oak of the bed.

"I'm your wife," she pointed out needlessly. She wasn't going to allow him to fend her off as she suspected he'd been doing for the last few weeks. "Does it still pain you?"

He still held her wrist but with considerably less force

now. "At times," he allowed.

She pressed a kiss to his shoulder. Something about the way he seemed so alone and broken was making her stomach feel as upended as a tipped teacup. Her emotions were riding a runaway carriage. The impasse that had fallen between them with its resulting gulf of anger and disillusionment no longer seemed as strong as it had only yesterday.

"Are you going to tell me what happened?" she asked, tugging her wrist from him.

He stared, seemingly waging an inner war. "I was shot in the back," he said at last, "by one of my own men. Fortunately, the bullet missed its mark and only resulted in an ugly flesh wound."

"You never told me," she murmured, "not in all this time. I hadn't realized."

Jesse shrugged, still radiating a wildness that made her ill at ease. "You can't go to hell without getting burned."

Bella turned his words over in her mind. While she knew precious little about the war, it seemed odd indeed to her that he had been shot by another Confederate. She had a feeling there remained something more to his story. "Why would a fellow soldier shoot you?"

He stiffened. "Enough. Leave off your questioning for this evening."

Her fingers grazed where his skin was puckered and dented once again. It was the only flaw on his otherwise broad and sturdy back. Someone had done him harm, caused him physical anguish, and she didn't like the feeling her new knowledge gave her. Unlike the gunshot, however, the emotional anguish had never healed. She wanted to make him whole again, but she wasn't certain if it was within her power to do so.

She looked back up into his guarded face. "Why won't you let me in, Jesse?"

"You don't want to be where I am, my dear." He looked away from her. "One spoiled apple rots the entire basket, as they say. I don't want to hurt you."

"You're hurting me by pushing me away," she countered. She began a pattern of slow, calming circles on his shoulders. "I told you many times that you cannot forever be a man alone."

"That was a very long time ago, Bella, and you were too naïve to realize what you were in for." His tone was self-deprecating.

"There's a difference between naiveté and love." The assertion was out of her mouth before she could think better of it.

His eyes jerked back to hers. "You don't want me. You said you wished I'd never returned."

She frowned, dismayed by her childish need to inflict the same hurt he'd dealt her. "I'm sorry. I didn't mean any of the awful words I said to you."

"Don't be. You're taking the Duke of Dullness for a lover, remember?" His lips quirked into a sneer.

Bella shook her head, once more ashamed by what she had done. "I don't want the Duke of Devonshire," she admitted.

"Ah." He frowned. "Who is it you long for then, my dear?"

Who did she long for? Blessed angels, there was only one man she wanted, only one man she had ever wanted. Bella stared at him, her heart aching with the love he seemed determined not to allow her to give him. "You," she whispered.

"But you already have me. I'm your husband."

"And yet you have been secreting away from me in this chamber, devoting yourself to business as if you can't bear the sight of me," she pointed out.

"I'm sorry. I never wanted you to see this side of me." His voice was as somber as his expression.

"Being husband and wife isn't about hiding ourselves from one another." She cupped his firm jaw. "I want to see all your sides, the witty, the dashing, the silly, the scared. If you're hurting, I want to know so that I may help you heal."

"I don't know, my love. There are parts of me I don't wish for you to see." He kissed her palm.

Bella was not about to be deterred by lovemaking, tempting though it may be. "Why did you keep all of this a secret from me, Jesse? Why did you not tell me? I could have helped you."

"By putting yourself in harm's way?" He scoffed. "It's my duty to protect you."

"I'm not afraid of you," she said, determined.

"You damn well ought to be," he replied harshly. "I've been violent, Bella. When I returned to London, I woke to bloodied fists and holes in my bedchamber wall. I cannot and will not subject you to my madness."

Her heart ached for him. "You aren't mad, Jesse. Don't you see? If your dreams have grown worse, there can only be one reason for it."

"Do tell."

The pieces of the puzzle seemed to unerringly fit together in that moment. "What are your nightmares about?"

He tensed, his eyes darkening yet again. "Battle."

Precisely. She felt as if all the answers were within her reach now. "And when you returned for Clara, where did you go?"

"Virginia." He frowned. "You know that. I've already told you."

"Yes, and where were you shot?" she asked, hating to blow the dust off his old pains, but convinced there was no other way to confront his demons, perhaps go a long way toward slaying them.

"Virginia," he bit out. "What the hell is this about, Bella?"

"It's about fighting the past," she said, unbothered. "You seem to think that hiding yourself down the hall and lying to me will fix your problems, but in truth it has only made them worse. We've grown apart when we should have been growing together. There must not be secrets between us any longer."

"I didn't want you to think me mad," he said, the admission seemingly torn from him. "I hoped the dreams would vanish on their own, in time. I had been able to control them before, but now it seems as if they seek to destroy me."

"I would never think you mad," she told him, meaning every word. "I believe I know the reason why your nightmares have grown worse."

"Indeed?" His tone was wry. "Then you must be capable of working miracles, for I've been trying my damnedest to figure it out for months."

"Yes." She hesitated, not wanting to further distress him but convinced she could help him better understand the dreams that had been blighting him. And perhaps with understanding would come healing. "You buried your memories of war away because they were too terrible for you to recall. When you returned to Virginia, it all came back to you."

He exhaled slowly, his skin becoming pale even in the low light. "You may be right." He closed his eyes. "Bella, there's something I must tell you."

She slipped her arm around his shoulders and drew him to her, trying to give him solace in the only way she knew how. "What is it, my love?"

He laid his head upon her breast as a shudder racked his strong body. "The man who shot me was Lavinia's lover. I was in Richmond. The whole city was on fire, or so it seemed. We were retreating when I was shot in the back. I'll never forget the smell, the crying of the wounded all through the night. A Union detail passed through but I lay there, pretending to be dead. At dawn, I dragged myself to a friendly encampment. Somehow, by the grace of God, they had a medic who attended me, or else I would have died like so many others."

Dear God. How horrible it must have been to be utterly

alone in the night, wounded and terrified. She ran a soothing hand over his hair, holding him tightly to her, wishing she could absorb his pain. "How did you know it was Lavinia's lover who shot you?"

He wrapped his arms about her waist, his grip so strong she feared he meant to snap her in two. "When I found my regiment, the war was nearly over, and our men were all readying to return to their homes. But there were those who had witnessed what he had done. By that time, he'd already deserted and run off with Lavinia and my daughter. It was too late for retribution."

"Oh, Jesse." Tears stung her eyes to think how much he must have endured. "I'm so sorry."

"Don't be." He looked up at her, his eyes glittering with moisture. "I never would have met you if not for my past. After what had happened, the South was in ruins. I was in ruins. I left without a clue where I was headed, and I never looked back."

"Until circumstances forced you to," she finished for him.

"I wouldn't trade you or Clara for a life of comfort and ease." He cupped her face in his hands. "I'd go to war all over again just for the chance to be your husband."

She released a sob then, part happiness, part sadness. "I love you so very much, Jesse Whitney."

"And I love you, my darling," he murmured before claiming her lips in a voracious kiss. "I'm sorry for not being entirely honest. I should have told you everything, but I was too damn afraid of losing you. Can you forgive me?"

"Of course," she said without pause. "I only want to ease your burdens. Promise me that from now on you'll no longer suffer in silence?"

"God, I don't know how I was somehow fortunate enough to find you." His voice was hoarse, his gaze intense.

Bella smiled, relieved for her tears to subside. How lovely it was to simply rejoice in the love they shared. "I feel precisely the same way."

He grinned, his dimple reappearing with irrepressible charm. "Maybe you can't get to heaven without first going through hell."

"However we got here, all that matters now is that we're here together," she said firmly. "And I'm not going anywhere."

"Nor am I." He pressed his forehead to hers.

"I mean it," she pressed on. "I'm spending the night right here by your side, tonight and every other night after."

His mouth flattened into a thin, stubborn line. "Bella—"

"Nonsense," she interrupted. "Nothing you can say shall change my mind. No more hiding away here on your own. We're in this together, Jesse."

"I never know when they'll come upon me, Bella. I won't have you hurt for all the world." He caressed her cheek. "You're too precious to me."

She shook her head, her decision already made a long time ago. "I don't give a fig about your nightmares. My place is by your side, and by your side is where I'll stay."

His eyes gaze burned into hers. "My darling girl, what would I do without you to slay my dragons?"

Heart bursting with love, Bella leaned into him to seal their mouths in a hungry kiss. "You'll never have to find out, my love."

"Thank God," he said on a groan, crushing her to him for another kiss that was as fiery as the passion burning between them. He lifted the delicate fabric of her nightdress over her head, and they both quite promptly forgot about everything but one other and the powerful bond of love they shared.

# Epilogue

"*I* DARESAY YOUR TIME IN ENGLAND THUS FAR has been a most improving experience for you, Miss Whittlesby. You aren't looking nearly as dowdy as you once were."

Bella suppressed a sigh as she glanced up from her dinner plate to the dowager, who was presiding over the family gathering like the proud—if a trifle rude—matriarch she was. Poor Clara was doing her best to maintain her composure. Dressed in a navy gown, she was looking quite the demure young lady. Her shopping escapades with Lady Stokey and her finishing lessons had truly transformed her. Looking at her now, one would never guess that she wasn't an English lady born and bred. She was settling in well to her London surroundings.

"*Maman*," Bella felt compelled to protest on her stepdaughter's behalf, for she had recently decided to be known as Miss Whitney rather than Miss Jones, and it pleased Jesse greatly. "You must cease insisting upon mispronouncing our family name. It's Whitney."

Her mother's hawk like countenance turned upon her. She raised an imperious brow. "Just so. That's precisely what I said. Is it not?"

Jesse gave her hand a gentle squeeze, as if to remind her that while the dowager had softened in some surprising ways over the last few months, she was still after all the dowager, a cunning curmudgeon who would never completely budge from her old ways. "It is indeed, my lady," he drawled, offering a quick wink to Bella.

She sent a grateful smile his way. Thank heavens her husband seemed to possess infinite amounts of patience, particularly where the dowager was concerned. She and her mother had begun to mend the damage between them. Bella wasn't entirely ready to forget the dowager's unwanted interference, but she was willing to forgive.

The dowager harrumphed. "I fear you've something in your eye, Mr. Whittlesby," she announced sharply.

"Perhaps it's a tear of joy?" Thornton suggested with a rascal's grin. "I'm sure he finds dinner with you to be a most improving experience, Mother."

Cleo pinned her husband with a halfheartedly stern frown. "Alex, must you forever be stirring up trouble?"

Bella couldn't help but laugh. What an odd assemblage they made, she and her American husband holding court for the first time at their Belgravia house. Life could take the most perplexing turns and twists sometimes, a bit like a maze designed by an overzealous head gardener. But in the end, she wouldn't trade it for a quiet life as the Duchess of Devonshire. Not for even a moment.

The dowager sniffed. "It would seem my son excels at stirring up trouble. He's been up to an awful lot of it recently."

Thornton grinned, unabashed. "At least no one can ever accuse the de Vere family of being boring."

"Much to the dismay of my weak old heart," the dowager bemoaned. "I shouldn't be surprised if it gives out on me altogether before too long."

"Funny that," Jesse whispered to Bella, "I'd swear she didn't have a heart."

"What was that, Whittlesby?" the dowager demanded, at her most regal. "I daresay you Americans have not heard that it simply isn't done to whisper at the dinner table."

"I'm sure we haven't, my lady," he murmured, somehow managing to maintain a serious expression.

It was Bella's turn to send him a wink. She'd never been more in love. Indeed, it seemed with each day that passed, the feelings she had for him only deepened. "Perhaps we ought to have sent you to finishing lessons with Clara," she suggested, enjoying the freedom of having her own household. She could occasionally bait the dowager without suffering any more serious consequences than a brutal harrumph.

"Don't be foolish, Arabella," her mother scolded. "I'm pleased to at least find you've enlisted a fine English cook here. Otherwise, I should despair." She took a bite of her roast. "There is nothing better in the world than good English cuisine. I simply can't abide by the French and all their sauces."

Bella didn't have the heart to tell the dowager that their chef was in fact a Frenchman lest her mother spit her roast upon the snowy table linens in her horror. "I'm pleased you're enjoying dinner," she said instead.

Her mother had made some progress, but she still detested foreigners. At least she no longer referred to Cleo as *that woman*. Some small battles had been won if not the war. For now, it was enough of a coup to simply have their family all seated around the same table. The sight of Thornton and Cleo, so clearly in love and blissful, thrilled her. Just a month before, they'd celebrated the birth of their first son. Clara too was smiling, more at home than she'd ever been, on the cusp of womanhood. Even the dowager managed a half-smile, but whether it was because of the roast or for Bella's sake, she'd never know for certain. What she did know was that they had all truly found their happiness.

"We shall have to make a habit of this," the dowager

said. "Now that we'll be planning Clara's comeout, I expect I'll be spending a great deal of time with you."

Bella looked at her mother askance. She hadn't realized the dowager was planning on aiding in Clara's entrée into society.

"Why are you looking at me as if I've sprouted a horn?" her mother groused. "I'm sure you'll need my aid."

She smiled, noting the brief look of horror on her stepdaughter's face. "Of course we shall. Thank you, *Maman.*"

"You've very welcome, I'm sure." The dowager sniffed and continued eating her roast.

The rest of the dinner passed in the comfort of familial ease. Bella was heartened to have her family all beneath one roof, their conflicts and troubles a thing of the past. The time had never been better to move forward into the glittering future awaiting them.

Later that evening, Bella eagerly awaited Jesse in her chamber. She'd taken extra care with her evening *toilette*, for she had a very important announcement to make to him. Smith had left her hair unbound just the way he preferred it, and she wore a nearly transparent nightdress she'd had imported from Paris. She dearly hoped he would be as thrilled as she was.

She thought then of Jesse and how far they'd come together. He'd been making slow but steady progress over the course of the last few months, and his inner strength never ceased to amaze her. He still suffered from nightmares but they were gradually becoming less frequent. She knew there was the possibility that he would be subject to them his entire life, but she also knew that together they could surpass any obstacles they faced. They hadn't stopped sharing a chamber since the night she'd found him down the hall. As a result, their lives were about to become even more complete.

The door between their chambers clicked open. She looked up with a welcoming smile as her husband sauntered across the carpet to where she sat before her mirror. He was handsome as ever, clad in only a dressing gown. When he reached her side, he stopped and took her hands in his large, calloused grip.

"Your nightdress is positively sinful," he murmured, his scorching gaze traveling over her body as he raised her hands to his lips for a lingering kiss. "I love it."

She allowed him to bring her to her feet. "How do you think dinner went?" she asked, curious for his opinion. She had missed her family's presence in her life, and with the Season in full bloom, she was glad to once more have them close at hand. The dowager seemed to truly be relenting. Bella couldn't believe her mother had actually deigned to offer her support for Clara's comeout.

"I think it went astoundingly well," he said thoughtfully. "Your mother kept her insults to a decided minimum and didn't so much as mention my troublesome treatment of vowels."

Bella laughed and gave his arm a playful swat. "How ungentlemanly of you to draw attention to my mother's shortcomings."

"I never said they were shortcomings," he countered with a grin.

"She's a bear and you know it." She slid her arms around his neck and leaned into the familiar, hard strength of his body. "At least she's taken to Clara."

"I am grateful for that." His hands settled possessively on her waist, anchoring her to him.

Bella was quiet for a few beats, gathering her courage before she plowed onward. "Jesse?"

He gazed down at her, his expression open and loving. "Yes, sweetheart?"

"Do you think Clara would like a brother or a sister?"

Jesse raised a brow. "I'm sure she wouldn't mind a little

scalawag scampering about one day. I suppose I haven't given the prospect much thought. Have you?"

She hesitated. "Rather a bit more in the last month or so."

"Bella?" His stormy blue gaze trapped hers, searching. "What are you saying?"

"I'm saying that I'm with child," she finally confessed on an exhaled breath.

His jaw went slack. "Are you certain?"

She nodded, still unaccountably nervous. "Quite."

A slow grin spread over his face, his dimple appearing in full force. "I'm going to be a father again."

"Yes, you are." She pressed her palm to his bristly cheek. "I hope you're pleased."

"Pleased?" He dropped a hard, quick miss to her mouth. "Hell, I'm ecstatic. I couldn't be happier."

Smiling back at him, she rose on her tiptoes to fuse their lips once more. "Nor could I."

"Ah, my own sweet Bella." He held her tightly, sounding slightly dazed by her revelation. "You've made me whole again. I have no idea how you managed it, but somehow you did."

"Love," she said simply. "All it required was love."

Read on for an excerpt of Book 3 in the Heart's Temptation Series, *Reckless Need.*

*Reckless Need*
Heart's Temptation Book 3

Heath, the Duke of Devonshire, has been living a passionless life of penance after losing the woman he loved. Determined to do his duty, he's in search of an innocent bride with a sterling reputation. A bride who's nothing at all like Tia, Lady Stokey.

The Duke of Devonshire may be handsome, but he's as boring as a bowl of porridge. Or so Tia thinks until he carries her to her chamber and undoes half her buttons while kissing her senseless.

The moment he scoops the delectable Tia into his arms, Heath wants her in his bed, and he'll stop at nothing to have her there. When they unleash the scandal of the century, they must face consequences that are deeper and far more dangerous to their hearts than either of them imagined. Will they find love, or was the reckless need between them doomed from the start?

## Chapter One

*East Anglia, England, 1882*

*J*F THERE WAS ONE THING IN THE WORLD THAT Tia, Lady Stokey, adored, it was parties. Give her a good *fête*, an army of new dresses, an entertaining assortment of guests and she was a happy woman.

Under ordinary circumstances, that was.

Grumbling to herself, she trekked through the maze at the Marquis of Thornton's hunting estate, Penworth, in search of her wayward charge. A mere hour after their arrival for a country house party, Tia had discovered Miss Whitney missing from her bedchamber.

"In need of a nap, my bottom," Tia grumbled, stalking around a corner. If only the hedges weren't so frightfully high and she so irritatingly diminutive in height. But of course, that would have rather nullified the purpose of a maze, she supposed.

The young Miss Whitney had declared the need for a respite after their travel through the countryside, and Tia had acquiesced. But suspicion had brought her round to collect the girl early, where she'd discovered only a note telling her that her charge had decided to take a restoring turn about the gardens instead.

"Restoring indeed," Tia scoffed, her ire growing with each step. She had a dreadful feeling that her charge was going to prove much more than a handful. After all, she recognized herself in the girl, and it was one of the reasons why she'd agreed to help introduce her to society.

The sound of gravel shifting interrupted her cantankerous musings. She stopped, holding her breath to listen. It sounded as if Miss Whitney was perhaps just around the next bend, behind the thick hedges obscuring Tia's vision. Smiling in triumph, she grabbed her skirts and hurried around the turn in the maze.

"Ah ha," she called out in delight. "I've found you now, you little minx."

But her moment of triumph was terribly abridged, for the noise-making culprit, seated on a bench before her, was not Miss Whitney. Nor, in fact, was it even a female. Quite the opposite.

Dear heavens. Eyes the same wistful color as a summer sky met hers, stealing her breath. She stopped, her heart thumping as madly as a runaway stallion's hooves. The man staring back at her, an open book in his large hands, a golden brow raised, was decidedly as far as one could get from the petite, Virginia-born Miss Whitney.

"I daresay I've been called a great number of things in my life, but never yet a little minx," drawled the Duke of Devonshire as he stood and bowed to her.

"I must apologize," she hastened to say, embarrassment making her cheeks go hot. "I mistook you for someone else."

A small smile curved his lips, drawing her attention to just how finely formed his mouth was. He had changed since she'd seen him last. He'd grown a beard. She swallowed, her heart continuing its mad pace. The duke had always been a handsome man, possessed of a rare masculine beauty that almost made him seem too perfect to be real.

But the neatly trimmed beard took the purity of his features and rendered them somehow sinful. Seductive. Her cheeks burned as she realized she was staring and, to her greatest dismay, he'd said something to her.

She had no earthly idea what.

Bother it all, what ailed her? She'd seen Devonshire scads of times before. The boring manner in which he conducted himself had long since rendered her immune to his undeniable good looks. He was quiet, uninteresting. For the most part, he didn't move in the same circles as she. In private, she referred to him as the Duke of Dullness. Why, then, was she turning into a silly schoolroom miss in his presence? A beard? An intense stare?

Tia released her skirts, allowing them to fall back into place as it occurred to her that she'd likely been revealing far more of her limbs than she'd intended. That bright-blue gaze of his followed her movement, making her feel almost as if he'd caressed her.

"By any chance, were you searching for a lovely young American, Lady Stokey?" he asked, saving her from further embarrassment.

She didn't know why, but she found it troublesome indeed that he thought Miss Whitney lovely. Tia shook the unworthy notion from her mind, reminded that she was charged with looking after the virtue and the conduct of a rather precocious young girl.

"I was, Your Grace," she acknowledged, dipping into a slight curtsy as her wits returned to her. "Have you seen her?"

"About half an hour ago," he confirmed, closing the distance between them. That smile still flirted with the corners of his mouth, almost as if he were enjoying a sally at her expense.

Half an hour. Tia frowned. The girl could be halfway back to America by now. "I don't suppose she told you where she intended to go next?"

"No."

A great lot of help he was. Tia tried not to notice how very broad his shoulders were, how lean his legs. She glanced instead to the book he held. It was a volume of poetry. She'd never had much patience for verse. "I'm sorry for the interruption," she told him, deciding the time for lingering was at an end. She needed to find Miss Whitney and bring the girl to task. England was not Virginia. She couldn't simply wander about as she chose, especially not as a young, innocent miss. She had a reputation to uphold.

"Think nothing of it, my lady." Devonshire still stood uncomfortably near to her, looking down with an unreadable expression upon his face. "I was merely enjoying a bit of solitude while I still could."

Solitude? Tia thought it an odd statement indeed but perhaps another indication of why she'd never been particularly drawn to the man. Aside from his undeniably arresting appearance, that was. She considered him now, her gaze dropping to his mouth of its own will before she forced herself to once again become ensnared in his riveting stare. "I confess I'm confused, Your Grace. Is not keeping the company of others rather the point of a country house party?"

He nodded, appearing a solemn, lonely figure suddenly. "I daresay it is, my lady. For most."

She couldn't help it. She knew she ought to be running after her errant charge, but there was something suddenly compelling about Devonshire. Here in the outdoors, the sun shining down upon him, the polish of his ordinary façade buffed away by the manner in which she'd caught him unaware…he seemed different to her. Almost dangerous. Certainly handsome. But sad too, as if he were a man who had never quite located his true place in the world.

"But not for you?" she asked him quietly.

"*Ça dépend*," he answered, stroking the binding of his book absentmindedly.

There was something about watching his long fingers that caused an ache deep inside Tia. It had been so very long since she'd been touched by a man. Too long, she reminded herself, else she wouldn't be mooning over the Duke of Devonshire. "On what does it depend?"

"The others with whom I'm expected to keep company," he answered cryptically.

"I see." She frowned again, supposing she really should have left well enough alone. She had the distinct impression he didn't want her there. "Then perhaps I should leave you to your seclusion after all. I don't wish to further inconvenience you. Good day, Your Grace."

She spun on her heel, determined to beat a hasty retreat before she made any more of a fool of herself, tarrying over conversation with a man who would prefer to be left alone. A man she didn't even like, no matter how attractive she found him. Yes, it was the beard, she decided as she hurried away. The beard had rendered him quite magnetic.

Lost in her round of self-chastising, Tia wasn't paying proper attention to her mules. They were delicate silk, horridly impractical for being outside and not at all the sort of things to be rushing about in. Her heel caught in the stones of the path, twisting her ankle and making her lose her balance at the same time.

Pain shot from her ankle up her leg as she landed in an inglorious heap on her hands and knees. She must have cried out, because the duke came rushing around the bend, all the better to prolong her humiliation. Her ankle aching, she stared at his trousers in misery, wishing she'd had the grace to fall somewhere out of his earshot instead.

He hunkered down at her side, his striking face coming back into her view. "Lady Stokey, are you hurt?" His voice was laced with genuine concern.

"Yes," she told him, grimacing when she flexed her foot and was met with another sharp twinge of discomfort. "My pride and my ankle are both grievously wounded."

He took her hands in his, turning them over to inspect her palms. They were bare because she'd been too intent on chasing after Miss Whitney to care. Devonshire was gloveless too, and the contact of his skin on hers gave her an unexpected jolt. He rubbed his thumbs over her lightly, lingering on the abrasions she'd earned in her tumble. "I'm afraid you're bleeding as well."

She glanced from her raw palms to his face. He was unbearably near, so near she had great difficulty catching her breath. Good heavens. She had to compose herself. "I shall mend," she said, trying for an air of unconcern. It wouldn't do for him to know the effect he had on her. Why, she didn't like the man. He was altogether unappealing. She preferred men who were eager and attentive, who knew how to kiss and woo a woman. Who were seductive and easy to understand and flirted with practiced ease. Men who didn't hide in the gardens reading poetry, of all things.

"Let me help you to stand," he said in a tone that allowed for no argument. "On the count of three. One, two—" He pulled her up without waiting for her compliance and without waiting to say "three".

Tia leaned into the duke as she stood, wincing when the pressure of weight upon her ankle produced more pronounced pain. Oh dear, perhaps she'd sprained it. However would she contain Miss Whitney if she were hobbled like an old dowager for the entirety of the party?

"I thought you said on the count of three," she groused, rather cut up about the entire situation.

First, her charge had disappeared. Then, Tia had reacted to Devonshire as if she were a smitten young girl straight off her comeout. Now she'd fallen in a heap before him. And she still hadn't located Miss Whitney. This fortnight was certainly off to a marvelous start.

"Put your weight on me," he ordered next, ignoring her. "I'll walk you to the bench, and then I'll take a look at your ankle to see what damage has been done."

"No." She tried to extricate herself from his grasp without success. "I don't require your assistance, Your Grace."

"Nonsense." When she continued to attempt her escape,

he caught her up in his arms.

Tia's hands went to his shoulders for purchase, finding them just as solid and strong as they looked. "Good heavens, put me down at once," she told him. If his proximity before had been tempting, it was now alarming. She could smell his scent, a deliciously masculine blend of soap, spice and the outdoors. She could feel the fine fabric of his jacket beneath her fingertips. His golden hair curled down over his collar, brushing against her as he moved. And she could detect the faintest flecks of gray in his otherwise perfectly blue eyes. It didn't escape her notice that he'd scooped her up without a bit of strain, as though she weighed little more than a handful of feathers.

He disregarded her request to put her back on her own two feet and carried her to the bench where he'd been sitting when she'd first interrupted him. He gently lowered her to its hard surface, and she had to secretly admit that she was somewhat disappointed to no longer be in his arms. When he sank to his knees before her, reaching beneath her skirts, her disappointment turned to dismay.

"Your Grace," she protested. "What are you about?"

"Hush," he dismissed her concerns, his hand closing around the ankle that was giving her pain. "I'm seeing to your injury."

"You needn't." She endeavored to pull her limb from his grasp, to no avail. His touch was warm and gentle through her stockings. A sudden rush of awareness threatened to swallow her whole. A wicked, luxurious heat settled between her thighs. She tamped it down. "For heaven's sake, I'm fine. I'm merely in a bit of pain, but it shall pass."

But his fingers were already gently at work, angling her foot this way and that. "It would be remiss of me not to make certain you haven't done yourself serious harm. You took quite a spill."

Oh dear. Little more than a dull throb plagued her ankle now, but another throb had taken up residence within her. A decidedly naughty one. She wet her suddenly dry lips.

"Truly, Your Grace. This is most improper."

He was insistent in playing the role of savior. "Does this hurt?" He pressed his thumb against her inner foot.

"No." Quite the opposite. It felt wonderfully good. Too bad he was not at all the sort of man for an inamorato. The wickedness in her pulled her skirts just a bit higher anyway, revealing the curve of her calf.

The duke's touch moved north as well, feeling suspiciously like a caress. "What of this?"

She flinched when he found the exact spot on her ankle where the soreness originated. "Yes."

He stopped his ministrations and glanced up, his gaze meeting hers. She wondered if he could tell she wasn't as unaffected as she pretended and hoped not. He moved her foot again with one hand while holding her ankle with the other. "I don't think you've broken anything, fortunately. But it does feel a trifle swollen. More than likely, you've sprained it. You'll need to rest for the remainder of the day."

Tia scoffed, doing her best to disregard his lingering touch. "I haven't time to rest. I have a wayward young American to locate and browbeat to within an inch of her wretched life."

"That sounds pressing indeed," he told her solemnly. "But I'm afraid you'll have to enlist someone else to help hunt your charge down for the life-threatening browbeating."

He released her ankle and pulled her skirts back into place. Tia felt the loss of his touch like an ache. This ridiculous reaction to him had to stop. She'd been a widow for several years, but she took great care with her lovers. She didn't simply set her cap for a man because he was beautiful and happened to touch her ankle and had a deliciously rakish beard.

Tia stared at him as he stood, an idea taking root in her mind. Yes, it was the perfect solution for her sudden, inconvenient and thoroughly foolish attraction to the Duke of Devonshire. After all, it would be a wonderful coup for

Miss Whitney to bring a duke up to scratch. "Perhaps you'll be so kind as to assist me in locating Miss Whitney?" she asked, giving the duke her most charming smile.

He nodded, picking up the book that he'd abandoned on the bench when he'd rushed to her rescue. "Of course, my lady. But in the meantime, I fear you'll need my aid to escape from the maze first." He offered her his arm.

Tia took it, allowing him to tug her to her feet. Her ankle still hurt but not nearly as badly as it first had after her inconvenient spill. "Thank you, Your Grace. You're most kind." And easily trapped, she hoped. For it would certainly be a boon to her if she could settle the troublesome Miss Whitney with a suitable gentleman at the first opportunity. A man very much like the Duke of Devonshire.

Heath aided Lady Stokey back to the main house, mindful of her limping gait and his painful arousal both. Had he known that touching her would prove so bloody dangerous to his restraint, he never would have so much as laid a finger upon her hem. But he'd been carried away by his concern, the need to make certain she hadn't broken a bone. From the moment he'd caught her up in his arms, he'd had a troubling suspicion that he was walking down a path from which there would be no return. Lady Stokey was an ethereal beauty, as golden as an angel with finely formed features, lush red lips and wide eyes the color of a meadow in spring. She'd smelled of violets.

He could still smell her now if he leaned near enough.

But the greatest folly of all had been lifting her skirts to reveal her trim, lovely legs. He'd stolen a peek all the way to her knees when he first lifted her silk and petticoats aside. He hadn't been able to help himself. And it had been worth it. Touching her had been intoxicating. He'd never before caressed a woman's limbs through her stockings, but he would now forever find the act unbearably erotic.

Unless he missed his guess, she hadn't been immune either. He'd caught the way her lips had parted, the way the green of her eyes had deepened, the way she'd lifted her hem even higher. It was too bad, really, that he was in search of a wife and not a mistress. If it had been a mistress he was after, he would have escorted Lady Stokey to her chamber and then joined her inside. To the devil with her nuisance of a young charge.

Instead, he was playing the role he'd honed well over the years. Perfect gentleman. "How is your ankle faring, my lady?" he asked, still desperate to distract himself from the inconvenient state of his cock.

She turned to him, her elaborately styled blonde locks glinting in the sun. In her haste to chase after her charge, she'd neglected to wear a hat and he was grateful for it. "In truth, it's still paining me, but I daresay it shan't be the death of me."

He'd always thought Lady Stokey something of a flighty woman. Though on occasion he'd traveled in the periphery of her circles, they'd never truly engaged in much conversation. That she was clever surprised him. In his experience, there ordinarily wasn't much substance to a woman of beauty. He'd known a few exceptions, of course, but they were just that. Exceptions.

A distinct expression of pain now furrowed her brow as she limped through the maze. He disliked seeing her suffering. "I would be more than happy to carry you to your chamber, Lady Stokey," he volunteered out of a combined sense of duty and desire. He had to admit that holding her in his arms once more would not precisely be a hardship.

"Heavens no," she objected immediately. "If I sap all your strength, you'll have none left to pursue Miss Whitney, wherever she may be."

She'd gone back to watching the ground before them, giving him her profile. He instantly regretted his hasty offer to locate her charge. Miss Whitney had indeed ventured past him in the maze, and though she was but a slip of a girl, he suspected she was a wily foe if the way she'd flummoxed Lady Stokey was any indication. He hadn't the patience for silly young girls.

"You'll not sap my strength so easily," he reassured her. Lady Stokey, for all her layers of dress, had been as light as a bird in his arms. And like a bird, she was a tiny, gorgeous creature.

"Oh," she exclaimed suddenly, her expression crumpling as she clenched his arm in a rigid grip. "Oh dear."

He stopped, sliding an arm round her waist, the better to give her purchase and keep weight off her injured leg. The maddening scent of violets enveloped him. "Perhaps you'll permit me to carry you after all."

"No," she denied even as she clutched his arm and her eyes glistened with unshed tears. "You mustn't. I can walk on my own. I may lack grace, but I'm no weakling."

A weakling she was not. A stubborn woman, however, she was. He decided not to allow her the opportunity for further argument. Heath tucked his book inside his coat, then bent and once more scooped her up.

"Your Grace," she remonstrated, her tone one of surprise mingled with disapproval. Her hands linked around his neck. Her lovely Cupid's bow of a mouth was so very near to his. If he but dipped his head, he could take her lips.

No, damn it. He could not. He forced himself to stare straight ahead and carry them from the maze. He'd come to Penworth in search of a wife, and he was determined to stay the course. Lady Stokey, tempting though she may be, was not the woman for him. Her reputation preceded her, and he didn't want a butterfly as his mate. Rather, he wanted a bookworm. A woman of substance. A woman of loyalty who was willing to respect her husband. Not a dazzlingly seductive widow with a string of lovers in her past and a penchant for throwing wild soirees. Regardless of how delicious she smelled and how alluring she felt in his arms.

"I'll not have another word of protest," he informed her coolly. "I cannot in good conscience allow you to carry on while in such obvious pain."

As he entered the house, Lady Thornton, his hostess and Lady Stokey's sister, appeared before him, having been interrupted in directing her housekeeper. The sisters were opposites in appearance, one dark, the other light, but both equally lovely. Worry clouded the marchioness's face. "What has happened?"

"I merely sprained my ankle. Tell this insufferable man to put me on my feet," Lady Stokey demanded in a queenly accent.

Heath exchanged a commiserating glance with Lady Thornton. "This insufferable man is attempting to keep her ladyship from doing herself further harm. If you'll be so kind as to direct me to her chamber?"

His hostess raised an inky brow at his request. He knew he could have simply deposited Lady Stokey in the drawing room, but he was on a mission now. He couldn't very well abandon his damsel in distress partway through his rescue. But if she thought his actions odd, in the end Lady Thornton chose to keep her misgivings to herself. "The east wing, third door to your left."

He nodded to her. "Thank you."

"You cannot be serious," Lady Stokey chimed in. "I'm perfectly capable of walking. Cleo, tell him."

"You mustn't take any chances," her sister called after them as Heath stalked in the direction of the stairs. "You'll not want to be injured for the party, dearest sister."

Heath gave his reluctant armful a victorious glance. "You see? Finally, a voice of reason. Listen to your sister if not me." He took the steps with ease, grateful that all the hard labor he'd been performing on his estate had finally rewarded him. He wasn't even winded.

The same could not be said for Lady Stokey, whose cheeks were pink and whose breath seemed too quick for a woman at rest. Her eyes snapped emerald fire at him. He had to admit she was even more captivating when irritated. "Voice of reason indeed." She tipped up her chin in a show of defiance. "Since when is carrying an able-bodied woman about as if she were a sack of turnips considered reasonable?"

"I would never carry a sack of turnips with such great care," he told her solemnly. There it was again, her heavenly scent, teasing his senses and his cock both. He forced himself to keep to the matter at hand. "Though I must confess I wonder what circumstances in life would require one to carry a sack of turnips to begin with."

"Bother." Her lips compressed and she turned her head away from him again, apparently too cross to even continue berating him.

She was pricklier than a cornered hedgehog. He rather enjoyed nettling her and a sudden, wicked impulse to continue hit him just then. "Oh dear," he said, feigning worry.

That deep, warm gaze swung back to his. "What is it?"

"I fear I'm going to sneeze," he told her.

"Good heavens." Her eyes widened and then narrowed as the grin he couldn't quite contain emerged. "You're not serious."

"No." He reached the top of the stairs and headed down the hall.

"That was not a kind jest, Your Grace," Lady Stokey chastised him.

He stopped before her chamber door. "Perhaps not kind but certainly humorous. Would you be so obliging as to turn the knob for me, my lady?"

Making a sound of irritation, she did as he asked. Something within him stirred as he stepped over the threshold into her private rooms. He pushed the door closed with his shoulder, trying to ignore the awareness creeping over him. Damn it, what was it about the small woman in his arms that made him want her so much? He'd seen more than his fair share of beauties. He'd long thought himself immune to the lure of a lovely woman. The lust coursing through him made little sense. He hadn't been so moved by the mere presence of a woman since Bess. The thought of the sweet, innocent woman he'd loved made his blood run a bit colder. She could not have been more different than the willful, decadent Lady Stokey.

Heath stalked the last few feet to her bed, stopping to carefully lower her to it. Lady Stokey's eyes were on his. Their noses nearly brushed. Her lips parted. The desire he'd been doing his damnedest to dash away returned, hitting him in the gut with the force of a punch.

"Thank you," she said softly. Her hands were still on his shoulders, burning him through his jacket, waistcoat and shirt.

"You're most welcome," he returned in a voice gone rough. He knew he should straighten, put some distance between them, ring for her maid and leave the chamber. But she was a temptation he couldn't resist. From the moment she'd rounded the bend in the maze and he'd caught sight of her, the sun glinting in her golden curls and twin patches of pink on her cheeks, her curves molded in a scarlet day dress, he'd been thinking of kissing her. Undoing the line of buttons on her bodice. Peeling her out of her gown to see if her breasts were as full and luscious as they appeared beneath her proper layers.

Before his conscience allowed him to change his mind, he lowered his mouth to hers. She opened to him and he took advantage, sweeping his tongue inside to taste her. Her fingers slid from his shoulder to his neck, sinking into his hair. An arrow of heat shot directly to his cock, making him instantly hard. One of his hands moved to her elaborate coiffure, itching to undo it and unleash her long blonde curls. With his other hand, he cupped her breast. She arched into him, filling his palm with the curve of her breast that wasn't contained by her corset, making a throaty sound of appreciation deep in her throat.

He wondered if her nipples were hard, and if they were the same pretty pink as her soft lips.

Damnation.

He hadn't meant to give in to his baser instincts. But now that he had, he couldn't seem to stop. He wanted more of her. Couldn't help himself from pressing his knee to the bed and leaning over her, the better to kiss her senseless. When her tongue ventured against his, a shot of unadulterated, reckless need blazed straight through him as if it were an inferno. He dragged his mouth down her throat, kissing the creamy skin he'd admired in the gardens. She even tasted of violets, sweet and floral, and for some reason, he found it incredibly erotic. The high lace collar of her gown served as an impediment for further exploration, so he released her breast to find the line of fabric-covered buttons keeping him from what he desperately wanted. He slipped them from their moorings, returning to her mouth for another deep, passionate kiss.

One, two, three, four. He counted each button he freed in his mind, eager to see and touch the skin he'd revealed. He wanted her so badly he ached with it. And if her response was any indication, she wanted him back with every bit as much fervor. Five, six, seven, eight.

Heath broke the kiss and raised his head to gaze down at his handiwork. Her red bodice had gaped over her breasts, exposing two generous swells above her white embroidered chemise. He met her gaze then, sensing her watching him. Her mossy eyes were glazed with passion, her lips swollen from his kisses. Several of her curls had come free of their pins, tumbling about her shoulders. Even mostly clothed, she was the most gorgeous creature he'd ever seen. He wanted to toss up her skirts, find the slit in her drawers and slide home. Deep inside her.

"Is this why you insisted upon carrying me to my chamber, Your Grace?" she asked, her voice breathless. Dazed. Slightly on guard.

He couldn't blame her. Her words sliced through the haze of yearning clouding his brain. Dear God. What had come over him? He'd meant to aid her, to keep her from harming herself. Instead, he'd closeted himself inside her chamber and all but ravished her. She was an incapacitated woman, for Christ's sake. It wasn't as if she could flee him.

"Of course not," he murmured, furious with himself for his weakness. He had not stooped so low ever in his life. He always treated ladies with care. He certainly never all but made love to them a mere half hour after chatting with them in a bloody maze. "I must apologize, my lady. I have no idea what came over me."

"I'm sure I do," she said, the saucy woman. She lowered her gaze to the obvious bulge in his trousers, which hadn't had the courtesy to abate even a bit. The minx. He should have been scandalized by her boldness, but it only made him harder. Damn it all.

As much as he wanted to continue what he'd begun, he knew he could not. It wouldn't be fair or right. Not for Lady Stokey and certainly not for himself. He was here to acquire a wife. Not a mistress. Even if that mistress was as ravishing and deadly to his sensibilities as the woman before him. He removed his knee from her bed and straightened, knowing he ought to keep his distance from her or else he'd be drawn back into her charms.

"Once again, I apologize. I shall ring for your maid to see to your ankle."

He bowed and turned on his heel, not waiting for her response. The need to flee was just as strong as the need to stay and finish what he'd begun. And Heath knew he must never embark on a seduction with a woman like Lady Stokey. It would only lead to ruin. He'd closed the door to passion a long time ago, and he had no intentions of reopening it now.

# About the Author

Award-winning author Scarlett Scott writes contemporary and historical romance with heat, heart, and happily ever afters. Since publishing her first book in 2010, she has become a wife, mother to adorable identical twins and one TV-loving dog, and a killer karaoke singer. Well, maybe not the last part, but that's what she'd like to think.

A self-professed literary junkie and nerd, she loves reading anything but especially romance novels, poetry, and Middle English verse. When she's not reading, writing, wrangling toddlers, or camping, you can catch up with her on her website www.scarsco.com. Hearing from readers never fails to make her day.

Scarlett's complete book list and information about upcoming releases can be found on her website.

Follow Scarlett on social media:

www.twitter.com/scarscoromance
www.pinterest.com/scarlettscott
www.facebook.com/AuthorScarlettScott

# Other Books by Scarlett Scott

## Heart's Temptation

A Mad Passion (Book 1)
Rebel Love (Book 2)
Reckless Need (Book 3)
Sweet Scandal (Book 4) (Coming Soon)

## Love's Second Chance (Coming Soon)

Reprieve (Book 1)
Perfect Persuasion (Book 2)
Win My Love (Book 3)

## Wicked Husbands (Coming Soon)

Her Errant Earl (Book 1)
Her Lovestruck Lord (Book 2)
Her Reformed Rake (Book 3)

44548059R00177

Printed in Poland
by Amazon Fulfillment
Poland Sp. z o.o., Wrocław